W9-BIS-659

CLEOPATRA'S
HEIR

Also by Gillian Bradshaw

The Wolf Hunt
The Sand Reckoner
Island of Ghosts

CLEOPATRA'S HEIR

GILLIAN BRADSHAW

A TOM DOHERTY ASSOCIATES BOOK NEW YORK

CLEOPATRA'S HEIR

Edited by Claire Eddy

Book design by Jane Adele Regina

A Forge Book
Published by Tom Doherty Associates, LLC
175 Fifth Avenue
New York, NY 10010

www.tor.com

Forge® is a registered trademark of Tom Doherty Associates, LLC.

ISBN 0-765-30228-4

First Edition: June 2002

Printed in the United States of America

0   9   8   7   6   5   4   3   2   1

TO MIKE

I know, it doesn't have any weather in it—
but I had to do something to say,
"Well done!"

FOREWORD

In the back of my mind I could hear the bewildered question, "Why are you calling Cleopatra a *Greek?*"

It's what she would have called herself. Pharaonic Egypt fell to the Persians in 525 B.C.; two centuries later the Persian Empire, including Egypt, was itself overwhelmed by the onslaught of Alexander the Great. In 323 one of Alexander's foremost generals, Ptolemaios, son of Lagos, a Macedonian Greek and a relative of the conqueror, became satrap, or governor, of the province of Egypt. Later he took the title "king," and English-speaking historians know him as Ptolemy I Soter. The dynasty he founded—known as the Lagids or Lagidae, after his father, or, alternatively, as the Ptolemies, after the name of every king in it—ruled Egypt for the next eight generations.

Ptolemy and his descendants unquestionably regarded themselves as Greek, and governed Egypt through a Greek-speaking administration initially drawn from a mixture of Alexander's soldiers and ambitious Greek immigrants. Egyptians, in their view, were peasants. (That was the theory. Practice was undoubtedly more complicated, particularly by the end of Greek rule, but even so, conducted in Greek.) Only one Lagid monarch even bothered to learn to speak Egyptian.

That Lagid, the last to govern Egypt, was Cleopatra VII. And yet, she wasn't *quite* the last. In compliance with the tradition that a queen could not reign alone, she made her eldest son king and official co-ruler when he was no more than a toddler. This boy was the fruit of Cleopatra's policy of partnership with the dominant superpower of the time, for his father was Julius Caesar—or so she claimed; her Roman enemies denied it hotly. The fifteenth and last King Ptolemy bore the cognomen "Caesar," and the populace called him "Little Caesar"—in Greek, Caesarion.

Cleopatra's plans for Rome, Egypt, and her son all came to nothing. Julius Caesar died, and Marcus Antonius, the Roman ally she chose in his place, was eventually defeated by Caesar's heir Octavian. (Caesarion could not be the heir: non-Romans could not inherit Roman property. Caesar had no acknowledged Roman sons, so in his will he adopted his sister's grandson.) At that time Caesarion was still barely of age. Octavian obviously did not want a natural son of Caesar to complicate his own position, and when he took Egypt in 30 B.C., he wanted Cleopatra taken prisoner.

But he wanted Caesarion dead.

CLEOPATRA'S
HEIR

CHAPTER I

His side hurt. He was aware of that before he was properly awake: the pain stabbed into his mind even through sleep. He shifted position, trying to ease it, but that only made it worse. He rolled over onto his other side and drew his legs up, then lay still, muzzily aware of himself.

It was bakingly hot, and he was thirsty. His tongue hurt. His head hurt. The pain in his right side was like a knife. He was lying on a heap of something rough and hard and uncomfortable. All around him was a dense, hot, purple shade, and a thick, choking smell of myrrh which could not quite drown the competing scents of blood, urine, and hot cotton.

He fumbled weakly at the pain in his side, and was rewarded by an exquisite thrust of agony. He moved his hand away again, rubbing swollen fingers together. They were wet.

I have had a seizure, he thought guiltily, and I must have

fallen on top of something. Mother will be angry. I hope she doesn't punish the slaves.

He felt for the fine gold chain around his neck, found it, hauled the little silk bag it held from under his tunic and pressed it against his nose and mouth. Peony root, cardamon, gum ammoniacum, bryony, cinquefoil, and squill: at least the latest remedy *smelled* nice. He drew in deep breaths of it and tried to remember where he was.

Dreamily, he thought of his bedroom in the palace. The floor was always smooth and cool underfoot, even in the hottest summer, and the polished marble was arranged in varicolored patterns, purest white, golden, deep, red-veined green. The bed was of cedarwood, inlaid with gold; in winter the coverlets were of quilted silk, in summer, of brilliantly dyed cotton. There was cool water in an alabaster jar, and a fountain played in the courtyard . . .

. . . when he was younger there'd been swimming in the big bath-house, with its pools paved with lapis lazuli, and the water taps that looked like golden dolphins, and the painting on the ceiling of Dionysos covering the pirate ship with vines while the sailors, fleeing into the green waves, were transformed . . . the water had felt so cool, so sweet, flowing across his naked flesh, swirling around his legs and arms . . .

Swimming will aggravate your condition.

By Apollo, he was thirsty! Why was he lying here alone? Where were the slaves to fan him, anoint him with scented oils, bring him cool drinks in sweating goblets? Where were the doctors with their potions? Why had he woken up alone? Had he had the seizure somewhere private, where no one could find him? How long had he been lying here?

It was so hot. He couldn't think clearly. He had to get out of this purple shade; it was cooking him.

Caesarion sat up slowly, holding his sore side, and found himself inhaling purple cotton. He pushed it away feebly, then realized that it was a covering—the awning of his tent, of course; it kept the sun off during the day, it must have fallen down. He turned onto his left side and began to squirm his way awkwardly out from under it, still with one hand clutched protectively over his injured side. Rough sticks of firewood wobbled beneath him, then slipped. He rolled jolting down on top of them into a blaze of sunlight. The pain stabbed red-hot, and he lay still, panting in anguish. Above him the sky was cloudless, colorless from the fury of the sun.

He was lying on something knobbly. He looked down and saw that it was one of the guards. The man's throat had been ripped open by a spear-thrust which had broken his jaw, and his tunic was thick with drying blood.

Caesarion recoiled, scrambled off hastily, and stood on hot stone, staring down in horror, wiping his left hand convulsively against his tunic. Then his stomach contracted toward his throat. He sank onto his knees and pressed the silk bag to his face again, squeezing his eyes tight shut. *No*, he thought, No, please, not now, not so soon. . . .

Nothing happened. No stink of carrion, no overpowering sense of dread, no memories. Only scorching stone against his knees, sun on his head, and the scent of the remedy. The ground was too hot to kneel on. He opened his eyes and stood up.

The dead guard was dressed only in his red tunic; his armor, weapons, and cloak were all missing. He lay upon his back, at an angle to the pile of purple-draped firewood. His arms had been at his side until Caesarion had fallen onto him and disarranged them, and one, jolted akimbo, still clutched a chunk of hard journeybread as an offering for the guardian of the Underworld. His eyes were shut, and one of the coins which had been laid upon them shone on the ground by Caesarion's feet. His name, Caesarion remembered, was Megasthenes; he was an Alexandrian of good family, twenty-two years old. He'd been specially selected for this mission because of his loyalty.

That loyalty had laid him on his funeral pyre. Caesarion glanced up at it: a stack of firewood, bulked up with camel saddles and grain sacks, piled six feet high and draped in the purple tent awning. He remembered now. Last night (or could it have been the night before last?) he had woken in the dark to the sound of shouting. He had jumped from his bed, fumbled in the dark for his spear, hadn't been able to find it. Someone had burst into the tent with a lantern, and he'd almost struck out before he realized that it was his tutor, Rhodon, who'd stayed behind in Coptos to get news. Rhodon was fully dressed, his normally sleek hair dusty and disheveled, his face pale and his eyes wild. He set down the lantern and grabbed the spear Caesarion had been searching for—it had been propped up by the entrance to the tent. "Here!" he'd shouted loudly. "Here, quickly!"

Caesarion had stretched out his hand for the spear—but Rhodon had leveled the point at him. "No," he'd whispered, and their eyes met and held. "Stand still."

"Rhodon?" Caesarion had said, unable to take it in.

"You're not worth my life," Rhodon said, with intense vehemence. "You're not worth any more lives. There are already too many dead who were whole and healthy." Then he shouted again, "Here! He's in here! Quickly!"

Caesarion remembered screaming in outrage and hurling himself at the traitor—but after that . . .

Bright, unnaturally vivid fragments: a dead sheep lying on an altar while a priest inspected its entrails; a butterfly fanning its wings on the eye of a corpse; the sound of a flute. There had been an . . . interval, and he had woken from it injured.

He looked down at himself.

A clotted mass of dried blood glued his tunic to his right side, and a fresh red trickle was crawling down onto his knee.

I didn't manage to hit him, he realized heavily. He betrayed me to the Romans, and I didn't even manage to hit him—or die nobly. I had a seizure; I was stabbed sometime during the course of it; and I've been lying since in a deep stupor. They thought I was dead. They put me on the top of the pyre, with the dead guard—guards—around me.

There was more than one guard, he saw that now. Another pair of feet stuck out from under the purple drapery beside Megasthenes' head. He walked slowly over to the still figure, bent stiffly to lift the covering. It was Eumenes, who'd commanded their small force. His left leg was almost severed, and there were stab wounds in his side and groin. His teeth were clenched and his face was set in an expression of agony; the coins on his eyes looked like beetles eating them. Caesarion replaced the covering with a shaking hand. His knees were trembling and he felt dizzy. He wanted to sit down, but the dead guards took up all the space on the edge of the pyre, and the ground was too hot.

There was a third body beyond that of Eumenes. He stumbled over to it, inspected it in turn. Heliodoros, the Cretan, stabbed through the heart. Odd that the mercenary should have died trying to defend Caesarion; he'd made it clear all along that he was only in it for the money. How would he collect his wages now?

He stood for a long moment, gazing at the mercenary's face. It was calm, the expression reflecting only a mild surprise. Heliodoros had been a handsome man who'd taken great care of his body, who'd combed his long black hair assiduously every morning and evening. Someone had combed it carefully now, and placed coins upon his eyes. His right hand clasped its chunk of journeybread, and his torn and bloodstained tunic had been carefully straightened. The body, like the other bodies, had not been washed—but then, the camp had been short of water even before an unknown number of the enemy arrived in it. The corpse had been properly anointed: scented oil gleamed on the calm face and made dark splotches on the scarlet tunic. At least Heliodoros and the others were getting a proper funeral.

Caesarion lowered the purple awning and raised his eyes to stare vacantly beyond the pyre. Red cliffs, dark, dusty soil, and the merciless desert sky. The sun was high; it must be about noon. Three dead bodies on the pyre. There had been thirty-eight people in the camp, not including himself: two files of royal guardsmen; Eumenes; Eumenes' secretary; Eumenes' valet; Caesarion's secretary and two attendants. Where were all the others? Where were the attackers? Who had arranged this funeral, then abandoned it with the pyre unlit?

It was too hot to light a fire now. Probably it had already

been too hot by the time the pyre was arranged, and now they were waiting for nightfall. He turned and looked behind him.

The camp his own men had made was still in place, clustered around the stone rim of the cistern which had been dug into the ground by miners a century before. A few scrubby acacias and dead thistles testified that this was a location which occasionally saw water during the winter, but now it was August, and the dry air shimmered like a kiln. The small collection of canvas tents huddled against the base of the near cliff, which provided shade during the worst of the afternoon heat. His own tent, in the center, looked oddly deformed without its upper awning—no, a corner was missing, and the tent had been pegged down lopsided. There were scorch marks on the cloth, just visible through the blur of heat-haze. Rhodon's lantern must have tipped over and set fire to it. The baggage animals—camels, mostly—were tethered a little farther along, and were lying motionless in the puddles of shade at the cliff foot. There were no new tents, but there did seem to be a few more animals, and a collection of military cloaks had been stretched out from the cliff face to provide a little shade, secured to the rocky soil by spears. Shields propped against those spears provided a little more shade, all the shelter that was needed in this hot land. They were tall, oblong shields, red, decorated with unfamiliar motifs. He began to count them, then stopped resignedly. Those were Roman legionary shields, and there would be eighty of them: a full century. A tall standard stood before them, the Roman eagle almost unbearably bright in the noonday sun.

The Romans had traveled light, he thought, forcing a numb

and weary mind to reason about what he could see. No tents, just a few baggage animals to carry food and water for the journey. They had chosen the right equipment and right number for the task they had in hand. They'd known where they were going, and how many men they had to deal with.

Rhodon must have sent them a message as soon as the rest of the party left him alone in Coptos. No—even before that: there was not time for a message to have gone from Coptos to Alexandria and a force of men to have sailed up the Nile in response. Rhodon must have sent his message when the royal party itself set off up the Nile. He had waited for the Romans in Coptos, led them up the caravan trail on forced marches—by night, since no one traveled the Eastern Desert by day if he could help it—and brought the enemy into the camp during the hours of darkness. Probably the attack had come just before the dawn, when men slept most deeply. He must have given the password to the sentries, so that no alarm was raised until it was too late. Then he had run to find Caesarion, because he knew that the men would surrender if their king were captured or dead.

Eumenes, Megasthenes, and Heliodoros had fought any-way—but perhaps that was just out of confusion, because they'd been woken suddenly by their enemies and didn't know what was going on. The others had indeed surrendered. Rho-don could truthfully claim that he had saved them from exile or death, which was all that they could have expected with Caesarion. There were no Roman bodies on the pyre, which meant that the attackers had succeeded in their mission without losing a man. They would be pleased about that, and would treat their prisoners leniently; they had, in any case, no reason to hate royal guardsmen who had no royalty left to guard. Probably Rhodon would be richly rewarded. Certainly the Romans *ought* to be grateful to him. He had eliminated a dangerous rival to their emperor, and secured them a chestful of treasure, without the loss of a single man.

Caesarion pressed the heels of his hands against his sore eyes. Rhodon had taught him philosophy and mathematics for three years now, and he'd preferred him to all his other tutors. He had *liked* Rhodon—liked his mordant sense of humor, his honesty, his penetrating mind and elegant wit. *You're not worth my life.*

No, he reasoned silently, passionately; no—but, Rhodon, it wasn't just *me* that you betrayed. It was all my ancestors as well; it was more! We in Egypt, we were last independent kingdom beside the Middle Sea. Now the Romans have it all. From this day the Greeks are a subject people. It should not have happened without a fight, Rhodon! It should not have happened through Greek treachery!

But there was no comfort there: Caesarion had failed, too, as ever. He had not fought: he had had a seizure. Now he was standing beside his own funeral pyre waiting for someone to notice that they'd made a mistake.

Were they all asleep? Hadn't they even bothered to post a sentry?

He sighed, rubbed his mouth wearily, then stopped and looked at his hand: it was dirty with dried blood which had covered his chin. He moved his tongue furtively in his dry mouth, and, yes, it was stiff and hurt horribly. He must have bitten it during the seizure. A fine figure he would cut when the Romans finally realized their mistake. Here he was, "King

Ptolemy Caesar," son of Queen Cleopatra and of the deified Julius—a dirty, bloodstained boy, barely eighteen, unable to speak clearly.

Maybe Rhodon was right, and he *wasn't* worth any more lives. He set his teeth against the all-too-familiar ache of shame. He had *always* fallen short of what he should have been. It wasn't anything new. He was obliged, still, to continue the struggle. He could not compound his failure by giving up. If he hadn't believed that, he would have killed himself when he first understood that his disease was incurable.

Dionysos! How *stupid*—he hadn't even *died* when he should. It was like some idiotic comedy, where the hero prolongs his death scene for so long that the rest of the cast pretend to club him over the head and set him on the pyre by force!

Except that the Romans *still* hadn't done so.

The Romans must have posted sentries. Romans always posted sentries. Antonius was very emphatic about that, and whatever else he was, the emperor Octavian was competent: he'd proved that by beating Antonius. There was no reason to think the camp was unwatched. The officer in charge had been entrusted with a task both important and delicate: he couldn't be a fool. He would undoubtedly have posted sentries even if he didn't have thirty-five prisoners and a treasure to guard. There were chests containing fifty talents of gold in that camp, enough to fund a small army for a year! Even if the prisoners were tied up, the Roman officer would have to take steps to see that his own men didn't pilfer it.

The gold had been in Caesarion's tent. Perhaps it was still there, and the Roman commander was sleeping beside it, as Caesarion himself had. Perhaps there were sentries there as well, but they were sitting inside the tent, out of the sun. It was really the most sensible place to sit, if you were a sentry.

They must be tired after their forced march. It was a long way to Coptos, and farther still to Alexandria, or wherever the Romans had been when they received Rhodon's message. They had traveled a long way fast, they had accomplished what they set out to do, and now it was very hot and they were resting. No normal sentry would be standing out in the sun, paying keen attention to the empty desert. He would be sitting quietly somewhere in the shade, and if he was watching anything, it wouldn't be the funeral pyre. There was nothing to fear from the dead.

Caesarion stood still, gazing stupidly at the camp. He *hurt*, and he was so tired. He had done everything he could, and he'd been defeated: surely now he could rest? If the stone weren't so hot he'd simply lie down where he stood. Did he have to try to *escape*? He'd only fail. He was wounded, and he had no water. He didn't even have a hat to keep off the sun. He wasn't a healthy man to begin with, and he'd just woken from a major seizure. Even if the sentries didn't spot him, he wouldn't last long in the desert. He'd be lucky if he made it as far as the caravan track two miles away.

There were waystations on that track, though, where he could find water. Kabalsi, the nearest, was barely five miles from where he stood. He could walk to the port of Berenike in only two days. There was a ship due in Berenike any day now; they'd been waiting for it for half the month. At first they'd planned to wait in the port itself, but Eumenes had been afraid that news of the treasure would leak out and attract robbers. So they'd camped instead in the secrecy of the desert, and Rhodon had betrayed them—but the ship might be in port. It would have friends, supplies, money. It had all been arranged.

Caesarion felt his eyes start to run, and he struggled to swallow the tears down. The effort hurt his tongue. He wiped at the tears miserably; the moisture was strangely cool on his hot face. He did not want to go on—and yet he had to try. He could not simply give up when there was a possibility that he might escape. His mother the queen had commanded him to flee to safety while she herself stayed in Alexandria to lead the resistance to the Roman invasion. No one had any hope that that invasion could be turned back. She might be suffering the final terrors of the siege that very moment, her only comfort the thought that her eldest son was still free. She would never forgive him if he surrendered and died.

The pyre had been built on an expanse of flat rock in the center of a wide dry riverbed; the path down to the caravan track ran along the foot of the near cliff, through the middle of the captured camp. Caesarion gazed hopelessly at the rough ground between him and the more distant cliff opposite—then began to stumble across it. Megasthenes lay half on, half off the pyre, arms akimbo, on a scatter of wood. Caesarion bent down—painfully and stiffly because of his wound—and straightened the limp arms, then hunted for the coins and set them back on the sightless eyes. The body was too heavy for him to lift back onto the pyre, but he tugged at the purple awning until it slid forward far enough to cover the dead man's face. Megasthenes had died for him. He deserved his funeral.

He picked his way slowly over to the farther cliff, then began the hot trek along it, past the camp and on toward the caravan track two baking miles and two hundred feet below. This cliff faced west, and, with the sun now just past noon, there was no shade even at its foot. The ground was uneven, strewn with rocks, and gave off a shimmer of heat. Caesarion walked very slowly, holding his side. Each step still jarred his wound horribly, and he felt sick and light-headed. He expected a sentry's challenge with each breath, and he began to count his footsteps for the grim satisfaction of seeing how far he actually got. One, two . . . He supposed that he was sweating, but his skin was hot and dry as the stone around him: the air sucked up moisture before it could even form a bead. Thirty-five, thirty-six . . . Herakles, the air was so dry it hurt to breathe. If only this were all over!

One hundred five, one hundred six . . . Perhaps he should have walked into the camp and had a drink of water before setting out? No. He had nothing with which to draw it from the cistern, and somebody would be certain to notice him . . . One hundred eighty-three, one hundred eighty-four . . . He wondered how badly he was wounded. The bleeding had stopped again, the trickle drying into a cake on his shin and foot, so probably it wasn't as bad as it seemed. He supposed he could stop and look at the wound, but what was the point? Taking off the tunic would tear the fresh scab and start the wound bleeding again, and there was nothing he could do about it anyway . . . Two hundred and fifty, two hundred fifty-one . . . Somebody had probably poured myrrh into the wound, anyway. All the bodies on the pyre had been anointed, and the sweet aroma clung to him as he walked. Myrrh, according to all the doctors, was the finest of all antiseptics. The wound had already been treated, so there was no point looking

at it. Three hundred twenty-eight, three hundred twenty-nine
. . . Of course, he was a fool to worry about infection anyway:
he was unlikely to live long enough for it to set in.

Three hundred ninety-four, three hundred ninety-five . . .
If he managed to get past the camp and the sentries, he was
probably safe until nightfall. No one was likely to worry about
him until they went to look at the pyre and found that he
wasn't there. Four hundred. Then they'd chase after him, of
course. Killing him was the whole point of their mission; getting the treasure, just an incidental benefit. He would have to
find a hiding place among the rocks by the first waystation.
No, he would have to keep walking for as long as he could;
otherwise the Romans could post men at the next waystation
in either direction and cut him off. Five hundred, five hundred
and one . . . Of course, they'd do that anyway. If he went to
the waystations for water, they'd catch him; if he didn't, he'd
die of thirst. Five hundred thirty-two. Apollo and Asklepios,
his tongue hurt! If only he had some water, just a little water,
to moisten it . . . Five hundred sixty-nine, five hundred sev-
enty. Oh, it was hopeless, useless! He wasn't going to get
away. What was the point of struggling on, suffering the heat
and the pain, when he was going to die anyway? Six hundred.

He stopped, breathing hard, and looked across to the opposite cliff, expecting to see the camp. It wasn't there. He
blinked, then turned slowly about and looked behind him.
Distance and the heat-haze had already reduced it to a pale
blur under the red cliff.

His heart gave a jolt, and all at once he believed that the
possibility was real: he might escape. For the first time, he

became afraid. He turned away from the camp, and stumbled on.

The wadi widened as he descended, and eventually he picked his way across to the path, afraid that if he followed the left-hand cliff he might miss the caravan track. He tripped on the rough ground, jarring the wound open again. Another trickle of blood was oozing down his calf when he reached the path, and he paused to wipe it away, so that the Romans couldn't track him by the spoor—though, as to that, they'd know at once which way he was headed. There was no escape for anyone without water, and no water apart from that in the buried cisterns in the waystations.

The east-facing cliff provided some shade, but the heat was still abominable; it made his head ache until he barely noticed the pain in his tongue. He thought of stopping to rest, but decided that he couldn't risk it. The Romans would come after him as soon as it got dark, and the shadows were lengthening steadily. He plodded on, following the path now, telling himself that he'd already done the worst part.

By the time he reached the caravan track, he knew that the worst part was still to come. The pain in his head had grown so as to eclipse that in his side, and he felt desperately sick and faint. Kabalsi waystation was still three miles away.

At this point the caravan trail ran almost due south, and he lost the cliff and the shade it had provided. Now he was in the open, stumbling over a wilderness of beaten soil and dark rock. The sun beat against his scalp like a blacksmith's hammer, and the scorched earth flung its heat back into his face. He remembered one of the doctors his mother had consulted during the first horrible year of his illness, when he was thirteen and she'd still expected that he could be cured. The man had recommended a course of purgation coupled with exercise, "to sweat the evil out of him." Caesarion had endured one foul-tasting laxative that made his guts cramp, and another vile potion to make him vomit, and afterwards had been required to run laps of the Garden Court in the sun. He had felt just like this then. On his fifth lap he'd had a seizure, which had at least ensured that that particular doctor was never consulted again . . .

He stopped: his stomach was contracting upwards, and he smelled carrion. He sat down quickly, shaking with a profound sense of horror, a fear of something unimaginably worse than the quick death that pursued him, and felt for his feeble little amulet of herbs.

There was the sound of a flute. His mother, wearing the red serpent crown of Lower Egypt and a robe of gold and crimson, smiled at him from beside an altar. There was blood on her hands. A black lamb lay on the altar, kicking feebly, and a priest was examining its entrails. His head was shaven, and the white linen of his robe was spattered with blood. He looked up, directly into Caesarion's eyes. His own eyes were very black, like caves in his head. He opened his mouth to speak, but the sound that came out was the high whistling rattle of the sistrum. Suddenly the lamb was a man, and it wasn't its belly cut open, but his head. "You see here the ventricles of the brain," said a voice out of nowhere, and Caesarion looked at the oozing cavities in the pulpy gray mass before him. The victim's hand twitched. "He's still alive," Caesarion said in horror—and his tongue hurt.

He was sitting on burning stone. It was unbearably hot, and he was in pain. He groaned and bent over.

After a minute, he found that his fingers were looped in the gold chain around his neck, and he hauled the little bag of medicaments up and pressed it against his face. He sat quietly for a long time, breathing in the scent. The events of the past hours gradually reassembled themselves in his mind.

I tried to hurry, he explained silently. I tried to hurry, but it gave me a seizure. I had to rest. Mother, it was so hot, it hurt to touch the stones, and I was wounded . . .

You could still walk? he imagined his mother asking. *How bad was the wound, then?*

I don't know, I didn't look. I tried to hurry, and I had a seizure . . .

A bad one? Did you fall down?

No, it was one of the little ones. I just remembered things and didn't know what I was really doing. But it was so hot, and I feel so horrible, please, you must understand, I had to rest . . .

If you don't hurry, the Romans will catch you and kill you. The ship is waiting for you in Berenike, Caesarion. It's only thirty miles or so, and there's water just a few miles farther on. You have another four or five hours before they realize you're missing. Four or five precious hours, and when those hours are gone, they cannot be called back. You must use those hours, Caesarion. I would use them. Your father would have used them. Do not fail me, my son. Do not fail me now.

Caesarion groaned and rose unsteadily to his feet. The caravan track swam before his eyes. O gods and goddesses, if he could only have some water!

Clutching his side, wavering like a drunkard, he continued on down the rough trail.

HE DIDN'T MAKE it to the waystation. The afternoon dissolved again into horror and stink and shards of memory, and when he came back to the present, the shadows were longer. He got up and staggered drunkenly on. Later he woke and found himself lying upon the hot ground. There were blue shadows all around, and the sun was going down. He tried halfheartedly to get up, and at once everything dissolved again.

He woke again in darkness. It was cold, and his hands and feet were numb. There was a thudding behind him of camel hooves and the creak of harness. He knew where he was— lying in the middle of a caravan track, some distance from the nearest waystation—and he knew that his attempt to escape was almost over. It didn't seem to matter much, though. If he lay perfectly still, the pain was small and unimportant, and soon it would be gone. He'd always known that he would fail. Probably, he decided, it was for the best. Rhodon was right. He wasn't worth any more lives.

The thud-creak-thud of camels drew closer, closer still. Then, sharp and cutting and oddly unexpected, a man's voice exclaimed in horror, "There's a dead man in the road!"

Caesarion lay still, waiting. After a vague period, somebody touched his face, and a voice said, "I think he's alive." He closed his eyes.

He was aware next of water. It ran wonderful and wet into his dry mouth. He swallowed, and his tongue hurt so much it made him gasp, and the water went down his throat the wrong way. He coughed, hurting his side, and tried to drink while he was coughing, and got water up his nose, and sneezed. The water stopped flowing, and he made a noise of protest and reached for it with his hand, and it began again. Nothing, he thought, nothing in all the world is so sweet as water, not gold nor health nor love; nothing. He whimpered with pleasure. The water spilled down the front of his tunic, cold in the night chill, and it was deliriously wonderful.

"That's enough for now," said a voice, and the water stopped. Caesarion lowered his head, found that he was resting it on somebody's shoulder, but didn't move. He wanted to thank whoever it was for letting him drink before they killed him, but it seemed too much effort.

"You're just a boy!" said the voice, sounding surprised. *I was eighteen in June,* Caesarion thought indignantly, but his tongue hurt too much to let him say it. "What sort of people would abandon you in a cursed place like this, eh?"

Caesarion didn't answer. Some small part of his mind, however, was beginning to stir in puzzlement. The voice wasn't Roman. It had the wrong accent. It was saying the wrong things. Gods and goddesses, it wasn't even speaking Greek, it was speaking Demotic Egyptian!

"Let's get you up," said the voice. The speaker tugged at him, and he tired to oblige and stand up. His legs refused to obey him, and his teeth began to chatter. The speaker swore, and somebody else came over and took Caesarion's arm. An elbow caught him in the ribs, just above the wound, and he caught his breath in pain.

"What's the matter?" asked the voice. Then it repeated itself in Greek. "Can you understand me, boy? What's the matter with you?" It had the singsong accent of Upper Egypt.

" 'M hurt," mumbled Caesarion.

"Where?" the voice demanded.

"Siidge," Caesarion slurred. "M' sidge hurt."

A hand touched his side, drew back when he whimpered. "All right," said the voice gently, speaking Demotic again. "All right, all right. Menches, he's injured on the right side. Bring the donkey: we'll sit him on that."

The next thing he knew he was sitting astride a donkey. There was an arm around his waist, steadying him, and his own left arm was looped around someone's neck, his head resting on their shoulder. The person smelt of old sweat, dirty linen, and fish oil, but his flesh was warm. The night was very cold, so Caesarion did not try to pull away. The man started humming to himself, a soft, rhythmic tune which Caesarion didn't know. The moon was rising, and the desert was stark black and pale gray. Everything was wonderfully peaceful.

After a while, the donkey stopped. The smelly man pulled Caesarion off and lowered him gently to the ground. The dust was soft, but it was cold, and he curled up on his left side, shivering. After a while, somebody put a covering over him and he fell asleep.

When he woke it was hot again, and light. His mind was clearer, but he was thirsty, and very weary. It seemed to require a lot of effort even to shift position. He lay quietly for a time, his eyes open, staring blankly at a camel saddle directly in front of him. After a while he moved his head to look around.

He was lying under an awning which was anchored at two corners with camel saddles and supported at the other two by thin posts. Outside the makeshift shelter was sunlight, bare earth, and the motionless shapes of camels.

This wasn't anyplace he'd ever been before, any situation he'd expected. He thought of the man who'd supported him on the donkey during the night—the smell, the soft humming of a walking song. *You're just a boy!* he'd said, in Demotic and a tone of shocked surprise.

He had no idea who I am, Caesarion thought, bemused by the strangeness of it. I was lying in the middle of the caravan trail, and an ordinary caravan came along, and helped me because . . .

. . . because I was lying there hurt and needed help. How strange.

It even seemed odd that at a time like this, with Alexandria under siege and Egypt on the brink of subjugation to Rome, there were still caravans on the trade routes—but the war had been going on for a couple of years now, and he supposed that merchants had to trade or starve.

So. What would happen now? Presumably the Romans would soon come along and ask the caravan master if he'd found any injured men. What would the caravan master answer?

Impossible to predict. He might hand over his find at once. He might ask for a reward. On the other hand, he might be afraid that admitting it would get him into trouble, and deny that he'd found anyone. He might decide to knock his dangerous acquaintance over the head and tip him down the next gully. *I have not seen the man you want. Probably he died in the desert.*

Or he might try to protect his guest. The smelly man had

seemed kind enough. Probably, though, the smelly man wasn't master of the caravan, but an assistant of some kind. He'd spoken Demotic, and even in Greek he'd had a native accent. A merchant able to mount a caravan from the Nile to the Red Sea would surely be a Greek, a member of the elite that had ruled Egypt for three centuries. Well, perhaps the caravan master, too, would be kind. A Greek ought to be sympathetic to a fellow-Greek in difficulties.

A lot depended, of course, on how the Romans actually phrased their question. If a couple of them tramped over saying that they were looking for a fugitive, that was one thing; if they marched up in force, saying that they were chasing the young king Ptolemy Caesar, and that to shelter such a personage was treason, that was something else. Even if the caravan master were patriotic, he was unlikely to risk his life for a cause that was already lost. Caesarion should keep his identity a secret—if he could.

A shape bulked blackly against the light outside, and then a man crawled in under the awning, on hands and knees since there wasn't room to stand. He looked to be in his late thirties, lean, with a heavy-jawed face stubbled with unshaven traveling, and the dark brown skin and slightly kinked hair sometimes found in Upper Egypt. He was dressed in a dirty linen tunic, with a coarse linen shawl tossed loosely over his head to provide some protection from the sun. Everything about his appearance proclaimed him a native Egyptian, a peasant, so probably he was one of the caravan's drivers. He looked annoyed about something, and when his eyes met Caesarion's, he gave an irritated grunt.

"So," he said sourly, in singsong Greek, "you're awake."

Caesarion recognized the voice: it was the speaker of the night before, the smelly man who'd supported him on the donkey. "Well, boy, there isn't any water. This thrice-cursed and god-hated place is out of it, and we can't do anything to clean you up. Have some beer." He held out a flask of coarse clay, stoppered with a stick wrapped in rag.

Caesarion remembered guiltily that Eumenes had been telling the men to drive the camels down to Kabalsi for water, to spare the supply at the camp. It seemed that they'd drunk the station dry. He wished they hadn't: he *wanted* water. Ordinarily he wouldn't have touched the thick beer favored by the native Egyptians, but now even that sounded delicious. He raised himself slowly up onto an elbow, began to reach for the flask, and found that the movement pulled painfully at his wounded side. He sat up properly and took the bottle with his left hand. The other man made a hissing noise through his teeth. He was staring at Caesarion's bloodied tunic.

"That doesn't look good," he remarked, gesturing at the injury. "What happened?"

Caesarion didn't know how to answer. He fumbled weakly at the bottle's stopper. The other took it from him, opened it, and handed it back. Caesarion drank greedily, hardly tasting the bitterness in the sweet fact that it was *wet*.

"Don't you understand me?" the other demanded sharply.

Caesarion lowered the bottle a moment and nodded cautiously. "Please," he croaked, manipulating his sore tongue with difficulty. "I'm thirsty." He glanced down at the flask, then, unable to resist, took another long drink. The beer stung his tongue and made it feel better at the same time.

"When we found you last night," said the other man softly,

"I thought either you'd been robbed, or you were a robber."

Caesarion lowered the bottle and stared at him in consternation.

"You're not, though, are you?" said the Egyptian. "You didn't get that," he gestured again at the wound, "in any beating. That came from a spear or a sword. You're sunburned, too, like a man who isn't used to the desert, and that tunic's military, and top-quality cloth, too. Even last night, I thought it was a damned strange robber who goes about drenched in expensive perfume. The myrrh was for the cut, was it? Why didn't you bandage it properly while you were about it?"

Caesarion, affronted, started to set the bottle down, then snatched it up again hurriedly as it began to tip over.

The Egyptian gave a snort of amusement. "Nothing to say for yourself?" he asked.

Caesarion looked down at the dry ground. Was this fellow playing with him? Had the Romans been here already? Certainly they'd had plenty of time to reach the waystation; in fact, he should have realized that. Was this some cruel game? He'd thought this man kind, but he certainly didn't seem so now.

"Boy," said the Egyptian, not unsympathetically, "a troop of Romans passed us on the road two nights ago, marching so hard they didn't even pause to steal from us. Last night there was a fire off to the right of the trail—a big one, a couple of miles away up a wadi. Tell me the truth. You were in the queen's forces, weren't you?"

Caesarion gazed at him incredulously. The Romans had *lit* the pyre? Burned the bodies? As though nothing had gone wrong?

Maybe they hadn't noticed he was missing. The purple awn-ing had covered the top of the pyre, and if they hadn't lifted it . . . He'd disturbed Megasthenes when he fell off, of course, but perhaps the Romans had simply assumed that one of their own people had done that. Or perhaps they hadn't even no-ticed. He'd pulled the awning down again, to cover the guard's face. Perhaps they'd just assumed that all was well, and thrust in the torch. All that scented oil, those camel saddles and sacks of flour—the pyre would have gone up with a roar and de-stroyed all traces of his departure.

If the Romans *did* believe he was dead and cremated now, would they realize their mistake when they tried to collect the ashes for burial?

"You're young to be a soldier," the Egyptian was continuing insistently. "From the look of that cut, you weren't wearing armor, either. Are you slave or free?"

He stared in confusion, at first too preoccupied by his own question to take in this one—and then bewildered by the in-solent implication. Finally his face stung with indignation. "Gods and goddesses!" he exclaimed hoarsely.

"Well?" asked the Egyptian, unimpressed. "I'll hear your story. If you're a slave, I want to know what's happened to your master."

"I am not a *slave!*" Caesarion cried furiously. His tongue was working again. "Zeus!" He set the beer bottle down with a thump. It promptly began to fall over. The Egyptian caught it, shook it, then drank down the last swallow of beer himself.

"So?" he asked, wiping his mouth. "Why weren't you wear-ing armor, then?"

"I was asleep," Caesarion said angrily. "Rhodon came, and . . ." He stopped.

"Rhodon your lover?" the Egyptian asked, with interest.

If he hadn't felt so weak, Caesarion would have hit the man. That a native, a peasant, should say such a thing to *him*—it passed belief. The queen would crucify anyone who showed her firstborn such disrespect.

"Well, I don't believe that soldiers on active service usually have supplies of perfume handy," said the Egyptian, responding to the glare of outrage. "—Though if they do, it explains why the queen's lost the war."

Caesarion's rage died suddenly. "The war's over?" he asked faintly.

The other nodded, warily now. "So they were saying in Coptos when we left it. Alexandria's fallen. The queen's lover, the general Antonius—he's dead, they say, and Queen Cleopatra has been taken prisoner. No word about the boy Caesarion, but he never counted for anything anyway. Egypt is a Roman province now."

Caesarion bowed his head, pressed the heels of his hands to his eyes. Alexandria fallen, Antonius dead, Mother . . .

She'd always sworn that she would never allow herself to be taken prisoner, never grace a Roman triumph. She'd sworn to burn herself alive in her own mausoleum, together with all her treasures, before she surrendered to her enemies. How had this fate—this unspeakable . . . How . . .

His stomach was starting to rise. He snatched the remedy bag up to his face and breathed deeply.

"I'm sorry," said the Egyptian quietly. Caesarion glanced at him quickly, then looked away again. His eyes were running, and he wiped them angrily without lowering the remedy. He could feel the seizure creeping toward him. Intense emotion often brought them on.

"So, you were of the queen's party," the other said, after a long silence. "What were you doing here?"

"Go away!" Caesarion ordered him indistinctly.

"There were nearly a hundred Romans in the troop that passed us," the Egyptian continued, ignoring it, "and they were in a tearing hurry. It must have taken something important to bring them so far inland, so soon—I never expected to see any of them, not until they'd settled the rest of the country. I'd guess you and some friends were sent in this direction on some important business—fetching or hiding something for the queen maybe?—and somebody told the Romans, and they hurried up and caught you, and there was a fight. They get the treasure—or whatever it was?"

"Yes," said Caesarion desperately. "Leave me alone!"

"Pity," said the other. "You're sure?"

"O gods and goddesses, leave me alone!"

"I'm sorry," said the Egyptian again, and went out.

Alexandria fallen, Antonius dead, Mother a prisoner—if what the Egyptian had heard was right, if she wasn't dead as well. He pressed his face against his knees, shaking. Even if she was still alive, she would die soon, she would die. She would never endure that, not to bow to Caesar Octavian, not to walk in chains in his triumph. She would die. It was all over. Why in the name of all the immortal gods hadn't he stayed on the damned pyre? Why hadn't he had the sense or the grace to die on cue?

He remembered her dancing in the shrine of Dionysos, deep

in the heart of the palace. Dressed in pearls and the skin of a fawn, her hair twined with ivy, she had vine-stepped about the altar by torchlight to the wild music of the sistrum and the flute. She was all fire and grace. Antonius, who was drunk, had blundered into the dance after her—and she had somehow made even that look as though it had been planned, a nymph dancing with a bear, a dolphin cavorting with a ship, so that even accident became perfection . . .

The scent of carrion, and an overpowering sense of horror. Mother was striding from the ship, wearing her purple robes and a gold-worked diadem. A woman flung herself forward out of the crowd, dressed in only in a tunic, her face and shoulders bruised. "Mercy!" she screamed. "Queen, my husband committed no crime!"

A fish was swimming in the deep green of a pool. Another fish lunged suddenly from among the weeds and seized it.

The man was tied to the table facedown, naked, his hands and feet secured to the table-legs with thick ropes. The back of his skull had been removed, and blood was trickling steadily into channels cut into the stone floor. "You see here the ventricles of the brain," said the doctor. He prodded the pulpy gray mass with a scalpel, and the man's hand twitched. "He's still alive!" Caesarion cried in horror . . .

He was sitting under an awning. It was hot. His side hurt. He straightened slowly, then lay down on his good side, trembling with exhaustion. He still had the remedy pressed to his face, but he couldn't smell it: his nose was choked with tears.

Why had he been forced to remember such things, at a time like this? The queen was brave, brilliant, witty; her magnificence left men breathless with admiration, her ambition covered the world. To remember *those* things . . . That man on the table had been a convicted criminal, condemned to death, and that woman's husband had been an enemy of the queen, executed at a time when the state was in danger. It was cruel ingratitude to rake up such things now, when the queen was either lying dead, or else a helpless prisoner. I'm sorry, Mother, he thought wretchedly. It was the illness that remembered it, not me.

It was no comfort. His illness had always been his worst, most unforgivable failure.

You must escape, his mother had told him, the last time they spoke together. That task was one he could still hope to complete. He must complete it. The knowledge that her son was still alive and at liberty was the only comfort he could offer the queen in her captivity, and his own survival the best memorial he could give her.

IT WAS LATE in the afternoon when the Egyptian came back: the shadows outside were long. Caesarion had slept, then woken with a raging thirst. When the Egyptian crawled in he sat up eagerly, but this time the man had no flask with him, only a piece of stale bread and couple of withered figs folded in a shawl. The Egyptian saw his disappointment.

"I told you: we've no water, and now we're almost out of beer," he declared, setting the food down. "We're saving our last pot of it for the journey tonight. You had more than the rest of us, boy: we gave you double rations this morning, and stinted ourselves. —What's your name, anyway?"

He suppressed a flash of irritation at the man's tone: he

didn't want this fellow to know who it was he'd been calling "boy." He considered answering truthfully, "Ptolemaios"—the name was common enough to attract no comment—but he wasn't sure he'd manage to answer to it. Nobody had ever called him Ptolemy: his nickname, Caesarion, "Little Caesar," had been used by everyone from his mother to the fishmongers on the Alexandrian quays—when they weren't calling him "king" and "lord," of course. He picked a name which sounded similar.

"Arion," he told the Egyptian.

"Huh. I'm called Ani." It was an Egyptian name, not even faintly Hellenized. "Arion," Ani went on, "would it be any use our sending up to that camp you came from to beg some water?"

"No," Caesarion replied, going cold despite the heat.

"They know we're around," Ani said reasonably. "They overtook us on the road. It's nothing to them if we take some water, is it? It's not as though they're planning to spend time up there. And we used the last of our own water this morning. It's a long walk to the next station if we have to go thirsty all the way."

"We were already almost out of water," Caesarion told him. "Eumenes was sending the camels down here to drink."

"Was he?" Ani cried irritably. "Well, bugger him! So, it's because of you that we're thirsty?" He was silent a moment, then said, "Your lot were up there for a while, were you?"

Caesarion hunched his shoulders uncomfortably. He was giving away more than he wanted to, but he couldn't think what else to do. He needed help from the caravan party if he was to reach Berenike and the ship; he was too weak now to do it on his own. "Yes," he admitted.

"With a treasure. You said the Romans had taken a treasure."

It was Ani, Caesarion remembered, who'd brought up the question of treasure: it had apparently been the first thing he'd thought of when he understood that a royal force had fought Romans in the desert. He looked at the Egyptian with distaste.

"Don't you try to hold out on me, boy," Ani said sharply. "I saved your life last night, if you didn't notice. Most caravan-masters find a boy lying half-dead in the road, they leave him there, you understand? Could be a decoy for robbers. I gave you water, put you on my own donkey, looked after you like you were my own. You can answer me."

"My debt is to the master of your caravan . . ." began Caesarion coldly.

Ani seemed to swell. "*I* am master of this caravan! Who'd you think I was?" He glared. "You think because I'm an Egyptian, because I don't speak la-di-da fancy Greek like you, I'm nobody? Your debt, boy, is to *me*. What were you doing with that treasure, eh?"

Caesarion fought to master his anger: if he said what he wanted to say, the insolent peasant would probably abandon him here in this waterless place. "We were waiting for a ship," he admitted. "It was supposed to meet us in Berenike sixteen days ago."

"Ah," said Ani. After a moment, he added slowly, "I heard how the queen had all her ships moved over to the Red Sea last winter. They said she was planning to sail off to the East, with all her treasure, and make herself queen of somewhere else. But I heard that the ships were burned."

"Yes," agreed Caesarion distantly. "They were all in the harbor at Heroonpolis, and King Malehus of Arabia attacked them and burned them. But there were a few that were salvageable."

Ani nodded. "So she decided to move some men and some money out of the country, to provide herself with a bolt hole if she lost Alexandria? And your lot were sent to take the treasure to Berenike, so that it could be loaded on the ship without any danger of the Arabs or the Romans finding out about it. Only the ship didn't come, and the Romans did find out."

"The ship may be there now," Caesarion told him. He had to give this greedy peasant a reason to help. "We know it left Heroonpolis. It's been delayed, but it should be in Berenike now. If you can take me to Berenike—they'd pay you for it."

Ani regarded him suspiciously. "I suppose they might, at that," he admitted grudgingly. "Worth something to them to know that the Romans have the treasure. What sort of treasure was it, anyway?"

"Fifty talents of gold."

He whistled. "And you're sure the Romans got *all* of it? Your lot hadn't . . . well, buried some of it, in a secret place?" He could not quite hide his eagerness.

"We didn't bury any of it," Caesarion replied with disgust. "It was royal treasure. It was supposed to pay men to fight for Egypt."

"Ah well," said Ani resignedly. "I'll have to make my fortune the hard way, then." He sat back, squatting on his haunches, and pulled thoughtfully at his lower lip—a peasant gesture, vulgar, like the man himself. "And you say there's no point trying to get water from your old camp?"

"We were almost out of water ourselves," Caesarion told him in a flat tone, wishing the fellow would go away. "Now there's a whole century of Romans there, and they have all our baggage animals in addition to their own. They're probably on short rations already."

"A whole what?"

"Century," Caesarion told him, with a faint sneer. "A division of a Roman legion. Eighty men."

"As I live, you may be a soldier after all! Very well, we'll have to do without water tonight. Do you know if there's still water at Hydreuma?"

Hydreuma was the next waystation, the last before Berenike itself. "There are *wells* there," Caesarion pointed out impatiently. There was, in fact, a small settlement. Eumenes had sent men there to buy vegetables.

"If your lot's camels haven't emptied them. Now, boy . . ."

"Stop calling me that!" Caesarion snapped, finally losing his temper. "I'm not a slave! I'm a freeborn Alexandrian and . . . and of good family. The queen herself sent me here. By Apollo! You Egyptian camel-driver, how dare you call me 'boy'!"

Ani's eyes narrowed. "Boy," he said deliberately, "are you able to walk to Hydreuma?"

Caesarion looked at the ground. He could feel his cheeks burning. He was certain that he could not. He doubted he could walk as much as a mile. What was worse, he had a nasty suspicion that if he tried, it would bring on a seizure. He'd had a lot of seizures in the past two days, many more than usual, and he could feel them pressing on him like a physical weight, crushing him: he didn't know how many more he could endure. Besides, Ani would probably abandon him at once if he knew about the disease. People tended to think it was contagious. Even in the palace, slaves had spat behind their hands before they picked up something Caesarion dropped, and they threw out his leftover wine rather than drink it. Ani had, so far, said nothing about the seizure Caesarion had had earlier that day, which undoubtedly meant he hadn't noticed it. That was to the good.

"So," said Ani sweetly, "you need help from this Egyptian camel-driver, don't you? Not a very good idea to insult me, is it?"

"No," whispered Caesarion, trembling with humiliation.

The Egyptian waited a moment; when no apology was offered, he apparently decided to accept the admission instead. "How bad's that cut?" he asked briskly.

"I don't know," Caesarion replied faintly.

"Don't know? Didn't you even look at it when you put that myrrh on?"

"I didn't put the myrrh on."

"You wear perfume all the time, do you?"

Be still my heart; you have endured worse. "The Romans anointed me for the pyre. They thought I was dead. The cut can't be too bad: I managed to walk as far as . . . I managed to get as far as the caravan track."

Ani was staring at him in disbelief. "They thought you were *dead*? And you got up and walked off?"

"Leave me alone!" Caesarion pressed his hands to his face,

choking. Mother murdered or a prisoner, Antonius dead, Egypt a Roman province—and he had to sit here, enduring the insults of a camel-driving peasant! "It was hot, they were in the shade somewhere, they weren't watching the pyre anyway. O immortal gods, I wish I'd never woken up!"

"Now, boy!" exclaimed Ani reprovingly; and, to Caesarion's horror and disgust, patted him on the shoulder. "You don't mean that. You're a young man, you still have your whole life before you . . . Here, let me look at what happened to you . . ." He tugged at the tunic.

Caesarion shoved his hands away furiously. "Leave me alone!" He caught his breath, struggled with himself, and went on, more moderately. "If I take the tunic off it will start bleeding again. It's got myrrh on it, it can wait."

Ani sat back, frowning. Caesarion glared back.

"You can ride the donkey again," said Ani, after a silence. "I pray to the gods there's water at Hydreuma. Whether or not you're telling me the truth, that cut's not good. Now, try and eat something: it's going to be a rough night."

CHAPTER II

It was indeed a very rough night. Caesarion afterwards re-membered it only in fragments: sitting stiffly on the donkey with the pain red-hot in his side; lying shivering on the ground in the moonlight during a rest stop; the almost unbearable delight of the last of the beer, drunk at midnight. He was certain he had at least one seizure during the course of that nightmare journey, but he was so light-headed with pain and thirst that it simply blended unnoticed with a waking delirium.

The caravan was smaller than he'd expected: eighteen cam-els, three men, and a donkey. The camels were very heavily laden with immense bales of what appeared to be linen cloth, and they were roped together in strings of six, with a man to lead each string. Caesarion gathered that until they picked him up the men had carried their own luggage on the donkey, and that now they had to carry it on their backs. It was, he decided, a very poor caravan, if there was no room on the camels for the drivers.

Ani's two assistants were called Menches and Imouthes; they were a middle-aged father and a son of about Caesarion's own age, both coarse, dark Egyptians, much like Ani himself. They objected to Caesarion's riding the donkey and having a share of the beer, and they argued about it in Demotic with Ani. Ani overruled them on the grounds that he expected money from Caesarion's ship.

They left the waystation about an hour before sunset. The donkey was thirsty and unhappy and inclined to kick, even when Ani took its head. The pain from Caesarion's wound started bad and got steadily worse, and it seemed to him that they would never reach Hydreuma, that he would jolt along in the blank darkness forever, enduring one endless minute after another after another. When at last they arrived, he did not at first realize it. By that stage he was lying facedown on the donkey's back, his arms folded around its neck, semiconscious and shivering. He only snapped back into awareness when he was pulled off. The flare of agony up his side made him scream, and he curled up in the dust, sobbing. It was dark and cold and there were people around him. A woman's voice said, "Sshhh!" into his ear, and he was carried inside a building and set down. An argument started over his head. He closed his eyes.

He woke up again when they gave him water. Everything was shadowy, illuminated only by the flame of a single lamp held by a woman standing over him. He was lying on a pallet next to a stone wall; above his head was what appeared to be a tent. He blinked at it muzzily. Another woman who was kneeling next to him began to splash water from a basin over his blood-encrusted tunic. She unfastened the pin that secured the cloth at his right shoulder, then slid a sponge under the tunic and dribbled more water down his side. The woman with the lamp bent over and took the pin.

"Here! That's not yours!" said Ani. Caesarion looked for and found him, standing in the middle of the house-tent and glaring at the women.

The woman spat on the grime-coated pin, rubbed it against the shoulder of her tunic, and examined it under the lamp. She was middle-aged, with a sour face. "This is gold," she told Ani.

"And not yours," replied Ani, taking it away from her.

"We're not thieves!" the woman complained. "You think we're going to rob him?"

Ani snorted. "Yes. You're already robbing me, the price you're charging. Here, you can give me his belt and sandals as well, and that amulet he's got round his neck."

The woman with the basin smiled at Caesarion. She was younger than the one with the lamp and darker: her teeth gleamed in the lamplight. She scooped more water out of her basin onto his side, then unfastened his belt, worked it out from under him, and passed it up to Ani. She reached for the silk bag of the remedy, but Caesarion was clutching it with both hands.

"No," he said weakly. "No, I need this."

"Huh," said Ani, squatting down beside him. "You're in your right mind again, are you? Boy, that amulet would be a lot safer with me."

"I need it," insisted Caesarion.

The Egyptian shrugged. "Suit yourself." He glanced up at the older woman. "I expect it to be here this evening—*and* the chain it's hung on. It's only a charm, anyway. There's nothing in it but herbs."

He must have looked in it himself to know that, Caesarion thought, with revulsion. He must have searched it for money.

The dark woman was unfastening his sandals. Ani took them, tucked them under his arm, and stood up.

"Where are you going?" Caesarion choked. He did not like or trust the caravan-master, but he trusted these women even less. They were going to hurt him. He could feel the water soaking into the mess of blood and linen at his side, and he knew that as soon as they'd softened the scab they were going to pull the tunic loose. Apollo and Asklepios, it was going to hurt!

"I'm going to see to my caravan," the Egyptian replied shortly. "Boy, I'm paying four drachmae for these two to look after you and clean you up. Tell me if they don't give you my money's worth. I'll be back this evening."

He went out, striding from the shadowy house-tent into a dusky outside. The dark girl smiled at Caesarion again and poured some more water on his wound. The older woman spat, bent over, and tugged at the tunic. Caesarion gasped in anguish. She spat again, and said something to the dark girl in another language.

The dark girl nodded. She stood, stepped astraddle Caesarion, and hitched up her tunic. Then she squatted and urinated directly onto the wound.

He turned his face away and pressed the remedy against his mouth. He was used to the torments and indignities of medicine. Fresh urine was supposed to be good both for softening a scab and cleaning a wound. He tried to pretend that the hot stinging ache was happening somewhere else—that it was there, in that vein of quartz upon that rock in the wall . . .

The older woman took hold of the tunic again and began to twist it back and forth, loosening it. The ache flared into white-hot brilliance. He choked, bit the remedy, felt his stomach rising with a familiar sense of utter horror . . .

They'd cut off the slave's nose, and it bubbled when he screamed, a horrible sound. The guards were flogging him. There were thorns knotted into the leather thongs of the whip, and they ripped great jagged holes in his naked back and buttocks. Caesarion wept. He ran over to his mother and caught her dress, and she looked down at him and smiled. Her hair was curled today, and the purple ribbon of the diadem she wore was stitched with pearls.

"Make them stop!" Caesarion begged her. "Please, make them stop! He didn't mean it!"

"He insulted you," Cleopatra told him. "My son, a king can never allow anyone who insults him to go unpunished. If he does, he loses authority, and if he loses authority, he is dead."

The slave screamed more horribly still. Bone gleamed white in the red ruin of his back. "Please, please!" Caesarion sobbed.

Someone was playing the flute. The sound floated up through the fragrant garden, sweet and clear and piercingly beautiful.

Then it was daylight, and everything was warm and quiet. He lay on his back looking up at the roof of the tent. He was naked apart from a linen bandage which circled his chest along the line of his lower ribs. His right side was very sore, and that puzzled him, because he couldn't remember how he'd hurt it.

I must have had a seizure and fallen on something, he thought dreamily—then remembered thinking that before, and waking . . .

Slowly, memory reassembled itself. He touched the bandage on his side. Under that lay a wound he still hadn't seen. He wondered again how bad it was. He felt for the remedy bag, found to his relief that it was still there, and pressed it to his face. He wondered if the women had told Ani that he'd had a seizure. He hoped not. It was still another day's journey to Berenike.

The dark girl came over presently, and seemed pleased to find him awake. She gave him a drink of water and spoke to him cheerfully in a language he eventually recognized as Trogodytic, the tongue of the natives of the Red Sea Coasts. His mother knew Trogodytic, but he had never learned it. "Speak Greek?" he asked her hopefully, but she laughed and shook her head. She made eating gestures, then went off and came back with a bowl. She helped him to sit up, propped him against the wall of the house-tent, and hand-fed him lentils stewed with coriander. He had not felt hungry, but the food settled deliciously into his empty stomach. He had eaten nothing but the two figs the day before—his mouth had been too dry and his tongue too sore to manage the bread—and he had had nothing at all the day before that. He remembered all the doctors who'd advised him that fasting would provoke seizures, and smiled sourly. The dark girl grinned back and said something encouraging. She helped him to lie down again, and fetched him a cushion for his head.

*   *   *

WHEN HE NEXT woke it was hot, but not unbearably so. The pain was receding, and he lay relaxed, listening. Goats were bleating somewhere nearby, and people were talking, their voices indistinct. Zeus, what a pleasant place Hydreuma was! Shelter from the killing sun, water in the bitter desert, company . . . She was pretty, that dark girl.

Maybe he should stay here for a few days. He suspected now that he'd been feverish the night before, that the wound was infected. It felt as though it had begun to heal now, but presumably traveling would make it worse again. His flesh recoiled from the prospect of climbing back onto that vile donkey—Dionysos, another night like the last one would kill him.

Ani undoubtedly intended to press on to Berenike in the evening, but did he really need Ani now? It was only about fifteen miles to the sea, and downhill all the way. He could say a long farewell to Ani and his insults, and go on to Berenike when he felt stronger.

He shifted uneasily, aware that Ani was expecting money and might not be willing to part without it. Well, there was the pin from his tunic—he could give the fellow that.

He frowned. He was pretty certain that he hadn't been wearing that pin on the night the Romans came. He'd slept in his tunic—they all had, both because of the chill of the desert nights and because it would save time if they had to leave in a hurry—but he hadn't worn the pin. It was a military tunic, stitched on the left shoulder, pinned on the right, so that you could unpin it and have your arm free for working.

A pin always bit into his shoulder when he tried to sleep, so he slept without one. He'd never slept in belt and sandals, either.

The Romans must have dressed him for the pyre. He found himself imagining them handling his body—pinning and belting the tunic, putting the sandals on his feet, arranging his head and limbs—and was sickened. Herakles, had he even woken wearing the same tunic he'd been wearing when Rhodon burst into the tent? He couldn't remember now. Picturing it to himself he saw only the thickly clotted blood, and couldn't recall any rips made by the spear. They might have stripped him and insulted his naked body: he wouldn't know.

Megasthenes, Eumenes, and Heliodoros had been set on the pyre wearing the torn clothing in which they'd died. But they hadn't been wearing pins or belts or sandals, now he thought of it. Of course, the Romans wouldn't have paid as much attention to them as they had to the son of the queen.

He realized abruptly that the Romans must have put him on display. They'd probably arranged him in the middle of the camp, decked out in his purple cloak and the royal diadem, and paraded all their own men and all their prisoners past him so that everyone could see him and agree that he was dead. Then they would have put aside the cloak and the diadem, together with his personal signets and whatever else they could find that he'd used to identify himself, so that they could provide the emperor in Alexandria with evidence that he was dead. If they'd been closer to the city they might have tried to take his body, or at least his head—but they hadn't wanted to carry a decomposing corpse on a ten-day trek across the desert and a fourteen-day journey down the Nile. Dionysos!

Had nobody noticed, in all that arranging and parading, that he was still breathing?

They hadn't known that he'd had a seizure; most of them hadn't even known that he had the disease. The queen had suppressed any discussion of her son's defect and ensured that only his close attendants were aware of it.

He'd been stabbed, and shown no signs of life thereafter. He must've bled from the mouth after biting his tongue, and been half-suffocated by smoke from the burning tent: probably they'd believed that the spear had pierced a lung. It must've been dawn when they set out his body for inspection, with the air still full of smoke, and he had been in a deep stupor. Of course they thought he was dead.

No wonder they hadn't checked the pyre before lighting it. That didn't mean, though, that the fire had removed all traces of the Romans' mistake. The bones would not have been consumed, not entirely. If the Romans continued to follow the proper funeral rites, they would collect the charred fragments, wash them in wine, and place them in urns for burial. Wouldn't they notice then that there were three skulls instead of four? Rhodon and some of the others knew all about his seizures. Wouldn't they begin to doubt, to send men out, just to be sure?

He supposed that he should be glad that the Romans had given him his belt and sandals. He never would have been able to walk across that burning desert barefoot. And the tunic pin: he needed something to pay off Ani. But perhaps he should not pay off Ani. Perhaps he should, after all, hurry on to Berenike at once, and hope that the ship was waiting.

Footsteps approached the house-tent and he sat up, hoping

for the pretty dark girl. Instead the sour older woman came in. She was carrying Caesarion's tunic over her arm; when she saw that he was awake she snorted and came over. Suddenly aware that he was naked, he looked about for something to cover himself.

She dropped the tunic across his lap. "So," she remarked, "you're feeling better."

He turned the tunic over and inspected the right side. It had been washed, but the blood had left a discoloring blotch on the rich crimson. Two ragged tears in the fabric—on the right side, exactly matching the level of the wound—had been clumsily mended with a coarse white linen thread. Thank the gods for that, anyway!

The woman squatted beside him, reached matter-of-factly for the bandage around his chest and deftly began to untie it. "You're lucky. Your friend is buying myrrh to put on this."

"He's not my friend," he told her irritably.

"No?" She paused. "Then why is he paying us to look after you?"

"He expects to be paid back handsomely."

She laughed. She had an unpleasant leering laugh which revealed blackened teeth. He looked away, wishing she'd sent the dark girl. "You're rich, aren't you?" she purred hoarsely. "He's seen that as well. You're one of the young men who were up in the mountains. A special detachment, they said, specially appointed by the queen herself. I thought to myself, Those must be fine rich young gentlemen; I wish they'd come here!" She stroked his shoulder with a crooked finger. "I could have found delicious entertainments for you."

He pushed her hand away and looked at her in cold offense. "What do you know about it?" he demanded.

She leered. "Entertainment? Oh, young lord, what don't I know about it?"

"The camp in the mountains!"

Another laugh. "Oh, come! Your commander sent men here to Hydreuma to buy vegetables: do you think we didn't know you were there? What happened to your camp and your friends, young lord? Did your enemies find you? Or was it bandits?"

He glared, not knowing what to say.

"That dirty caravan-master who isn't your friend said he found you on the road," she confided. "He says that Alexandria has fallen. Please tell me what happened, young lord! If it was the barbarians, I'm afraid they might come here next, and carry off my girls."

She didn't look afraid; she looked eager. This woman, he realized abruptly, would "entertain" barbarians as happily as Greeks, and if they tried to carry off her "girls," her only concern would be to get money from them first. What was more, she'd sell *him* if she thought she had a market. She'd approach any Roman who appeared in Hydreuma looking for water or vegetables or information. She might even send up to the camp to inquire whether anyone wanted a girl or a fugitive.

"Do your business!" he ordered her sharply, then sat still while she untied the bandage, wondering what he could say that would convince her to keep her mouth shut. Threaten her? With what? He was wounded and powerless, and the care she was providing had been paid for by another. Give her the pin in exchange for her silence, then? She'd take it and still sell him. She was a whore and a whore-mistress. Why had Ani put whores in charge of him? He drew a deep breath in indignation, then winced as the bandage came off.

There were two wounds on his right side: a deep puncture between the lower ribs, and a short gash leading down to it from above. A linen pad which had been tucked under the bandage was stained liberally with blood, and the skin around the cuts was puffy and red. Caesarion stared at his own torn flesh in fascinated revulsion.

The woman tut-tutted. "Bandits hereabouts use the bow from a distance, and knives and clubs for close quarters," she pointed out. "Oh, young lord, it was the foreign barbarians, I know that! Why don't you want to talk about them? Are they chasing you? Did you kill one of them?"

"Be quiet!" he snapped desperately, and tried again to think of some way to make her stay that way.

She raised her eyebrows, but stopped talking. Fetching a basin and a sponge, she began dabbing at the wounds. The water was salt, and it stung. He bit his lip, then pressed the remedy against his face and breathed deeply.

More footsteps crunched up to the house-tent, and Ani came in, disheveled and bad-tempered. He saw what the woman was doing, grunted "So!" and came over to stand behind her and stare while she cleaned the wound. He looked, Caesarion thought indignantly, as though he were inspecting a purchase.

"Better than it might have been," he commented, as the woman finished and got up to empty the basin. "The way you screamed this morning I thought you were about to die. Heard you right over by the camels."

Caesarion said nothing. He had been told that he shrieked horribly at the start of a falling fit. He had never heard himself: he was always unconscious when the cry was uttered.

"I'm setting out in about an hour," the Egyptian went on. "But I think you should stay here for a couple days more. I can take a letter to your ship. You can write, can't you?"

"Of course I can write!" Caesarion said with contempt. "But I can't give you a letter."

"Why not?"

Because I don't trust you, he thought. Ani would undoubtedly read a letter before handing it on—or find someone else to read it for him, since the fellow was probably illiterate. If he knew who Caesarion really was, he'd sell him as readily as would the whore.

"You think that if your friends on the ship know what happened, they'll sail off without waiting for you?" Ani asked sweetly.

"Yes," Caesarion said tightly. It was as good an excuse as any, and it was probably exactly what the ship would do if he sent them a letter written under a false name.

"True and faithful friends!" Ani remarked, hooking his thumbs in his belt. "Boy, I still think you should rest for a couple days more. Last night you were raving, and the way you screamed this morning—Scylla told me the pain gave you some kind of fit."

"He thrashed about and foamed at the mouth," agreed the whore-mistress, coming back with a clean pad of linen to put inside the bandage. "It was horrible to see him."

"I'm better now," said Caesarion grimly.

Ani let out his breath through his nose. "Those Romans aren't going to come after you," he said matter-of-factly. "They've just taken fifty talents of gold: they're not going to waste time chasing after one hot-headed boy, even if he did kill one of their comrades. They're probably on their way home already."

"Fifty talents of gold?" shrieked Scylla. "Fifty *talents* of *gold?*" Her mouth was wet with awed avarice.

"That's what he said," Ani told her, with a nod toward Caesarion. "It seems his lot were waiting to put it on a ship. But the Romans have it now. You think they're sitting around waiting for every thief in the neighborhood to hear they've got that sort of money? I don't."

Caesarion glared at him. Tell one stinking peasant a secret, and you've told the whole world. "I will start for Berenike tonight," he said stiffly. "I can walk there on my own."

Ani shrugged. "If you insist!" He set down a bundle that appeared to be Caesarion's sandals wrapped in his belt, then dug a small jar out of a fold of his shawl. "Myrrh," he said, holding it out to Scylla.

She took with a leer, opened it, and sniffed appreciatively.

"I want the jar back when you've finished," Ani told her flatly. "—With anything leftover still inside it, understand? And I'm going to stand here and watch."

Scylla snarled, took the jar, and rubbed the precious ointment onto Caesarion's side with quite unnecessary force.

They set off not long afterward. The dark girl reappeared to feed Caesarion another meal—flatbread with cheese and olives—before they left. She talked to him in a worried tone as he ate, apparently telling him that he was too ill to leave. She helped him to dress, however, fastening his sandals for him and wrapping Ani's shawl about his head with earnest and incomprehensible instructions. When he at last stood up and walked unsteadily out of the house-tent, she hovered beside him anxiously.

Hydreuma was less pleasant than he'd imagined—dust; a few house-tents clustered around a well; some date-palms and summer-withered vegetable patches; and a long colonnade thatched with palm leaves where a flock of goats and a few camels were sleeping. Behind him the sun was setting, and before him the caravan trail swept down the mountainside in pale loops like a dropped string. The Red Sea shone deep-indigo beyond it, and there, on a curve of that shining coast-line, lay a lagoon like an emerald, with a tiny grid of red-and-white sparkling beside it: Berenike. Ani's caravan was waiting for him in the road, with Ani in front holding the donkey.

"I'll walk," Caesarion told the Egyptian, eyeing the little animal with loathing.

"Boy, you shouldn't be up at all," Ani replied. "You can't walk to Berenike!"

"I'll walk as far as I can!" he insisted, and, without waiting for the others, started out.

"Mush choi!" called the dark girl after him. It took him a moment to understand it as Greek: "Much joy." He stopped, searched in his memory and found one of the few phrases of Trogodytic which his mother had impressed on him: the words that meant "Farewell."

The dark girl laughed with delight. She ran down the track

and kissed him. Smiling stupidly, he repeated his phrase, and she returned it. When he reached the first bend in the road, he looked back and found her still standing there. She waved. He waved back.

"Nice girl," said Ani, joining him. Imouthes had the donkey, and the caravan-master was on foot. The setting sun cast their shadows long and blue into the pale dust. "How is it you speak Trogodytic?"

Caesarion grunted resentfully and started walking again. "I don't. Just 'Greetings' and 'Farewell.' " But he could not dismiss the question of the girl so quickly, and he found himself asking, "She's a slave, isn't she? That foul whore-mistress rents her out to passing camel-drivers."

"And profits handsomely from it," the caravan-master agreed equably. "Ah well, somebody will probably buy her before long, and take her away to better things. A nice girl like that won't stay a whore for long."

"I don't understand how anyone could have sold her to a brothel to begin with!"

Ani gave him an odd look. "Most poor people will sell a surplus daughter, and the people round here can't be rich. Mother Isis, I've never seen such barren country!"

Caesarion was surprised. "Haven't you been this way before?"

For once the Egyptian looked abashed. "No," he admitted. After a moment he added, "It was an opportunity, see. I know a man who invests in shipping, only this year he decided that, with the war and all, he wants to keep his money, not spend it. I had some money, and I'm willing to risk it. You Greeks have kept the Red Sea trade all to yourselves since it started.

I reckoned I should take my opportunity while it offered." He glanced back at the train of camels with nervous pride. "I was born in Coptos. All my life I've seen the caravans setting out for Myos Hormos and Berenike and coming back laden down with the riches of the East. Now I've got a caravan of my own."

Not much of one, thought Caesarion. Resentment boiled up again. "Why did you leave me in a brothel?" he demanded.

Ani stared, then gave a loud bray of laughter. "Isis and Serapis, that offended you? I can't imagine it was the first time you've ever been in one."

Caesarion's cheeks burned: it *was* the first time he'd ever been in such a place. "That vile old whore was trying to find out if the Romans would buy me!"

"Yes, but the Romans are on their way home," Ani pointed out. "I made sure she knew that. Boy, where else could I leave you, in that dung-heap? Apart from Scylla and her girls, there's nobody in the place but a few goatherds and gardeners. They looked after you well, didn't they?"

He glowered uncomfortably and did not respond.

"Why are you so worried about the Romans chasing you, anyway? They're not baby-eating savages. All the ones I've ever met speak Greek and admire Greek culture: they wouldn't kill a well-born Greek boy like you unless you gave them good reason. *Did* you kill one of them?"

It was, he supposed, a reasonable explanation for his urgent desire to get away. He ought to use it. "I may have," he said carefully. "I don't know. It was dark." Then he added sarcastically, "So you don't still believe I'm a runaway slave?"

Ani shrugged. "You'll admit that when I first saw you, you

weren't at your best. When you started talking, I realized pretty fast you had to be a gentleman. 'Myi dehbt is too thee mahstair of your cahrahvahn . . .' " He mimicked Caesarion's long-voweled Attic Greek with mincing exaggeration. "I never would have believed anybody *really* talked like that, but you were too ill to pretend. And the troop you were with pretty plainly weren't regular army: the queen would never put the regular army in charge of fifty talents of gold." He fished in his purse and brought out the tunic pin. "Here."

Caesarion took it. It was, he saw, the gold annular one with the emerald, a more lavish affair than the plain gold fibula he'd usually worn in the camp. He stopped, tugged his tunic straight and pinned it.

"A runaway slave wouldn't *wear* that," Ani remarked with satisfaction. "He'd hide it. Where are you from?"

He began to walk again without answering. His side was starting to hurt more fiercely.

"You said you were Alexandrian?"

"Yes," he admitted.

"Never been there," Ani informed him, "but if this venture succeeds I'll see the city next month when I go there to sell my cargo. Your family's there?"

Mother a prisoner, if she was still alive, Antonius dead. "You said the city's fallen," he said, suddenly urgent. "Do you know anything about . . . about *how*, about what happened?"

"Ah," said the Egyptian. After a moment, he said, "It wasn't sacked, that's what I heard. Your family should be safe."

"What *happened*? Surely people said?"

"What I heard was that the army deserted to Caesar Octavian without a fight. They've been doing that all year, of course, ever since it became clear that the queen and Antonius were going to lose, but once Octavian was camped in the hippodrome it went like cloth unraveling. Men peeled off in all directions. Then the fleet went over as well. They weren't mercenaries or Romans like the others that went; they were Egyptian, and everybody'd expected them to stay loyal to the queen. Antonius apparently concluded that the queen was abandoning him as well, and he ran about threatening to kill her. She was so frightened she had her servants tell him she'd killed herself already. I suppose she meant to come explain herself when he'd calmed down, but he killed himself. Couldn't bear life without her and fell on his sword. That was the end. The general was dead, the war was over, and the city fell without a struggle. The queen locked herself up in her own mausoleum, along with all her treasure, and threatened to set fire to it unless the Romans allowed her to leave the city, but the Romans tricked their way in and took her prisoner."

It had the bleak sound of truth. He recognized it all. Desertion, treachery, deceit were bitterly familiar: he'd been hearing that story for years. His mother had said she would burn in her mausoleum before she surrendered to the Romans, but if they tricked their way in . . . it was probably true. Everyone had betrayed her, in the end. He wondered if she knew that Rhodon had betrayed her as well.

"A calamitous business," said Ani piously. "The fall of such a great and ancient house, and a queen who claimed the favor of the holy goddess. But at least the war is *over* now, thank the good goddess, and there'll be no more fighting, and no more war-tax. And I've heard that the Roman king is promising clemency."

Caesarion gave a snort of contempt. "Caesar Octavian has always been a cold-blooded liar and a murderer."

"You think there'll be reprisals?" Ani asked, with a shade of anxiety.

"He has never kept any promise which became inconvenient," Caesarion said bitterly. "He has broken treaties, and pretended it was the other side's fault. He has had thousands of his own countrymen put to death—and Romans are far more reluctant to shed Roman than foreign blood. He pretends that the deed was forced on him—but he keeps all the estates he confiscated from his victims. A crocodile is more clement than Octavian."

"Be that as it may," Ani said, after a moment's hesitation, "I haven't heard of any executions. I expect you could go home. In fact, if you like you could . . ."

"Do you know what happened to the queen's children?"

He had said good-bye to his half-brothers and half-sister when he left Alexandria in June. Little Ptolemy Philadelphus, who was six, had refused to let his big brother go, and had followed him all the way to the stables. He remembered the tiny figure in its miniature purple cloak, standing forlornly in the stableyard biting its fist as he rode away.

Ani blinked. "No. I heard that the young king wasn't in the city when it was taken. How many other children did she have?"

Caesarion stared at him in shock. "Don't you *know*?"

Ani made a rude noise. "Boy, I've lived all my life in *Coptos*!

I know more about what's happening in the world than most people there, because I'm interested and I make a point of talking to travelers and getting all the news I can, but people don't say much about anyone except the queen and the king, and a lot of what they say about *them* is rubbish. I know that the queen and Antonius had children—but it's not as though they've ever come up the river, or are ever likely to, now."

"She had them proclaimed kings and queens!"

Ani looked surprised and doubtful. "I haven't seen their names on any decrees or documents."

"Not kings and queens of Egypt! Of Armenia and Media and Macedonia and Cyrenaica! And she proclaimed herself 'Queen of kings,' and her son 'King of kings'!"

Ani again looked surprised, then thoughtful. "Oh. Yes. I suppose I did hear something about that. There was a big ceremony in the gymnasium of Alexandria, wasn't there? People talked about it. I heard the ceremony was the most magnificent thing ever seen, but that most of those places have kings of their own already, so if anything ever came of it, it would mean more wars. Thank the good gods, I suppose nothing will come of it now. Well, I'm afraid I don't know anything about it, or about the queen's children. All I heard was that the queen was taken prisoner, and that the young king wasn't in the city . . ." He stopped, as though suddenly struck by something. "Maybe you know more about *that* than I do, too."

Caesarion felt the blood throbbing fast and hard in his side. "What do you mean?"

"He's the most obvious person for the queen to send treasure to," said Ani. "Maybe you're planning to go join him."

Caesarion's heart slowed down again. He said nothing.

Ani apparently took silence as an admission that his guess was right. He gazed at Caesarion doubtfully and pulled at his lower lip. "I wouldn't have thought Caesarion was a good person to follow into exile," he said, with concern. "I heard a rumor that he's a leper. I heard he's been shut up in the palace for years."

Caesarion glared furiously. Sometimes he suspected that his mother's attempts to keep his condition a secret only meant that there were dozens of rumors about him instead of just one. This, however, was one he hadn't heard before. "That's a lie!" he declared indignantly.

Ani lifted his hands in concession. "If you say so, I believe you. You're an Alexandrian; I'm from Coptos. I told you we don't hear much news, only rumors from the traders and bargemen who come upriver, and even though I don't know what the truth is, I can tell *they're* full of lies. Most say the queen is a holy goddess who goes about working miracles; some, that she's a drunken harlot. Some say that the young king is a god manifest; others, that he's a half-wit or a leper. To tell the truth, to Coptos it doesn't matter much. But even if the king deserves your loyalty, have you asked yourself whether he'll welcome you if you arrive without the money— particularly now you're wounded?"

The question of what he would do without the money presented itself. Caesarion pushed it aside: the task now was to get safely out of Egypt. "I'll worry about that when I get there," he said, and let Ani believe what he liked.

Ani made two or three more attempts to probe his origins and intentions, but Caesarion did not respond. His side was hurting more and more and his breath was short, and eventually the Egyptian realized this and gave up.

They walked until it was fully dark; paused for a rest and a drink of water, then rose and continued on. At midnight they ate a meal of flatbread and cheese, and set out again when the moon rose. About half an hour later, Caesarion finally gave up and asked to be allowed the donkey.

The caravan stopped again about an hour before sunrise. Caesarion was once more in a daze, his consciousness so crushed by pain that he could take in little else. He knew only that he had a chance to stop jolting and rest, and he slid off the donkey and lay down on the ground, wrapping his arms about himself for warmth. After a few minutes, Ani came over and draped a blanket over him.

As the pain receded a little, he realized slowly that the others were pitching a camp. Awnings were rigged, bedrolls unpacked, camels tethered. A fire was lit, a stewpot was suspended over it, and presently there was a scent of pork and onions. A little while later, Ani came over again. He had a piece of flatbread rolled into a cone and filled with the stew. He bent over to offer it. When Caesarion didn't move, he squatted down beside him, took the limp hand, positioned it upright, placed the bread in it, and folded over the fingers.

Caesarion groaned and sat up. He looked at the bread with distaste, then glanced around. The light had brightened to a lucent pearl-gray, and he could see that the awnings had been pitched on a flat sandy area broken by a few scrubby bushes. Along one side of the sand there was water, and to the right were buildings—real buildings, of brick and tile, not the flimsy house-tents of the desert.

"Are we in Berenike?" he asked hoarsely, hardly daring to believe it.

"We are indeed!" replied Ani, grinning at him. "Eat your supper and get some rest. We'll go over to the harbor this evening."

Caesarion looked at the cone of bread. He had no appetite, but he forced himself to nibble a corner. "We'll go this morning," he corrected Ani, when he had swallowed it down. "I'll rest for a couple of hours, then go in."

The grin disappeared. "Boy, I'm not going to do business looking like a peasant. I'm going to have a sleep and a meal, and then I'm going to wash and put on my good clothes. You can wait until evening."

"I'll go on my own. This morning."

"And run off without paying me? You swore I'd get money from your shipmates."

"How much do you expect to be paid?"

Ani looked at him with narrowed eyes. Caesarion took another bite of the bread and swallowed it, refusing to meet that gaze. He did not know why he suddenly felt ashamed. Around them the light brightened.

"I paid Scylla four drachmae," the caravan-master said slowly. "I paid another two drachmae three obols for the myrrh, and one and five obols for the bandages. You've eaten food—oh, call it four drachmae's worth. You rode my donkey and enjoyed our protection for two days: call that another eight drachmae as a hiring fee. The cloak you're wearing cost me twenty drachmae . . ."

"You can have it back," Caesarion said, with a faint sneer.

Cloak! The garment was barely more than a headdress!

"I reckon you cost me twenty drachmae, then, and that I'm owed another ten for the trouble."

"I will give you the pin. The stone on it must be worth more than that."

The response startled him: Ani made a rude noise, and glared in anger and exasperation. "Boy, that pin is the only valuable you have! You are in a strange city hundreds of miles from your family and any source of money, and you're heading off into exile. How, by all the good gods, do you think you're going to survive if you throw away your only valuable?"

"Stop calling me 'boy'!" Caesarion shouted at him, stung.

"If the stone on that pin is real, it's worth sixty drachmae!" Ani shouted back. "And it belongs to *you*, not your oh-so-reliable shipmates. Think, you young idiot! Are a few *hours* worth that much?" He got to his feet, towering over Caesarion. "And look at yourself! You've a hole in your side and you can barely stand. Sweet Lady Isis, if you had a grain of sense in your head you would've stayed at Hydreuma and let that pretty little whore look after you! What's so wonderful about exile, eh?" He paused, caught his breath, then went on. "Well, I'm not taking your god-hated pin. You can come to the harbor with me this evening, or you can go off by yourself this morning knowing that you owe me twenty drachmae—and your life—and couldn't be bothered to pay."

Caesarion had no idea how to answer. Ani waited for a reply, then, seeing that his antagonist couldn't think of one, stamped off with a satisfied air. He stopped after a few steps, however, turned back, and said, "You can sleep there." He pointed at an awning rigged up against a bush. A bedroll lay enticingly open beneath it. "You'll want shelter when the sun comes up."

Caesarion sat nibbling the stew until Ani had disappeared into his own shelter. Then he crawled over to the awning, lay down on the bedroll, and went to sleep without even bothering to take the pin out of his tunic.

HE WOKE UP when it got hot, and crawled awkwardly out from under the awning to find some water. It was still before noon, but the sun was like a furnace, the white sand of the campsite hurt the eyes, and the air above the sea gleamed like silk with the heat. Two other awnings were stretched nearby, with the linen bundles heaped between them and secured to them by a rope. Ani was asleep under the nearer one, his face hidden in the bedroll and one arm flung out above his kinked hair. The donkey was stretched out asleep in the shade between its master and a bush, and the tethered camels were lying down, chewing stolidly at pile of fodder.

A public fountain stood only a few yards away, a plain stone basin with a tank which could be filled for animals. Caesarion staggered over to it, drank from the tap, then splashed more water against his wounded side, which was burning. He took off Ani's shawl and ran water over his head. He drenched the shawl and draped it over himself again, then sat a moment, leaning against the cool stone and dangling his hands in the water.

You must avoid cool, moist things. They will aggravate your condition.

To Hades with that: hot, dry things didn't seem to be doing his condition any good.

He ought to go find the ship. He was, he admitted to himself, desperately afraid that the ship would not be there after all. Since the middle of July they had waited for it, and it had not come. Why should he trust its captain to stay loyal, when so many others had turned traitor? To be sure, the captain had been selected for trustworthiness—but so had Rhodon, and all those others who had peeled away from the queen like cloth unraveling.

Eumenes had posted a man in Berenike to watch for the ship. Didymos, that was the man's name; he was lodged at an inn called the Happy Return. The thing to do now was to go into the town, find the inn and the man, and learn from him how things stood.

What would Ani think when he woke and Caesarion wasn't there?

It didn't matter. If the ship was there, Caesarion could send him the thirty drachmae and end the connection. If the ship wasn't there . . .

Ani would resent being sent thirty drachmae without seeing the ship for himself. He would feel that Caesarion had behaved very badly. Why he should feel that way, Caesarion could not say, nor could he explain why part of himself agreed with the verdict.

What did it matter? Ani was an insolent peasant who had insulted him. Cleopatra would have had him flogged.

It did matter, though. The caravan-master had saved his life. He might not like that, but it was true. And—little as he wished to admit it—apart from the insults, Ani had treated

him with great kindness. His own donkey. The last of the
beer. The myrrh. The stew and the bedroll.

Ani could have taken the pin from him at any time, but
he'd refused it even when it was offered. He wondered why.
The Egyptian had sounded almost . . . *concerned* . . . for the
safety of his guest. Perhaps that was it! He regarded Caesarion
as a *guest*, to whom he had a host's obligations. Perhaps that
was why Caesarion felt ashamed at the thought of walking out
on him: it would be a breach of hospitality.

Or perhaps it was something else. Perhaps Ani was a lover
of boys, and he had taken a fancy to Caesarion.

Caesarion sat very still, struck through with disgust and
utter revulsion. He remembered how Ani had steadied him on
the donkey that first night—the man's arm around his waist,
his own head resting on the shoulder of the dirty tunic. Had
he thought that *kind*? He remembered the proprietary look on
Ani's face as he watched Scylla cleaning the wound—suddenly
saw himself sitting naked in the shadows of the house-tent,
with the old witch dabbing myrrh onto his bare flesh, and the
crude peasant ogling . . . He had been unconscious in Ani's
presence several times—the man had examined the remedy
without his knowledge—what *else* might the fellow have done?

He pressed a hand to his mouth, sick with humiliation. He
was the son of a queen who claimed to be the living incarnation
of the goddess Isis, and of a man greater than any king—a
man whom even the Romans worshiped as a god! He had been
given divine titles of his own, "Theos Philopator Philometor—
the God Who Loves His Father and Mother"; he had been
called "Lord of the Two Lands," and then "King of Kings"; he
had had a temple built in his honor. Maybe he was unworthy;

maybe all the titles were propaganda for the ignorant masses—but to be the object of a camel-driver's lust . . . He ought to *kill* the brute!

That would be a poor return for his life, which the brute had saved. Ani had not, in fact, actually *done* anything to him—not while he was awake, anyway. It might even be the case that Ani's feelings were, after all, only friendly and hospitable; he had no real evidence that it was not so. No: he would put the disgusting idea from his mind. Moreover, he would leave Ani the pin—a more fitting reward than a mere thirty drachmae. But he would go into the city on his own now, and have nothing more to do with the man.

He went back to the awning, knelt down, and set the tunic pin on the bedroll where he had slept. Satisfied, he rose laboriously to his feet and straightened the shawl.

Against his will he remembered that he'd told Ani he wouldn't keep the garment. With the sun this fierce, though, he had to have some kind of head-covering, and he had no money to buy anything else. Well, the pin would pay for it and more.

His feet crunching in the coarse coral sand, he set off slowly toward the town.

Berenike was a small city. There was a central marketplace, flanked by a moderately sized temple dedicated to the god Serapis; there was a fort that could hold a small garrison, but which had been empty for some years; there were a few streets of rather flimsy houses—and there were more warehouses, shipping offices, and inns than would have seemed reasonable in a place three times the size. Berenike had been founded for the Red Sea trade, and apart from that trade, had no existence.

The market was almost empty on this quiet morning, and the streets were deserted. A month before, the town had bustled—but that had been in July, when the monsoon blew from the west, and the ships of the India trade had set out for the East, making the sea blaze with their bright sails. Now it was too late in the year to sail eastward, and the ships would not return to the west until February, when the winds had changed. The coastal trade, southward along the shore of Africa, was not seasonal, and caused far less stir.

Caesarion paused in the marketplace to drink water from the fountain and to soak his shawl, which had dried out on the short walk from the campsite. A couple of old women, spinning as they sat selling melons in the shade nearby, stared at him curiously and whispered to one another. He hesitated, then braved the stares and came over. "Women," he said hoarsely, "do you know of an inn called the Happy Return?"

The two of them looked at one another, as though amazed he could speak, but then one of them nodded and informed him, "It's on the Harbor Street, child, about halfway along. Young man, you look very ill. Do you want to sit here and let me fetch your friends?"

"No," he told them. "Thank you." He turned left out of the marketplace, and paced stiffly down to the street which flanked the harbor.

Berenike had no deepwater harbor. Ships were drawn up on the shallow, sheltered beach, and loaded by ramps, or by men who waded out to them from shore. There were three or four ships run up on the beach now, their sterns lapped by the turquoise water of the lagoon, but one of them caught his eye at once. The others were round-bellied merchant vessels, but this was a galley, long, thin, and light. He started toward it, his heart speeding up, and soon there was no doubt. It was a triemiolia—a heavy trireme from which the top bank of oars could be removed to allow long voyages under sail—and the prow was decorated with a robed figure which held something round. He felt his face cracking in a manic grin. The ship for which they'd waited so long was a triemiolia called *Nemesis*, and the goddess Nemesis was always depicted as a woman holding a wheel of fire. He was going to get away.

If he hadn't reached the Happy Return first, he would have gone straight to the ship. However, he noticed the inn's sign on his way—a painting of a harbor and a ship safely anchored, with the name picked out in red lettering—and he decided to stop and check whether Didymos was there and had anything to tell him.

The Happy Return was one of the grander inns. A two-story building, it stood proudly at the center of the harbor front. He pushed open the plain door and walked through a dark entrance passage into an open courtyard flanked by a portico. Vines in pots set into the packed soil grew over the portico, creating a deep shade with their thick leaves, and bunches of black grapes, now ripe, dangled over the tables. A couple of men were sitting at one of the tables playing draughts; otherwise, the place was empty.

Caesarion sat down at the nearest table, glad to be out of the sun. One of the draughtsplayers noticed him, left the game, and came over. "Wine, master?" he asked, smiling.

"I'm looking for a man called Didymos," said Caesarion.

The smile vanished, instantly and absolutely. "He was arrested day before yesterday. He owes me money."

Something inside Caesarion seemed to go numb. The certainty of deliverance winked out like a lightning-stroke.

"Are you a friend of his?" the waiter demanded. "He owes me for ten days' lodging."

"Who arrested him?" Caesarion asked faintly. "What for?"

The waiter spat. "The ship he was waiting for arrived, day before yesterday—he was expecting queen's men, wasn't he?—but the Romans had taken the ship, and when he went on board they arrested him. You one of his friends? I want my money."

"The Romans?"

"You heard me. They've conquered Egypt, so they say; the war's over, the queen's a prisoner, and Antonius is dead. They had some information about the ship, and they went to Myos Hormos, where it was undergoing repairs, seized it, and brought it up here. My guess is they wanted to catch Didymos and his friends. You probably know more about that than I do; you're one of Didymos' friends, aren't you?" The waiter leaned over the table and looked Caesarion implacably in the eye. "I want my money."

"I don't have any money," Caesarion told him. He was trembling.

"Your friend owes me that money. Give it to me, or I'll run down to the ship right now and tell the Romans that somebody has turned up asking for Didymos."

"The Romans took our camp," Caesarion whispered. "I barely escaped alive. I can't give you any money—and the Romans won't, even if you hand me over to them. All they'll do is ask *you* questions about why Didymos and I were here."

The waiter's eyes raked him, taking in the coarse shawl

over the rich but crudely mended tunic; the right side of the tunic hanging down because its owner lacked even a pin; the complete absence of a purse. Then he spat, this time directly into Caesarion's face. "Get out!"

Caesarion rose unsteadily to his feet and staggered back down the dark passageway and out into the blast of sun from the lagoon. Lapped by the calm waters, *Nemesis* mocked him. He wiped spittle from his face, rubbed his soiled hand against his thigh. It was hard to breathe. His stomach rose, and suddenly he smelt carrion.

O gods, he cried silently, O Asklepios and Apollo, no, please no. Not here! He dropped to his knees in the street and tried to grab the remedy, but his fingers tangled in the shawl and it evaded the clasp of his hand.

CHAPTER III

Ani woke around noon. He lay still for a minute or two, telling himself that it would be foolish to get up, that if he didn't get enough sleep he'd feel the want later—but he knew that it was no use. The immense, joyful excitement inside him made it completely impossible to go back to sleep.

He sat up and looked out from under the awning. There, only twenty yards away, was the sea. The Red Sea! He, Ani, son of Petesuchos, was camped on the shore of the Red Sea— with his own caravan! He offered up an ardent prayer of thanks to Isis, his favorite divinity, who had allowed him to make a boyhood dream come true.

He crawled out into the blaze of sunlight and ran through a quick check. The pile of trade goods was undisturbed—as it should be, roped as it was so that the camp awnings would shake if anyone tampered with it. Good enough for now, but

he'd have to do something about getting the goods warehoused; rent a tent to put up as well, or everybody in the city
would think he was a nobody. The camels were all there,
placidly chewing their cuds, and no thieving bugger had
touched the donkey. Apart from his own small party, there
was nobody in sight. Ani grinned to himself. Menches, who'd
been here often, swore that this was the main camping place
for caravans, that in July and in February it was like a fair-
ground, and that he'd never seen it so empty. That was undoubtedly because of the war, and it was good, good, good!
There'd be nobody else to bid for the cargo of that fine, richly
laden ship, and the captain would have to take what he was
offered. Not that Ani was offering a bad price—but it was
less than the usual, and Greeks were always reluctant to give
bargains to Egyptians. In the circumstances, though, the captain might even be willing to accept an Egyptian as an investor
and partner—Fortune grant he was!

Ani went over the fountain, gloating over the fact that they
were *right next to it*, in the prime location that would normally
have gone to a great caravan, while small poor ones like his
own were pushed out to the fringes of the ground. He had a
drink, splashed some water over his head, and looked around.
The red-and-white houses of Berenike were only yards away,
and if he followed the sweep of shoreline, he could make out
ships on the beach. One of those was undoubtedly the *Prosperity*, which he had come to meet. *Prosperity*. The very name
was a good omen!

The sea shone enticingly in the sun. It was so *big*! He'd
heard that you couldn't see the edge of it, but it had been
impossible to imagine such a thing, and nobody had mentioned

the *colors*—the peacock-greens and -blues, the deep-indigo of sunset and fires of dawn. He had always thought it must be red—with mud, like the Nile when it was in flood—but it was the least muddy of any water he'd seen.

He glanced around again. He'd wanted to rush into the sea when they first arrived—to touch it, to prove to himself that he'd really arrived; to taste it, to see if it was as salty as everyone said; to swim in it, and wash the smell of twelve days' travel from his parched skin. But he hadn't dared to jump in, not in front of Menches and Imouthes. He was the caravan-owner who employed them. Sober and professional caravan-owners did not celebrate their arrivals in Berenike by rushing into the sea with all their clothes on; still less did they tear their clothes off. Menches had told him, too, that the Red Sea was full of poisonous creatures that stung like scorpions and that he himself would never venture into it. Ani could not imagine staying out of it, and he had decided that it would probably be safe enough if he was careful to touch nothing, but he didn't want to offend Menches, who knew the caravan route and the city. Menches and Imouthes were asleep now, though. They *were* asleep, weren't they? They hadn't gone off into the city without telling him? He crunched around the pile of trade goods to check, and yes, father and son snored side by side under the largest awning. He looked at them with approval: decent, reliable men who were neighbors of his back in Coptos, who wouldn't cheat him.

He went over to the third awning to check on the boy Arion before his swim—and found that Arion wasn't there.

He gaped at the empty bedroll. He'd thought better of the boy; he'd thought the talk this morning had knocked some sense into that proud and stubborn head. Obviously not: Arion felt no obligation to a mere Egyptian, and Arion had run off without paying—and taken the cloak with him.

Then Ani noticed a glint of green and gold from the center of the coarse linen. He bent over, and found that the boy had left the pin.

Well, the gods destroy him! He'd told the young fool he wouldn't take the god-hated thing, but here it was. He picked it up and turned it in his fingers. The stone on it was the size of his thumbnail. Worth more than twenty drachmae, the youth had said, with the ignorant assurance of a young man who's rarely paid for anything himself. Ani hadn't liked to admit that, until the other had set that value on the "stone," he'd thought the pin was adorned with nothing more valuable than glass. It blazed now in the bright sunlight with a rich green fire no glass ever possessed. Sixty drachmae, he'd told the boy, but that had been just a guess: he had no idea how much an emerald this size would cost. It might well be more than that.

He wondered again just how rich and important your family had to be before a queen would trust you to escort fifty talents of gold to her son on his way into exile. Nobody from an obscure or questionable background would be picked for a job like that; probably no Egyptians would be chosen, either. Probably you had to be somebody the army officers of the royal court in Alexandria *knew*, and that meant purebred Greek, and wealthy. Arion's arrogance proclaimed as much, as did his beautifully cultured voice. Ani himself was a peasant by birth, but he could recognize aristocracy when he met it. It still seemed a tragic waste, to have so much and to throw it all away to follow a nonentity of a king into poverty and exile. Loyalty was all very well, but probably the young king wouldn't even *want* the burden of another mouth to feed, particularly one belonging to a man who was too ill to be any use to him.

He told himself that he'd refused the jewel and Arion had still given it to him: he ought to give up and keep it. He was not satisfied. The image of Arion's face that morning rose before his eyes: sunburn peeling off the strong beak of a nose, the skin around the eyes ash-white, the whole pinched and drawn in an extremity of pain and exhaustion—but still determined. What did that passionate, brave, and completely impractical young man think he was going to do without money? He was going to need medicine and care; he was going to need food and clothing. Perhaps he expected his friends on this mysterious ship to provide for him, but he'd admitted that those same friends would sail off without waiting for him if they suspected they were in danger. Perhaps he relied on the young king Caesarion—which was even more foolish, for no king by the name of Ptolemy was going to spend money on a wounded follower who'd lost him fifty talents of gold.

Ani blew out his cheeks in disgust. There was nothing for it: he couldn't leave an inexperienced youth penniless and injured in a harsh world. He would have to go after him and give him his pin back. If Arion responded with twenty drachmae, good; if he didn't, well, an act of charity to a stranger in need ought to please the gods, and bring good luck—which, the gods knew, he was going to need over the next few days.

He pictured himself telling his wife and daughter about his act of charity, pictured his wife's anxious pride and his sixteen-year-old-daughter's wide-eyed admiration. Tiathres always worried that people were taking advantage of her husband's generosity, but Melanthe was sure that her father was just as wise as he was kind. He smiled: it was worth twenty drachmae to be able to play hero to his household. He crunched back round to Menches and Imouthes, squatted down, and tugged the older man's foot. Menches woke up with a grunt and picked himself up on an elbow.

"Arion's gone off," Ani informed him.

"Ill-fortune to him!" Menches replied at once. "I told you he would cheat you."

"He left this," Ani said, waggling the pin between thumb and forefinger. "I'm going to go after him and get him to give me my money instead. I should be back in a couple of hours. Stay with the goods."

Menches grunted and lay down again. "He'll deny that he ever met you," he warned gloomily. "No Greek will admit a debt to an Egyptian."

"We'll see," said Ani, and started off toward the city.

When he had gone thirty paces, he glanced back, saw that Menches wasn't watching, and diverted down to the sea. There was time for just a *short* swim first.

The water of the lagoon was warm as blood, salt as tears, and astonishingly clear. There were fish unlike any he had ever seen: bright yellow, iridescent blue, or striped like butterflies in black and white. Weeds waved vivid green in muddy patches on the bottom, and where the bottom was stony there grew trees of what appeared to be pale stone, and clumps of red-and-green flowers with long petals that swayed in the languid currents. O gods, he thought, in passionate delight, Melanthe would love it!

He trod water, trying to memorize everything, so that he could describe it to his daughter when he got home. A fish brushed one of the flowers, and—incredible sight!—the "flower" seized it in its long petals, and drew it, struggling, into a mouth which had appeared in its center. Isis and Serapis, Melanthe would *love* it! He wished she could see it: he could picture her dark, eager face with its eyes wide and shining with excitement.

His other children would like it, too, of course, and Tiathres, his wife, would exclaim in amazement—but Melanthe was the one who would feel as he did. The little ones were too young to appreciate it, and Tiathres was too . . . practical. *Good* thing to be, of course, but sometimes, sometimes . . . the world was so astonishing: one had simply to draw one's breath and cry out at the wonder of it. Isis and Serapis, a flower that ate fish: who could have imagined such a thing?

He swam reluctantly back to shore, careful to touch nothing until he was over clean white sand. He waded out, pulled on his dirty clothes, and set out again for Berenike. His anger and exasperation with Arion had faded. He had seen a flower eat a fish: sweet Lady Isis, what a world!

He did not take the road into the marketplace, but walked instead along the beach until it ended in a ramp and a paved road along the harborfront. Arion was undoubtedly headed for his ship. Given that it had been despatched by the queen, that ship would probably not be a merchant vessel. It should be easy to find.

He identified it almost at once—the long shape of the galley stood out among the trading craft like a hound among sheep— and strode briskly along the Harbor Street toward it. He paused, however, when he saw the small crowd outside the inn—then stopped as he realized that what they'd clustered around was a body. Moved by a cold premonition, he crossed the street, joined the crowd, and saw that the body was indeed Arion's. The young man was lying on his injured side, one leg folded under him at an awkward angle. His head was thrown back, and his chin was shiny with spittle. The cloak Ani had lent him was tangled around his neck and left arm. He did not appear to be breathing, and his face under the sunburn was still, stricken, and pitifully young.

"Holy Mother Isis!" Ani whispered in horror.

"He fell over in a fit and died about an hour ago," a tall man in the crowd told him. "We need to remove the body, but we don't know where to take it. Do you know who he is?"

"Yes." Ani swallowed, unable to look away from the still face. "His name's Arion. He's an Alexandrian. He came into the city with me this morning."

At that everyone stared. One of the men, a slight, cold-eyed Greek in a blue tunic, said, "Are you another friend of Didymos?"

"I don't know any Didymos here in Berenike," Ani replied. "I'm from Coptos." He squatted down beside the boy and gingerly began trying to untangle the trapped arm. The flesh was warm—hot as the afternoon, in fact—but completely inert. A remote part of his mind registered that, by touching a corpse, he was involving himself in the rituals of death. He would, he realized resignedly, end up paying for the funeral. It would be costly, it was not by rights his burden—but he had been responsible for this lost child and simply could not leave his body to rot and his ghost to wander. At least it would be a Greek funeral, quick and hot, and not a mummification.

"I mean Didymos who was staying at my inn," said the man in the blue tunic. "He was arrested day before yesterday. He owes me money."

"Who?" Ani asked, not paying attention. "What?"

"Didymos," said the man in the blue tunic, more loudly. "I said, he owes me money. This one came into my inn asking for Didymos, and you say he was with you. The Romans arrested Didymos. They're on that ship there, the *Nemesis*. Shall I go tell them that you're asking for Didymos, or do you want to pay the debt one of your friends owes me and go bury the other one quietly?"

Ani looked up into the cold eyes. Slowly, he got to his feet. There were three men besides the one in the blue tunic, and at least two of them looked to be Greeks. All four were citizens of Berenike while he was a stranger. It didn't matter: he was too angry to be afraid of them. "I already told you: I don't know this man Didymos," he said evenly. "I'm a caravan-owner from Coptos. I met this young man on the road, and brought him with me because he was injured and needed help. But if I were an innkeeper, and I had just threatened a young man who came into my inn hurt and alone, looking for friends and help—threatened to turn him over to his enemies if he didn't pay me money he didn't have—and if I had then seen him die of grief and fear on my own doorstep —*I* would not be threatening the man who came to take away the body. I would be praying to Zeus the Guest to forgive me a great sin, and I would be afraid that my next guest would offend the laws of hospitality as greatly as I had done."

The innkeeper flushed angrily. The tall Greek who'd spoken first—a well-dressed man of middle age—asked, "Is that what you did, Kerdon?"

"He said he was a friend of Didymos!" complained Kerdon. "Yes, I asked him to pay his friend's debt, but when he said he didn't have any money, I told him to get out. I didn't go to the Romans!"

"If you had got money from him," said the tall man, "it would have been accursed." He looked out at the galley bleakly. "Our enemies have taken our country by the spear, and brought that ship here to trap the queen's servants. You were going to betray a Greek youth to *them?*"

"I didn't go to them!" protested Kerdon, sweating now. "Archedamos, times are hard, you know that. I need that money, and I asked for it. But I didn't go to the Romans!"

"You threatened that you would," said the tall man, his voice quiet but heavy with condemnation. "And the young man, who was ill, is now dead. I will remember this, Kerdon." He turned to Ani. "Friend, my name is Archedamos, son of Archelaos; I am supervisor of the port of Berenike, and I was summoned here to deal with the body of this unfortunate young man. Are you truly willing to undertake the expense of the funeral? I must tell you that if you are not, I am at a loss. The city cannot pay for anything at the moment. The Romans on that ship have informed us that we are now their subjects, and the council has no idea whether we have any revenue or any authority to spend it."

Ani swallowed. Port supervisor. This man's goodwill could ease any business he had here; his enmity would doom it. With a mixture of resignation and resentment, he realized that he would never know now whether he was paying for the funeral out of kindness or because he wanted to win this man's help. "I'll cover the costs," he agreed, "—though I'd be pleased if the citizens would help out. I'm an Egyptian, as you've probably realized: I don't know much about Greek funerals."

"May the gods reward you for your piety," said Archedamos warmly. "Tell me where you want the body, and I will help you move it."

It turned out that one of the other men was a municipal slave assigned to the port supervisor's office, and that he'd brought a cart with which to move the body. Ani helped him to lift Arion's limp form onto it, then paused to unwind the tangled cloak. Poor boy, he thought sadly. So young—he should have had a whole life ahead of himself. Rich, too, and well born and well educated, or I'm no judge at all. Here he lies, thrown away—and *I* could have used him, even if he had no use for himself. Isis and Serapis, shelter and Heaven to all mankind, receive him kindly.

In the vaguest of hopes, expecting nothing, he checked for a pulse under the lax jaw. It beat under his thumb, slow, regular, and strong.

Ani gaped, then found himself grinning maniacally. "He's alive!" he exclaimed to the others. "Great is the goddess! He's still alive!"

"What!" cried Archedamos, and came to check for himself.

"Ha!" exclaimed Kerdon, both relieved and indignant. "You

accused *me*, but the fellow simply had an epileptic seizure. He
has the sacred disease!"

"He does not!" Ani replied at once—then suddenly suspected that he did. He remembered the young man's response
when the old whore at Hydreuma had told him he'd had a fit:
no alarm, no surprise, just a sullen and resentful "I'm better
now." That was not a normal reaction to such disturbing news.
He found himself startled and oddly touched by the notion
that the arrogant young Greek might suffer such a despised
illness, but he continued as though the suspicion had not occurred to him. "He's wounded and feverish. He's lost blood
and gone short of water in the heat. He's traveled two nights
with a hole in his side, and you threatened him and took away
his last hope. A man doesn't have to have the sacred disease
to fall down in a faint after all that. We need to get him out
of the sun."

"I'm not having him in my inn!" exclaimed Kerdon at once.
"I don't serve the diseased." He stalked off into the building
and slammed the door.

Archedamos looked at Ani. "I'll help you bring him to your
caravan," he offered.

A house would be a better place for him, Ani thought—
but he did not say it. The last thing he wanted was to offend
the port supervisor.

"You say he was wounded?" asked Archedamos, as they
started back along the Harbor Street toward the caravan halt,
the slave pulling the cart and Ani and the port supervisor
pushing it.

Ani nodded. "Wounded in the side, and sunstruck as well.
I found him unconscious in the road three nights ago. I tried

to persuade him to stay and rest at Hydreuma, but he insisted on coming down to the city to meet that ship."

"I'm glad he has someone to care for him," said the port supervisor. After a moment he went on in a low, angry voice, "The neighbors told me that when he fell down, Kerdon came out and shouted at him to move. They say he kicked him. It cut me to the heart to think a young man like this—a loyal servant of the queen—should have died like that, with a greedy oaf cursing and kicking him."

"No one should die like that," Ani agreed.

Archedamos grunted. After a moment he went on, in a different voice: "Was he with the camp near Kabalsi? I knew of it—I had instructions to render assistance to its commander if he asked. Is . . . is it worth my while sending the commander a warning? Or going up there to . . . salvage . . . anything?"

He knows about the gold, thought Ani, or at least he suspects that it was there. "Salvage," my arse! "No," he replied levelly. "The Romans took the camp. According to Arion, there was gold there, and the Romans took that, too. A troop of them passed my caravan on the road from Coptos, four nights ago, and Arion said that he himself barely escaped them."

Archedamos sighed. "They were thorough: one troop to take the camp, another troop to take the ship, in case the first failed. Father Zeus, that I have lived to see Egypt fall to a foreign conqueror!"

My own people have seen it before, Ani thought. He did not say that, either.

"You said you came with a caravan?" the port supervisor

went on, inspecting Ani's dirty tunic and shabby cloak with evident doubt.

He ducked his head. "A small caravan, Lord Archedamos, but yes, I am the owner—Ani, son of Petesuchos, of Coptos." He was painfully aware how uncouth his Egyptian name sounded to this elegant Greek, and he hurried on. "Please excuse the way I'm dressed. I was concerned about Arion, and when I realized he'd gone into the city on his own I went to look for him without stopping to change out of the clothes I wore for the journey." No need to mention the swim.

"Your concern does you credit," said the other, approvingly. "As does your resolution. Your caravan is the only one here. Most gentlemen are waiting to see what comes of the war before investing their property in anything risky. It's a difficult time for the city."

It was a natural opening, and Ani firmly believed in seizing opportunity when it presented itself. "To be honest, Lord Archedamos, it's because of the war that I'm here. I own some property and a clothing manufactory in the town of Coptos, and for some years I've supplied linen goods to a gentleman who invests in the coastal trade. This year, though, he isn't investing, although his ship's returned safely; he took his profit from the last voyage but will provide nothing for the next. I thought I would go in his place. I've always wanted to see Berenike."

Archedamos smiled. "What ship are you investing in?"

"Hoping to invest in," Ani corrected, smiling back. "It may be that I'll have to content myself buying what I can of the present cargo and leaving it at that. But the ship concerned is the *Prosperity*."

Archedamos clicked his tongue in pleased recognition. "I wondered if it was, as soon as you said the investor had backed out. The captain's a friend of mine: Kleon, son of Kallias. He's been moping about the city for days, wondering how to dispose of his cargo. Normally . . ." the port supervisor's eyes flicked over him again, ". . . normally he would be reluctant to take on a completely new and unknown investor, particularly, if I may say so, one who lacks the freedoms of a Greek— as I presume you do."

Ani nodded fractionally. He'd been aware from the start that his birth was against him. Egyptians paid taxes from which Greeks were exempt, and were barred from positions of power which Greeks could hold. They could not ordinarily use Greek courts of law, and were forbidden to intermarry with Greek citizens or to themselves become citizens of any Greek city. An Egyptian obviously had several disadvantages as a prospective business partner for a Greek.

"However," Archedamos went on, "I will tell him of your piety toward strangers—and of your resolution in coming here despite the uncertain times. Would you care to come to dinner at my house, tomorrow night, and meet him?"

O Lady Isis, Ani thought fervently, thank you, thank you, thank you! "Thank you," he said at once. "That's very kind of you."

They had reached the ramp leading down to the beach, and they stopped, since the cart could not traverse the deep sand. Ani could see his caravan, undisturbed beside the fountain, an untidy little pile of awnings, goods, and camels.

"We only arrived this morning," he told the port supervisor hastily. "We haven't rented a tent yet."

"I can see you've not yet warehoused your goods, either," said Archedamos. "I have a warehouse of my own standing empty, as it happens, at the corner of Market and Harbor Streets. Kleon usually keeps his cargos there until he's ready to load them."

"I can think of nowhere better for my own goods," Ani said at once.

"Bring them round this evening, then," Archedamos said, with satisfaction. "Come two hours before sunset and I'll see them safely stowed. And my neighbor Kratistes could rent you a tent."

"I'd be glad of that. Arion certainly needs better shelter than an awning if he's to make a good recovery."

They both looked down at the still form on the cart. Archedamos sighed. "I will be honest with you," he said, in a shamed voice. "I know I should take the young man into my own house, but I'm afraid of Kerdon. If he goes to the Romans and says, 'Archedamos is harboring a fugitive' . . . I'm known as a supporter of the queen. The accusation could cost me everything. Will he be all right with you?"

And if Kerdon says, *That Egyptian caravan-owner is harboring a fugitive* . . . ? Ani thought sourly. *I'd* lose nothing? To Archedamos, however, he smiled and said, "I think he'll be all right if I can persuade him to rest quietly for a few days. I'll go fetch the donkey to carry him the rest of the way to my camp."

He hurried across the sand, untied the little animal, and drove it over and up the ramp. The slave helped him to load Arion across its back. Arion groaned when they lifted him, which Ani welcomed as a sign of recovery.

"May the gods reward you for your kindness to strangers," said Archedamos, satisfied that he'd disposed of a dangerous problem without burdening either his house or his conscience. "I look forward to seeing you at the warehouse this evening."

WHEN ANI LED the donkey back up to the camp, Menches was up, standing by the fountain looking bewildered. He hurried over. "As the gods live!" he exclaimed, gazing at the helpless shape draped over the donkey's shaggy back. "What happened to him?"

"He fell over in the street." Ani slung one of the boy's arms over his shoulder and eased him to the ground. "The port supervisor was called to take charge of his corpse. But it's all right, he's still alive. Help me put him back on his bed."

"You should have left him," said Menches, making no move to help. "He's nothing but trouble and bad luck. You'll never see any money from that ship."

Ani laughed. "No, I won't see any money from that ship," he agreed, and was pleased by Menches' confusion. "It seems that the Romans sent men to take charge of it before it got here, and it's sitting at the quay waiting to snap up strayed Greeks."

Menches was surprised, then dismayed. "You mean to keep this Greek beggar in *our* camp? For how long?"

"I don't grudge the boy the care," Ani replied happily. "The port supervisor was so struck by my piety toward Greek strangers that he's asked me to dinner—to meet the captain of the *Prosperity!*—and he's virtually promised that he'll recommend me to the man as a partner!" He laughed again. "May the gods reward me indeed! If you won't help me put Arion to bed, go fetch some clean salt water. I want to see to his wound."

Arion whimpered when Ani cleaned the wound. When Ani applied the myrrh, his eyes fluttered open. He stared around himself blankly, as though he had never seen the place before.

"Easy," Ani told him, laying a hand on the young man's bared chest to prevent him from rising.

The dull eyes flashed to sudden life, and there was a rush of color to the haggard cheeks. Arion struck his hand away with surprising force and rolled over, getting to his knees in the sand. "Keep your hands off me!" he snarled.

"Sit down!" Ani replied impatiently. "You're going to get sand in your wound."

The young man glanced down at himself wildly. Ani had slipped the tunic off his left shoulder, but left it belted at the waist. His skin was pale, and the wound stood out against it, livid and swollen. New bruises showed red here and there. "What were you doing?" he demanded furiously.

"Treating your god-hated wound!" Ani snapped back, beginning to be annoyed. "Boy, you fell over in the street outside an inn, and, from what I heard, were soundly kicked by the innkeeper while you lay there senseless . . ."

"Oh, Herakles, the ship!" cried Arion in anguish.

"Taken by your enemies," Ani replied levelly. "I heard. I'm sorry."

Arion ignored the condolence. "Why am I here?" he demanded. "Why did you go after me and bring me back here, if you know I can't pay you? I'm not . . ." his voice thickened with loathing and disgust, ". . . a slave you can use as you wish! I am not nor ever will be your *boy*. Gods! What were you *doing* to me?"

"Mother Isis, is *that* what you think?" exploded Ani in outraged astonishment. "I was cleaning your wound! Do you think I was about to bugger you?"

It was, clearly, exactly what Arion thought. He glared at Ani, his eyes blazing.

"Why in life should you think such a thing of me?" Ani demanded, bewildered and angry. "I've treated you with nothing but kindness." He paused, still watching the furious young face opposite him. "As I live," he whispered, "that's how it is among rich Greeks, is it? If anyone treats you with kindness, you immediately ask yourself what he wants from you?"

The fierce eyes finally dropped, and Ani felt a moment's discomfort. There *was* something he wanted of the boy. He preserved his indignation by telling himself that it was nothing like *that*, and that he'd been prepared to let the boy go without even mentioning it.

"As it happens," Ani said, sitting back on his heels, "I'm not a lover of boys. I'm a married man—married to my second wife, in fact, since the first one died in childbirth—and I have three children. Even if I *were* a lover of boys, though, I would not take advantage of one who lay injured and helpless under my protection: may the gods destroy me in the worst way if I would ever commit such a crime! Shame on you for condemning me for it, when I never gave you the least cause!"

Arion was trembling now. He fumbled for the amulet around his neck, then pressed the little bag against his face, as he often seemed to do when he was distressed.

"I saved your life!" Ani went on, growing angrier by the

minute. "I paid for your care; I walked here and let you ride; I fed you; I refused to take your precious pin even when you offered it to me, and when you left it anyway I went to give it back. I found you supposedly dead, and I brought you back here and cared for you with my own hands—and in return you've given me not one word of thanks, only this shameful accusation!"

Arion remained where he was, kneeling on the sand beside the bedroll. "O Dionysos!" he said, in a low voice.

"An apology would be accepted," Ani told him shortly.

He did not seem to hear. "O gods, why am I still alive?" He covered his face and began to weep.

The ship, Ani realized. *Now that he's decided I'm no threat to his pure, manly, and Hellenic virtue, he's back to the problem of the ship. Great goddess, Menches is right: I should have left the selfish little swine lying in the road.*

"Boy," he said impatiently, "Fortune blessed you when she kept you off that ship. Even if it had still been in your friends' hands, it would only have taken you into exile, but now you can go home—home to your own people in Alexandria, who'll look after you . . ."

"They're dead," Arion said thickly. "I can't go home."

That made a huge difference. Ani suddenly found he had some sympathy for the young man after all. No family—and probably no money, either. An orphan, barely of age, who had taken up arms and fought passionately in the queen's cause, was not going to be able to lay claim to any property in Alexandria, even if his parents had been as wealthy as his own manner indicated. The Roman conquerers would want to reward their friends among the citizens, and there was never any difficulty in finding friends who claimed an inheritance.

"Even so," he said, after a short silence, "you're young, you're educated, you're a citizen, and when you're well again . . ."

That brought a noise of derision, and Ani remembered his earlier suspicion, and realized that Arion did not expect ever to be completely well again.

"Do you suffer from the sacred disease?" he asked bluntly.

The head came up, and the wet eyes regarded him with fear and shame. The little bag of herbs was still pressed against the mouth.

"What's that?" Ani asked quietly, touching the silk. "A charm against seizures?"

Arion hesitated a moment, then lowered the bag. "Yes," he said, with great bitterness. "—Or rather, a remedy, to clear the brain. I don't know: it might be worse without it."

Ani did not know what to say. The sacred disease. He did not share the common fear that it was contagious. A woman he knew in Coptos had had falling fits every day since she was a tiny child. She had lived all her life with her family—first with her parents, then with her brother and her brother's family. No one else in the family had ever had a seizure. Nor had anyone else in the neighborhood, though the whole neighborhood drew water from the same well, and borrowed clothes and cooking pots freely. No, the sacred disease wasn't contagious. It was, however, a fearful illness which commonly aroused disgust and horror in those who witnessed its effects, and a sufferer who had it as an adult was likely to be afflicted all his life.

He found, however, that the fact that Arion suffered from

it made him like the boy much better. The wariness, the refusal to confide anything about himself, were not simply arrogance, but a fear of being rejected if he gave himself away.
And—Isis and Serapis!—the boy was brave. To reach Berenike
he had fought not merely the wound, the thirst, and the desert, but his own disability—fought them all to a standstill,
without mercy to himself or pride in the accomplishment.

"I should have died," the young man said now, very quietly.
"Sir, I apologize for burdening you, and for my suspicion,
which I admit was unjustified. I thank you for your many
kindnesses. I will go now. You may keep the pin."

Ani gazed at him in surprise and despair. *Still* Arion couldn't
seem to trust or even understand kindness, and still, apparently, the boy presumed the worst of him. "Sit down!" he
ordered. "You're in no shape to go anywhere. I'm not afraid
of the disease, and if I was ashamed to leave you helpless when
you were wounded, I'd be doubly ashamed to do it when
you're wounded and epileptic. You can stay here until you're
feeling stronger. In fact . . ."

He hesitated. From the first moment he'd appreciated the
beautiful modulations of the young Greek's voice, he'd badly
wanted to make him an offer—but he wasn't sure how such
a proud and headstrong youth would respond to it.

"Thank you," said Arion, without interest, "but that's not
necessary."

It took him only a moment to work out why it wouldn't
be "necessary." Then he spat. "What do you plan to do? Hand
yourself over to the Romans, or kill yourself?"

Arion gave him a startled look, as though there were something surprising about Ani having worked it out, as though he

hadn't made his feelings blazingly clear all along. He had thrown himself heart and soul into the queen's cause, and that cause was lost. He couldn't conceive of surviving its ruin.

"What good does it do anybody if you die?" Ani asked him. "It's just one more wasted life at the tail end of a wasted war. Why not live, and try to repair some of the loss?"

Arion pressed the remedy to his face again. "You don't know what you're saying. The loss is irreparable."

"There are always things to be done."

"Leave me alone!" Arion begged indistinctly from behind the herbs.

"Don't you want to go back to Alexandria?" Ani asked him cunningly. "You must have friends there, even if your family is dead. I could see, when you asked about the city, that you were worried about *somebody*. Don't you even want to see how they are? Don't you think that they may be worried about you, hoping that they'll see you again? Doesn't it matter to you what they'd feel if they heard that you destroyed yourself?"

A long silence. Then Arion leaned slowly forward onto the bedroll and folded up on it. He curled up on his good side and began to cry again, silently, pressing a hand against his eyes. The lips of his exposed wound gaped with each sharply drawn breath.

"Child!" protested Ani, touching his shoulder. The skin was hot with fever. "Child, there's no point in dying. There's no need. It would be a waste."

"Don't touch me!" Arion snarled, and pushed the hand away. He lay weeping for a moment, his hand over his eyes, and then, without moving, said, "It is twelve days' journey from Berenike to Coptos, and another fourteen down the river from Coptos to Alexandria. What are you proposing? That you should carry me all that way out of *kindness*?"

"Well," Ani admitted. "No." He took a deep breath. "You could repay me by writing letters."

Arion still didn't move. "Writing letters."

"Writing letters in good Greek to the gentlemen I want to do business with," agreed Ani. His stomach had gone tight and his breath was short. He did want this, he realized: he wanted it more than he'd been willing to admit. Aristodemos, whose place in Berenike he was trying to usurp, was a gentleman, an educated Greek, and the men he dealt with—in Berenike and down the river in Alexandria—were Greeks. They regarded illiterate Egyptians with contempt. Ani could read and write a bit, but letters . . . anything he could produce would be poorly penned, badly phrased, and full of spelling mistakes, and the fine gentlemen would laugh at it and throw it away. He had thought he might hire a scribe, but the sort of scribe he could get, a half-trained villager, would be only a slight improvement on his own clumsy hand. Arion, though—an Alexandrian from a rich family, member of a select unit especially appointed by the queen—Arion could probably write letters that would make Aristodemos look uneducated! And Arion could tell him other things—the layout and rules and manners of Alexandria; how to drape those damned Greek cloaks the way gentlemen did; how to behave at a dinner party, which—gods!—he'd need to know tomorrow night. He needed a gentleman, and gentlemen, by definition, weren't for hire. He needed Arion.

Arion lowered his hand and looked at him in disgust. His eyes were still running. "You want *me* to work for you," he said flatly. "To be your *secretary!*" It was clear he thought this only marginally less degrading than the position he'd previously believed Ani had intended for him.

"Informally," Ani said hastily. "We don't have to make out a contract. You could write letters and advise me on Greek customs, and I would provide you with transport to Alexandria, and with, um, food and clothing during the journey. When we reach Alexandria, you'll be free to forget about me and go where you please." He leaned forward. "You owe me your life and twenty drachmae already. I'd take your agreement to this as full payment of the debt. I don't deny that I'd profit by it, but you would, too. It would get you home to your own city, and at the very least you'd have the comfort of knowing how your friends are. Perhaps they'll be able to help you."

"They will not be able to help me," Arion said, in a very faint voice, "but I would like . . . I would like . . ." He stopped.

"You can go to Alexandria," coaxed Ani. "There's no sense dying, or in handing yourself over to your enemies. There's no point throwing yourself away." He started to touch the boy's shoulder again, then stopped himself. "I'll get you some water," he said instead, "and you can lie there and think about it. Whatever you decide, there's no hurry. You can stay with us as long as we're in Berenike, and we'll be here for the next five days at the least. Tonight we're getting a tent, and it will be more comfortable for you."

"I should have died," was Arion's reply, but he did not move from the bedroll for the rest of the afternoon.

*   *   *

TWO HOURS BEFORE sunset Ani, shaved and dressed in his best clothing, led the procession of laden camels to the warehouse at the corner of Market and Harbor Streets. It was a sturdy building adjoining a grand house which, as Ani immediately guessed, belonged to Archedamos. The port supervisor saw their goods stowed with considerable satisfaction, collected a month's warehousing fee, and took his new friend across the street to meet his neighbour Kratistes, who was very pleased to rent out a tent to the city's only customer. They loaded it onto one of the camels, brought it back, and were in the middle of pitching it when a company of armored men marched down the ramp onto the beach.

Ani saw them coming, and he dropped his guy-rope and stared in alarm. Eight of the men wore mail shirts over short red tunics, and carried tall spears and oblong shields—red, decorated with a pattern of lightning-bolts and wings in yellow. Another man, probably an officer, wore a gilded cuirass and had a sword. The setting sun gleamed off nine polished helmets crested with red horsehair. Archedamos, walking huddled up among them, looked drab, small, and very frightened.

The party marched up to the caravan and halted, the soldiers grounding their spears in the sand with a thudding hiss. The officer surveyed the caravan with an air of condescending interest. Menches and Imouthes stared back, frozen beside the half-erected tent.

"Um," Archedamos muttered unhappily to the Roman officer. "Um. This is Ani, the caravan-owner I told you about. Umm, Ani, here is centurion Gaius Paterculus, from the Roman party aboard the *Nemesis*. He, um, heard of the incident at the Happy Return, and he, uh, wishes . . . wishes to speak to your guest."

Ani felt sick and numb. So, Kerdon had indeed gone to the Romans. Clearly Archedamos had thought he might, but somehow Ani had never expected them to take any interest. Now they were here, and there was nothing he could do. He could neither hide Arion nor protect him—and, faced with this wall of metal, he abruptly thought to fear for his own safety as well. The Romans might well arrest him for sheltering a fugitive, and who knew what sort of treatment he could expect then?

He had a sudden intense vision of his wife and children in Coptos sitting down in the main room of his house for the evening meal, as they would at this time of day. Melanthe would say, "I wonder if Papa is in Berenike now?" and Tiathres would reply, "I only want him to come home." Sweet Lady Isis, he prayed, only let me get home.

"I was told," said the centurion, in clear though heavily accented Greek, "that you have given shelter to a soldier of the queen, a fugitive from the camp at Kabalsi."

Ani swallowed several times. Tell the truth, he commanded himself. There is nothing shameful about giving help to an injured traveler, and if they punish you for it, the disgrace is theirs.

"Sir," he said respectfully, "I found a young man lying injured and unconscious in the road near Kabalsi. I took him up and brought him with me here to Berenike, because he would have died if I'd left him. Sir, he's very young, not more than eighteen. He was wounded and unarmed. The gods command us to show piety and to be merciful to strangers and travelers."

"Were you at the Greek camp at Kabalsi?"

"Me?" said Ani, caught by surprise. "No, of course not! I'm from Coptos: I came here with a caravan of linen trade goods. Archedamos can vouch for that: my goods are in his warehouse."

"He has already done so," the Roman admitted. "Did you ask this young man who he was and what he was doing lying in the road?"

"Sir, he was unconscious when I found him." Let the Roman understand he'd given help first, and asked questions later! "I asked him when he woke, the following day. He told me that his name is Arion and that he's from Alexandria. When I questioned him more closely, he said that he and some others had been encamped in the mountains, waiting for a ship to arrive in Berenike. He said that your people had come to the camp, that there'd been a fight—which the Greeks lost—and that he had escaped. He wanted to go to Berenike to warn the ship what had happened." He drew a deep breath. "Sir, I am very sorry if you're offended because I helped him, but I did not think one injured youth was a matter of any importance to the masters of Egypt."

"It is not," said the centurion, "but I was charged with seeing that no one escaped from that camp. Where is the fugitive?"

Helplessly, Ani gestured at the awning.

Arion was asleep, his tunic still around his waist and the cloak draped loosely over his unbandaged chest to keep the flies off the wound: Ani had decided that exposure to the hot dry air would benefit the cut. The centurion looked at him a moment, then barked an order to his men. Two of them at once pulled loose the front posts of the awning and folded it back. Arion opened his eyes. He saw the centurion and began to sit up—then lay back again, his face settling into an expression of resignation.

"Your name is Arion?" asked the centurion.

The young Greek looked surprised.

"You went today to an inn called the Happy Return," the centurion told him. "You asked for Didymos."

"Yes," Arion agreed. He seemed confused.

The centurion smiled. "A truthful answer. You are from the camp at Kabalsi?"

"It wasn't at Kabalsi," replied Arion. "It was about five miles away, up in the mountains."

The centurion snorted. "You do not dispute, though, that you were in the camp of King Ptolemy Caesar?"

Archedamos gasped. The Roman glanced at him and asked sharply, "What?"

"The *king*?" asked Archedamos. "I thought . . . I thought they had gold there."

"You did not know?" asked the centurion, amused. "Queen Cleopatra's bastard and colleague was there. He is dead now— dead and burnt." He made a dismissive gesture. "There was gold as well."

Ani looked at Arion. The boy had shut his eyes and set his teeth as though in pain. He had never confirmed that he served the king, let alone that the king had actually been in the camp. Perhaps he'd believed that Caesarion had been able to escape while he and his comrades defended the camp, and only now realized that his protective silence had been pointless.

"I didn't know," said Archedamos numbly. "I had orders to

assist the camp commander, who was called Eumenes. I knew nothing about the king."

"The secret was kept well, then," said the centurion. He seemed pleased at that, and glad of the chance to tell them about this victory for his own people. "There was a traitor— the young king's tutor, a man called Rhodon. He sent a message to our general, and our general sent my friend Marcus Avitus and his men to take the camp, and myself and my men to take the ship on which the king planned to escape from Egypt. I and my men marched to Heroonpolis, commandeered a galley, and took the king's ship before it could reach Berenike, cutting off his escape. This morning, however, I received a messenger from Avitus to tell me that there was no escape, since his own mission was completely successful. He and his century sailed up the Nile to Coptos, where Rhodon, the traitor, met them. He led them to the king's camp, gave the password, and ran to find the king. He took the king's own spear and meant to hold him prisoner, but when the king understood what had happened he was so angry that he threw himself at his tutor and ran himself through the heart on his own spear. Probably it's true what they say, that he was feeble-minded. Just as well: none of Avitus' people wanted to be named as the one who killed him. He was called Caesar, even though he had no right to the name."

Arion's eyes flew open again. "That's a lie!"

The centurion was amused. "The queen is no better than a whore. She told Julius Caesar that the child was his, but who knows who the real father was?"

"Julius Caesar knew her better than you," replied Arion sharply, "and he thought so highly of her that he set up her statue beside the altar of his divine ancestress, in the heart of the city of Rome. The father of *Octavian* was Gaius Octavius. The one with no right to call himself Caesar is *your* emperor, centurion."

There was a moment of silence—and then the centurion laughed. "A warlike answer! I believe now that you fought to defend your king. Avitus said there wasn't much fighting. None of our people died, and only a few of the enemy."

"I am sorry for that," Arion declared, with staggering disdain for his own safety.

"You lost, little bantam cock," returned the centurion. He still seemed amused. "Your king is dead, and you're unarmed and penniless and flat on your back. I was surprised to hear that anyone from the camp had arrived here. Avitus said no one had escaped."

"I did," insisted Arion, glaring. "I have not surrendered."

"So I see. Well, it was dark when Avitus attacked, and there was some confusion. One wounded boy running off into the night is easily missed. What was your position in the camp, Greekling?"

Arion simply continued to glare.

"Were you a slave? An officer's catamite, perhaps?"

"No!" exclaimed Arion in outrage. "I am freeborn, an Alexandrian and a gentleman!"

The centurion smiled again: Ani was sure that he, too, had recognized an aristocrat when he heard one, and had made the other suggestion only to bait the young man. "And what was your position in the king's camp?"

Arion subsided sullenly. "Staff officer. With Eumenes. The commander of the king's bodyguard."

The centurion nodded: staff officer was exactly the kind of position one would expect a young aristocrat to hold. "That explains the wound," he remarked. "Avitus said that the commander was one of the few who fought."

"Yes," agreed Arion, his jaw set. "He died bravely."

The centurion nodded, as though this matched with what he had heard. "He would have done better to surrender, and you with him. Then he would have kept his life, and you'd have a whole skin. Well, Avitus has seen to it that your commander had a royal funeral: he was cremated along with your king. Avitus is marching the rest of your friends back to Coptos now, apart from the few who died in the attack. They're prisoners, but they won't be harmed. You would not have been harmed, either."

Arion's eyes were hot. He began to speak, stopped himself; started again. "If you wish to kill me, do it." He glanced proudly round the others, then added hastily, "All I have to say is this: Ani helped me only because he is a pious man who believes that kindness to strangers is pleasing to the gods. He is not a supporter of the queen or an enemy of Rome. To punish him as well would be unjust."

Ani was surprised, moved—and deeply relieved, particularly when the centurion shook his head and declared, "I am not going to punish him."

Then the Roman lifted his head and announced loudly, "We have made Egypt a Roman province. Your queen is a prisoner. We killed your king and took possession of his treasure. It is the custom of the Roman people to spare the defeated, and our emperor, Gaius Julius Caesar Octavianus, son of the deified Julius, wishes to begin the Roman rule of this province with clemency. He has decreed that there will be no reprisals against anyone who fought for the queen, provided that they lay down their arms now."

He looked down at Arion, and his lips quirked in a smile. "You've lost your weapons, little cockerel, so we will agree that you have laid them down."

Arion glared, and the centurion's smiled widened. He bent, and set his hand on the young Greek's side. Arion flinched, but the centurion had merely laid two fingers alongside the wound. "That is infected," he said matter-of-factly. "And you have fever. I would take you back to Alexandria with us, but you'd need nursing, and even if we provided it, the voyage would probably kill you." He straightened again. "I am going to leave you here, Arion of Alexandria, in the care of this pious caravan-owner. I have seen you and spoken to you, and I am convinced that you were at the king's camp, but that you are no threat to anyone. Good health!"

He snapped his fingers, and his men stood to attention. He walked past them, and they fell in behind him with a stamping of feet. Helmets and spear-points glinting in the last of the sun, the Romans marched proudly off the beach.

The others watched them go. When they had stamped their way up the ramp and onto Harbor Street, Archedamos let out his breath in a long sigh. "I thank Serapis and all the gods and heroes!" he exclaimed. He hurried to Ani and slapped him on the back. "I was very much afraid for you, my good man, and for our young friend. But *clemency*, ha! That is an official policy I can support!"

Ani said nothing, but forced himself to grin and nod. He was perfectly certain that Archedamos had fingered him for the Romans the moment they turned up at his door. That he'd also vouched for Ani's status as a genuine merchant meant nothing—he could hardly have done otherwise, with the goods in his own warehouse. Still, there was no point making an enemy of a man he needed as a friend.

Archedamos went over to Arion. "I am pleased that you're out of danger, young man."

Arion had been sitting up on an elbow, glaring after the centurion. He gave Archedamos a bewildered look and said nothing.

"And you fought to defend the young king!" the port supervisor declared admiringly. "It was well done, even if it was done in vain."

"Who are you?" Arion asked in confusion.

Archedamos smiled. "Of course, you were unconscious when I saw you last. I am Archedamos son of Aristolaos, supervisor of the port of Berenike. And you are Arion son of . . . ?"

Arion shook his head. He lay down suddenly, curled up on his good side, and covered his face. He was trembling.

"Ah, you're ill!" cried Archedamos sympathetically. "You're injured—a fearful wound!—and to be questioned like that was a shock, I'm sure, though you answered the barbarians bravely. I'll leave you to rest. I'll send my doctor to see to you in the morning, shall I? Good health. Ani, I'll expect you tomorrow an hour before sunset. Good health!"

He left, walking with a light step and his head held high—a result, Ani was sure, of the just-announced Roman policy of clemency. At least he'd send a doctor.

Ani went over and knelt beside Arion. "Are you all right?"

"Leave me alone!" the boy snarled, from behind his remedy.

Cheated of martyrdom, and dismissed as no threat to anyone: a dreadful humiliation. The fact that he was, remarkably, still alive and at liberty did not seem to impress him. He could not reckon the value of his own life any better than he had that of the jewel, and he would dispose of it as casually.

Ani thought again of his wife and children sitting down to supper in Coptos: Tiathres, perhaps, holding their younger boy, Isisdoros, on her lap, while the elder, Serapion, told her about some small adventure of the day, and Melanthe looked out the window and wondered when her father would come home. He could almost see the evening sunlight shining on the table, and smell the fresh cumin bread. He would return to them whole and safe, and they would welcome him. That was a thing more precious than any jewel, more valuable than the cargo he hoped to gain. Lady Isis, he prayed, you who ordained that the True should be thought good, I thank you, great goddess, for my life and freedom.

Menches came over. "Those are our new rulers?" he asked.

"So it would seem." Ani looked around for the guy-rope he'd dropped when the Romans first appeared.

"I thought they would take the Greek boy." Menches sounded disappointed that they hadn't. Probably he had not understood enough of the conversation to realize that his employer was in danger, too: his command of Greek was largely restricted to the ordering of camels. "What does 'clessimy' mean?"

"*Clemency*. It means mercy. It seems that the new king has

decreed that there should be no reprisals against those who fought for the queen."

"Huh. Better news for the Greeks than for us, if he means it."

That was true: clemency to the defeated would mean Greek rights and property untouched and no new opportunities for Egyptians. Ani comforted himself with the knowledge that reprisals would have meant not just Arion's death, but chaos throughout Egypt and a collapse of trade. He sighed and went back to work on the tent.

They had just got it up when he remembered the light he had seen in the north the night he found Arion: the light of a great fire, a couple of miles away up a remote mountainside. That, he realized, had been the funeral pyre of King Ptolemy Caesar, the last of the Lagid dynasty.

He had never entirely believed in the divinity of kings. The gods raised up kings and queens to be rulers of men, but the gods brought them down again at their own pleasure. Cleopatra had claimed to be the living incarnation of Isis, and no doubt that was true, in the sense that the goddess had granted her power over Egypt—but it was Isis alone who governed the thunderbolt and could overcome Fate, and she had ordained an end to Cleopatra's reign. He pondered that a moment: the Lagid kings fallen; the order of the world changed forever. The gods alone remained: great was the goddess.

He himself must have been one of the only Egyptians to have seen the funeral of the last of the Ptolemies. He would have to tell Melanthe: she would understand what it meant, to have seen the end of an era with his own eyes.

Tiathres would just be pleased that he was home safely.

Tiathres would kiss him, draw him into the dark little back room which was their private place, and welcome him home into the sweet sanctuary of her own body. Tiathres, he thought fondly, always had had good sense.

CHAPTER IV

Archedamos' doctor arrived early in the morning, when the Egyptians were still feeding the camels and cleaning up about the camp.

Caesarion had spent a miserable night tossing and turning on his bedroll, trying to find some position where the pain from the wound was bearable. It burned him; his head ached savagely and he felt very sick. By the time the doctor arrived, he was certain that he was going to die. He wished fervently that he'd done it before, and spared himself the tortures and humiliations of the past few days. He'd had to beg Ani's pardon for a ludicrous suspicion, he'd been spat upon and, apparently, kicked by an innkeeper, and been called a bastard and a 'little bantam cock' by a swaggering centurion. It would have been better to have died.

Even more humiliating—and far more frightening—was a

horrible sense that his very identity was slipping. As far as the world around him was concerned, Ptolemy Caesar was dead, and he was Arion, a foolish young Alexandrian who was no threat to anyone. If he lived he would have to take the job Ani had offered him. He had, he realized with horror, absolutely no idea how else to support himself—and he wanted to go back to Alexandria: there was nothing for him anywhere else.

Alexandria would be dangerous, of course. There were far too many people there who knew him, and now the city was in Roman hands. His mother was there, though, and his brothers and sister, together with whatever remained of the royal court. He had nothing to live for and no way to escape, so he might as well try to accomplish something worthy of a king before he died.

If he set off for Alexandria as a camel-driver's secretary, however, who would he be by the time he reached the city? Would he still be Caesarion, a deposed king hoping somehow to free his mother, or at least his brother, from captivity? Or would he be indeed Arion, a feeble and epileptic ghost, helped out of pity and ridiculed out of scorn? Better, much better, to die here in Berenike.

To die from an infected wound, though, burning and stinking and in pain—it was a horrible end. Perhaps, though, it was what he deserved, since he had refused the royal death that had been offered him first.

The doctor, however, was optimistic. "There is some infection," he announced, after a careful examination. "However, it is still in its early stages, and I judge it can be controlled by cleaning and proper care, combined with rest and a low and cooling diet." He pronounced the wound itself not too dangerous: "The lower cut is deep, but is confined to the flesh between the ribs: it has not penetrated any of the vitals. The upper stroke has cracked a rib, but apart from that, is of no significance."

He gave Caesarion a drug to reduce the fever and dull the pain, a bitter-tasting concoction of opium and black hellebore. Then he cleaned the injury with a solution of vinegar and biting herbs and stitched the torn flesh together, leaving channels for the pus to drain.

Caesarion endured it in silence, pressing the remedy against his face. The drug dulled the pain and his mind both. He felt as though he were suspended in a gray fog by a hook in his side—suspended and twirling slowly in a disintegrating world.

The doctor finished stitching and applied a poultice. "What is this?" he asked, taking the remedy from his lax grasp.

"I need that," Caesarion protested in alarm, reaching for it.

The doctor opened the little bag and shook some of the contents into his palm. "Cardamon," he commented. "Gum ammoniacum. Bryony. Cinquefoil. What's this, cyclamen?"

"I need that," Caesarion repeated, more urgently.

The doctor sniffed at the wizened chunk of vegetable matter. "No, peony root . . . These are heating and drying herbs, no help for wounds or fevers. Why do you have these?"

Ani emerged out of the grayness. "He has the sacred disease."

The doctor stared. Then he tipped the herbs back into the little bag and silently handed it back. Caesarion pressed it to his face and drew a deep breath of the piercing scent. The world was still swirling.

"I should have been told this before," the doctor remarked irritably. "It affects his treatment. How long has he suffered this disorder?"

Ani shrugged and grimaced in expressive ignorance. The doctor turned back to Caesarion and repeated the question.

Caesarion was still spinning in the fog. "It began when I was thirteen," he answered dreamily. "I remember coming into the house, and then I was in bed, with a doctor looking at me. I hurt all over and my clothes were wet. They said I fell down. It can't be cured. They've tried. We consulted lots of doctors. They tried drugs, and they tried bleeding and purging, but nothing worked. One of them wanted to cauterize my brain, but Mother wouldn't let him. I don't have fits that often."

"How often?"

"At home, I fall down maybe once a month . . ." He came back to the present with a jerk. He was not supposed to discuss his condition with anyone unless the queen had approved it. "Have you sworn the oath?" he demanded.

"Which oath?" asked the doctor. He was frowning. He was an elderly man, well dressed, bearded like a philosopher. He looked wise and kind, but Caesarion never trusted that in a doctor. They all tried to look that way—their livelihoods depended on it—but some of the treatments they recommended were little short of torture.

"The Hippocratic oath. 'Whatever I see or hear, professionally or privately, which ought not to be divulged, I will keep secret and tell no one.' You must tell no one that I have the disease."

"I have sworn the oath," the doctor said reluctantly. "However, in this case, Archedamos is paying my fee, and he asked me to report to him."

Ani appeared out of the gray again. "Archedamos wants to know about the wound," he pointed out. "There's no need to tell him about the disease. Come, the boy's ashamed of it, you can understand that, can't you? He doesn't want the whole town pointing him out as an epileptic and spitting at him."

The doctor appeared to accept this. Caesarion was vaguely aware of him giving Ani instructions as to his care—drugs, diet, dressings for the wound. "I'll be back tomorrow morning," he finished. Caesarion hung suspended in the fog, twirling slowly.

After an indeterminate time, Ani appeared again and began doing something to the dressing. "You shouldn't have told him I have the disease," Caesarion reproached him.

"Told who?" asked Ani.

He realized that the doctor had left hours ago. I should not have accepted the drug, he thought, though without urgency. It's too strong. I may give myself away. I must not. "That doctor."

Ani gave a snort of disgust. "Boy, he's a doctor! He had to know. You heard him yourself: it affects your treatment." There was a wonderful coolness up his side as a fresh poultice settled on the hot flesh. "At home you fell down once a month, eh? You've had two fits since I met you."

More than that, he thought dreamily—but the small seizures had passed unnoticed. "It was easier at home," he said faintly. "It wasn't so hot. The condition is exacerbated by hunger and by thirst, by too much exertion or too little, by suffering and by strong passion."

"Wasn't a good idea to become a soldier, then, was it?" The Egyptian's face hung over him, sharply etched and unnaturally distinct. "Passion exasperates it? Isis and Serapis, what does that mean? You're supposed to avoid women?"

He thought of Rhodopis, with whom he'd fallen in love when they were both sixteen. She had such a beautiful laugh—such a joyful, free, uninhibited laugh, such bright eyes, such lovely breasts . . . She'd been a palace slave, however, and when his mother found out that they were sleeping together, Rhodopis had been sold in the public slave market. "I'm sorry," Cleopatra had told him, when he went to her in tears to protest, "but you know that it would have aggravated your condition."

"I'm supposed to avoid women," he agreed bitterly.

"Sweet Lady Isis, what a fate!"

He thought Ani said something else then, but when he asked him what, he found that the Egyptian was no longer there.

He woke without being aware that he'd slept, and Ani was there again. The world had stopped whirling, and his head was clear enough for him to realize that this was because the drug was wearing off. The pain, however, did not seem nearly as hot as it had been that morning.

"Arion," said the Egyptian nervously, "I need some help."

You must, Caesarion thought sourly, if you're willing to use my name.

"Archedamos invited me to dinner," Ani went on. "It's a Greek dinner. Should I wear a cloak?"

Caesarion was quiet a moment, trying to order his disjoined mind, to work out why he'd been woken up for such a trivial question. Ani watched him anxiously, and he realized that for

Ani it wasn't trivial at all: the overbearing caravan-master was completely daunted by the invitation to a dinner party. It was a surprising realization, and a gratifying one: Ani might be sharp, shrewd, and forceful, but he was no gentleman and he knew it. For a moment Caesarion contemplated misleading the fellow so he'd make a fool of himself—but no, he couldn't do that. As Ani kept reminding him, he was in debt to the wretch for his life. "What time is it?" he asked.

"Now? About two hours till sunset."

"No, the dinner! What time does the dinner begin?"

"Oh. In an hour."

"And how many guests?"

"I . . . He said he was inviting Kleon, the captain of the *Prosperity*."

"Who?"

"The captain of the *Prosperity*! Sweet Isis, the man this whole venture depends on! I want him to accept me as an investor, a partner, and not just a customer!"

"Archedamos is unlikely to invite just two guests," Caesarion said judiciously. "That would leave the couches unbalanced. And the hour is early for an informal occasion, though not early enough for a banquet. There will probably be six to supper, and three courses. You should wear a good cloak, but you shouldn't bring a garland."

Ani looked more anxious than ever. "O gods, it's going to be *formal*? And I have to wear a long cloak? I can never get those god-hated cloaks to hang properly. *Couches*, you said? I'm going to have to eat lying down—in a bit of god-hated Greek drapery?"

Caesarion sat up, found that he was light-headed but not

too uncomfortable. "Fetch the cloak," he ordered. "I'll tell you what to do."

ANI SET OFF for the dinner party three-quarters of an hour later, uncomfortably swathed in a long cloak, his head swimming with instructions. Caesarion lay down again, tired but satisfied: he had saved his host from making a fool of himself, which did something to redress the balance between them.

One of the Egyptian camel-drivers—Imouthes, the young man—came into the tent carrying a bowl of broth. He set it down by Caesarion's head, stood a moment frowning, then left in silence. "I gave it to him," Caesarion heard him say from just outside the tent.

"Good," said Menches, the older man. "If he gave Master Ani bad advice, I hope it turns his stomach."

He spoke, like his son, in Demotic. Caesarion wondered if they realized that he could overhear and understand. Greeks from the cities usually spoke no Demotic at all. The queen, however, had learned the language of her subjects—the first of her dynasty to do so—and she had insisted that her son learn it as well. He picked up the bowl and sniffed it cautiously. It smelled harmless—pleasant, in fact: barley broth sweetened with a little honey.

"Why did the master need advice on how to eat dinner?" asked Imouthes. It sounded as though the two were settling to eat their own supper just outside the tent.

Menches spat—a loud hawking and a distinguishable plop of spittle striking sand. "You ever been invited to dinner by a Greek? They don't usually ask Egyptians, not even the likes of Master Ani. These Greeks have rules about how to sit and how to chew and which hand to use for what, and if a man doesn't know them, they think he's a dirty peasant. They *invent* rules like that, to set themselves apart. No Greek ever wants an Egyptian as a friend and partner."

"You don't think Master Ani will get his partnership?" The young man sounded disappointed.

"Better if he doesn't!" Menches replied darkly.

"What's wrong with Master Ani becoming a rich merchant?" Imouthes protested. "He's come by his money fairly, and he always spends it where it helps his own."

There was a silence, and then Menches said, in a significant tone, "Why did he hire just us and our own camels, when he really needed another man and at least three more beasts?"

"Because he didn't want to hire from Sisois," said Imouthes, plainly mystified.

"And why didn't he want to hire from Sisois?"

"Because Sisois is a fornicating dog," replied Imouthes promptly.

Menches gave an abrupt bark of laughter. "Apart from that!"

There was a puzzled silence.

"Because Sisois serves Aristodemos," Menches explained triumphantly. "If Master Ani had gone to him for camels, Aristodemos would have found out what he was up to."

"So?" asked Imouthes. "Aristodemos isn't investing this year. Why should he care what Master Ani does?"

"Why should an impotent man care if somebody else sleeps with his wife? He *does* care, that's all. Aristodemos isn't going to like this, and Master Ani knows that. He wants it all done before Aristodemos finds out, because he thinks that then Aristodemos will have to swallow it. I say, though, that if it's just a question of Ani buying up one cargo, Aristodemos will swallow it—but if it's the partnership, there'll be trouble. The Romans said that their policy will be 'clemency'—and that means the Greeks keep everything, and *that* means that Aristodemos will want to put money into trade, after all. The *Prosperity* has done four voyages for him. It's a good ship, with an experienced captain who knows the coasts and the people. Aristodemos won't give it up without a fight—not to an Egyptian. And if it comes to a fight, he'll win, won't he? He's richer than Master Ani, and all the magistrates are Greek. No, it would be better for Ani if this ship captain decides he's a dirty peasant, and that he wants to look for a Greek partner."

They began to talk about the caravan-masters and merchants of Coptos, and Caesarion stopped paying attention. He drank the barley broth, rolled over onto his good side, and tried to sleep.

He was startled out of a doze a few hours later to find that it was dark and that Ani and another man were standing over him with a lantern. The light from it jittered drunkenly about the shadowy tent, and there was a strong smell of wine.

"Good health!" said Ani. He sounded extremely cheerful. "You feeling any better?"

Caesarion pushed himself up onto an elbow and squinted at him. The man beside Ani squatted down by the bedroll. He was a balding, big-boned man of middle age, probably Greek, wearing a good cloak askew; his forearms were scarred and the hands draped loosely over his knees were heavily callused. "Ani says you've agreed to write his letters," he said. His breath reeked of wine, and he seemed every bit as cheerful as

Ani. Caesarion suddenly suspected who he was.

"This is Kleon," Ani confirmed happily, also squatting down. "Captain of *Prosperity*. He wanted to meet you."

"Archedamos thinks you were a companion of the king," confided Kleon, loud with wine. "A Kinsman, or at least a First Friend."

Caesarion gazed at him in alarm. Archedamos had decided he was a high-ranking member of the royal court? How? Why? Were his accent, his loyalty to the queen's cause, and the position he'd claimed, as "aide to Eumenes," enough, or did Archedamos remember seeing him? He could not remember ever meeting Archedamos, but that meant nothing: he'd often stood before the crowds on ceremonial occasions and been stared at by thousands. If Archedamos had seen him, and re-membered that he was a member of the court, would he eventually remember more?

"You were with the king in that hideout up in the moun-tains, weren't you?" Kleon went on. "Aide-de-camp to the commander, Archedamos said. He's been telling the whole town about it, and about what you said to the Romans when they came to question you. He's overcome by admiration— now that the Romans are going to be clement. Always did adore royalty, our port supervisor. Were you at the court?"

"I was a Friend of the king," Caesarion replied cautiously. That was the third rank of courtier, below the Kinsmen and the First Friends.

"Good enough, good enough!" Kleon roared delightedly, and slapped Ani on the back, nearly knocking him on top of Caesarion. "By the Two Gods, that's something, a Friend of the king to write your letters! That bugger-arsed Aristodemos never had anything like that. And you think you can get the tin?"

Ani spread his hands. "If it's to be bought at all."

Kleon laughed admiringly. "That's the kind of man I like to deal with! Aristodemos always was a whiner—'Can't do this, can't do that; my health, my lands, my resources do not permit . . .' Would've dropped him last voyage, if I could've found someone else. So, we've got the linen, you're sure you can get the glassware, and with a king's Friend to write letters, you think you can get the tin. You feeling better, Arion?"

Caesarion regarded him with distaste. His sleep-dull mind caught up with the fact that his agreement to Ani's proposition was being assumed—that it appeared to have been included among Ani's advantages as a prospective business partner. He had *not* agreed to it. Ani had told him there was no hurry, and left him to think about it.

"Did Menches give you the rest of the medicine?" Ani asked, before Caesarion could think how to object.

"No," said Caesarion, irritated to find that Menches should have done so. "But I don't want it. The pain is better. I . . ."

"Oh, you want to take it!" Kleon at once assured him. "Fever in the summer is deadly, but hellebore will see it off. Purges you, you see, as well as dulling pain; clears all the poison out of you."

Caesarion was well aware of its purgative effects—he could feel them in his gut at that minute—and they were not, in his view, an advantage with an injured side.

"I was wounded once in the stomach," Kleon continued expansively. "—Pirates, down to the south by Ptolemais Theron. Would have died of the fever, if it hadn't been for the hellebore; would have died of the infection, if it hadn't been for the myrrh. I'll send some myrrh tomorrow—top-quality stuff from Opone—a gift, eh? For the noble assistant of my new partner."

"Thank you," said Ani at once. "It's the best thing for in-fections." He jumped up, then came back with a glossy black flask. "Here's the drug," he told Caesarion. "You'd better take it. The doctor said you should have it at sunset. Menches probably thought there wasn't any need because you were asleep. He did give you the barley broth, though, I hope?"

"Yes," agreed Caesarion, staring up at him sullenly.

He could announce that he had *not* agreed to assist Ani. But . . . Ani had helped him. Ani had, in fact, saved his life. Ani was providing shelter, food, medicines—and a way to reach Alexandria. He wanted to reach Alexandria. Berenike had be-come dangerous—Archedamos might have recognized him, and the Romans were still here. But in Alexandria he might, still, be able to do something—*something!*—to help his mother, his family, his cause.

If he didn't turn into a secretary on the way.

In the end, he took the black flask and drank the bitter drug without saying anything.

THE DOCTOR CAME again the following morning, and was pleased with his progress. The inflammation of the wound had gone down, and the fever had abated. The doctor cleaned and bandaged the injury and offered another dose of the drug, but, to Caesarion's relief, did not press when it was refused. Then he asked more about the remedy—who had prescribed it and what was in it. He had no questions, however, about Caesarion's experience of the disease, and when he wrote down the ingredients, Caesarion realized that his interest was in the medication, not the patient. It was a mistake to have named the doctor. This local physician would boast of his prescription derived directly from a luminary of the royal court, and Archedamos would hear about it, and perhaps remember the real status of the man whose medical bills he'd agreed to pay.

Were the Romans still in Berenike? Would Archedamos go to them if they were? Or would he gossip—"tell the whole town about it"—as he had before?

He had to get away from Berenike as soon as possible.

When the doctor was gone, Ani came over again. "Anything I can fetch you from the city?" he asked. He was in a very good mood that morning: he had gone about the camp tunelessly bellowing fragments of drinking songs and patting the camels.

Caesarion looked at him with dislike. "You told the captain I'd agreed to write your letters," he pointed out coldly.

Ani sobered quickly. "Boy, you're not going to change your mind *now*!"

"What do you mean, 'change my mind'?" Caesarion demanded indignantly. "I never made it up!—and don't call me 'boy'!"

"By all the gods!" exclaimed Ani, equally indignant. "Why shouldn't you do it? I saved your life!"

"You only saved it because you thought you could use me!"

"No!" Ani answered at once. "I saved your life when I didn't know who or what you were. It was only *afterward* that I found out that there was something you could do for me in return.

And I'm not asking for anything that would hurt you; in fact, you'd benefit. Sweet Isis, you can't back out *now!* Kleon's going to sign the contract today!"

"You had no business telling him I'd do it when I hadn't agreed!" Caesarion protested.

"Are you saying you won't do it?" Ani snapped back.

They glared at one another for a long moment. "I didn't say that," Caesarion admitted at last. "I didn't say I wouldn't. But you had no business telling that drunken sea-captain that I had agreed, when I haven't."

Ani relaxed slowly. "Well." He blew his cheeks out. "The truth is, boy, that I *didn't* tell him you'd agreed. All I said was that I'd made the offer. Kleon just assumed that you'd agreed, and he was so pleased with the notion that I didn't contradict him. I was sure, anyway, that you would agree: you'd be a fool not to." He sat down on the floor of the tent, cross-legged. "So—will you do it?"

Caesarion grimaced. "Why is this business so important to you, anyway?"

Ani grinned. "I want to be rich. I do better than most, but you can't get rich—not really rich—out of growing flax. The taxes get you coming, and the linen monopoly gets you going, and the most you can hope for is twelve percent profit in a year. Trade'll get you two hundred, if you pick your ship carefully and Fortune smiles. You know anything about the coastal trade?"

Harbor dues and tariffs; rich cargos arriving from royal vessels; petitions for the queen to improve the roads and the harbors, to put down piracy and banditry. Nothing, really, that he could admit to.

"The ships set out from Berenike, or from Myos Hormos up the coast," said Ani. "They go south down the Red Sea, sometimes as far as Opone, which is on the Indian Ocean. They can take over a year to go and come back again. To fund a voyage, the ship's captain—or the syndicate that owns the vessel—looks for investors who fit out the ship and take a share of the profits on its return.

"Now, Kleon, as it happens, owns *Prosperity* outright—he bought her from the syndicate that built her. He also buys up cargo on his own account, and owns about half what the ship carries. The other half comes from a partner. Kleon's partner *was* a rich landowner from my own town, a man by the name of Aristodemos. In the ordinary way of things, when the ship came in, Aristodemos would send a caravan to collect the cargo, both his share and Kleon's. He took it overland to Coptos, and then down the river to Alexandria, where he'd sell it on—at a handsome profit—and buy up goods for the outward voyage.

"This year, though, as I think I've mentioned, Aristodemos was afraid of the war. He wanted to keep his money safe, and he certainly didn't want to go to Alexandria when it was going to be besieged. He sent a caravan that was half the usual size, unladen and traveling very fast, to get to Berenike before the war. He took his own share of the cargo, and left Kleon and his share sitting in Berenike."

Caesarion had begun listening to this account of petty mercantile dealings with disdain, but it had dawned on him that, little as he liked it, the circumstances were likely to dominate his life over the next month, and he was now paying close attention. "Kleon couldn't take his share to Alexandria himself?" he asked.

Ani flashed another grin. "He could, of course, but it would cost him plenty."

Caesarion looked blank.

Ani spread his hands expressively. "This city is perched on the edge of the most desolate piece of desert the gods ever cursed. There isn't much pasturage even in the winter, and in summer there's none. There isn't much water in the cisterns, either, to irrigate more than a few vegetable patches. Costs a lot to keep a camel if you have to import all its food across three hundred miles of desert. There aren't many beast to be hired here during the summer, and those there are, are expensive. No, caravans of camels come to Berenike from the river—and then go back there. Kleon would need to go to Coptos, hire camels and drivers, come back here with them, load the cargo, take it to Coptos, hire a boat, take it to Alexandria, conduct his business, sail back up the river, hire more camels—and hope his ship was still in good shape when he returned to it, because ships need careful managing, and hired help is never going to manage anything as carefully as an owner. No, he needs a partner—and, as it happens, I'm more than willing to take Aristodemos' place."

Caesarion thought of what Menches had said—that Aristodemos would make trouble if Ani took his partnership. He thought Ani must be right to disregard that: Aristodemos couldn't possibly expect Kleon to take him on again. He had left the captain comprehensively stranded. Ani, in contrast, had come to Kleon's rescue—and hoped to profit by it, just as he hoped to profit from his rescue of Caesarion.

"You brought trade goods here before you even met Kleon," Caesarion pointed out. "But you said you've never been to Alexandria."

"I brought the linen clothing," Ani agreed. "That part of the cargo Aristodemos always bought from me. See, *Prosperity* usually sails with a cargo—an outbound cargo—of linen clothing and dyed linen cloth, along with glassware from the workshops in Alexandria and tin from overseas. Yes, I took a risk bringing the linen before I knew I had a buyer for it—but I was pretty sure Kleon would be pleased to see it, and I had it ready waiting for Aristodemos anyway. I was certain that Kleon would take the linen in exchange for some of his own cargo, and that alone would make the trip worth my while. I thought he'd be pleased enough that he'd agree to let me take the rest of his cargo down to Alexandria for him, on commission. But what I wanted—and, I thank the Lady Isis, what I'm getting!—is partnership on the same terms he gave Aristodemos."

Caesarion thought of the overloaded camels on the way from Kabalsi. "If the linen is only a part of the cargo," he asked doubtfully, "do you have the camels to transport what you'll get in exchange, and all of Kleon's goods as well?"

"The linen's an investment!" Ani corrected him at once. "My stake in the business. The whole of what we take to Alexandria will be Kleon's, and all I'm getting on it is commission. We'll use some of Kleon's profit to buy up the rest of what we need. But you don't need to worry about overloading the camels. We'll be able to carry spare water going home, and we'll be able to ride most of the time. Incense doesn't weigh much, compared to linen of equal value."

"Incense?"

Ani grinned broadly. "Three hundred pounds of top-quality myrrh from Opone," he said reverently, "and another five hundred pounds of myrrh of lower quality. From Mundus, four hundred pounds of cinnamon and two hundred of frankincense, plus another three hundred of assorted fragrant gums. Then there's tortoiseshell, also from Opone, and ivory from Adulis. It won't burden the camels, but do you *know* what it's likely to fetch in the market of Alexandria?"

He did not know. He did know, though, that incense was sold by the ounce, and weight for weight was worth more than silver. This was a valuable cargo even by the standards of his own dynasty. "You'll want guards for it," he said, startled.

"Kleon's sending a couple of sailors with us, to keep an eye on things and help out. But guards—well, it's the wrong time of year for bandits: they don't sit out in the desert in summer, not after the India trade has left the ports. And if you're worrying about the Romans or the remains of the queen's army—there's nothing we can do about them, with guards or without them. No, boy, I'm not going to worry about robbery." Grinning, he patted Caesarion's shoulder—an irritating familiarity. "What we need to worry about is tin. That's what Kleon delivers to Opone in exchange for the myrrh and the tortoiseshell. Aristodemos knows a merchant who imports it to Alexandria, but he's a friend of Aristodemos, and he may not deal with me. That's why I need someone who can write the sort of letters gentlemen write—I need to persuade some rich Alexandrian importer that I'm a real merchant."

Even though you're not, Caesarion thought, with a mixture

of scorn—for the deceit—and admiration—for the determination and daring.

He did not like the idea of providing a spurious authenticity to a peasant's prentensions. But he did want to reach Alexandria. *You were worried about somebody*, Ani had said. *Don't you even want to see how they are?* And he had thought at once of his little brother standing in the stableyard biting his fist.

So how *was* little Ptolemy Philadelphus—son of Marcus Antonius and of Cleopatra—"King of Macedonia," according to his parents? Executed? Imprisoned? Weeping for his mother—and perhaps for his older brother? What did Caesar Octavian, ruthless new lord of Egypt, have planned for the last son of the Lagid dynasty?

He had never been close to his older half-siblings, the twins Alexander Helios and Cleopatra Selene. When they were growing up he'd been healthy and active; he'd been busy with tutors or with companions of his own age, and he'd rarely even seen them. But the disease first struck him when Philadelphus was only two. For the first year or so he'd been very ill—more from the attempts to cure him than from the disease itself—and he'd frequently found himself playing quiet games with his youngest brother. Philadelphus had adored him—a glamourous *older brother* who would *play* with *him!*—and that adoration had helped him to survive the crushing humiliations of that dreadful year. After that he'd looked for Philadelphus, talked to him, listened to him whenever he could.

If he could reach Alexandria . . . his first duty, of course, was to his mother the queen. He would have to see if there was any way to rescue her from her captivity—but he suspected that, one way or another, she would be beyond any help he could provide. Philadelphus, though—he was young enough that nursemaids, not soldiers, might have been set to guard him. If he was still alive, if Caesarion could help him . . . he had to try.

"I can write letters," he told Ani.

"So you do agree?" asked the Egyptian, grinning widely. "Good, good! Can I get you anything from the city now, then? Papyrus? Pens?"

"You expect me to start *now?*" Caesarion asked in horror.

Ani waved his hand calmingly. "No, no! It's just that I need to have the customs documents ready when we arrive in Coptos, and by the look of things, we'll be setting off as soon as you're able to travel. I don't know how much opportunity I'll have for shopping, so I might as well start on it now. Papyrus, pens, ink, wax tables . . . anthing else?"

Caesarion regarded him a moment with dread. His flesh rebelled at the thought of facing the desert again. On the other hand, there was Archedamos—and the Romans. Yes, go as soon as you can, he thought. Wait for health, and you'll wait forever. "A hat," he said.

"A shawl round the head is better," Ani advised him. "A coarse one, that you can breathe through. Keeps out the dust."

"I want a hat," Caesarion declared obstinately. "A *petasos,* with a wide brim, to keep the sun off. And a short cloak, for traveling—the sort *Greeks* wear for traveling."

Ani thought about it. "Fair enough. You'll have to wait until you're on your feet again to try on hats, but I'll fetch you a cloak out of the warehouse."

*   *   *

THE CLOAK APPEARED later that day. It was a startling shade of orange, bordered with blue. Caesarion gazed at it with revulsion. All his life he'd worn purple, with occasional white and gold or crimson. Obviously he could not wear purple now, but still—*orange!* He remembered sitting enthroned before the multitude in Alexandria at a festival, the smoothness of purple silk against his skin, the ribbon of the royal diadem tight around his head—remembered the smell of incense and the acclamations of the crowd. The afternoon heat made the tent stifling, and he felt giddy. The wound had started to itch. *Orange!* Purple was for kings: what was *orange* for? Cameldrivers' secretaries and drooling epileptics?

"It's a good cloak," Ani told him proudly. "Made in my own workshop. Dyed with saffron and root madder, and the blue is real indigo. It won't fade. Kleon says that in Mundus they'd give you its weight in frankincense."

"It's too bright!" Caesarion complained. "It's vulgar. I want something darker. Blue, or . . . or green. Or black." That, he thought, would be the most appropriate: black for loss, for mourning.

Ani scowled and pulled his lip. "There isn't much. They like bright colors in the south, so that's what I brought along—what I've got."

"Then go buy . . ."

Ani's scowl deepened. "Boy, I'm not *buying* you a cloak, not when I've got perfectly good ones in the warehouse. Besides, you don't want anything dark, not to travel in, and you don't want white, either. The dust ruins either in half a day.

This," he shook the cloak out, "this travels well, and won't mark. This is a good cloak, boy! Even in Coptos you'd pay fifty drachmae for a cloak like this—and fifty drachmae is a good salary for a month's work!"

It took him a moment to make the connection. A *salary*. Zeus, Ani reckoned that fifty drachmae a month was what *his* labor was worth—he, Ptolemy Caesar, who'd been worshiped as a *god*! Speechless with indignation, he could only glare.

Ani, unimpressed, dropped the cloak on top of him. His stomach seemed to contract away from it, and there was a sudden whiff of carrion. The whole world began to seethe with an inexplicable horror.

"O Apollo!" he muttered, dreading what came next. He fumbled hurriedly for the remedy, got it to his face. Ani was staring at him. He seized the disputed cloak with his free hand and pulled it over his head to shut out the staring eyes. The stink of carrion drowned the scent of the spices. One breath, two . . .

There were fish in the pond. He stretched his hand into the water, trying to touch them, but his arm broke in a slanting line at the surface. The water smelled of decay.

A man in black was half dragged, half carried past by a party of guards. He was moaning, clutching the bloody stump of his right arm. "They caught him fiddling the accounts," Eumenes said disapprovingly.

The coins lay on Eumenes' eyes like beetles burrowing into the flesh.

Philadelphus had fallen over and bumped his nose. It was bleeding. The blood poured down over his purple cloak and white-and-gold tunic, and his little face was screwed up and

red with crying. Caesarion ran over and picked him up, and
the blood ran onto him as well.

Blood trickled steadily from the back of the man's head and
ran into the stone channels cut into the floor. "You see here
the ventricles of the brain," said a voice from nowhere, and
the man's hand twitched . . .

It was hot, and his side hurt. A man was holding his shoulder and staring into his face . . . a dark, heavy-jawed man . . .
Ani. He looked worried.

Caesarion turned his face away, pushed the intrusive hand
off, found the remedy again, and sat breathing deeply.

"Sweet Lady Isis!" said Ani.

There was a silence. Then the Egyptian asked, "What . . .
happened to you?"

"I had a seizure," Caesarion replied flatly. "A small one."
He could smell the remedy properly now, a sweet, warm,
piercing scent. He imagined the vapors going up into the ventricles of his brain . . .

No. Don't think about it.

"You didn't fall over. I thought . . ."

"Sometimes I fall over," he said coldly. "Sometimes I just
. . . have a seizure like that one."

There was another silence. Then Ani's hand came back onto
his shoulder and pressed it. Caesarion looked up angrily—and
was utterly taken aback by the compassion in the Egyptian's
eyes. "You looked as though you were having a vision of Hades," Ani said quietly.

Caesarion did not know how to reply. He stared at the
caravan-owner in confusion.

"Does that happen about once a month, as well?" The voice was still gentle.

"No," said Caesarion. He looked away, embarrassed, and wiped his face with the back of a hand. "More often. Every three or four days, when I was at home. But it's not . . . not like the big seizures. It's over in a few minutes, and then I can go on with what I was doing. It isn't . . ." He realized sickly that he was going to have to tell Ani more: he would undoubtedly have seizures during the journey, and Ani would be in charge of him. "When I have a big seizure," he said, nerving himself, "I fall down in convulsions. When I have a small one, I . . . They tell me that I mutter and stare . . ."

"You looked like you could see something terrible," said Ani. "I shook you and shouted at you, but you didn't hear me or see me."

"I don't hear or see anything around me—but I don't fall down, not even if I'm standing or walking when it happens, so it isn't dangerous. Usually I know when it's about to happen, though, and I try to sit down, in case the seizure is a big one. I can't tell from the warning how big it will be, you see, and the fall can be dangerous. So I sit. Apart from that, it probably looks worse than it is. I'm not aware of anything around me between the warning and waking up afterward."

"You were sobbing . . ." Ani was confused, concerned.

"Memories. I see things that happened before, usually things that frightened me, that I hated. But it's not . . . not danger-ous. Sometimes I'm a little confused afterward, but that passes quickly. If it happens when I'm in company, I try to get away, but it's not anything to worry about. You can ignore it. It's happened a couple of other times since we met, but you didn't notice because we weren't speaking together at the time.

"The big seizures . . . as I said, they don't usually happen more than once a month. I've had more recently, but that's because of the heat and the pain and . . . and the grief. Usually I manage to sit down before it starts, and I'm not hurt. If you're with me when I have one, don't do anything about it unless I'm going to knock something over or fall under something. The fit will pass by itself, and nothing that's done will help; it's more likely to hurt. After a big seizure I'm in a stupor for a couple of hours—an unusually deep stupor, the doctors say, deeper than those of most other people who have the disease. I don't feel anything, I don't know anything that's happening to me. If it's possible, I prefer to be left as I am to sleep it off. I hate it when I wake up and find that people have been doing things to me and I have no way of knowing what they've done. Obviously, if I fall down on the road you'll have to move me—but I hope that won't happen. With luck I shouldn't have another big seizure until we've parted."

Ani was still watching him with a sober, pitying expression that confused him, annoyed him, and made him ashamed. "I will pray to the gods that they spare you," he at last promised solemnly.

Caesarion looked away. "The gods have no more to do with this than with any other ailment."

Ani blew his cheeks out. "Well, but they call it the sacred disease, so it must be special to them. In Coptos some people say it's caused by demons."

"It's a disease of the brain."

"Really?" Ani sounded so intrigued that Caesarion looked

back at him in surprise. "Is that what your Greek doctors say? Why do they think that?"

"The brain is the seat of consciousness and of intelligence. In this disease . . ."

"In Coptos they say that the *heart* is the seat of consciousness."

"They're wrong. You can see that plainly. If a man is struck hard above the heart, he may fall over and have trouble breathing, but he won't lose consciousness. If he's struck on the head, he will. Men who've been wounded in the head may suffer loss of their speech or sight or memory, even after they've recovered, and even though their tongues or eyes are unharmed."

"This is true!" exclaimed Ani. "I never thought of it. Is that how your Greek doctors reason? What do they say the heart is, then?"

"A fire, or furnace, which heats the vital spirit and drives it with the blood about the body."

"I've seen blood vessels in the hearts of chickens and pigs. I hadn't thought about it, but you're right, all the blood goes from the heart to the body. So what do your doctors say happens in the sacred disease?"

Why, he wondered suspiciously, was Ani so interested?— then, looking at the Egyptian's intent expression, discovered that he knew the answer to that question. Ani was interested because he possessed a forceful and curious mind. If he'd been content with the ideas he was born to, he wouldn't have come to Berenike. He had seen Caesarion tormented, and he wanted to understand why.

It was disconcerting, to find that he knew that about Ani—

that, in some peculiar way, he admired it—that he wanted this insulting peasant to . . . what? Listen to him? Understand him? *Like* him? He found himself giving the full explanation, as it had been given to him. "Within the brain there are hollow passages for the vital spirit which the doctors call ventricles. In some people of a moist and phlegmatic humor, these can become clogged with phlegm. Then the brain is choked and obstructed, and the body convulses in at effort to clear it."

Ani thought about this. "Sort of like a sneeze?" he suggested.

"Yes," agreed Caesarion, obscurely comforted. The knifing attacks of memory, the horrors of waking ignorant and unclean after profound absence—no more than a sneeze.

Ani considered him critically. "So the doctors think you're of a moist and—what's the word again?—*phlegmatic* humor? Isn't that the one that's supposed to be cold, sluggish, and unemotional? That's not how I'd describe you."

Caesarion felt his cheeks heat. He had wondered about that himself. "Your bodily humor doesn't necessarily determine your mental temperament," he said loftily—though, from all he'd understood, it was supposed to do just that.

Ani considered that, too. "Your Greek doctors know all this. But they can't cure you."

"No," he admitted. "I suppose the fault runs too deep. Some of the remedies help, though."

"Those herbs?"

"I think they help. Breathing them is supposed to clear phlegm from the head."

"That makes sense. But—avoiding women?"

His cheeks went hot again. "Anything that adds moisture to the body, or anything that chills it, will aggravate the condition. The body is moistened by congress with women."

"You said the heat made it worse."

He shrugged. "It feels like that. I suppose it's simply that all extremes are bad, because they disturb the natural balance of the body."

Ani wasn't satisfied. "It still seems to me that if your doctors had it right, the disease ought to be unknown in the desert and common as fever in swamps. I don't think they've grasped the whole of it. Whatever the cause, I will pray to the gods that you have no trouble on the journey. In the meantime . . ." he got to his feet and picked up a crumpled heap of orange linen which had been lying neglected by the bedroll, "I'll see if I can find you a cloak more to your liking."

Caesarion found himself unexpectedly embarrassed. In some corner of his mind, he was aware that it *was* a good cloak— good quality cloth and expensive dyestuffs, at least—and that Ani had been generous in offering it. "You don't have to do that," he said impulsively. "I . . . It's just that that one is . . . different . . . from what I'm used to. I can . . . get used to it, I suppose. I suppose I *have* to get used to it."

There was a moment of silence. Ani looked at him uncertainly.

"It will be all right," said Caesarion. "If you say it will do well for the journey, I'll trust your judgement. I'm . . . sorry if I was ungracious."

He was ashamed as soon as he'd said it—but he was not certain whether the shame was because he was apologizing to a camel-driver, or because he had, indeed, been ungracious to a man who had been kind to him.

CHAPTER V

Melanthe was worried about her father.

He had left Coptos in the evening, twenty-nine days before. The Nile had been in flood then, a shallow brown lake across the whole countryside, and the town and the villages had been muddy islands. Now the river had gone down again, all the way back to its own channel, and he wasn't home.

Tiathres said that yesterday was the very earliest they could have expected him, and probably he wouldn't be home for another few days. Tiathres, however, was nearly as worried as Melanthe. Barbarians had set off on the road to the coast a few days after Papa's caravan passed that way—a whole troop of Romans, armed, armored, and grim, with a Greek to guide them and some camels for the luggage. Melanthe's first, panicked thought when she heard of it was that they'd find her father on the road and kill him. Then she'd reasoned with herself: there was no reason for them to kill him; he wasn't their enemy. They'd simply rob him. He'd be home early, without the linen and without the cargo of spices he'd gone to Berenike to buy—but he'd be home.

Only he hadn't come home early, and three days ago the Roman troop had marched back into the city. They had a lot of Greek prisoners, and their commander announced in the marketplace that they'd taken the camp of the young king Ptolemy Caesarion, and that the king was dead. They had an urn with his ashes in it, wrapped with the royal diadem, and they'd paraded it about the city on a litter draped with the king's purple cloak. Melanthe's little brother Serapion, who'd managed to get close enough to see, said that there was blood on the cloak.

Melanthe was sick at the thought that Papa might have been caught up in this desperate last stand. She wanted to go to the Romans and ask if they'd seen him, but Tiathres forebade it. "He'll be home," she told Melanthe, very firmly. "There's no reason for him to have been anywhere near the king, and if the Romans were chasing the king, they won't have been in-terested in caravans. We can't go questioning the Roman army—who knows what the barbarians might do to us? No: we will keep Ani's house safe for him to come home to."

She had, however, gone that evening to the temple of Isis, and given the goddess a basket of cakes and a necklace as an offering for her husband's safe return.

Now the Romans were gone again, in a flotilla of boats down the river, with their prisoners and their luggage and their purple-draped urn, and still Papa wasn't home. Melanthe got up that morning feeling as though the whole universe were pregnant with catastrophe, and she could find nothing for herself to do except to sit staring wretchedly out at the beaten earth of the courtyard.

"Melanthe," Tiathres said, after breakfast, "will you run down to the market for me and see what the news is?"

Melanthe jumped up and hugged her gratefully. Her stepmother was only ten years older than she was, and had never been like a mother—but she'd always been a wonderful big sister, and *kind*, to give up this errand to her stepdaughter when she must ache to run it herself. Melanthe ran to fetch her cloak, and called Thermuthion, the household's eleven-year-old slave girl, to accompany her. They set off into the quiet sunny morning, glad to escape the dreadful silence of the house.

It was hot, and the air was heavy with the smell of the retreating floods. The house lay about a mile from the town of Coptos, and though the two girls picked their way carefully through the maze of puddles, their clothes were still mud-spattered by the time they reached the marketplace, and their feet were filthy. Ordinarily Melanthe would have tried to wash the mud off before going on into the marketplace—there was always a chance of meeting one of the boys who admired her—but today it didn't even occur to her.

The marketplace was half deserted, but there was a knot of people outside the customs house, where the public notices were displayed and where the barbers and water-sellers gathered to collect gossip. Melanthe crossed the square to join them.

She saw, even before she reached the crowd, that there was a new notice up, a wide sheet of papyrus marked with bold black lettering. She also saw, however, that one of the men who'd clustered about to read it was Aristodemos, formerly her father's most important customer. She was certain that he must know by now that Papa had gone to Berenike in his place, and she stopped, deciding not to come any closer until he'd gone. He was the richest and most important man in the district, and she was sure that he wasn't pleased about what Papa had done.

It was no use. Aristodemos said something about the new notice, glanced round to see how his audience had taken it—and noticed Melanthe, hovering at the edge of the crowd.

"Ah," drawled Aristodemos. "You're Ani's daughter, aren't you?"

He was a tall, loose-limbed, sneering man who always looked as though he were half asleep, and he managed to look elegant even though his long blue-and-white cloak was as muddy about the hem and his feet as dirty as her own. Melanthe had never liked him. She ducked her head politely and held a corner of her cloak over her face—a piece of modesty that was appropriate in a girl of marriageable age, but also a convenient way to hide her expression. "Yes, Lord Aristodemos," she said humbly. She found herself wishing that Tiathres had run this errand after all: Aristodemos wouldn't have questioned Tiathres. She didn't speak Greek and he refused to speak Demotic. Everyone knew, however, that Ani regularly spoke Greek to all his children, and had paid to have them educated.

"Your father's not come back, has he?"

"No, sir," Melanthe admitted. It hurt to say it.

Aristodemos smiled. "He was on the road at the same time

as the Romans, wasn't he? *I* thought it was much too risky to travel during the war. Your father, of course, thought he knew better . . . How long has he been away now?"

Melanthe looked at the ground. She decided that she would have to answer. "Twenty-nine days, sir."

"Late." Aristodemos nodded in satisfaction.

One of the other men in the crowd stirred. "Berenike and back easily takes that long, if you have business and want to rest the camels," he objected.

It was what Melanthe had heard, but Aristodemos plainly wasn't happy with it. "He's late," he declared authoritatively. "It was not a safe time to travel, and he was a fool to go. Tell me, girl: was he intending to talk to Kleon, of the *Prosperity?*"

"He didn't discuss his business with me, sir," Melanthe said stolidly. That was a lie: Papa talked to her about anything and everything—including the need to make sure that Aristodemos couldn't interfere with his great venture.

"He took the linens, though."

"Yes, sir." She couldn't easily lie about that.

"A pity. I might have wanted them after all." Aristodemos turned back toward the new notice and regarded it thoughtfully. Melanthe edged close enough to pick out the heading— she could read, thanks to Papa's insistence on education. *The Senate and People of Rome* . . . she read: and, further down, the words *clemency* and *province* and *governor*. It's announcing a new administration, she realized, with a thrill of horror. The war's over, and everything's going to be orderly and peaceful, so Aristodemos thinks it's safe to trade after all. He's going to be furious if Papa succeeded in Berenike!

The man who'd spoken up before, sniggered. He was a local

shopkeeper, not—like many of the others present—a dependent of Aristodemos. "You think your ship's captain is still waiting patiently for you to come back?" he asked.

Aristodemos turned the half-asleep sneer on him, and the shopkeeper sobered. "Everyone's waited for the end of the war," he said. "—Everyone except the son of Petesuchos. Yes, I think my partner will be pleased to see me again. Ani could have sold me his goods, instead of losing them, as I fear he must have done, to barbarians or fugitives. But he was always greedy."

"No!" Melanthe protested, too indignant to be cautious. "He isn't greedy at all. He's good and generous and kind. He's brave, too, and he went to Berenike when you were too afraid even to keep the bargain you'd made with your partner."

Aristodemos' lazy expression disappeared, and in its place was something far darker and more savage than the indignation she'd anticipated. He *hates* my father, Melanthe realized in alarm. It's not just that he thinks Papa's an upstart: he *hates* him.

"You insolent little bitch!" snarled Aristodemos. "Your father is a stinking peasant without even the intelligence to understand where his own place is. He tried to set himself up as a gentleman—to run a caravan—and if he's lying dead on the road to Berenike, it's his own fault. *I* had more sense than to try the trade routes with a war on. It's his own pride— and his insatiable greed!—which have left him to rot in the sun on a road even the vultures avoid!"

Little Thermuthion began to cry. Aristodemos' eyes brightened with triumph. "You may well cry," he told her. "What's your house going to do now, without its master?"

"You're saying he's dead because you hope he is!" Melanthe objected, though her legs had started to tremble at the thought that Aristodemos might be right. "He's not really even *late* yet!"

Aristodemos raised his hand warningly. "He got the fate he deserved!"

One of his dependents applauded. Another grinned. Melanthe, not knowing what else to do, turned on her heel and walked proudly away. Thermuthion followed her, still crying over the thought of kind Master Ani lying dead. That thought was pressing on Melanthe's mind, too, making her shake, but she made herself keep walking. She would not, she decided, give Aristodemos the satisfaction of seeing her afraid. She would not, she would not, she would . . .

There were camels in the road on the other side of the square.

She stopped dead. Thermuthion bumped into her and stopped as well, rubbing her face, her mouth round with surprise. The lead camel swung out of the shadowy road into the sunlit marketplace, and it was Menches riding it, with a long string of camels after him, all carrying packs . . .

"Papa!" shrieked Melanthe, and went racing across the square toward them.

A donkey came galloping up alongside the camel train before she reached it, with a dear, wonderful, infinitely familiar figure bouncing on its back. Papa leapt off and ran over to hug her. He was dirty and smelly and unshaven, but he was *alive*, solid, whole. "Well, Melanthion!" he said, and held her out at arm's length to look at her. "My pretty sunbird, I didn't think I'd see you till I got home!" "Sunbird" had been his pet name for her ever since she was tiny, because, he said, sunbirds were quick, pretty, colorful, and loved sweet things.

She laughed and held on to him tightly. He was *home*, safe, alive! "I came in to see if there was news." Then she remembered, and said urgently, "Aristodemos is *here*, Papa—just there, by the customs house, and there's a proclamation from the Romans and he wants to trade, after all. He's going to be very angry if you got the cargo!"

"Then he's going to have to be very angry," Papa told her complacently. He caught the donkey's reins and her hand, and began strolling on toward the customs house. "I need to pay the duties on my caravan." He nodded to Thermuthion and switched to Demotic. "Little one, can you run home and tell your mistress that I'll be back shortly, with guests, and we all want a bath?"

Thermuthion, who'd gone from tears to beaming smiles, nodded happily and skipped off toward the house.

"Guests?" asked Melanthe, glancing up at the line of camels. Menches on the lead; Imouthes leading the second string; and there did seem to be another figure in an orange cloak riding further back, with a couple more at the end.

"Two sailors sent by my new partner," said Papa, switching back to Greek, "and . . . a kind of secretary, though don't, by the immortal gods, call him that to his face or he'll be offended."

"Your *partner*?" repeated Melanthe, apprehension quivering through her new happiness. Tiathres, she knew, had been hoping that Papa would fail to get the partnership he craved. She'd wanted him to obtain the cargo, make a profit on the trip, and finish the venture. A partnership, she thought, would make him enemies among the Greeks of Coptos—particularly Aristodemos.

"My partner, Kleon," Papa announced, with immense satisfaction. "My girl, I got everything I wanted, and we're going to be rich . . . Good health!"

This last was to Aristodemos. They had almost reached the customs house, and the landowner had moved forward to stand directly in their path. He was scowling, his fists clenched at the side of his blue-and-white robe. One of his slaves and a couple of his dependents stood behind him, blocking the way completely. The crowd was still there; in fact, it had grown, and Parmenion, the customs officer, had come out onto the steps of the building and was surveying the scene apprehensively.

"What's this?" demanded Aristodemos, his eyes on the camel train behind them.

"A caravan, Lord Aristodemos," said Papa, in a matter-of-fact voice. "If you will excuse me, sir, the law requires me to pay duty on the goods." He gestured toward the customs house steps. Aristodemos didn't move.

One of the ridden camels came trotting around the rest of the animals, which had piled into a milling mass behind Papa, kicking at one another and grunting. It stopped, jerking its head irritably. The rider was a youth not much older than Melanthe, still beardless. He was dressed in the Greek fashion, in a wide-brimmed hat and a short orange cloak, and he sat very straight, one knee hooked over the front of the camel saddle. He had a proud, disdainful face, with a strong, hooked nose and fierce dark eyes like a hawk. "The documents are in the left-hand saddlebag," he told Papa. He had the most beautiful, most educated voice Melanthe had ever heard. He sat motionless on the camel while Papa went over and opened the saddlebag, making no move either to dismount or to get the documents himself.

Papa took a sheaf of papyrus out of the saddlebag, glanced at it, then handed it up to the young Greek. The Greek sorted through the papers and handed one back. "That's the schedule of goods," he informed Papa. "And this," another paper, "is the power of attorney for you to act on Kleon's behalf. The officer will want to see both. He should keep the schedule, and return the other to you."

Papa nodded.

"Power of attorney," repeated Aristodemos, in a grinding tone.

"I am presently acting as agent for Kleon, son of Kallias," agreed Papa calmly. "I am taking his cargo to Alexandria and selling it, on commission. Two of his men are here, and can vouch for it." He jerked his head at the two strangers who'd brought up the rear of the caravan, who were now both busy trying to prevent the camels from biting one another.

Aristodemos' face had gone pinched and pale. "And the partnership?"

"Kleon and I," said Papa, still frighteningly calm and matter-of-fact, "have agreed to a partnership for his next voyage."

"You had no right!"

Papa shrugged and spread his hands apologetically. "Lord Aristodemos, Kleon has a right to make a contract with anyone he pleases."

"Is *this* Aristodemos?" asked the young Greek, from his height on the camel. "I thought you said he was a gentleman."

For a moment there was no sound in the square but the oblivious grunting of the camels. Everyone in the small crowd stared, stunned, at the young man who'd just questioned whether the richest man in the district was a gentleman.

"Umm," said Papa, now—finally—worried. "This is Arion, of Alexandria. He was a Friend of King Ptolemy Caesar. He was wounded when the Romans attacked the king's camp near the waystation of Kabalsi, and I, uh, helped him. He's agreed to, umm, assist me, until we reach Alexandria."

There was a perceptible relaxation, from shock into uncertainty. An Alexandrian, a Friend of the king, might indeed find fault even in Aristodemos. Coptos was a rich market-town, hub of the caravan routes, but it was far from the manners, the grace, the *Hellenism* of the capital. Even Aristodemos' blank outrage eased. "A *gentleman* has agreed to assist *you?*" he demanded indignantly.

Arion's lip curled slightly. "Ani saved my life," he stated. "I am indebted to him. Sir, I am sorry if I offended you just now, but I assumed that a gentleman would use a horse when the roads are muddy." He looked disdainfully at Aristodemos' muddy cloak and dirty feet—and the most important man in the district flushed brick-red.

"If you're questioning the validity of Ani's contract," Arion continued loftily, "I suggest you go to a magistrate. In the meantime, there are customs fees which must be paid for these goods before they can be warehoused, and you are standing in the way. Do you mean to prevent the government from receiving its due?"

Aristodemos was still red. "Th-this is . . . !" he stuttered, couldn't find the word for it, gathered himself up and tried again. "Young man, this greedy Egyptian is trying to cheat me out of a valuable partnership!"

"Cheat?" repeated Arion in surprise. "How? You broke off your partnership with the son of Kallias. He's still very indignant about it—and you cannot reasonably have expected him to be otherwise. Kleon would never have dealt with you again even if Ani had never left Coptos, or so he himself asserts. He found another partner, and you're free to do the same. There are plenty of ships. Sir, I must ask again: are you trying to prevent us from paying the tariff on these goods?"

Aristodemos bit his lip, trapped. The new administration of the province would undoubtedly collect its dues as zealously as had the old administration of the kingdom: it was never a good idea to come between a government and its tax. Slowly, he stood aside, and motioned his cronies to do the same. Papa, looking both anxious and amused, edged past him and onto the customs-house steps. Parmenion, with a worried glance at Aristodemos, took the two papers, and they went inside.

"I will not allow this," Aristodemos said in a low voice. "I will not submit to being robbed by an *Egyptian*." He looked up at the young man on the camel. "You fought against the Romans, did you?"

Arion nodded. "But I am not a fugitive. A centurion by the name of Gaius Paterculus spoke to me in Berenike, and was satisfied that I was of no interest to the Roman state."

Aristodemos' jaw clenched with anger. "I will not endure this!" he exclaimed. He tugged his cloak straight and marched off. His followers hurried after him, casting nervous glances over their shoulders.

Arion watched them go. His look of disdain faded, and he pulled a small bag of something out from underneath his tunic and pressed it against his face. Melanthe wondered if he was ill—then remembered that Papa had said he'd been wounded. She wondered if she ought to offer to fetch him some water from the fountain—but she didn't have a cup.

He noticed her staring at him. His cheeks flushed angrily— he had, she realized, very fair skin, that showed the color readily—and he looked pointedly away. Melanthe looked down, ashamed because she'd offended him and she hadn't even spoken to him yet.

Magnificent, she thought, almost at random. That was the word she wanted. The way you dismissed Aristodemos was magnificent! she wanted to say.

He himself looked magnificent, too, sitting up there on the camel in that fire-colored cloak, gazing proudly into the distance. She itched to speak to him, and didn't dare.

Papa came back out of the customs office and down the steps. He went over to Arion's camel and put the legal document back in the bag with the other papers. Then he paused, looking up at the young Greek. "It's about another mile," he said in a low voice. "Are you going to last?"

Arion nodded without looking at him.

"You can lie down then," Papa told him. "On a bed, out of the sun, with a cold drink."

Arion nodded again. Papa gave him a hard look, slapped the camel, then turned back to catch the donkey. He smiled at Melanthe.

"You want to ride, Sunbird?"

"I'll walk with you, Papa," she said, and he grinned. They started across the square together, leading the donkey, and the caravan rearranged itself behind them.

Melanthe looked back: Arion was falling into place in the middle of the camel train. "Is he very ill, Papa?" she asked anxiously.

Papa blew out his cheeks. "Arion? He has a wound in the side. It was infected, but it's mostly healed now. That road to the coast is a bitter hard one, though, and it's been hot as a furnace. The boy swore at Berenike that he was fit to travel, but he plainly wasn't. He has the sacred disease, and heat, hunger, thirst, and pain make it worse: he's been having two or three fits every day—mostly in the mornings, when he's tired. Sweet Lady Isis, it's good to be back at the river!"

"*He* has the sacred disease?" Melanthe exclaimed, with another backward glance.

Papa grinned. "Wouldn't think it to look at him, would you? That boy makes Aristodemos look humble." He laughed. "O gods! 'I assumed that a gentleman would use a horse when the roads are muddy'—and *Aristodemos* stood there blushing and trying to hide his feet!" He laughed again.

Melanthe did not laugh. "Papa, Aristodemos went off saying that he wouldn't endure this."

"Nothing he can do," Papa replied cheerfully. "It's legal. Oh, he may think of sending some of his tenants to smash up the boat or the cargo, but he won't do it if he's got any sense. I'm on good terms with my neighbors, and he's not. His tenants would come back bloody-nosed."

"But what if he goes to the magistrates? They're Greek, they'll favor him . . ."

"Kleon's Greek, too," Papa pointed out. "The cargo's *Kleon*'s property, Sunbird, not mine—and I've got Arion to speak for me. Doesn't he have a beautiful voice?"

"Yes," agreed Melanthe fervently. "But Papa . . ."

"That boy was a find, for all the trouble he's been."

"Did you really save his life?"

"By the immortal gods, I did, too! Found him lying unconscious in the road, and picked him up. Had no idea what he was, until he started talking. He's very cagey—still hasn't even told me his father's name—but it's clear he's a gentleman the moment he opens his mouth. Aristodemos knew at once, didn't he? He's agreed to write letters and advise me until we get to Alexandria." He looked at her, suddenly very serious. "My sweet bird, you're to keep your distance from him. I think he's a good-enough boy at heart, but he's proud—he thinks I'm a dirty camel-driver—and you're pretty, and he wouldn't respect you. I don't think he'd mean to hurt you, but he could. So you just make sure you don't let him."

She rolled her eyes. Papa had been telling her to keep her distance from boys since she was thirteen and first got interested in them. It was annoying, because the boys didn't want to keep their distance from *her*, and some of them were very sweet. Still, it was good advice, well meant, and she ought to listen to it. She wanted to marry a boy who was kind and clever and good-looking—someone with a little education, someone she could *talk* to—and for that she had to be a respectable virgin.

Then her heart sped up: it sounded as though Papa was expecting her to see quite a lot of this Arion, and that implied . . . "Papa, does that mean I can come to Alexandria?"

she asked breathlessly. They'd discussed it before he left for Berenike: whether the whole family could boat down the Nile to the capital with the cargo. They had the boat—a heavy barge normally used to move flax and farm equipment—and there was space on it; the only question had been whether the journey would be safe for women and children.

"The war's over, and the Romans seem inclined to keep everything peaceful," Papa said reasonably. "I don't see why you shouldn't come along."

Alexandria! The most glorious city in the entire world! She gave a little scream of joy. Papa laughed and tousled her hair.

They'd reached the road out of town. Papa walked directly into the first puddle he came to and stamped, splashing mud and water up to his knees. He drew a deep breath of the scent of sunlit mud, and tossed back his head. "Isis and Serapis, it's good to be back in a living world!" he exclaimed joyfully. "That desert's a terrible place." His eyes meeting hers were bright and happy and wise—her father, back from the desert, with a cargo of spices and a contract and a Friend of the king to speak for him. Had she really woken this morning, afraid she'd never see him again?

"I'm so, so glad that you're home," she told him, from the bottom of her heart.

The house, when they reached it, was buzzing like a wasp's nest. Thermuthion had arrived with her message, and household slaves and farmworkers were clearing out the storerooms, fetching water from the well, and sweeping everything in sight. Papa led the donkey past the drying sheds and up to the front door, and Tiathres burst out and threw herself into his arms, followed rapidly by Serapion, who was six and embraced his father's hips, and Isisdoros, who was two and hugged his knees. Everyone was talking and laughing at once, and Melanthe almost lost track of the caravan. When she next looked, half the camels had been unloaded, and their packs were being carried into the storeroom. Two strangers—Kleon's sailors, she realized—had come up and were waiting to be welcomed to the house. Papa introduced them as Apollonios—a wiry, middle-aged Greek—and Ezana, a tall and ferocious-looking black man from the port of Adulis, at the other end of the Red Sea. Melanthe looked around for Arion, and saw him sitting tall and aloof on his camel, the little bag still pressed against his face. She glanced at Papa: he was busy with Kleon's men. She walked over to Arion, thinking that he ought to come in with the others.

"Sir," she called up to him, "do you want to . . ."

She stopped. Arion's eyes were wide, and he stared fixedly at nothing with an expression of desperate horror. He was grinding his teeth behind the bag of herbs, and his face was pale and drenched with sweat.

"Sir?" she repeated.

He did not seem to hear her. She touched his knee, but he did not look down. She could feel that he was trembling. He gave a choked sob that sounded like "No!" then muttered incomprehensibly.

"Sir!" she said, really frightened now. "What's the matter?" Hurriedly, she tapped the camel on the shoulder, the way the drivers did: it knelt down with a groan. Arion swayed in the saddle, almost falling off, then sat rocking back and forth, still gazing at nothing, grinding his teeth and muttering. She stared at him helplessly, wondering if she should throw water over him, or pull him into the shade.

Arion moaned. His eyes rolled upwards in his head—and then shut. He shuddered and bent over, pressing the bag against his face. The muttering had stopped.

"Sir!" she said helplessly. "Sir, are you . . ."

He looked up, gazed at her a moment with a dazed expression. He looked around at the half-unloaded camel train, the slaves, the house. He looked down at the camel he sat on, then eased one leg over the front of the saddle and swiveled his foot.

"Are you all right?" Melanthe asked nervously.

"Who are you?" he asked, mystified.

"Melanthe, sir. Ani's daughter. Are you all right, sir?"

"I had a small seizure," he said flatly. "I'm subject to them. I'm fine." He stood up, swayed, and sat down again.

"I'll get someone to help you," she said hurriedly.

"I'm fine!" he repeatedly, angrily this time, and got to his feet again. He stood very stiff for a moment, then stalked off toward the house. Melanthe started after him, then remembered the sheaf of papyri in the saddlebags—important documents—and went back to rescue them.

When she got to the house, Arion had already disappeared. Papa and the sailors were still talking in the courtyard. She gave Papa the saddlebag with the papers.

"Thank you," he said—then, looking at her more closely: "What's the matter?"

"Arion had a seizure," she told him—and found that her eyes were stinging with tears.

The Greek sailor, Apollonios, groaned.

Ezana, the Auxumite, shrugged. "At least we do not have to carry him to the house."

Papa was looking at her intently.

"I thought people fell down when they had seizures," she told him.

"He does that, too," said Apollonios. "Twice since we left Berenike. But he has staring fits every day."

"The gods have cursed him," said Ezana. He had a strange, heavy accent, weighting the beginnings of his words.

Apollonios made a noise of agreement. "I think the gods are punishing him. He says that during the staring fits he sees memories—and it is clear they're hateful memories."

"We all have things we'd prefer not to remember," said Papa slowly—and from the grim look on his face she thought he was remembering her mother's final illness. "He says his family's dead. A man can have terrible memories without having done anything terrible himself."

"I don't like it," declared Apollonios, giving Papa a hard look.

"I don't think Arion likes it, either," replied Papa mildly.

" 'He's still alive!'—that gives me nightmares. Who's still alive, and why is it so horrible that he should be? He won't answer any questions—have you noticed that?—about that or about anything else. I think he's committed some unholy crime, and that the gods are punishing him."

"I think he has a disease of the brain," replied Papa sharply, "which he endures with considerable courage—and there's nothing odd about not wanting to talk about something the world regards as shameful. —What's the matter, Sunbird?"

Melanthe felt the hot tears overflow her eyes and run onto her cheeks. In the marketplace, facing Aristodemos, Arion had been like a god. To see him staring and muttering to himself had been inexpressibly horrible. All that magnificence, twisted, broken, lost!

"You pitied him?" said Papa gently.

She nodded. She did pity Arion—and, in the pity, lost something, she did not know what, that she mourned bitterly.

Papa put an arm around her and kissed her head. "My gentle girl. I do, too; Isis grant that no child of mine ever suffers the like! But we're back at the river, and things should be easier now."

CHAPTER VI

Caesarion woke the following morning, and lay quietly in bed for a long time, listening to the sounds of the house. Two women were talking nearby, chattering to each other in Demotic, occasionally laughing. Outside someone was watering the garden, a regular tramp-tramp-*splash!* as buckets of water were tipped over the herbs which sat in their terra-cotta pots in the courtyard.

It was a bigger house than he'd expected—a low rambling collection of buildings surrounded by date palms, outside the city, with stables for animals and storerooms and workrooms for the linen business, pools for soaking flax and sheds for drying it. There were slaves, maybe a dozen of them, and there were linenworkers and farmworkers who appeared to be dependent upon Ani in some way or other—they could not be actual tenants, because this was Crown land and linen was a royal monopoly, but still they clearly regarded Ani as in some fashion their superior. It was something of a relief to see that Ani was not, after all, just a camel-driver. He might not be precisely *rich* as an Alexandrian would understand the word, but he was clearly a man of substance in Coptos. Well liked, too: that had been very plain from his welcome.

Odd people. He thought of Ani being embraced by his daughter, Ani being embraced by his wife and sons, Ani shaking hands and back-slapping with everyone in the neighborhood. They touched one another a lot, these Egyptians. It was . . . well, vulgar and contemptible, of course, but very affectionate and warm. It made him feel . . . left out—which was stupid, because he had no desire whatever to be embraced by these people. It would be better if he could get away from them.

He might do that. They were back at the river. His side was healing; Ani had said he would fetch a doctor to take the stitches out today. He could, conceivably, say good-bye to Ani *now*, sell the pin, make his own way to Alexandria . . . only . . . he owed Ani too much. In Berenike thirty drachmae would have settled the debt; he doubted that a hundred would cover it now. There was the cloak and the hat; there was the food and water and the camel; there was that long, abominable journey, where the fits had struck every day, and twice he had woken up in the heat and dust, hurting all over, with Ani sponging his face, while Menches and Imouthes, or Apollonios and Ezana, muttered that he was unclean, bad luck, ought to be left to die by the roadside . . .

He owed Ani too much. It frightened him, how much he owed Ani. He was entangled in the man's affairs, and the royal shape of his own purpose was becoming blurred, like a spear-point dropped in a garden and overgrown with beans.

There was a sound from the doorway, and Caesarion looked over and found a small brown boy gazing at him with large dark eyes. He was dressed in a good white tunic, and wore a protective amulet on a thong around his neck. Not a slave. No, of course not, this was one of Ani's sons—Serapion, that was the name. A name which, though it honored an Egyptian god, was Greek in form. All of Ani's children had Greek names, to prepare them, no doubt, for the status of gentry which their father was eager to bestow on them. He'd noticed that their father made a point of speaking to them in Greek, though their mother was confined to Demotic.

"You're awake!" said the child, in Greek, with a mixture of pleasure and anxiety. "Papa said if you were awake to tell you that we're going down to the boat this afternoon, and if there's anything you need from Coptos you should say now."

Caesarion sighed and sat up. The wound pulled a little with the movement, but not too painfully. They'd arrived yesterday; today they would load up the boat, and tomorrow morning they would set off for Alexandria. Ani was energetic and industrious; Ani was also, he suspected, more worried about this fellow Aristodemos than he wished to admit, and eager to get away before his rival found some way of stopping him. He supposed he'd rested long enough—but he was weary still, very weary. The boat, though, would be far better than a camel, and the Nile . . . wide, brown, rich-smelling river, source of life for all Egypt . . . the Nile was infinitely better than the desert.

"Where are my clothes?" he asked the child. His own things

had disappeared yesterday, and he'd eaten supper in a borrowed tunic of bleached linen.

Serapion looked around vaguely, then went out to the corridor and said something. The women's voices clucked impatiently, but stopped chattering. He came back. "They'll fetch them," he announced proudly. "—I'm going to Alexandria, too."

Caesarion straightened the sheet. "Are you?"

Serapion nodded. "And Mama, and 'Dorion, and Melanthe. And Senhuris—she's our nurse. Papa said we could. What's Alexandria like?"

He thought of Alexandria, the city where he had been born, which his ancestors had created. Beautiful, spacious, wealthy; teeming, squalid, and chaotic. A passionate city, much given to rioting and disorder, where the mob had raised up and brought down kings; an intellectual city, where the best minds assembled in the Museum and famous Library; a mercantile city, the world's greatest port. At Alexandria were desperate poverty and immense wealth, wild ignorance and unparalleled learning. Altogether it was the richest, most dazzling, and most violent of all cities in the world.

"A bright torch set on top of a termite nest," he told Serapion sourly. So, King Ptolemy Caesar would arrive back in his capital on a peasant barge loaded with women and squalling brats? "Why is your father taking all of you to Alexandria?"

"Because we want to go," replied the boy instantly. "Papa says there's a tower there, as tall as three temples stacked on top of each other, and at night they light a big fire at the top, so you can see it for miles and miles. Is that why it's like a torch? Why's it like a termite nest?"

"Because it's crowded. I thought your father had never been to Alexandria."

"He *heard* about it," said Serapion, disappointed. "Isn't there a tower?"

"Oh, there is. The Pharos, it's called—one of the wonders of the world. It lights the entrance to the harbor."

The child grinned, his eyes shining. I have a little brother about your age, Caesarion suddenly thought of saying, and he always loved the Pharos. Once we went up there, him and me, and had the men show us the machinery they use to raise the fuel for it, and the mirrors that reflect the light. We used to watch it together every evening after that, and see the light brighten and extend out into the night.

He did not say it. But he found he could not simply send the child away. "There's a big park which you'd probably like, too," he volunteered. "It's called the Paneion, because it's sacred to Pan—that's the Greek name of the god you Egyptians call Min, the god of wild places. It's built up as a kind of artificial hill, and there's a path with steps which winds about it to the top. From the summit you can see the whole city— the lake and the sea, and the Pharos, and the ships coming and going. And there's a menagerie, in the palace quarter near the Museum, where there are many strange and wonderful animals. There's a snake there as thick around the middle as a man's waist."

The boy's eyes widened. "Does it bite?"

"No. It's from somewhere far in the south, where the snakes grow very big but aren't poisonous. That one's tame, in fact. She'll rest her head on her keeper's shoulder and lick his ear."

"I want to see it!" exclaimed the child delightedly.

"You'll have to see if the palace quarter's open," Caesarion told him, belatedly remembering that it might not be. "There's a wall between it and the rest of the city, and the Romans may have closed the gates. But even if that's shut, there are things to see in the temples. In the temple of Serapis there are some wonderful mechanical devices. There's a machine which pours libations when you burn incense. It has little figures of a man and a woman, worked in gold, and when you burn incense on the altar, the figures pour libations of wine." He remembered admiring the magical device himself, and Rhodon explaining to him how the heat of the fire caused the air inside the altar to expand, and forced wine hidden in the pedestal up into tubes which led to the figurine's hands. Even when he knew how it worked, it still seemed magical.

Serapion laughed. "I want to see it!"

His sister, Ani's daughter, swept into the room, followed by a slave-girl who carried Caesarion's clothes. "See what?" she asked, smiling.

Caesarion scowled and hurriedly pulled the sheet higher. He knew that he had disgraced himself in front of Ani's daughter the morning they arrived, and he had noticed her watching him since with an anxious, pitying expression, as though she expected him to fall down foaming at the mouth at any moment. What made it worse was that Melanthe was disconcertingly pretty—dark as her father, with a mass of thick, wavy, very black hair, and a wide, white, delicious smile. She was eminently kissable. To be the object of her pity was intolerably galling.

"A magic machine in the temple!" Serapion told his sister eagerly. "Arion was telling me. And he says there's a mana

. . . a mener . . . a place with lots of animals, which has a big snake!"

"You may not be able to see that," Caesarion put in hurriedly. "It's in the palace quarter. They close the gates when the city's troubled. I should think the Romans are in the palace now, with the gates to the city shut tight."

He found himself imagining the Romans in the palace: the heavy studded sandals of the legionaries scarring the marble pavements; Caesar Octavian ordering his men to carry off the gold dolphins from the bathhouse to ornament his own palaces in Rome. Was anyone using his own rooms? Was Marcus Agrippa, the emperor's right hand, sleeping on the cedarwood couch, under the richly worked cotton bedspread? Or had Octavian had the rooms pillaged, stripped down, and their contents carted off to his ships?

Alexandria fallen; Alexandria in Roman hands.

"The machines may not be there, either," he added harshly. "The Romans may have taken them. They can't make such things themselves, and they like them."

"*I* want to see the sea," declared Melanthe, her eyes bright. "The Romans won't have taken that away! Papa said that in the Red Sea there were flowers that ate fish."

He was taken aback. "What, anemones?"

"Is that what they're called? Do they have them in the Middle Sea as well?"

"I think they live in most seas," said Caesarion. This was Ani's daughter, indeed! "They're not flowers. The philosophers say that they're a kind of animal, like a snail."

"Papa said they looked like flowers."

"There are insects that look like leaves, or twigs."

"That's true! And they have these . . . anemones? . . . in the sea at Alexandria?"

"They live all over the harbor walls," said Caesarion, smiling again in spite of himself. "I used to throw them snails. They'd suck in the snail and spit out the shell later on."

"I want to see them," she announced decisively. She gestured for the slave to set down the clothes on the bed. "Serapion, let Arion get dressed. Sir, the girl will fetch water if you want to bathe." She escorted her brother out.

He had the girl fetch some water, and he washed and dressed himself. His tunic had been cleaned and mended again. The coarse stitching from Hydreuma had been taken out, and the careful replacement showed only a very slight mismatch in the color. It was, in fact, hard to tell that the tunic had been damaged at all—but then, the linen manufactory presumably had thread in all colors. The girl had brought a bronze mirror along with the water, and she offered to trim his hair for him.

He sat holding the mirror while she snipped. It had been awhile since he looked in a mirror. His face was thinner than he remembered it, and stamped around the eyes and at the corners of the mouth with the traces of fresh pain. His hair which the girl trimmed back had grown in black tangles over his ears. But there was also—strange sight!—a shadow on his upper lip. He touched it with a hesitant finger: the hair was still thin and downy. The beard to go with it was confined to a faint bloom on his cheeks.

Should he shave? It would be something of a landmark, to be able to say that he'd lived long enough to shave.

No. In the present circumstances a moustache, even a thin

shadowy one, was a gift from the gods. Here in the south there were only a few who had seen him: in Alexandria there were thousands. Obviously, anyone from the court would recognize him, but there were also public slaves—like the ones at the Pharos—city officials, and people who'd once stood in the front rows of a crowd to watch a parade. A moustache wouldn't deceive the court, but it might deflect recognition by a more casual acquaintance—particularly when coupled with a wide-brimmed hat, an orange cloak, and a boatload of noisy Egyptians. It ought to give him time to determine the city's state of mind, to work out who of the queen's friends might still be willing to help him, to find out what had happened to little Philadelphus . . .

And to the queen, of course, if no deadly news of her reached him first.

Haircut finished, he put on the orange cloak and went out into the courtyard. Ani was seated at the far end, under a fig tree, holding his youngest son and listening to a skinny old woman who appeared to be reporting to him on the state of the linenworkings. The toddler was eating a fig, and there were sticky red handprints on his father's tunic.

"Good health!" said Ani cheerfully. "Feeling better this morning?"

"Yes, thank you," he replied awkwardly.

"Good, good! Thought of anything we need to buy before we set out?"

"I was wondering about weapons," he said hesitantly. "There may be fugitives or bandits."

"No," Ani replied at once, very firmly. "Anybody who comes at us with weapons is likely to have more of them than we do. If we were armed, they'd kill us. Anyway, there aren't any fugitives or bandits, none that I've heard of . . . apart, I suppose, from the odd soldier on his way home." He grinned sympathetically at Caesarion. "I wouldn't be planning to take the children if I'd heard there was likely to be any danger. Everything I've heard says that the policy of clemency is real. Still think the emperor is a crocodile?"

"A crocodile with a full stomach," Caesarion replied sourly, and sighed. Octavian needed money to pay his army and the debts he had incurred in the war: reprisals would only destroy sources of revenue and would gain him nothing, since he already had everything he'd fought for. He knew, however, that the imperial clemency would not extend to himself. He could see the sense of Ani's refusal to carry weapons. He would, nonetheless, have felt happier if he knew he could lay hands on a spear if he needed one—not because he thought it would keep him safe, but because it would give him another chance at a noble death. On the other hand, Ani, very reasonably, did not want a noble death, and, in fact, had probably never been taught even how to hold a spear.

"Then, no," Caesarion said regretfully. "I can't think of anything we need to buy."

The boat was drawn up at a private landing, next to a field belonging to Ani. It was not a convenient arrangement in this season: the field still lay under several inches of water, so that anyone going on board had to wade through the fresh mud. Caesarion suspected that dread of Aristodemos lay behind the decision not to load the cargo at the public quays in Coptos, and was exasperated: the man hadn't looked such a dire threat to him.

The boat itself was a sailing barge, battered and dirty, but solidly built, with a capacious cargo hold and a thatched cabin amidships; there were a dozen oars, but it was planned to manage the craft with only eight, manned by four of Ani's slaves, two of his dependents, and Kleon's two sailors. When Caesarion arrived, Ani's wife was already on board, arranging the accommodations.

Caesarion stopped in the flooded field, up to his ankles in mud, and regarded the vessel in dismay. It was clear at a glance that there was not enough space for him to have a room to himself. He thought of his own sailing barge, the *Ptolemais*, on which he had sailed to Coptos, only two months before at the rising of the flood. Forty oars, and space for sixty men; the sails were purple, and the prow was worked with gold. He'd had a spacious chamber in the stern, with a separate dining room lit by golden lamps . . .

He'd sent *Ptolemais* on up the river after disembarking; it had orders to sail up to Thebes, and then return to Alexandria, to mislead any spying eyes. His own boat was long gone, it was the ebb of the flood, and he was coming home in this . . . craft.

"Arion, good health!" called Tiathres, smiling at him with shy goodwill. She turned to her stepdaughter, and went on in Demotic: "Melanthe, can you tell him the sleeping arrangements?" He had already noticed that her Greek was rudimentary.

"I speak Demotic," he said abruptly, and waded unhappily forward, sandals in one hand, cloak edge fastidiously high in the other.

"Oh!" exclaimed Tiathres, taken aback by his declaration.

He had not admitted his knowledge before, and he realized that he should not have done so now. It removed another of the barriers between himself and these people. It was too late, though, to take back what he'd said. Tiathres cheerfully began to rattle away at him in Demotic, telling him that he could sleep in the stern cabin, with Ani and Kleon's men, that she and the children and the nurse had the forecabin, that the others would sleep on deck—quite comfortable, really, in this weather.

It was dismal, squalid. It would have to do. He nodded, not trusting himself to speak, climbed onto the gangplank, and washed off his feet in the Nile before he came on board.

The cargo of spices was carried down to the river on donkeys—Menches and Imouthes had taken the camels back to their stables—then transported on heads and shoulders across the flooded field and stowed safely. It was dusk by the time the work was finished. Ani and the people who were going exchanged noisy and effusive good-byes with the people who were staying, and then the slaves and farmworkers were splashing away with the donkeys across the field, and the boat was bobbing quietly on the river under the brightening stars, moored fore and aft to stakes driven into the bank. Tiathres lit a fire on a small, carefully insulated stone hearth on the foredeck, and soon the air was full of the scent of flatbread and stewed lentils.

Ani came over to Caesarion where he sat morosely at the stern. He drew a deep breath and stretched happily. "This is the way to travel!" he declared.

Caesarion looked at him sideways.

"I always hoped I could use this boat properly," Ani went

on, and slapped the wooden side affectionately. "Up till now it's done nothing but move flax."

Caesarion's lip curled. "Does it have a name?"

Ani shook his head. "*I* call it 'my boat.' Everyone else calls it 'Ani's boat.' I bought it two years ago. The last owner drowned, which made it unlucky—and cheap. I had a priest bless it, to change the luck, and I had the old name taken off, but I didn't want to rename it until I had a *real* use for it."

"You were already thinking about becoming a merchant two years ago?" Caesarion asked, curious.

"I've been *thinking* about it most of my life!" replied Ani. "I just haven't had the money and the opportunity until recently." He leaned on the low rail. "When I was a boy I used to watch the caravans leaving the marketplace and think that I would run away with one someday—go off and see the world!" He laughed. "In the last few years, I've been more worried about the way that bugger-arsed Aristodemos has cheated me over the linens."

"Has he?"

"Sweet Lady Isis, yes! Ever since I started selling to him, and every time I've improved the product he cheated me more." He glanced down at Caesarion indulgently and went on. "See, I keep improving the product, making it more what the people down south want. Kleon got more for it, Aristodemos got more profit on his share—and I got the crumbs. I was sure Aristodemos was lying to me about how much he was making, and Kleon has confirmed it. That thieving bugger made himself the richest man in the district on the back of *my* hard work!"

"I thought the real business was the goods from Alexandria."

"Huh. Up to a point. Kleon has a man in Opone who wants the tin for bronzeworking. That's the backbone of his trade: tin for incense. The fat—the *increase* in the profits over the last few years—has been from my linens. See, I started off selling undressed linen cloth, and not much of it, just like my father did. Then I looked at what I had to pay in licenses to the royal linen monopoly, and I decided that nobody was ever going to make money making linen—except the queen, of course. So I branched out into clothing—no license needed, see? I made money on that, so I persuaded some of the neighbors to sell their flax to me, and spare themselves the license fee. I started selling to Aristodemos then, and I thought I was doing well. I bought some new looms, and improved the quality of the cloth, which meant I could charge more, and I gave the neighbors wives cheap loans so they could buy new looms as well. Then I started getting the cloth dyed, with good dyes and strong mordants, in bright colors, the way they like it in the south. It's top-quality stuff now, what I make, and Kleon says that in Adulis and Mundus and Opone they're mad for it. It sells for twenty times the price of undressed cloth—and Aristodemos never passed on more than a fraction of that increase to me. He's the grand Greek merchant, I'm the humble farmer, so the profit is his—but *I'm* the one who increased that profit. Now I'm a merchant as well, and I'm going to take what's mine."

Caesarion felt a slight uneasiness. If this was true, then it explained why Aristodemos was so angry, and why Ani was worried about him. A new partnership would not replace the profits which Aristodemos was losing with the old one. Aristodemos must bitterly resent Ani's trip to Berenike.

"You're right, though," Ani went on, regaining his good humor. "The boat ought to have a name, now it's a proper trading vessel. Come on, then, what's a good, well-omened *Greek* name for a merchant boat?"

Caesarion glanced along the battered and dirty hull. "*Soteria?*" he suggested.

It was a sarcastic suggestion—"*Salvation*" was a grand and divine name, given to warships as often as to merchant vessels. Ani, however, was delighted. "That's good! They call Lord Serapis and Lady Isis the Saviors. And your Greek Dioskouroi are called the Saviors, too, aren't they? and they're gods of seamen and merchants. You Alexandrians celebrate a festival called the Soteria in their honor isn't that right?"

"In honor of the first Ptolemy and his wife," Caesarion corrected, suddenly unhappy. The name he had suggested to mock Ani's pretensions had twisted and mocked his own. "They're the ones who are called the Savior Gods in Alexandria." Ptolemy, son of Lagos—Ptolemy Soter the Savior—had founded the glorious dynasty which was now reduced to riding this battered hulk.

"That's even better!" exclaimed Ani. "The first king's wife was Berenike, wasn't she? The one the port's named for! It suggests where we go. And better still, it sounds *safe. Soteria!* Huh. Well done!" He slapped the side of the boat, then walked forward to where the evening fire cast its marigold light over the quiet water of the river. "Arion's suggested a name for the boat," he told his family happily. "What do you think of *Soteria?*"

*   *   *

SOTERIA SET OUT at dawn the following morning. Ani pulled out the forward mooring stake; Ezana removed the one aft, and Apollonios steered the vessel out onto the wide brown current. Serapion cheered and waved at the empty shore, then ran to hug his father as Ani climbed dripping back on board.

All that day they ran downriver, the oarsmen rowing only hard enough to give them steerage. It was even more dismal and squalid than Caesarion had feared. There was no *space*. If you tried to walk along the deck, you were always ducking around the men who were on the oars and stepping over the ones who weren't. If you sat down, people pushed over and around you—particularly the children, who were constantly pelting from one end of the vessel to the other. And there was no privacy. The Egyptians pissed over the side, the men contesting who could piss farthest and making disparaging comments about each other's equipment; they defecated over the stern. The women were more modest, and put up a screen first, but it was impossible to copy them without being mocked.

Most of the Egyptians didn't like him. Ani's authority en- sured that nobody insulted him openly, but they only stopped ignoring him to scowl at him. And they behaved as though he were unclean—not surreptitiously, as people had for much of his life, but openly and aggressively, spitting if he happened to brush against them, washing anything he had touched. Ani didn't, and seemed to have prevailed on his wife to behave naturally as well, but the rest were noxious—except for the children, who didn't care, and Melanthe, who simply gave him looks of deep pity.

Apollonios, who as the only other Greek in the party might

have been expected to be sympathetic, was the worst offender. Caesarion understood why, and had nothing but contempt for it. The man had made a tentative sexual advance toward him when they first left Berenike, and he had rejected it with disgust. Apollonios had then decided that he didn't want Caesarion anyway, that the disease rendered him detestable, and spread the attitude as far as he was able.

Occasionally Caesarion tried to imagine what Cleopatra would have done to Apollonios, but it was not much comfort. The queen was a prisoner, her allies deserted or dead, and neither she nor he would ever hold power again.

At night the boat was moored by a sheltered bank. There were mosquitoes. His sleeping mat was next to that of Apollonios, who made an ostentatious point of edging away from him. The river gurgled noisily under the keel. One of the Egyptians on the deck snored.

In the morning, when the others were still getting up, he left the boat and walked away from the river a little, just to get away from the smell and the noise. He went as far as a grove of date-palms and sat on the edge of a well for a while. There were birds chattering among the leaves, and somewhere not far away cows lowed. He considered staying there, and allowing *Soteria* to leave without him.

He owed Ani too much. He sighed, and started back to the boat.

He met Melanthe while he was still ten minutes' walk away, hurrying along with her skirts hitched up. She had nice legs.

She saw him and stopped, dropping the skirts. "Oh!" she exclaimed in relief. "There you are. We're ready to leave. Why did you go off on your own like that?"

He set his teeth. "To escape the company."

He tried to stalk past her, but she fell in beside him as though she expected him to need support. "You shouldn't go off on your own," she told him solicitously. "You might fall down."

"So might you," he snarled.

"I'm not ill!"

"You might slip in the mud, or trip. Far more common causes for a fall than a seizure, even for me. If you don't worry about that, why should you worry about the other?"

"You haven't seemed well. I was worried."

"Without cause, I assure you," he told her coldly.

They walked on for a minute in silence, and then she said hesitantly, "I'm sorry the men are unpleasant to you. It would help, you know, if you joined in the work. If you helped fetch firewood or wash up, they'd see that at least you were trying, and they wouldn't feel you were just a burden."

He stopped short with a glare of amazement. "You're suggesting that *I* fetch firewood and wash cooking pots?" The phrase *Don't you know who I am?* came to his mind, but remained unspoken. She did not know, and he dared not tell her.

"Everybody else helps with whatever has to be done," she said, taken aback by his outrage. "Papa takes a turn at the oars, too, same as the other men. You may be too ill to do that, but . . ."

"I am not 'too ill' to row. I do not do it because *gentlemen* do not do menial work. Dionysos! Do you really need that explained to you?"

Her look of surprise gave way to one of offense. "*Papa* joins in the work."

"Your father, girl, is not a gentleman. It's why he made an arrangement with me. And he will have to stop degrading himself to the level of his slaves if he wants any gentleman to do business with him."

She gaped, then flared up. "My father is the most respected Egyptian in Coptos!"

He gave a snort of deep contempt. "Oh, indeed, the most respected *Egyptian* in the great and wonderful town of *Coptos*! In Alexandria they hire people like that to sweep floors. If he wants to be accepted as a merchant, he'll have to behave like one. Pissing over the side with his slaves, and letting his wife squat over a fire and do the cooking! Zeus!"

"What's wrong with Tiathres cooking?"

He rolled his eyes. "*Ladies* have slaves to cook for them. If a woman does the chore herself, it means she has none."

"But we have slaves, you know we do! Tiathres is just being *helpful*—unlike some people! She's always helpful and kind. And she likes cooking; she does it better than anyone else in the household."

"Then she should do it at home. It disgraces your father, to have her doing it in the sight of anyone who goes by. And why doesn't he have her speak Greek?"

"Because he cares for her feelings. She's shy, she gets embarrassed when she makes mistakes, she doesn't like trying to speak Greek. If he made a fuss about it, she'd worry that she wasn't good enough for him. He *thinks* about things like that!"

"If he wants to be a merchant, he'll have to think less of that and more of his own dignity."

"I hope he never does!"

Caesarion was momentarily taken aback—not by Melanthe's words, but by the fact that he agreed with them. He was far too angry, however, to admit it. "Then he'll never amount to more than he is now."

"He saved your life!"

"Which is the only reason I'm still here! Otherwise I wouldn't *spit* on that filthy hulk he calls a boat."

"I felt sorry for you," Melanthe informed him hotly. "I won't anymore. How can you talk about my family like that?"

"I'm saying nothing but the truth," he replied, "but if it spares me your pity, girl, I'm delighted."

They walked the rest of the way back to *Soteria* in hot silence. The boat was, indeed, ready to depart, and all the crew were annoyed with him because he'd made them wait. He went on board and walked straight into the stern cabin without speaking to any of them.

THERE FOLLOWED ANOTHER miserable day. Late in the afternoon they reached the town of Ptolemais Hermiou, where Ani apparently considered the threat of Aristodemos sufficiently abated to put in at the town docks. There he and the sailors promptly engaged in a discussion of trade and the hazards of the next stretch of river with the crews of some of the other boats at the mooring. Tiathres was impatient to get to the market, to buy fresh vegetables for the party before the stalls closed. Melanthe was eager to see the town. Caesarion just wanted to get off *Soteria*, and he found himself escorting the two women into the city. Melanthe had cooled down a little since the morning, but she still wasn't speaking to him.

The marketplace of Ptolemais was set well above the level of the floods, and hence was some distance from the docks. The main street was busy, with the evening crowds buying and selling after the heat of the day. Tiathres bought leeks and parsley, coriander, cucumbers, and figs, which she put in a basket she had brought along for the purpose. Some of the things went into a second basket, which was handed to Melanthe. Nobody suggested that Caesarion carry anything, which relieved him of the necessity of refusing such a menial chore.

When they arrived in the market square itself, Melanthe was sufficiently excited by the attractions of a new town that she forgot her indignation. "Look at that temple!" she exclaimed delightedly.

It was a graceful building in the Greek style, facing the marketplace from behind a forest of statues and votive altars. It was, Caesarion supposed, different from the rather heavy native style of the temples of Coptos. Ptolemais had been since its foundation a Greek town, a center of Hellenism in the deeply traditional reaches of Upper Egypt.

"It looks so light and elegant!" the girl went on. "Can we go see it? Please, Tiathres?"

"Which god owns it?" Tiathres asked Caesarion nervously. She was clearly uneasy, here in this town where she knew no one, and she didn't want to go worshiping any strange deities.

Caesarion had never visited Ptolemais before and was not entirely certain, though he had an idea. They crossed the marketplace to find out, and the altars proved his suspicion right: they were dedicated "to the Savior Gods Ptolemy and Berenike" and "to the Loving Brother and Sister Gods, Ptolemy and

Arsinoe." The temple had been founded by the first Ptolemy, and was dedicated to the dynastic cult of the Lagids.

Melanthe and even Tiathres were delighted by the dedications "to the Savior Gods," and at once decided that worshiping the patrons of the renamed boat was practically a necessity. Tiathres bought some wine and oil to offer, and they went on through the open doorway into the shadowy sanctuary.

There were more statues here. They stood along the walls, singly or in pairs, twice life-size, dressed in robes of faded purple worked with gold, their stiff marble faces painted with smiles, their glass eyes gazing solemnly down upon their worshipers. Many of the altars were dark, but some flickered with lamps, and in the unsteady light the statues seemed alive. Caesarion felt suddenly unable to breathe. He took a step backward, his heart thundering. They're merely statues of men and women, he told himself. Calling them gods is just propaganda. Anyway, even if they were gods, they're my ancestors, and they'd want to help me.

It was not what he felt. These generations of Lagids were staring with shame and anger at the degraded outcome of what they had so nobly begun.

Melanthe caught the edge of his cloak. "What's the matter?" she asked. The alarm on her face added silently, *Are you about to have a fit?*

"I will wait outside," he said, with an effort. "This . . . this is all lost now, and I can't bear it."

"In truth, it is hard for anyone to bear," said a voice from the shadows behind them.

They all turned, and saw that a priest had been burning incense at one of the side altars. He wore a white cloak, and his head was covered. He came forward into the light from the open doorway, and became at once less mysterious and more ordinary, a middle-aged, middle-class, Greek official. "What do you want?" he asked anxiously.

"We have an offering for the Savior Gods," said Melanthe, after a hesitating look at Caesarion.

The priest was silent for a moment, and his anxiety relaxed into relieved approval. "This is good," he said. "The spirits of the Savior Gods are still with us, still working to benefit their people. I'm very glad that you have come to make offerings to them, especially at a time like this." He looked keenly at Caesarion. "You are a Greek, and just now you spoke like a man who was loyal to the queen and distressed by her fall. Don't go outside. Go up and make the offering to the Savior Gods with your friends, and then make another offering, to the spirit of the divine Cleopatra. That will ease your distress."

The whole world seemed to go faint and blurred. A cold numbness grew about his heart. *I will not have a seizure*, he thought desperately. *Please, no! I owe her that much!*

"Friend," he said, breathlessly, "I have been out of Egypt. The last news I heard was that the queen had been taken prisoner. If you have heard more news since, I beg you, tell me!"

The priest frowned, taken aback by his intensity. "Haven't you . . . ?" he began—then deliberately rearranged his face into solemnity, and said, "The news came up the river days ago. The queen is dead. She refused to bow to the will of Caesar Octavian, and she took her own life. They say that she had a serpent smuggled to her in a basket of figs. They have buried her body next to Antonius, but her spirit is immortal."

Caesarion fought for breath. He had known, all along he had known, that she would not endure captivity, that she would refuse to walk behind Octavian's triumphal chariot and suffer the jeers of the crowd. She was a great queen, a Lagid, the last heir of all these smiling divinities . . .

. . . apart from himself, who had stupidly survived to be spat upon by slaves.

"Where is her altar?" he asked the priest.

The man pointed back to the place where he'd been standing, the place immediately to the right of the door. An onyx bowl of incense smoked on the small altar, and lamps on a gilded stand cast a soft light on a smiling statue: Cleopatra, wearing the serpent crown of the goddess Isis, holding a child in her arms.

She had had many such statues made; she had even set a similar image on her coinage. Isis was usually shown holding her son, whom the Egyptians called Horus and the Greeks Harpokrates, and Cleopatra had adopted the pose after Caesarion's birth. She had identified herself with Isis and Julius Caesar with Serapis, king of the gods; later she had mourned Caesar as Isis had mourned her murdered husband. Later still, she had claimed that, just as Serapis had been restored from the dead, so the god had found a new human incarnation and come back to her in Marcus Antonius. Caesarion was familiar with every cynical manipulation of the myth—and yet, faced with the image of his mother cradling the infant that was himself, he found himself trembling, his face wet with tears. He had known that she would die, yet still the event struck on an unguarded heart.

"Friend, do you have a knife?" he asked the priest. "I wish to mourn for her."

Puzzled, the priest handed him a small knife of the sort used to cut off sections of incense. Caesarion went over to the altar with it, pulled off his hat, and began to hack at his hair, cutting it off in handfuls and dropping it onto the bowl of incense. The black strands crinkled and burned, momentarily making the sweet smoke stink. He sliced his scalp, and felt the blood trickle down onto his ear, but the pain was almost unnoticeable in the roaring agony of grief.

"Arion!" said Melanthe, shocked.

He ignored her. Hair cut raggedly short in mourning, he stood staring at the coals, breathing hard, the knife hilt hard and slick in his sweating hand. Behind him, Tiathres was anxiously demanding to know what was going on—she had not understood the Greek conversation with the priest. Melanthe began to whisper a Demotic explanation.

"Do you know what happened to the queen's children?" Caesarion asked the priest, without turning round.

"The young king Ptolemy Caesar is dead." He sounded nearly as shocked as Melanthe. "A Roman troop passed this way five days ago, carrying his ashes."

"We know that," Melanthe informed him, breaking off her whisper to Tiathres. "Arion was a Friend of the king. He was wounded trying to defend him."

"He never counted for anything," Caesarion said harshly. "I meant the queen's other children—Ptolemy Philadelphus, and Alexander Helios and Cleopatra Selene. Do you know if they are alive?"

"No," said the priest, still shocked, though now impressed as well. "I've heard nothing about them."

Probably they were dead. Even if they lived, how could he do anything to help them? No one had helped his mother while she lived, and who was going to oppose the Romans now that she was dead?

The edifice of excuses in which he'd lived since Berenike collapsed around him. There was *nothing* he could do in Alexandria. He should have died as soon as he realized that there would be no escape from Berenike—no, he should have died on the pyre. The queen had taken her own life rather than accept humiliation by Rome, but he had blindly and stupidly submitted to every sort of degradation, to preserve a life which even Rhodon had known was worthless. He looked up again at his mother's face, glassy-eyed and smiling under the serpent crown. Once again, as so very often before, she had had to show him what to do.

"I'm sorry," he told her, aloud. "I failed you. Forgive me. I will make what amends I can." He looked vaguely at the knife in his hand, then brought the edge down hard across the base of his left thumb.

"Arion!" screamed Melanthe. She threw herself at him and tried to snatch the knife. He shoved her off, and dragged the sharp little blade across his wrist once more. Blood spurted out, hot and red, hissing on the coals. The same blood that ran in Ptolemy the Savior, he thought triumphantly, unclean and degraded perhaps, but still capable of being purified in death.

Then there was a blow against his side, and he found himself on the floor with the priest on top of him. The man's knee caught his right side. The wound flared agony and he screamed. Melanthe wrested the knife out of his suddenly nerveless fingers.

"How dare you profane this temple!" shouted the priest furiously.

"Profane it?" Caesarion gasped, trying to free himself. "No! Never! O Apollo!"

Tiathres caught his injured hand and began winding the hem of her cloak about his wrist to stop the bleeding.

"You pollute the altar with human blood," said the priest, more calmly. "This does not honor the queen's memory, young man; I tell you, it does not!"

He moaned, catching the first whiff of carrion: still less would it honor the queen to throw a fit over her altar. "Let me up," he pleaded. "Let me go out, where I won't pollute the temple."

The priest got off him. He tried to get his hand away from Tiathres, failed, staggered to his feet with her still pressing it. Pain he had not felt a moment before hammered in his wrist. He leaned against the altar, clutching his side. The bowl of incense had stopped smoking, drowned in blood, and the statue's robe was spattered with dark droplets. The priest took his arm and tugged, escorted him as far as the door. He stood swaying in the evening sun, fighting the seizure. Tiathres was still pressing her cloak to his wrist, holding the wound closed. "Give me a bandage," she begged the priest, "—or a knife to cut a strip from my robe. He's still bleeding."

She spoke Demotic, and the priest only looked at her blankly. Melanthe, her voice thick with distress, translated.

"Take it off!" Caesarion begged, shaking his arm weakly.

"I'm not polluting the temple now." Tiathres did not let go, and moving the hand hurt and made him dizzy. The priest caught his arm again as he staggered.

"Come to my house," said the priest, gathering himself together and addressing Melanthe. "It's across the street. My wife will help you bandage him and clean up. You can't go through the marketplace like that: somebody would call the guard." Caesarion, stumbling, allowed himself to be led down the steps. The world was swinging around him in circles, and it reeked of carrion.

The stink and the fragmentary images gave way at last to a paved courtyard. He was sitting on the ground, his back against a column. Tiathres was kneeling beside him, dressed only in her tunic, wrapping a strip of linen around his wrist and hand. Beyond her another, unfamiliar, woman was filling a tub with water.

Melanthe came over, holding a cup of unglazed pottery. She, too, had stripped to her tunic, and her bare upper arms glowed the color of dark honey. She knelt down, on the other side of him from Tiathres, and held the cup to his lips.

He was thirsty, so he drank. It was watered wine, mixed with a little honey and something bitter. He drained it, not caring what drug he was swallowing. Melanthe set the empty cup down and looked at him angrily.

"You're awake again, aren't you?" she said. "Why did you do that?"

He was beginning to feel that he had indeed done something stupid and disgraceful, and he tried to defend himself. "She had the courage to kill herself," he explained hoarsely. "I should have had it, too. It was a mistake, thinking there was anything left for me to do."

"Why should you kill yourself?" she demanded. She was almost in tears. "*Why?* What good would it do anyone?"

"I do no one any good alive," he told her. "I have never counted for anything, and I never will. My life was a burden to me before, and now I am a deadweight on the earth. Everything I lived for is gone. I only survive by betraying everything I was."

"Cleopatra wasn't even a *good* queen!" objected Melanthe.

He glared. "How dare you utter such a foul lie!"

"All those wars!" Melanthe protested tearfully. "All those taxes to pay for all those wars, and the tin in the coinage, and she never paid for anyone to repair the dykes and the ditches, or the roads. And she killed her sister and her brothers and . . ."

"Hush!" said the strange woman, coming over from the washtub. "I agree with you, dear, but it's just as well my husband's next door, or he'd turn you out of the house. He always believed in the queen, and he's been in mourning ever since she died." She squatted down in front of Caesarion. "And you're another of the same breed, are you, young man? Herakles, what a mess you've made of your hair!"

He looked at her vaguely. She was stout, dark, dressed in a white linen shift, and he'd never seen her before in his life. Why should she be worried about his *hair* when all he wanted was to die? He looked questioningly at Melanthe, but she only frowned.

The stout woman took his left hand from Tiathres and inspected the bandage. "That should hold it," she said in Demotic. "Sweet Isis, what a thing to do! Not a good time to do it, either. The Romans are here in the city, and there'll be gossip. People will have seen you coming out of the temple all covered in blood, and they'll talk. —I've got your things soaking, sister. Fresh blood comes right out, and your cloaks should be fine once you've wrung them out."

"We are very grateful," said Tiathres, and went over to the washtub. When she squatted down over it, Caesarion belatedly remembered how she'd used her cloak to stop his bleeding. He realized dimly that someone had taken his own cloak as well . . . and Melanthe's. He must have got blood everywhere. The strange woman must be the priest's wife; the priest had said she'd help them clean up. He wondered for a moment where the priest himself had gone—then remembered that he'd got blood all over the altar and statue as well. The pious man would want to clean it off.

He had been spectacularly stupid and foolish. Cleopatra had planned her death carefully. He had cut himself wildly, in the fury of a moment, in front of people he should have realized would try to stop him. All he'd succeeded in doing was making a fool of himself—and dirtying his mother's statue. His eyes stung, and he wiped at them wretchedly with his good hand.

"The Romans are *here?*" asked Melanthe anxiously.

"They arrived from Panopolis about noon," replied the priest's wife. "A great army of them. Their emperor has sent one of his generals up the river to secure the kingdom. They're camped outside the city now, but they've announced that tomorrow the general will come into the city to receive oaths and hear petitions. My husband has been sitting in the temple all afternoon, worrying about whether he should give his oath."

"Does he have to?" asked Melanthe.

"He's on the town council," said the priest's wife unhappily. "The whole council will be required to swear. I don't know what will happen if he refuses. And the Romans are demanding that the town hand over the temple treasuries, to pay for the war, and my husband . . ." She trailed off, afraid to say what her husband might do, then glanced anxiously at Caesarion. "I don't like to ask, but—is he a fugitive?"

"No," said Melanthe at once. "Papa said the Romans came and questioned him at Berenike, but they discharged him. Papa offered to take him to Alexandria with us, if he'd help by writing letters along the way. My papa is a merchant." She added the last with pride.

The priest's wife nodded in relief. Caesarion guessed that she knew that her husband would have insisted on sheltering a fugitive Friend of the king, and that she'd feared the family would suffer for it. In the middle of his own misery, he felt a pang of shame that these good, kind people should expect to suffer for their loyalty to the house of Lagos.

A door banged, and the priest came into the courtyard. He was carrying Tiathres' two baskets and Caesarion's hat. He set them down beside a column and came over; his white cloak was still smeared with blood.

"We gave him some hellebore," the priest's wife told her husband, getting to her feet. "I don't think the amount of blood he lost was as much as it looked. He was prevented in time."

The priest nodded in acknowledgement and squatted down in his wife's place. "Young man," he said sternly, "I understand your grief. I share it. But such desperate actions do no honor to the queen. If you were, as your friends said, a Friend of the king, then remember that the queen sent her son out of Egypt to keep him safe, and sent you with him. If you destroy yourself, you defeat her purpose. It is by our lives and worship that we honor the gods, not by bloody self-murder."

"I am sorry, sir, if I polluted your temple," Caesarion replied faintly—the uncomplicated truth he could utter, rather than the muddled and desperate one he could not.

"I fully believe that you never intended any disrespect to the gods," said the priest, relenting. "Were you truly a Friend of King Ptolemy Caesar?"

"As much as such a man *has* friends," he replied—and wondered why he didn't just tell them the truth. Why go on pretending, when all he wanted to do was die?

He would continue to conceal the truth, he realized, because he was ashamed. King Ptolemy Caesar ought to stand in that hall of statues, regal and serene, and he, bloody and tear-stained and diseased, could not.

"And the queen?" the priest asked in a low voice. "Did you know her as well?"

He caught his breath painfully. "Yes."

"Ah." After a moment, the man went on. "I met her once, when she stopped here on her way to Thebes. I thought her the greatest and most godlike being I have ever encountered. Tell me, since you were in the party she trusted to accompany her son—did she ever say anything about . . . about what her supporters should do if . . . when the war was lost?"

Caesarion looked into the worried face. "She said that they should do what was necessary to save themselves," he declared without hesitation. Cleopatra had, in fact, discussed it very little, except to curse those supporters who fell away before the end. "Sir, your wife has mentioned that you have been wondering whether you should swear loyalty to Rome and allow them to confiscate the treasury of your temple. I can tell you that the queen would wish you to do nothing else. The lives of her supporters were dear to her, and I think she would have agreed with you that we honor our gods by living worship, and not by self-destruction. You were right to say that, and I was acting from passion, not reason. She has gone to join her ancestors, and for you to swear loyalty to the new Lord of Egypt is no treachery. Remember, also, that the Roman emperor is the adopted son of Caesar, whom the queen loved. Though she opposed Octavian, she did not consider him unworthy."

The priest's face brightened and his shoulders sagged in relief. Behind him, his wife beamed at Caesarion gratefully. Caesarion blinked, startled by the strength of his own pleasure in that gratitude, in the knowledge, amid the bloody shambles of his life, that he had done one small thing right.

CHAPTER VII

It was dark when they left the priest's house. Arion was not quite steady on his feet, and Melanthe watched him warily, wondering whether he was more likely to faint or to have a fit. She thought he'd had a fit while they were getting him to the priest's house, but he might simply have fainted: they'd all been in such a state that it was impossible to say anything for certain. At least he seemed calmer now, though perhaps that was simply the drug he'd been given. She shut her eyes for a moment, trying to blot out the image of Arion's wild-eyed stare as he hacked at his hand. Maybe he'd been *in* a fit then, and that was why he'd done it. Or did the sacred disease unbalance your mind even when you weren't actually having a seizure?

At least they looked respectable now, and attracted no attention from the few people still about. Their cloaks were still wet, but the night was hot, so that was no hardship, and the darkness hid the damp. Arion was wearing his hat again, which concealed the ragged mess he'd made of his hair—not that anyone would have noticed *too* much, in the dark. His face, in the light of the occasional torch affixed before a grand house, was white and haggard, but reserved.

"They were good people," remarked Tiathres, meaning the priest and his wife. "If there's time, I'd like to go back there tomorrow and give them some linen to say thank you. And we could make our offering to the Savior Gods."

"I think they're going to be busy tomorrow," said Melanthe doubtfully. "They said that the Roman general is coming into the city to take oaths." The thought of a whole Roman army encamped somewhere nearby was alarming, and she glanced anxiously at the shadows of the roadside, hoping that the soldiers had not been allowed into the city. There did not seem to be any of them on the streets.

They walked on in silence for a few minutes. Then Tiathres said, "Ani will be worried."

Papa *would* be worried. They were going to be back very late, and he'd probably heard about the Roman army from the men at the docks. Maybe he was looking for them now. She hoped *he* didn't run into any Romans. She cast an angry look at Arion, and wished she dared say something reproachful.

She didn't. It might unbalance him again. He might take the bandage off; he might seize a knife and cut open the other wrist. He might attack *her*—no, he wouldn't do that. It was probably the disease that had made him try to destroy himself. It was a terrible affliction. It must be dreadful to have to live with it. And she supposed that the attitude of the others on the boat hadn't helped.

She winced at a stab of guilt. She was keenly aware how *she* would feel if the others behaved toward her as they did toward Arion, and Papa had explained to her that Arion was from a grand family and probably felt it even more than she would. She'd been wrong, Papa explained, to suggest that Arion should help out with the work of running the boat. "You wouldn't expect Aristodemos to do anything like that," he'd pointed out, "and this boy sneers at Aristodemos. He feels he's degrading himself by agreeing to write letters: you can't expect him to wash pots."

It was true, she could see it, and she was sick at the thought that perhaps she'd helped push Arion into that desperate gesture at the temple—but she *still* resented his arrogance and his contempt for Papa and Tiathres. The horrible bloody assault on his own life had shaken her to the core.

His mind was diseased. To come all this way after the king died, and then try to kill himself because the queen was dead—she just couldn't understand that at all. After all, he was supposed to have been the *king's* Friend, not the queen's. There was something very wrong with him. She wished he would go away, and leave *Soteria* and her family alone.

As they descended the hill toward the docks, Melanthe saw torches burning beside one of the boats, their light reflected redly in the dark Nile. As they drew nearer, she recognized the blunt shape of *Soteria*. She wondered if Papa were assembling a search party, and quickened her pace. On the quay she broke into a run, cradling her basket of vegetables and leaving the other two to follow at their own pace.

The torches were tied to poles beside *Soteria*'s mooring posts, three of them, and as she ran Melanthe realized that there were men sitting on the quayside between the torches—and that they wore armor.

She stopped abruptly. One of the men, who had heard her running and glanced around, got to his feet. He wore a long mail-shirt and a helmet with a crest of red horsehair, and there was a sword slung at his side. She saw, with a thunder of the heart, that the poles to which the torches had been fastened were, in fact, spears.

She stared at the soldier; stared at *Soteria*. The boat's deck held a litter of scattered ashes from the cooking fire, a dropped cloak, a broken bottle. There were no people there, no light from within the cabin, no sound or sign of life at all. She looked back at the soldier. He grinned and started walking toward her. She stood frozen, torn between the instinct to flee and the agonized necessity of discovering what had happened.

"What you want?" the soldier asked her. He spoke Greek with a strange heavy accent.

"That's our boat!" she exclaimed, stunned. "What's happened? Where's my father?"

"Your boat," repeated the soldier, and nodded. He looked beyond her to the approaching forms of Tiathres and Arion and jerked a hand upward. At once the two other soldiers behind him got to their feet, picking up javelins which had lain on the ground beside them.

"No run," the soldier ordered them all, with a significant gesture toward the javelins.

The other two had stopped. Tiathres was aghast; Arion . . .

had an expression she did not recognize. It might almost be relief.

"You Arion, of Alexandria?" the soldier asked him directly.

At that the young Greek looked surprised and puzzled. "Quem quaerite?"

There was a sharp silence, and then the first soldier demanded in astonishment, "Loquerisne Latine?"

"Sane loquor." Arion surveyed the man a moment. "*Arionem* quaerite?"

"Nonne Arion es, Alexandrinus quis, hostis populi Romani?"

Arion blinked. "Sum Arion," he declared, "sed haud hostis Romanorum. Pater mi ipsi Romanus est!" He rattled off a question, to which the soldier, surprised but pleased, responded.

"What's happening?" Tiathres asked in anguish. "What are they saying? Where's Ani—where are the children?"

"I don't know!" Melanthe hissed back. "Tiathres, they aren't speaking Greek—you must be able to hear that! I think it's Latin. They're Romans."

Tiathres stared at Arion and the Roman, who continued to jabber at each other. Then her face set in an expression of bitter hatred that Melanthe had never seen on it before. "Aristodemos!" she spat.

Arion and the Roman in charge glanced round at that. Arion began speaking again. Melanthe caught the names "Aristodemos" and "Coptos" and "Alexandria." Arion gestured at *Soteria*. The Roman shook his head. Arion appeared to insist. He gestured emphatically, at himself, the boat, the two women. He spread his hands in surrender. The Romans looked doubtful, but one of them set down his javelin and walked rapidly away down the docks. Arion sighed, said something else, then sat down on the quay and leaned wearily against a mooring post, crossing his arms upon his knees. The fresh bandage shone in the torchlight, and the wide hat shadowed his face.

"What's happening?" Tiathres demanded desperately into the silence. "Where's Ani? Where are my children?"

"Quietly!" commanded Arion. "They don't speak Demotic, and they may object to us speaking it. Let me ask permission." He asked the soldier a question, received a nod, and turned back. "Ani and the others have been arrested and taken to the Roman camp. The tessararius doesn't know why. His orders were simply to arrest me if I came back here, and he was told that I'm an anti-Roman agitator. I'm . . ."

"Tessarius?" asked Melanthe, with an anxious glance at the Roman.

"Tessararius—watch-commander, a non-commissioned rank, subordinate to a centurion. This honest fellow here. I'm sure you're right, and that this is the result of a false accusation by Aristodemos. I've said that to the tessararius, and he's inclined to agree, at least as far as I'm concerned. I'll ask him about the children."

He turned back to the Roman and asked a question. The Roman replied at once, gesturing at one of the neighboring boats. He smiled at Tiathres and nodded encouragingly.

"He says that when they took the others away, they told your neighbors there to look after the children and the nurse," Arion supplied. "He says you and Melanthe can go join them if you want. He has no orders to arrest any women. But he says you mustn't try to go on board your own boat. It's been confiscated and will be kept under guard, at least for the time being."

Tiathres leapt toward the boat that contained her children— then halted again. "What about Ani?" she wailed. "Where is he? What are they doing to him?"

"He's in the Roman camp," Arion replied patiently, "and the tessararius here doesn't know more than that." He hesitated, then added, "They're going to take me into the camp presently, but I persuaded the tessararius to ask if they should collect the documents from *Soteria* first."

"Documents?" asked Tiathres blankly.

"The customs documents and the goods manifests—which, taken together, prove conclusively that Ani is a merchant and not whatever Aristodemos may have said he is. If the documents are secure in Roman hands, it also means that the guards won't feel free to pilfer the cargo. I'll be able to find out what the charge actually is when I get to the camp, and I hope that I'll be able to disprove it. Do you still have those figs you bought?"

"Figs!" exclaimed Tiathres, with a sob. "Yes. What should I do with them?"

"Offer some to the soldiers here, to show that you're grateful to them for letting you go—and give me some, as well. At the moment they're listening to me. If I have a fit, they may not, and I'm more likely to have a fit if I'm hungry."

Tiathres, beginning to weep, offered the Romans figs from her basket. They took some, with smiles and polite "Tank you"s. Arion also picked up a handful, and set them down on an edge of his cloak. He began to nibble one delicately.

"What about Ani?" Tiathres asked again, piteously. "*He* hasn't eaten, and . . . and he doesn't know what's happened to us. Can I bring him food?"

Arion relayed the question and received a lengthy reply. "He says, not tonight. The gates of the camp are shut. He says you should come in the morning. He says you can ask for him—Gaius Simplicius, of the First Century of the Second Legion—and he'll try to find out where they're keeping your husband and get you permission to see him. He says, don't worry, if your husband's innocent he has nothing to fear."

Tiathres stammered, "G-Gaius Sima . . ."

"Gaius Simplicius," Arion repeated, "of the First Century of the Second Legion."

Melanthe repeated it carefully. Simplicius smiled at her and nodded. He said something more and gestured again toward the neighboring boat, which contained two undoubtedly very frightened children who would surely be overjoyed to see their mother. Tiathres bowed to him, touched Melanthe's arm, and started toward it.

Melanthe didn't come. "Ask the Roman to let me go with you," she told Arion. "I want to help."

Arion shook his head. "There's nothing you could do. You'll be much safer here."

"What if you have a seizure?" she demanded. "What if you faint, or go mad and kill yourself? You're unbalanced, and you despise my father anyway. I don't trust you with his life!"

Arion looked up at her, his head far enough back that the torchlight fell on his face: his eyes had all their old ferocity, and his pale cheeks were stained with their quick color. "I'm epileptic, not insane! And I will not kill myself while your father is in danger. I do not despise him: on the contrary, I respect him enormously and I am well aware of the debt I owe him. I don't think that the best way to repay it is to take his beautiful virgin daughter into a camp full of armed men who might, if things went wrong, abuse her. I will be a prisoner, and have no power to protect you. Go help your mother, and ask for your father in the morning. I hope you'll have better news then."

"Why do you speak Latin?" she demanded.

His face went proud and calm, giving nothing away. "My father was Roman."

She remembered something she'd once heard—that, just as Greek citizens could not legally marry Egyptians, so Roman citizens could not legally marry foreigners of any nation. Arion, who made Aristodemos look humble, was a bastard.

He was also a Friend of the king. She wondered if he had obtained that status through royal intercession, and if that was why he'd been so acutely distressed when he heard that the queen was dead. After all, the queen herself had borne children to Romans, and might have chosen Arion as a friend for her son when most monarchs would have had no time for him at all.

She'd misjudged him, she realized slowly. He was not unbalanced. He was a young man who'd lost his family, seen the cause he'd believed in go bloodily down, and who had no hope of ever regaining the status and position he had held before. His situation on the boat must have galled his very heart. It wasn't surprising that he wanted to die. He was injured, weary, distraught, weak from loss of blood—and he was preparing to do battle with the Romans for her father's liberty.

The Romans had marched Papa off without pausing to collect the documents that proved his innocence. If Arion hadn't spoken Latin, they would have done the same to him. Ani, Melanthe knew with absolutely certainty, belonged to a class where to be accused by a superior is to be convicted. Arion did not—she had to admit that he did not—and he could speak the Roman language. He was Papa's only hope of deliverance.

"I . . . I'm sorry," she stammered. "I didn't mean . . . I shouldn't have . . ."

"Your mother's waiting," he told her implacably. He lowered his head again, and his face disappeared once more into the shadows.

She bobbed her head and hurried over to Tiathres. She felt his eyes watching her, though, all the way to the next boat.

THE LEGIONARY WHO'D been sent off to the camp came back with a clerk, to Caesarion's great relief: he hadn't been certain that the centurion would agree to the request. After a brief discussion, the Romans allowed their prisoner onto *Soteria* long enough to point out the location of the official documents. The clerk collected the papers and, after some grumbling, issued him with a receipt for them. They posted one man as a sentry and set out for the Roman camp, walking upriver away from the docks.

"Muddiest damned country I've ever seen," grumbled the tessararius, looking for somewhere to scrape the mud off his hobnailed sandal. "I thought Egypt was supposed to be dry and sandy!"

"Walk a few miles uphill," Caesarion told him tolerantly. He felt he knew these men. They had the same accents and habits and complaints as Antonius' legionaries.

"The river floods every year?" asked Simplicius, in the tone of one who'd often heard that it did but wanted it confirmed one more time.

He discussed the flooding of the Nile and the chances of seeing hippopotami most of the way to the camp. He was vaguely astonished at his own calm. Perhaps it was because he'd suffered such an emotional storm earlier in the day; perhaps it was something to do with the dose of hellebore he'd had at the priest's house. Whatever the cause, he felt peculiarly confident that he'd succeed—that no one would recognize him, and that he would manage to convince the authorities that whatever charge had been brought against Ani had no more grounds than the malice of a disappointed rival.

The legionaries were all entirely convinced of his own innocence, which was a start. They had never before encountered a Greek who spoke fluent Latin: Greeks in general expected people to master their own tongue, and considered it demeaning to learn anyone else's. No young man who had departed so far from the usual Hellenic arrogance could possibly be an anti-Roman agitator.

On the other hand, he could undoubtedly expect strict questioning, after being arrested on such a charge. He was probably secure from torture—gentlemen were not normally subjected to such degradations—but he could expect to be executed if found guilty. This would be a military affair, too, conducted by an army of occupation: he could not expect to receive a trial. At most there would be a hearing before the general, and even that would depend on what impression he made on his first interrogators. If the matter did go to the general, that had its own hazards. He had met a number of Octavian's generals. Earlier in the year the Second Legion had been commanded by Gaius Cornelius Gallus, whom he knew by reputation as a talented commander and, unusually, as a poet, but whom he had never met. It was possible, however, that someone else was in charge of this expedition.

The camp was about a mile to the north of Ptolemais. It was utterly standard: a ditch and rough palisade surrounding neat rows of tents. They were admitted at the south gate, and turned left past the standard of the Second Legion.

Simplicius marched his party directly to a particularly large tent at the end of the central row. So: the interrogation was to be, in the first instance, by the centurion of the First Century. The first century of a legion was always a double-strength one, and its centurion outranked all his fellows, a senior and trusted man—though not as senior as the legionary commander or his tribunes. That gave some idea of how much importance the Romans attached to this case: it was serious, but not worth the attention of the high command. Simplicius halted outside the tent, and announced himself with a stamping of feet. A grizzled head poked out the tent flap, surveyed the party, and said, "Very well, bring him in!" in an irritated tone.

Caesarion ducked his head and entered the leather shelter behind Simplicius. It was comparatively large, but otherwise very plain: one camp bed, a chair, a scribe sitting on a stool and holding a set of wax tablets, three oil lamps—and the centurion, a thin, scowling, wiry old man in a red tunic, out of armor, but with his vinewood staff-of-office thrust into his heavy leather belt. The centurion stared at Caesarion a moment, then cast Simplicius a reproving look. "You should have bound him," he complained.

Simplicius shrugged. "He didn't give us any trouble—and he's hurt his arm."

The centurion glared at Caesarion's bandaged wrist and grunted. He sat down in the empty chair and surveyed his prisoner with dislike. "I'm told you speak Latin," he said, in that language.

"Certainly," replied Caesarion, and made his opening move. "Sir, I believe that this false accusation against myself and my associate, Ani, son of Petesuchos, emanates from one of my associate's business rivals, a man by the name of Aristodemos. May I ask, sir, if Aristodemos brought this charge—whatever it is—in person, and, if he did, whether you have him in custody as well?"

The centurion flushed. "*I* am asking the questions!" he snapped.

Caesarion inclined his head. "I will answer your questions, sir, very readily. But I believe Aristodemos should answer, as well. He is attempting to pervert the majesty of Roman law to satisfy a personal grudge."

"Hercules!" muttered the clerk, staring.

" '*Majesty*,' " repeated the centurion. "You know what that means? —Yes, you do, may the gods destroy you!" The dislike on his face was joined by resentment. *Maiestas* was the charge of treason, and by using the term in connection with his accuser, Caesarion had made his counteraccusation impossible to ignore.

Caesarion inclined his head again. "I do not presume to

dictate your course of action, sir. I merely assert that this accusation is false and malicious. The accuser probably brought it because he thought the Roman people were too savage and stupid to investigate it thoroughly. I trust that you will prove him mistaken."

"You speechify like some cheating lawyer!" snapped the centurion. "Where did you learn Latin?"

"My father was Roman," Caesarion replied evenly, "and he wished me to learn it. There were always Romans at court who were happy to speak it with me." He glanced around. "May I sit down?" His legs were weak and his head was starting to hurt.

"No," the centurion said flatly. He glared at the prisoner. "You said you would answer my questions. Your name is Arion? Son of . . . ?"

"Gaius," Caesarion told him truthfully.

"You are not the *son* of a Roman," responded the centurion. "Romans have no *sons* by foreign women."

"Sir, my mother was a woman of rank, and the connection was formal and recognized. I do not claim my father's Roman status or property, but he acknowledged me as his, and I do not reject him as mine. To do so, in my mind, would require me to reject and despise Rome itself. I have never done so: do you wish me to?"

The centurion glared and yielded the point. "Gaius what?"

Caesarion took a deep breath: he'd prepared for this. "Valerius." It was probably the most common Roman family name, as Gaius was the most common personal name. It would be impossible for the centurion to pin down any particular Gaius Valerius who might have lived in Alexandria eighteen years before. "He came to Alexandria with the deified Julius, and met my mother, who was an attendant upon the queen."

That seemed to satisfy the centurion. "And you became a friend of the king, Ptolemy so-called Caesar? You were given a position on the staff of the commander of the king's body-guard, and accompanied him on his attempt to escape from Egypt?"

"In that much your reports are correct."

"And after the king's death, you fled back into Egypt, in-tending to raise opposition to the Senate and People of Rome. You received assistance from a troublemaking Egyptian by the name of Ani . . ."

Caesarion took another deep breath and proclaimed loudly, "Lies! Outrageous lies! I surrendered, in Berenike, to a cen-turion by the name of Gaius Paterculus. He discharged me in accordance with the emperor's policy of clemency, as I am sure his own report will show. Ani, son of Petesuchos, a pious and decent merchant who helped me when he found me wounded on the road, offered to let me travel with him from Berenike back to Alexandria if I assisted him with his letters. He has a cargo from Berenike—on which the tariffs have been paid!—and power of attorney to act for the ship captain who owns it. The clerk there has the documents."

The clerk who'd come to the ship hefted them and nodded. The centurion leaned back, scowling. "You say you were wounded? When was this?"

"When your people took the king's camp. Twenty days ago, I suppose."

"Then why are you wearing a fresh bandage?"

There was a glint of triumph in the old man's eyes. He'd

heard of the incident at the temple, Caesarion realized. Some-one had already reported it—human blood poured out on the queen's altar, a ferocious condemnation of the new order and an attempt to invoke malign ghosts to curse it. The centurion had realized the significance of the bandage the moment he saw it. It didn't matter, though: Caesarion had already worked out what he was going to say.

"I was wounded in the side," he said mildly. "This," he lifted his wrist, "was an accident this afternoon."

"An accident?"

"A stupid accident," he agreed. "We went to the temple to make an offering to the Savior Gods, who are the patrons of my friend Ani's boat. The priest there told me that the queen was dead, news I had not heard before. I was very distressed, and I tried to cut my hair in mourning as an offering to her spirit, but the knife slipped and cut my hand."

The old man glared at him indignantly. "You tried to cut your *hair?*"

Caesarion took off his hat and showed him. "I made a mess of it." He smiled appeasingly. "It was a small, sharp knife. I should have waited and used scissors." Behind him, he heard Simplicius swallow a laugh.

"It was reported to *me*," declared the centurion furiously, "that a young man matching your description slit his wrists before the altar and prayed for vengeance on Rome!"

Caesarion raised his eyebrows incredulously. "Zeus! Who-ever reported to you, must have been drinking. I cut my hair and the knife slipped—or do you think I normally wear my hair like this? You can ask the priest whether I prayed for vengeance—or, indeed, prayed for anything except a bandage, fast. He led me over to his house and gave me one. I suppose your informant saw us coming out of the temple and invented a more exciting story."

The centurion kept glaring. "You were very devoted to the queen, were you?"

"Yes," Caesarion replied, without hesitation. "I fought for her and for the house of Lagos with all my strength. If that is a crime, you may kill me for it—though you will have to kill many thousands of others as well, including the half of the Roman Senate who supported Antonius. I was told, however, that Caesar has proclaimed a policy of clemency to those who surrender and lay down their arms. I surrendered, I am unarmed, and since I left Berenike I have neither spoken nor acted against the Senate and People in any way. What is the emperor's clemency worth, if it weighs less than a malicious lie from a second-rate merchant who's lost trade to a rival? You have *evidence* there in your clerk's hands that my friend Ani is engaged in lawful and honest trade. What *evidence* has Aristodemos offered to the contrary?"

"You are a very insolent little bastard!" snapped the centurion. He glanced at Simplicius and commanded, "Strip him."

Caesarion straightened, his face heating. "I am an Alexandrian of good family! You may not treat me like a slave! I demand to see your superior!"

"Oh, you *demand*, do you, Greekling?" snarled the centurion. He nodded to Simplicius, who, rather hesitantly, took hold of Caesarion's cloak and hauled it off.

Caesarion wrapped his arms protectively around his tunic, quivering with outrage. Nakedness was not the issue: like all Greek boys, he had exercised naked in the gymnasium. But to be stripped, by soldiers, so that he could suffer beating or the-gods-knew-what at their hands—it was inconceivable! "Yes, I demand!" he exclaimed furiously. "What else can I do, when my interrogator violates imperial policy? Aristodemos stood in Coptos marketplace and swore, in the hearing of half the city, that he would not endure the loss of his partnership to an Egyptian. Send to Coptos, if you don't believe me! If you accept his bare accusation over our evidence, you dishonor the Roman name and you mock the policy of the emperor!" He glanced imperiously at the scribe. "Have you written this down, man? And will you show it to this oaf's superiors?"

"May the gods destroy me!" The centurion pulled out his vinewood truncheon and slapped it against his palm. "Oaf, is it? You're a proud boy, and I ought to beat some of that arrogance out of you. —Hold him."

Simplicius seized Caesarion's arms and wrestled them behind his back. Caesarion struggled, hurt the wrist, was forced, panting, to his knees. He glared up at the centurion. He was far too angry to be afraid. "You *dare*!" he gasped, in outraged incredulity.

The centurion prodded him in the chest with the end of the truncheon. "Very proud, aren't you, for a mongrel and an epileptic bastard?"

Caesarion caught his breath, aware of sudden shock of hurt even through the anger. Ani had told this unspeakable man about the disease—recounted all of Caesarion's humiliation and suffering during his own interrogation, in an effort to shift blame from himself.

Maybe it hadn't been Ani. Maybe it had been Ezana and

Apollonios. They would have been interrogated as well, and he would expect such behavior from *them*.

"Should we spin a wheel in front of you?" jeered the centurion.

It was a test for the sacred disease, often performed on slaves before a sale. Caesarion had never been bothered by spinning wheels, but, in his weakened state, *thinking* about having a seizure was enough to bring one on. He caught the first scent of carrion, and the dread suddenly swallowed him whole. "O Apollo!" he begged frantically. "No!"

"What . . ." the centurion began—but the rest of his words were lost.

The criminal stopped breathing. His face was pale, covered with sweat, but calm. The asp sat coiled on his chest, its black scales gleaming in the light. Mother inspected it with a twisted smile on her face, her eyes fearfully bright. "That doesn't look painful," she observed. She trailed the edge of her purple cloak across the coiled snake, and it mantled, lifting its body so that it echoed the serpent on her crown.

The doctor frowned at him and relaxed the ligature. Caesarion watched the red rivulet flow down the inside of his arm from the puncture just above the elbow. It twisted like a snake. "So we release the poison," said the doctor, with satisfaction. He wiped the bloody lancet on a rag.

Rhodopis smiled at him, stretched out on top of the silk coverlet. Her body seemed to glow in the summer heat. "I don't think you're full of poison," she told him.

An anemone folded its red petals around a snail. Waves lapped against the quay.

Mother's flagship, the *Antonias*, was sailing into the Great Harbor, her purple sails shining against the blue sea. Distant on the air came the wailing of the mourners, and the air smelled of smoke, incense, and cremated flesh.

He was kneeling, half naked, on the muddy floor of a tent. His left wrist hurt. A thin old man in a red tunic was examining the livid, scabbed-over wound in his side. Others were standing around him, staring with horror and disgust. He bowed his head, trembling with humiliation and weakness, and reached for the remedy.

It wasn't there. His fingers fumbled blindly for it against his bare skin. The centurion straightened and prodded him in the shoulder. "Finished?" he asked.

Caesarion realized that they'd unpinned his tunic, pulled it down around his waist, taken the remedy away. Had they done anything else?

He thought not. Not much time seemed to have passed. It had been only a small seizure. "Please give me the herbs back," he asked, his voice shaking with shame and exhaustion. "They're for the disease. They help."

"Didn't even need a wheel," remarked the centurion. "*Very* proud, you are, for someone so sick. The thing I don't understand," a poke of the vinestaff, "is what a proud boy like you is doing working for an upstart peasant. The rest of what you say might be true and you have, you insist, evidence— but I just don't see a young man with such a high opinion of himself agreeing to write letters for an illiterate farmer. The thing *I* would have expected you to do in a strange city would be to attach yourself to a gentleman of your own class. There must be some, even in Berenike. —Well?"

Caesarion looked away. His left wrist hurt savagely, and he could feel a warm dampness on the bandage. His head was swimming; it was even harder than usual to distinguish the world present from the fragments of the seizure. "Ani saved my life," he said faintly. "I owed him a debt."

"Go on."

"When I escaped . . . When I left the king's camp, I was wounded. I had no water. I walked as far as the caravan trail, but it was very hot. I . . . had a seizure. Several. I couldn't go on. Ani found me lying unconscious in the road and saved my life. He gave me water and he paid for people to look after me. I tried to give him my tunic pin, which was the only valuable I had, but he wouldn't take it. He said I would need the money. When he asked me to write letters for him, I had to agree. I had no other way to repay him—and it would bring me home. I was ill on the journey, and he looked after me: I am more deeply in his debt now than I was before. And . . . he is a good man. He helped me when he didn't expect anything in return. I've never met anyone like that before. I trusted him because I had no choice, but he didn't fail me, not once."

There was a long silence. Then the centurion nodded at Simplicius.

The tessararius gave Caesarion the little bag of herbs. He clutched it hard, breathed the warm, familiar scent. He did not try to get up. Instead he inspected his bandaged wrist. A splash of red had blossomed on the white linen. When had that happened? He sank back on his heels, shuddering, and cradled his arm against his bare chest.

"Let me see the documents," the centurion ordered the clerk.

Caesarion remained on the floor, breathing in the remedy and hugging his wrist while the centurion thumbed through the cargo manifests, contracts, and tax receipts. His head hurt. The resolution and resources which had brought him this far had all run out. He wanted only to lie down.

"So," said the centurion at last, "tell me about this Aristodemos. I take it he used to be the partner of this fellow Kleon?"

Caesarion listlessly detailed the arrangements, explained the Greek financial terms in the documents. The old man listened, asked questions. At last he turned to his scribe. "Run over to the general's tent," he said. "If he's still up, ask him if he'll see me. Tell him it's about a malicious charge brought by a Greek merchant against a rival, and I need to know how he wants to proceed."

Caesarion looked up, not daring to believe it. The centurion gave a snort of laughter. "Simplicius," he ordered, "give the young man a cup of wine. He looks like he could use it." He tossed the tunic pin over to the tessararius. "Do up his tunic for him, too. I don't think he'll be able to manage it himself."

Caesarion was just finishing the wine when the scribe came back, saying that the general was up and would see the centurion.

"Bring him along," the old man ordered Simplicius, and Caesarion was pulled to his feet, draped in his cloak, handed his hat, and marched out the door. The shock of the night air cleared his head a little. He hung the remedy around his neck and pulled the hat on straight as he walked. It was, he realized, looking at the stars, still before midnight.

They went up along the rows of tents to a main aisle, then right to a large pavilion—the general's quarters—in the center of the camp. They stood a moment waiting while the centurion was announced.

"Is your general still Cornelius Gallus?" he asked Simplicius. The extreme lassitude which had followed the seizure was beginning to wear off, and his mind was clear enough to let him worry.

"You know of him?"

"We heard enough of his victories," Caesarion replied, relieved. "And I'm familiar with his poetry."

The old centurion looked around sharply, seeming alarmed—but at that moment one of the general's attendants summoned them in.

There was no air of virtuous simplicity about the pavilion of General Cornelius Gallus. The tent was divided into rooms by curtains worked with crimson and gold, and lamps on gilded stands burning scented oil revealed rich carpets and elegant tables and couches. The attendant showed them through an entranceway into an inner room where the general, resplendent in a long crimson cloak and the purple-striped tunic of his rank, sat examining papers at a table of ivory and polished citronwood.

Gallus looked up. He was a handsome man of middle age, fair-haired and clean-shaven. The centurion saluted him crisply and stood to attention.

"So," said Gallus pleasantly. "Centurion Hortalus. You said

it was about a malicious charge by a Greek merchant."

"Yes, sir," replied Hortalus. "Yesterday a Greek from Coptos, Aristodemos son of Patroklos delivered a sworn accusation to your staff in which he stated that an Alexandrian named Arion, a former Friend of the king, had set out from Coptos with the intention of stirring up anti-Roman sentiment during your expedition up the river. This Arion, he claimed, had fled Berenike after the king's death, and had brought with him a cargo of valuable incense, which he intended to sell to fund his activities. He was assisted, claimed Aristodemos, by an Egyptian, Ani son of Petesuchos, a known troublemaker from the Coptos region. Aristodemos said that he wished to prove his loyalty to the new government by informing us of this, and provided a description of the men and of the barge on which they were traveling. Inquiries about him confirmed that he is a wealthy merchant and landowner, an important man in Coptos, where he has at one time or another held most of the civic offices.

"The matter was placed in my hands, and I had men keeping a watch for the barge, which duly docked in Ptolemais this afternoon. I arrested Ani son of Petesuchos and the men with him, but Arion had, they told us, gone into town with Ani's wife and daughter before our troops were able to arrive. I sent some men into the town to look for them, and I set a watch on the boat."

"That's Ani, is it?" Gallus asked, surveying the prisoner doubtfully.

"No, sir: Arion. —May I finish? When I questioned Ani son of Petesuchos, he at once swore that Aristodemos had brought the charge out of malice, because he himself had supplanted Aristodemos in a partnership with a Red Sea trader named Kleon. He claimed the valuable cargo—which does indeed exist, and is on the barge—belongs to the trader in question, and that he is transporting it to Alexandria to sell on commission. Arion, he said, was merely a young Greek officer whom he had found half dead in the road near Berenike after our forces took the king's camp, who had agreed to write letters for him in exchange for his passage back to Alexandria. Ani persisted in this story under strict questioning, and the men with him confirmed it, very noisily, I will add, with many curses of Aristodemos and quite a few of Arion. I was determined to find Arion before I believed a word of it."

"It seems you found him."

"Indeed, sir. And I am now confident that the charge was indeed malicious. Arion has provided documents which demonstrate convincingly that the cargo belongs to Kleon, that Ani is acting on Kleon's behalf, and that the cargo has been legally imported and taxed. As for Arion, I cannot believe that he is an anti-Roman agitator. He's half Roman himself, and speaks fluent Latin."

"Does he, by Jupiter! I thought he looked as though he understood us."

"Too well, sir. He at once suggested that Aristodemos' accusation amounted to an attempt 'to pervert the majesty of Roman law.' "

"Did you?" Gallus asked Caesarion directly, frowning.

Caesarion bowed, though his head was still swimming. "General, he was attempting to abuse you to satisfy his personal grudge against Ani. The town of Coptos would have no doubt whatever that the charge was false—Ani and Aristode-

mos are both well known there, and after he lost the partnership Aristodemos swore openly that he would do something
to revenge himself. For you to believe the charge and punish
Ani would damage the respect the people of Coptos ought to
have for Rome. But I am far more concerned about Ani and
myself than I am about Aristodemos."

"Jupiter!" exclaimed Gallus, startled. "I don't think I've ever
heard such fluent Latin from a Greek. You're half Roman, and
were a Friend of the king?"

"Yes, lord. Sir, I beg you—may I sit down? I am not well."

"Give him a chair," ordered Gallus. Caesarion sank into it
gratefully, nursing his wrist.

"What's the matter with your hand?" asked the general.

"He cleared up that other matter," supplied the centurion
Hortalus, with an air of grim amusement, "the story about
vengeful prayers and blood sacrifices in the temple of the Lagids. This young fool tried to cut his hair in mourning for
Cleopatra, and accidentally caught his hand with the knife."

"True?" asked Gallus sharply.

Hortalus gave a snort of laughter. "I can't think of any other
reason why a proud young man of good family would have a
haircut that looks like it was done with a kitchen knife." He
reached out and removed Caesarion's hat.

"I take your point," said Gallus, smiling. "See that the story's
spread around, will you? The men don't like blood curses."
He leaned back in his chair, regarding Caesarion tolerantly.
"So—Arion. You don't care what happens to Aristodemos?"

"I can understand, lord," Caesarion said slowly, "that you
are extremely reluctant to do anything against a wealthy Greek
landowner on your first visit to the region, when the local

gentlemen are all extremely anxious about what a Roman administration will be like." That fact had been very clear to him
from the beginning.

There was a moment of silence. "There speaks a courtier,"
remarked Gallus thoughtfully. "So what, in your opinion,
should be done about Aristodemos—if I accept that he is guilty
and you are innocent?"

"Persuade him to withdraw the charge," Caesarion replied
at once. "Have him brought in, present him with the evidence—he was not aware that I am half Roman, and he undoubtedly expected you to accept what he said without an
investigation. When he sees that he was wrong, present him
with some way to say that it was an honest mistake. If he
withdraws, you need take no further action."

"A neat solution," said Gallus. "And for yourself and this
Ani?"

"Release us, the boat, and the cargo, and let us continue
on our way. I ask nothing more."

Gallus smiled. He gestured to one of his attendants, who
fetched him a cup. He sipped it. "Very forgiving," he remarked. "Yet Hortalus has been rough with you, hasn't he?
Aren't you angry?"

Caesarion felt his face heat. He could see clearly now that
the centurion had tried, quite deliberately, to break him—and
had succeeded. "You were told a lie of a sort no general could
ignore," he said wearily. "It had to be investigated. We would
have done exactly the same to a suspect accused of a similar
offense. I think"—he glanced warily at his white-haired interrogator—"I think he was skilled, and used no more force than
was necessary. I would be a fool to object to it."

"A practical attitude. You appear to be making a practical accommodation, too, to the fact of Roman rule. Yet you were willing to go into exile with the king, and you cut your hair in mourning for the queen. Are you *really* that practical, young man? Or have you been lying to us?"

"I was willing to live and die for the house of Lagos," he replied evenly, "but the house is fallen, and nothing I do now can ever bring it back. 'Stop playing the fool: when you've seen something die, call it dead.' "

"Gods and goddesses!" exclaimed Gallus in amazement. "You've read Catullus?"

"I love Catullus. What's wrong with that?"

"An Alexandrian who loves *Latin* poetry? Gods and goddesses, most of you people think we're all barbarians who don't even have an alphabet!"

"I like Latin poetry, and our own as well—as I know you do. Your love elegies are very Alexandrian, very witty and elegant."

"You think so?" cried Gallus in delight, and Caesarion suddenly saw the reason behind the centurion's look of alarm. Here was a man susceptible to flattery.

"Yes, I do," he said at once. "The one about Lycoris' treachery and the raven—it was worthy of Kallimachos himself."

In fact, he didn't dislike the poems, but the main reason he was familiar with them was that Gallus' love elegies were directed to a "Lycoris" who was actually an actress named Cytheris—a former mistress of Marcus Antonius. Antonius had occasionally read the verses at dinner parties, with comments on the lady's charms and jeers at Gallus' virility. His friends had found it very funny. Caesarion had no intention of saying so.

Gallus beamed at him. "I don't think I've *ever* met a Greek who was familiar with my poetry before I introduced him to it."

"It deserves to be better known," Caesarion said shamelessly. This was a royal road out of the clutches of the fearful Hortalus.

Gallus beamed again. "Have you dined this evening? Perhaps, if you're feeling well enough, we could have a late collation together, and a little wine. I've had little opportunity to discuss poetry for months, and the sweet Muses know that I adore them above all the immortals."

"I would be delighted," said Caesarion. "I, too, have been missing civilized conversation for a long time. And if you had any small work in progress, I would be enchanted if you would honor me with a reading."

"Sir!" said Hortalus, looking dismayed.

Gallus glanced at him impatiently. "What is it *now?*"

"The other prisoners—Ani son of Petesuchos and his men. What shall we do with them?"

"Release them. —No, wait, we have to make the Coptos landowner withdraw the charge. Well, bring in Aristodemos first thing tomorrow morning, show him the evidence, and tell him that he can be charged with *maiestas* unless he drops the charge. When he drops it, release the others, and release the boat and cargo. See that they're treated gently, as innocent men. —As it happens, Arion, I *do* have a little work in progress: a poem on Apollo's shrine at Gryneum, a little thing in dactylics, which I'm quite proud of . . ."

"I would love to hear it," lied Caesarion.

CHAPTER VIII

A ni did not sleep that night.

The Roman encampment lacked a proper prison, so he and the others had been tied up in the workshop area near the center of the camp. Their arms were secured behind their backs, and ropes around their necks fastened them to stakes driven into the ground; their legs were hobbled. They lay, all nine of them, on the hard ground, which seemed to find out every bruise they had—and they were all of them covered in bruises from their arrest and from their brutal interrogation, though Ani, as leader of the party, had suffered most. They were all desperately thirsty.

Worse than the physical discomfort, though, was the horror of the situation. Ani could not get out of his mind the screams of his children when the Romans came. Over and over through the night he saw Serapion sobbing frantically and beating with his small fists against a man's armored flank—saw him tossed aside to fall weeping on the quay—saw little Isisdoros held aloft, kicking madly, as an iron-clad barbarian, faceless under a beetlelike helmet, carried him off *Soteria* and dumped him shrieking on the muddy ground.

The Romans had ordered the men on the next boat to take the children and their nurse. The men had obeyed. He'd spoken to those neighbors before the troops arrived, and they had seemed decent-enough sorts—but a bit rough. Charcoal vendors, he thought they'd said, three brothers and a cousin. What would they do with children? What would happen when Tiathres and Melanthe got back? Would the men give Tiathres the little boys—or would they keep them to sell as slaves?

O gods, O dear Lady Isis, no. Not Serapion and little 'Dorion, no, please, Lady Isis: I'll give you anything, but please, keep my little boys safe!

And what about Tiathres and Melanthe? Would the Roman soldiers waiting at the boat respect them? It did not seem likely that they would. They were pretty women, both of them, and the Romans would believe them to be the wife and daughter of an enemy. Ani squeezed his eyes shut, trying to shut out the tormenting images of rape. The soldiers would not be allowed to do that, he told himself, not in a town which was scheduled to swear its loyalty next day. It would generate ill-feeling which the general must be eager to avoid. The soldiers would leave Tiathres and Melanthe alone. As for the charcoal vendors, they'd seemed decent men. Surely they would give the children back to their mother? Probably they'd be relieved to get rid of them! The nurse had been completely hysterical, and would have been no help at all.

But what would the women and children do then, lost in a strange city with no way to get home?

He told himself that perhaps the Romans would investigate his account of himself, and decide that he was innocent—but he could not convince himself. The Romans had a sworn accusation from Aristodemos, that respectable and important Greek, and they'd barely even *understood* his own story. That brutal old centurion spoke fairly good Greek, but it was not his native language, and he had plainly found the local accent difficult to follow. Ani had tried to force himself to speak slowly and clearly, but it hadn't been easy, and when everyone else began shouting and talking at the same time—which had happened a lot—the centurion had ordered them all to be silent, and given Ani no more opportunity to explain. He had wanted to speak to Arion, and Arion . . .

. . . was a hotheaded, passionate youth. He might try to fight arrest, or run away and get himself killed with his version of events untold. Or he might denounce Rome with the wild defiance he had used in Berenike, and convince the foul old interrogator that he was, indeed, a ferociously anti-Roman agitator, and that they were all guilty and ought to die.

Ani bit his lip, aching with shame. The others had all been cursing Arion. This was Arion's fault as much as Aristodemos', they said. Arion was bad luck, probably guilty of something unspeakable, and undoubtedly an enemy of the gods. Perhaps they were right.

Only, he *liked* Arion—felt that underneath the arrogance and wariness were reserves of loyalty and affection that no one had ever tapped. Certainly the boy was brave and intelligent, articulate, and well educated. And—this was the thing that pinched his heart—he couldn't help feeling that if Arion were killed it wouldn't be Arion's fault, but his own. If Apollonios and Ezana—and Pasis, Mys, Harmias, Pamonthes, Achoapis, and Petosiris; his own people—if they died, it would be because of him. If Serapion and Isisdoros were sold into slavery, and Tiathres and Melanthe were raped and left to beg in the marketplace, it would be because of him. He had indulged in an ambitious and vainglorious attempt to set himself up as a gentleman, had fatally underestimated the strength of his opposition, and had lost not just the enterprise, but himself and everyone around him.

Why had he done it? He'd had a very good life—prosperous farm and business, loving wife, fine, healthy, intelligent children. He was about to lose it all because of—what? A boy's dream of seeing the world, and a man's resentment of the conceited fool who'd cheated him?

Not worth it, not worth it—O gods, no. He rolled from his stomach to one side then the other, and finally lay still, pressing his face against the earth and praying to the gods to spare his family.

The night passed very slowly, but eventually the world turned gray. Trumpets brayed from the gates of the camp. A horse neighed loudly nearby. Light reshaped the world, and men arrived in the workshop next to their makeshift prison and began to repair a torn banner. Presently, one of the soldiers who'd arrested them came up, with a small group of others. They untied the prisoners' hands, gave them water to drink, and led them off to a latrine in groups of two.

"That Aristodemos come," Ani's guard informed him, when it was his own turn to piss.

"What, now?" Ani asked, in dread. "Here?"

"Here," agreed the guard—but he pointed south, toward the camp entrance. "Talk to Hortalus." He grinned. "You friend Arion here."

"In the camp?" Ani asked, relieved that at least Arion had not been killed trying to escape. "Why isn't he with us?"

"With general," the guard replied.

He did not understand that, but when he tried to inquire, the guard didn't understand his questions. The fellow patted him on the shoulder and brought him back to the others.

They were not tied up again, and after a little while another soldier appeared carrying a pot of barley gruel and some bowls: it seemed that the prisoners were to have breakfast.

They were in the middle of this unappetizing meal when there was a shriek of "Ani!" and Tiathres came hurtling up out of the middle of the camp, closely followed by Melanthe. Behind them was yet another soldier.

Tiathres flung her arms around her husband where he sat on the ground, kissed him, kissed his black eye and swollen ear, and wept. Ani hugged her hard, careless of the bruises, immensely comforted by the warmth of her body against his, but at the same time terrified to see her. "What are you doing here?" he asked.

Tiathres was sobbing too hard to answer. Melanthe was the one who replied. "They told us we could come in the morning, Papa," she said, hugging him in one of the spaces Tiathres had left vacant. "The tess . . . tessa-ra-rius Gaius Simplicius said we could ask for him, and he'd show us where you were. Oh, Papa, they've beaten you!"

"And the rest of us!" muttered Apollonios jealously.

Ani impatiently waved one hand at him for silence. "You're not hurt? I thank the gods! What happened to Serapion and Isisdoros?"

They were fine, it seemed, with the nurse and the charcoal vendors. The men had been kind, very kind; they'd looked after the little boys, they'd let Tiathres and Melanthe sleep on their barge, and they'd provided food and a promise of shelter until Ani's case was settled.

"And what happened to Arion?" Ani asked, weak with relief.

"Isn't he here?" asked Tiathres, lifting her head from her husband's shoulder and looking around.

"O Kastor and Polydeukes!" moaned Apollonios. "Save us! He's escaped: they'll kill us for certain."

"He didn't; I'm sure he didn't," Melanthe said hotly. "He went with them willingly so that he could prove we were innocent. He made them take all the documents from *Soteria*. He was going to tell them all about Aristodemos. He can speak Latin."

"What?" Ani asked in astonishment.

"His father was a Roman," Melanthe informed him. "He started talking Latin the moment the soldiers came up to us, and they were so pleased that he knew their own language that they listened to everything he had to say." She said this with a slightly defiant air, as though it were an argument she had employed many times already, perhaps to convince the charcoal vendors that it was safe to help, perhaps simply to confort Tiathres and herself. Ani stared at her in confusion.

"*Arion's* father was a . . ." he began.

"Ani son of Petesuchos!" shouted a harsh voice.

Ani's body remembered that voice before his mind did, and

jerked in fear. The evil old centurion had come upon them while they were talking, and was now standing over him. The old man was very grand and severe this morning, in a polished breastplate covered in silver medallions, his wiry arms adorned with gold armbands. His scowl was exactly the same.

"Your accuser has withdrawn all charges," he announced shortly. "You and your men are free to go." He gestured sharply, and a clerk came up from behind him and offered Ani a stack of papyrus. "Here are the documents for your cargo."

Ani let go of Tiathres, staggered to his feet. His head was spinning, and he could not take in what had just been said. *Your accuser has withdrawn all charges?*

The clerk frowned. "Here are the customs documents for your vessel," he said pointedly, thrusting the sheaf of papyri at him. Ani took them numbly. "Here are the legal papers giving you authority to act for your partner Kleon," another set, "and here is a letter of discharge from your arrest, and a note explaining the circumstances of your detention which you may show to the authorities if you are questioned again."

Ani looked down at the last papyrus. It was written in a language and alphabet he did not know. Latin. Discharge, from the Roman authorities. Free to go. Lady Isis, sweet, merciful goddess! So quickly, so . . . simply?

Why would Aristodemos withdraw the charges?

Ani could answer that: because Arion, who spoke Latin, had managed to convince the Romans that those charges were false and malicious.

"Simplicius," the centurion said, and the soldier who'd arrived with Tiathres snapped to attention. The centurion gave him an order in Latin, and the soldier saluted.

"Tessararius Simplicius will escort you back to your vessel," declared the centurion, "and he will dismiss our sentries. I congratulate you upon your innocénce." He turned and began to walk off.

Ani closed his gaping mouth, then managed to open it again and stammer, "L-Lord?"

The centurion stopped and turned around again. "What?"

"The young man Arion, who was accused with me . . . Is he free, too?"

The old man's face darkened. "He's with the general." He began to walk back toward his erstwhile prisoners. "What do you know about that boy? Is he honest?"

"I think he is," said Ani, startled and alarmed, taking a step back. "I don't know much about his family, but he's been honest with me."

"He talks too fast and too prettily to be honest," said the centurion darkly. "And he lies like a Greek, but in good Latin. And he's diseased. Why did you bring that boy here?"

"I'll be happy to take him away," Ani replied faintly.

The centurion glared at him for a long moment, then shook his head angrily. "The general wants him now." He turned on his heel and stamped away again.

"Hortalus no like poetry," said the Roman called Simplicius. He seemed to think it was funny. "No like clever Greeks. Come. We go boat." He tapped Ani's arm and pointed in the direction they should go. Ani blindly started off in the direction indicated.

When Simplicius showed the bedraggled party to the camp gates, Ani expected the guards to refuse them passage. When they were through the gates and making their way back to the docks, he kept expecting a troop of armed men to quick-march after them and haul them back. When they finally arrived at the quayside, he expected to find no boat.

Soteria was there, just as he had left her. Simplicius and the sentries exchanged a few cheerful words, slapped each other on the back, waved to the Egyptians, and marched off back to their camp, leaving them alone and free on the docks. The charcoal vendors, who'd waited for the Romans to leave before emerging from their own boat, came running over to ask what had happened. Serapion and Isisdoros and the nurse came with them, the woman shrieking with relief. Serapion flung himself onto his father, locked his small arms around Ani's neck, and sobbed against his shoulder.

Only then did Ani find himself able to believe that he was free. He sat down on the quay, shaking; nearly dropped the papers in the Nile; kissed his sons, and burst into tears.

IT WASN'T UNTIL after noon that Ani felt able even to try to make sense of his release. It was necessary first to wash, to rest, to eat, to sort through the boat's cargo and be certain that nothing was missing, to thank the charcoal vendors, to comfort his family and his men. From the center of Ptolemais, far up the hill, came the occasional sound of a crowd cheering, but there was no hint of any disturbances. The crew of one of the other barges—not the charcoal vendors, who had seen more of Romans than they wanted—ventured up the hill to see what was happening.

About the middle of the afternoon the barge crew came back to say that the town of Ptolemais Hermiou had officially accepted Roman authority and sworn its loyalty to the emperor. The townsfolk had acclaimed the general's proclamation of imperial clemency to the province of Egypt, and cheered his announcement of a gift to the town's royal temple to pay for an altar to Julius Caesar.

"That young man who was with you was standing behind the general," a bargee informed Ani. "He whispered in the general's ear. People were saying that he's the one who suggested the altar to Caesar. They say that he's the one who polluted Queen Cleopatra's altar, and that he suggested a new altar so as to make amends. Caesar was the queen's first husband, and she erected a temple to him in her own city, so she should be pleased with it."

"Arion polluted the queen's altar?" asked Ani helplessly. It didn't seem very likely, but neither did the idea of Arion whispering suggestions to a general.

"Hadn't you heard? Apparently he cut his hair in honor of the queen, and accidentally cut his hand and polluted her altar with blood."

"I hadn't heard," Ani said. He shot Melanthe a look of mystification, and noticed that his daughter was looking bewildered.

"He didn't accidentally cut his hand," Melanthe told him, in a whisper, when the barge crew had gone and he was able to talk to her privately. "He tried to kill himself. It was horrible. The priest told him that the queen was dead, and he went over to the altar and cut his hair in mourning, and then he told her statue that he was sorry for failing her, and tried . . . tried to cut his own hand off. He didn't even seem to feel it. There was blood everywhere. The priest had to knock him down to stop him." She paused, then went on. "But I suppose it's much better to say that he just cut himself accidentally. Nobody's going to worry about that. The priest's wife was very worried about what the Romans would think of it otherwise. They were very kind people, Papa, that priest and his wife. I'm glad Arion persuaded the general to give money to the temple."

"Arion speaks Latin?" Ani asked again, still unable to believe it. "He told you his father was a Roman?"

Melanthe nodded solemnly. "He never told you?"

"No." He remembered, though, the way Arion had replied to the centurion in Berenike—declaring that Caesar had thought highly of the queen, and had erected a statue to her in his ancestral temple in Rome. That, he now realized, had been a *Roman* response to criticism of the queen, not mere Greek defiance.

"I think probably the queen interceded for him," said Melanthe soberly. "She gave him a place at court even though he's a bastard, because her own children are half Roman. I think that must be why he was so upset when he heard that she was dead. She was his benefactress, and she sent him to protect her son Caesarion—only, Caesarion's dead and so is she—and he thinks he's failed everybody and will never have another chance."

It was, Ani thought, perceptive and very probably true. He wondered if Arion had had some wild scheme to rescue the queen when he reached Alexandria. It seemed likely.

He could believe that when the boy had learned he was already too late, he'd tried to pour out his life at the queen's feet. He found it far more difficult to imagine Arion standing behind a Roman general and whispering in his ear.

Was he there of his own free will? He'd been arrested on a charge that had been withdrawn, so presumably he was free to go, and the barge crew had the impression that he was high in the general's favor. So, come to think of it, did that foul bugger Hortalus: that had been why he was so angry. But . . . *was* Arion there freely? Perhaps the general was a lover of boys and had taken a fancy to him. Perhaps Arion was trying desperately to get away without offending the man. Or perhaps the general still suspected him, and he was, despite appearances, a prisoner.

The way to find out would be to go to the Romans and ask, but the thought of doing so made Ani cold all over. The centurion had beaten him with that vine stick—over the back and shoulders when Ani insisted that Aristodemos was lying; on the side of the head when he tried to speak after an order to be silent. The centurion had shouted at him and kicked him and done everything he could to force him to admit that he was guilty. The thought of meeting the man again, of asking his *help*, made his stomach curl up with dread. He would wait for a while, and see whether Arion showed up.

The afternoon wore on. When it was almost time for the evening meal, Apollonios came over and suggested that they leave Ptolemais while there was still light, and put a few miles between themselves and the Roman army.

"We'll wait for Arion," Ani told him at once.

Apollonios scowled. Ani was aware that Kleon's man had been sent primarily to keep an eye on the cargo, and that as a Greek he disliked taking orders from an Egyptian. Ani had tried, hitherto, to avoid giving any cause for offense.

"Arion's with this general," Apollonios protested. "From the sound of things, well in with this general, and we're well rid of him. He always was more trouble than . . ."

"Silence!" Ani hissed, suddenly very angry. "Do you really think we'd be standing here free if it wasn't for Arion? Aristodemos was always going to lie; it's just a miracle of the gods that Arion was able to prove he was doing it. We'll wait for Arion. If he isn't back here by tomorrow morning, I'll go to the Roman camp and find out whether he's planning to come with us or not. We will not simply sail off and abandon him."

Apollonios scowled more fiercely, and went off to complain to Ezana. Ani cursed himself as a fool for committing himself.

They ate supper. Evening faded into dusk. Ani sat down at *Soteria*'s stern, watching the path which led along the riverbank up to the Roman camp, trying to accustom himself to the idea of walking up it again in the morning.

As the first stars flowered in the dark blue of the sky, a light appeared on the track, startling gold in the soft air.

Ani got to his feet, watching it draw nearer, hardly daring to breathe. Soon he could make out that there were two people coming down to the docks: a drably dressed man carrying a torch and a basket, and a man in a short orange cloak and wide-brimmed hat walking in front.

"I praise Isis," Ani whispered, and rested his head on his hands.

Arion speeded up when he saw Ani waiting for him. "Ani, good health!" he called breathlessly as he reached the boat. The light from the torch fell on his face as he tilted his head back, and showed the look of gladness and relief. Ani jumped off the boat. He wanted to hug the boy, but somehow this was something he could not quite dare, and he contented himself with seizing Arion's hands in both his own and squeezing them hard.

"Careful!" exclaimed Arion, extracting his hands quickly. The left wrist was heavily bandaged. "Ani, what happened to you?"

"You know," Ani told him. "By the immortal gods, boy, I thought we were all going to die. I couldn't believe it when Melanthe told me you spoke Latin, that you could talk to them. Are you all right?"

Everyone else in the party was on the quay as well now, staring at the returned wanderer with relief—or, in the case of Apollonios, resentment. Melanthe was beaming, and her eyes shone; Serapion jumped up and down with joy—though there was something about Arion which forestalled an embrace, even from the children. Tiathres emerged from the cabin last, carrying a lamp.

"I'm fine," said Arion. He looked, in fact, tired but well, his face flushed and his eyes bright with pleasure. He was wearing a new tunic, Ani realized in surprise—a good one, bleached linen bordered with a pattern in blue, undoubtedly not cheap. "I need to write a letter to the general. Can someone get me my pen-case and a sheet of papyrus?"

Melanthe darted back onto the boat and fetched them. Arion got the man with the torch to lift the basket, braced the sheet of papyrus against the wickerwork, and wrote a short note. It was not Greek, Ani saw, watching the confident strokes of the pen. Arion could not only speak Latin, but write it. He blew on the ink to dry it, rolled the papyrus into a scroll, and handed it to the man with the torch. The torchbearer set down the basket, bowed and said something; Arion replied, and the torchbearer bowed again and departed.

"Has he forgotten his basket?" Tiathres asked nervously.

"No," said Arion, picking it up. "It's mine. My old tunic and some books. He's just a slave the general sent to light me back." He picked up the basket and climbed confidently onto *Soteria*.

"Are you really all right?" Melanthe asked him, following.

"Yes," said Arion, sitting down heavily in the middle of the stern deck, "though if I hear one more precious mini-epic I am going to have a fatal seizure and die. Dionysos, I thought I'd never get away!" He took off his hat and tossed it into the cabin. His hair had been cut down to an even quarter-inch of dark fur. There were scars on the back of his head which had been hidden before—narrow parallel bars, too regular to be accidental. "He offered me a job. Zeus, he didn't so much offer as insist! I told him I had the disease, and he said it didn't matter. I told him my family in Alexandria were very worried about me, and he told me to write them a letter. In the end, he accepted that I had to go and see how they were . . ."

"I thought you said they were dead?" interrupted Ani in bemusement.

"I *lied*. To him, not to you. I've been lying like a lawyer and flattering like a whore. I suppose it's too dark for us to leave now?"

"Who are you talking about?" Ani asked weakly. "Who offered you this job?"

"Gallus," Arion said, rolling his eyes.

"Gallus?"

"The general," Arion expanded. "Gaius Cornelius Gallus.

Soon to be governor of Egypt, if you believe him, and there's no reason not to. He's got the qualifications—military achievements, fluent Greek, *no* senatorial rank to feed private ambitions, and the emperor's already shown his intention by appointing the man to do a tour of the province and receive the oaths and petitions of the people. I don't think he's the man for the job—though don't for life's sake, repeat that."

"He's going to be governor of Egypt and he offered you a job?" Ani echoed, in consternation.

"Mm. He has two secretaries already, one for Latin letters, one for Greek, but neither of them can read the other's language, neither of them speaks a word of Demotic, and neither of them knows much about poetry. They both hated me. If I'd taken the job, I would have had to hire a wine-taster."

"What's poetry got to do with it? Isis, I hope you don't mean he's in love with you!"

Arion laughed, ran his hands over his cropped scalp. "Gallus writes poetry. Four books of love elegies—to a *woman*, Ani, don't worry, to a blowsy actress!—and a miscellaneous assortment of mini-epics. Not bad, actually, though not as good as he thinks they are. I told him they were wonderful, elegant, delicate, so charming, the best things ever written in Latin . . . Apparently I'm the first Greek to have read his works before I met him, but I doubt very much that I'll be the last. In love with me? No, but oh, how deeply in love he is with praise! Not good, not good at all, not in this country. Attend to flattery, and you allow into your heart maggots that will eat you alive. Flatterers always want something. I did—us out of here—and I got it, and now I want to get away."

"Are you really all right?" asked Melanthe, gazing at him steadily.

"I'm tired," he told her, "and I've had too much to drink—celebration dinner with General Gallus—*io triumphe!*—another town surrendered to the province, a toast to the genius of Caesar! and another to General Gallus, conquerer of Cyrenaica, pacifier of Paraetonium! What could I do but drink? If I'd stayed sober, my heart would break for the loss of my country." He caught several sharp breaths, and added, more quietly, "And my wrist hurts. I didn't dare change the bandage, in case someone realized that I was lying about how I hurt it. I put a fresh one on top."

"I'll get some brine to clean it," Melanthe said at once, "and some myrrh."

Arion nodded, wearily now. "We need to get away from here," he said, in a low voice. "As soon as we can. One more lie, and I may start telling the truth out of desperation."

"We'll leave at first light," Ani promised him. "What was the letter you wrote?"

He dismissed it with an airy wave. "Thanks for his kindness; thanks for the books, gush, gush. They're his mini-epics, mostly, and some eclogues by a friend of his. The eclogues are extremely good."

"Boy—Arion . . ."

The cropped head lifted, the proud dark eyes met his own.

"Thank you very much for what you did," Ani said with deep feeling. "You saved all our lives."

Arion's cheeks flushed again, and he looked down. For the first time since Ani had met him, he seemed shy. "I saved my own life, too," he said, in a whisper, "but it is your lives that please me."

GENERAL GALLUS DID not send anyone to retrieve them before dawn, and at first light *Soteria* pulled up her mooring stakes and stole quietly away down the broad current of the Nile. Then ran down the river for another nine days without a single incident to cause them a moment's anxiety.

The flood was over now, and everywhere people were clearing ditches and preparing fields for the plow. The only signs of the Roman conquest of Egypt were the notices pinned up in marketplaces, and the occasional new altar to Caesar erected in a place of civic worship. There were, perhaps, fewer traders on the river than there might normally have been, but there were plenty of boats plying up and down, moving seed and fodder, charcoal and straw.

There was no sign of Aristodemos, which did give Ani moments of doubt. On the one hand it seemed unlikely that, after such a disastrous failure, the landowner would try again to stop them; on the other hand, Ani had never expected any bold moves from him in the first place. Aristodemos had not wanted to risk going to Alexandria while the war was on; he had feared to take a full caravan even to Berenike. Ani had never expected him to approach the Romans, despite the proclamation of clemency in Coptos marketplace. And yet, that was what he'd done. He must have set out from Coptos the day before Ani's party, and gone straight to the Roman army. True, he'd withdrawn the accusation as soon as he'd realized that it had failed, but Ani had no idea whether that failure had frightened him. He wished that he'd *seen* Aristodemos while they were in Ptolemais, that he had some idea of the man's state of mind. But Aristodemos had appeared neither to gloat nor to plead forgiveness, and Ani could only guess what he intended to do next.

Most of the time, though, he told himself that Aristodemos must have been so badly frightened that he'd turned around and gone home. He was enjoying the trip too much now to want to worry about him. Every day brought a new sight—a temple to an unfamiliar god, an antique tomb, the biggest crocodile he'd ever imagined, sunning itself on a bank—or a new and surprising piece of information to ponder and delight in.

Most of the information came from Arion, who was finally losing some of his wariness and gaining a willingness to talk. The fits seemed to have eased their pressure on him: he had not had a major seizure since the last one on the road to Coptos, and the staring fits now came only once every two or three days. His wrist was healing cleanly, his side no longer seemed to hurt him much, and he seemed far more cheerful and relaxed than he had been since Ani first met him.

Some of the cheerfulness could undoubtedly be accounted for by the complete reversal of the attitude of the crew. The "accursed epileptic" had saved them all; more than that, he had been offered a job by the next governor of Egypt, and he had chosen instead to stay with Ani. The men were suddenly convinced both that Arion's haughtiness was justified (a governor's secretary was *entitled* to be arrogant) and that his continued presence on the boat showed a noble and generous spirit. In the face of their gratitude and admiration he became far less cold and disdainful. He would smile, say "thank you" for small courtesies, laugh at jokes, even venture hesitant, sidelong pleasantries of his own. With Ani his attitude became one of real friendliness, and talking to him became a huge pleasure.

Most of the discussions began as practical instruction, aimed squarely at getting Ani accepted by the merchants of Alexandria, though they kept expanding into long, fascinating digressions.

"The thing to aim for is 'honest country landowner embarking on business,' " Arion decreed. "You're never going to pass for an educated gentleman." Ani had to agree: "honest country businessman" was going to be difficult enough. To begin with, there was a whole new way of standing and moving: don't pick your nose or your teeth or pull your lip; if you spit, do it out the door, not on the floor; if you're sitting on a chair, don't cross your legs or sit with your knees apart—tuck one foot under the chair instead, like that; don't fart or belch or scratch yourself in public; stand up straight; don't bend over at the waist to pick something up, bend at the knees instead . . . He realized as they progressed that Arion lived this advice, that he had never seen Arion in any position which was not poised and graceful, except in the aftermath of a seizure. It was this, he realized, almost as much as the voice, which left everyone Arion met convinced of his status as a gentleman, even though they knew nothing of his family and he told them less.

Ways of speaking mattered as well, though. Ani found himself being advised on how to adjust his accent, on words and constructions which would be considered irredeemably vulgar. Trying to imitate Arion was of only limited value. "You'd never pass for Alexandrian," Arion said ruefully. "You simply want to avoid sounding like the sort of peasant Alexandrians refuse to associate with." It wasn't easy.

The question of formal manners was, in many ways, the easiest thing to change. What to wear, how to drape a cloak, how to greet people and which hand to use for food (one finger for salt fish, two for fresh), were simple compared to remembering not to pick his teeth. Even the problem of How a Gentleman Treats His Slaves was solvable. Ani hated to sit doing nothing while others worked—he had always detested laziness and arrogance—but the crew forced him do just that as soon as they understood that he had to make a good impression on the Greeks if their venture was to succeed. "A gentleman wouldn't do that," they informed him, and eagerly strove to preserve a dignity which he had never before felt he owned.

He was not sure that he liked dignity. It was as restrictive and uncomfortable as the new way of draping a cloak. Arion's digressions were his compensation, his reward for putting up with all the rest. Arion knew so much! He had read philosophy and history; he had studied music and poetry; he had heard the great powers of the world debating everything from religion to trade routes. He had clearly had exceptional tutors, and he had traveled—there was a casual reference to Athens, and another to Ephesus. He could tell you what Aristotle said about sea anemones, explain why the king of Arabia had burned Cleopatra's ships, or quote Euripides by the yard.

Ani never felt ashamed of his peasant manners, but occasionally he winced at his own ignorance—his meager education in the bare scrapings of the alphabet and simple accounting;

the experience which had been confined almost entirely to flax-growing and linen-making in Coptos. Mostly, however, he was aware only of the glorious opportunity of having the book-learning of Alexandria at his side, obtainable every minute by a question.

The only subject Arion remained unwilling to discuss was himself. Such personal details as emerged were revealed incidentally, in fragments. One came out while Ani and Melanthe were asking him about Romans.

"Are they *all* called Gaius?" Melanthe asked.

Arion laughed. "No, though it often seems like that! All Roman citizens have at least two names: a personal name, like Gaius or Marcus or Titus—they only have about six to choose from—and a family name, like Valerius or Julius or Antonius. Most have a third name as well, but some don't."

"Like 'Caesar'?" suggested Melanthe.

"Exactly. The third name, the *cognomen*, can be the name of part of a clan—like the Julii Caesares—or it can distinguish two clans which have the same name—like Cornelius Gallus; his family are Cornelii from Cisalpine Gaul, not the great senatorial clan from Rome. Sometimes the cognomen can be a second personal name—non-Romans who are given the citizenship usually use their own name as a cognomen, and there are traditional cognomina which run in families. The name that counts among the Romans, though, is the family name. They're obsessed with family."

"Is that why they don't recognize marriages between Romans and foreigners?" Ani asked—then wondered if this was a sensitive question.

Arion, however, did not seem at all offended. "Partly. I

think the *real* reason for that, though, is property. They don't want Roman property in foreign hands. They have another law which says no Roman may make a will leaving any property to a foreigner."

"So you can't inherit anything from your own father?" Melanthe said—a still more sensitive question, and one which Ani at once suspected she'd ventured as a deliberate test. She was certainly watching the young man very intently.

Still Arion wasn't offended. "I did, though," he replied, grinning. "Despite all the laws in Rome, I did—and I wish I hadn't. I inherited the sacred disease from him. It just goes to show: blood's stronger than any amount of ink."

Melanthe wasn't sure whether to be amused or sympathetic. She laughed and exclaimed, "Oh no! He had it?"

"He did! Though nobody actually *told* me that until I was struck with it myself. Then my mother said, 'This came from your father!' I was astonished, because nobody had ever mentioned it to me before, though it turned out half the city knew. I still don't . . ." He stopped abruptly, with an air of alarm, as though he'd realized he was giving away more of himself than he'd intended.

"Didn't you know him?" Melanthe asked in surprise. "I thought he taught you Latin."

"He died when I was very young," Arion said, and went back to the topic of Romans generally.

Another fragment emerged when he was telling them about the Alexandrian library. Melanthe's jaw hung open when he informed them it contained over three hundred thousand books. "I wish I could see it!" she exclaimed longingly.

Arion smiled. "Well, you will very soon, won't you?"

"Are women allowed in?" she asked in surprise.

"Anyone's allowed in—unless they're noisy, or drunk, or take books off the racks without permission. I've seen plenty women there."

"The library in Coptos is only open to men," said Melanthe resentfully.

"There's a *library* in Coptos?" asked Arion in amusement.

"A small one," Melanthe admitted. "It's at the gymnasium."

"Oh, a *school* library," Arion said dismissively. "That's not the same thing at all. Obviously they wouldn't let you into that, but you're probably not missing much." He did not, however, go on to tell them more about the Library in Alexandria, but instead gazed at both Ani and Melanthe a moment curiously. "What do you do for books?" he asked. "Are *you* allowed to use the gymnasium library, Ani?"

Ani shook his head glumly. The Coptos gymnasium, like its counterparts throughout Egypt, was a center of Greek culture, and did not admit Egyptians. The native temples trained a few scribes, but ordinary Egyptians like himself had the choice of a private tutor or nothing. Most chose nothing. "I have never read a book," he admitted quietly. Then he added, defiantly, "I bought Melanthe a copy of the first book of the *Iliad* last year. She's been reading it with her tutor."

"I haven't got very far," Melanthe admitted, looking down in shame. "I don't understand it very well."

Arion hesitated a moment, then shrugged. "Homer isn't easy to begin with. His Greek is so different from the way we speak these days that it's almost another language. Everyone finds it difficult at first."

Melanthe looked up again and regarded him with bright

eyes. "A lot of people told Papa he was a fool to buy me a book at all. They say that there's no point in educating females."

Arion curled his lip in disdain. "What nonsense!" Then he laughed. "Zeus, if anyone had dared tell *Mother* that there was no point in educating females . . ." He broke off, laughing, and shook his head. "Dionysos!"

Melanthe beamed at him. "Did your mother used to go to the Library?"

"Frequently! She loved books. Once she . . ." He stopped abruptly, again with that air of alarm, and once more changed the subject.

Ani worried, often, about what Arion would do when they finally reached Alexandria. In Berenike the boy had invited the Romans to kill him; in Ptolemais he'd tried to do the job himself. He seemed happier now, but would that outlast the arrival? Wouldn't it crush him again to return to his own city, and learn all over that everything that had made it home was lost? He would not discuss his plans. It was clear, though, that he had little hope for himself.

Several times he considered suggesting that Arion accept some form of partnership with Kleon and himself; each time he held back, fearing a proud rejection. If Arion wanted a job, he had a prospective governor of Egypt waiting for him; he could do much better than a minor Coptos merchant. There was another thing, too, which caused him considerable unease: Melanthe. She liked listening to Arion. Ani couldn't blame her—what Arion had to say was fascinating, she was his own daughter, she had always felt the same urgent need as himself to question and understand. On the other hand, ever since

Ptolemais she'd regarded Arion worshipfully, as her family's deliverer (a humiliation in itself), and she was so pretty that he could not believe Arion was indifferent to it; indeed, it was noticeable that Arion was far more talkative and agreeable when Melanthe was present. Perhaps he had been advised that sexual congress would "exasperate" his condition, but Ani considered his own nature at eighteen, asked if that advice would have stopped *him*, and answered himself with a resounding *no*.

He could not reasonably order Melanthe not to listen to Arion when he was listening himself; certainly he couldn't give any such order on a boat the size of *Soteria*. Of course, a boat the size of *Soteria* provided no opportunities for privacy for any other purpose, either. But when they reached Alexandria . . . he could easily imagine Arion offering to show Melanthe the sights of the capital, and Melanthe eagerly agreeing, and . . . well, maybe it was a good thing that Arion was planning to disappear when they reached the city. Safer for Ani's peace of mind and Melanthe's happiness.

Only he didn't *want* Arion to disappear when they reached Alexandria. Apart from anything else, he'd be very useful in the business. Elegant Greek letters would probably be enough to persuade the gentlemen-merchants to grant Ani an interview; acceptable manners might get them to pay attention to his offers—but it would be much *more* impressive to call upon the merchants with Arion in tow. Better yet, stay on the boat and let Arion call upon the merchant. *I've come on behalf of my partner, a Coptos merchant . . .*

He itched to offer the boy a partnership—half my fortune and my daughter's hand in marriage. The thrill of pleasure that struck him at the thought of Arion as a son-in-law was disturbing—humiliating, really: he'd always sworn he was as good as any Greek, so why should the notion of having one in the family give him such pride? It did, that was all: when he imagined introducing people to *Arion son of Gaius, my son-in-law* and watching their faces change and their attitude become distinctly more respectful, it gave him a greedy thrill of delight. He felt, too—unhappily—that Melanthe would like the idea even more than he did. He feared, though, that Arion would regard it as an insult. Such a marriage couldn't even be legally binding: Greek citizens couldn't marry Egyptians. Arion, he felt increasingly, did not belong in the same world as himself. His presence there could only be fleeting, like a fish dropped on a mudbank that beats its way across the earth into its native element.

Only that native element had, according to Arion himself, become hostile, and the boy had made it very plain that he didn't *want* to work for General Gallus. So . . . he might, just, welcome another option. He seemed to regard Ani as a friend now, and a *partnership* wasn't the same thing as employment. A *partnership* with a Red Sea trader was respectable enough, surely? And the boy would be so *useful*. Arion could be dignified, and Ani could be practical . . . he ought, at least, to *ask*.

The valley broadened, and the river branched into the Arsinoite region, the drained lakeland and the rich towns of Oxyrhynchus, Arsinoe, and Karanis. They followed the main branch of the Nile, however, until the current slowed and, nine days after leaving Ptolemais, they reached the green flats of the Delta.

The first Romans they'd seen since Ptolemais were guarding

the customs post at the apex of the Delta, next to the town which was called Babylon, like the Mesopotamian city. The Lagid kings had had a fort there, since the town's position gave easy access to all the branches of the Nile, and it seemed the Romans were maintaining the arrangement. The guards made no trouble, however, after Arion explained the customs documents to them in Latin, and *Soteria* was allowed to continue on, onto the Canopic branch of the river and westward toward Alexandria.

Here the Nile was wide, slow, and full of boats. *Soteria* ran down it for another two days, past Terenuthis; past Naukratis, which had been the first Greek settlement in Egypt, and at last, on the evening of the second day from Babylon, found a mooring by the entrance to the Canopic canal which led from the Nile to Lake Mareotis and their destination.

Here at last Ani managed to dare the question which had been preying on his mind. The whole party was finishing supper on the foredeck. The stars were starting to come out, the lamps were lit, he had lashed out on a skin of wine, one of the Egyptians was playing snatches on a flute, and everyone was in a relaxed and holiday mood.

"So," he began carefully, addressing himself to Arion, "how long will it take us tomorrow?"

Arion leaned back, hooked an elbow over the railing, and grinned. He was wearing only the red tunic and a pair of sandals, and for once looked much like any young man. "We'll be docked by noon," he said. "The Canopic canal is worth seeing in itself, though, so you don't want to hurry. People have summer houses along it, big ones with gardens. Hermogenes has one with a lot of statues along a riverside terrace, animals dancing and playing musical instruments."

"I want to see it!" exclaimed Serapion. He'd said that frequently in the past few days.

"So you shall, child," replied Arion easily. "They're designed to be seen from the water."

Ani cleared his throat and tried again. "When we reach the city . . . I don't know what your plans are."

Arion stopped grinning and unhooked his arm. The rest of the party fell silent. Even the flute-player stopped his tune midnote.

"You're very welcome to stay on with us for a few days," Ani said hurriedly, feeling his face heat. "You're welcome to stay as long as we do, in fact. In fact . . . well, in fact, if you wanted you could leave with us, as well. I could . . . if you wanted some kind of partnership, we could arrange something. I would like that." He sensed rather than saw the stir from Apollonios, and added quickly, "In respect of my own investment, not Kleon's, obviously. You can think about it, anyway. If you're interested, we can talk more."

"Ani . . ." Arion began—then shook his head. His hand stole to the front of his tunic, and there was a glint as he wrapped the chain that held the remedy around a finger.

"You don't need to tell your family's grand friends," Ani went on—and despised himself for being so humble. "You can just say you've been offered a partnership by a Red Sea trader. That sound respectable enough, doesn't it?"

Arion shook his head again. "Ani, it isn't like that! I . . ." Again he stopped, but this time resumed, suddenly very earnest. "There's a . . . a question of an inheritance. A disputed inheritance. The man who has it won't want me around. He's . . .

rich and powerful, much more so than Aristodemos. I don't want to draw trouble to you." His eyes met Ani's, level and entirely sober. "You've been very kind to me. I don't want to repay you by bringing you this man's enmity. It would destroy you."

There was a terrifying certainty to the last words. Ani stared at the young Greek, trying to reason it through and see if it could possibly be justified. He had known that Arion's family were rich and powerful and had had a high position at court; Arion had said that they were dead; he himself had guessed there would be other claimants to the estate . . .

"This man's a relative?" he asked.

Arion's mouth twisted in bitter amusement. "Second cousin once removed."

And presumably legitimate. The second cousin had control of the estate and would not be at all happy to find the family bastard, last seen heading into exile, turning up in the city. What Arion had said, however, implied something more serious than mere social embarrassment. There must be money at stake. It could not be a legacy—a bastard could not legally inherit. It must be some property which had already been settled on Arion, a legal title which he feared he could not enforce.

So why *try* to enforce it? Why not just let it go?

Ani sighed: *he* had taken a stupid risk because he resented the way Aristodemos had cheated *him*, and he was older and far less proud. If Arion felt that he was being deprived of his birthright he *would* fight it, even if he thought it would kill him. "What are you risking?" he demanded. "What is this man likely to do if he finds you're back in the city?"

Arion hesitated. "Ani, believe me, you can't help, and you don't want to try."

"Being half Roman wouldn't help you?"

Arion shook his head quickly. "Being half the wrong Roman is no help at all."

Romans had fought on both sides during the war. In Ptolemais any sort of Roman had been acceptable, but in Alexandria they were, presumably, more choosy. "Your cousin's friendly with the Romans on the winning side, then?"

Another twisted smile. "Yes. Very much so. Ani, this isn't a trivial matter. This is dangerous. You don't want to know any more, you don't want to touch it. We will part in Alexandria, exactly as we agreed."

Melanthe made a noise of protest. "But what will *you* do?" she burst out angrily.

He glanced at her quickly, then looked away again. "I will go to some of my mother's friends and see if they're willing to help me."

"Help you fight?" Melanthe asked. "You don't have to fight this man, Arion! You don't *need* him, you can . . ."

"I'm not going to fight him." Arion interrupted. "I'm just going to ask some of my mother's friends to help me. Maybe one of them can suggest somewhere I can go, something I can do . . ."

"*Papa* suggested something you could do!" exclaimed Melanthe furiously. "Why are you too proud to do it? You think you're degrading yourself to work with dirty peasants like us? You despise us that much?"

"No."

The two of them were looking at each other now as though

no one else in the world existed. Melanthe's eyes, bright with tears, held an emotion which Ani had never seen in them before. Oh, sunbird! he thought, shocked. I didn't realize it had already gone that far. For a moment he hated Arion—and yet, Arion had done nothing except be himself. This was Ani's own fault. He had brought the boy into the family, encouraged him to talk. *He* had wanted the guest to stay. What had he expected Melanthe to feel? She was at the age when girls fall in love. Arion spoke not only to her mind, but to her blood.

"I don't want you hurt," Arion said abruptly. "I don't think anyone else has ever been kind to me without wanting something for it. I don't dare stay with you beyond tomorrow." He got to his feet. "I'm going for a walk."

He climbed off *Soteria* onto the bank, and strode off into the dusk.

"Well," said Apollonios, after a silence. "Seems we'll be rid of him in Alexandria after all."

Melanthe jumped up, sniffling, and ran into the cabin. Everyone else, even Ezana, glared at Apollonios, who muttered and fell silent. Tiathres glanced reproachfully at her husband, then got up and went after Melanthe.

Ani sighed, rested his chin on his hands, and wished that he had sent his daughter to play with her brothers every time he asked Arion a question.

He also wished that he had told Arion, *Never mind the danger: we'll help you.*

That was one thing he could not have done. Aristodemos had shown him that. Arion said his second cousin was richer and more powerful than Aristodemos, and everything about Arion himself suggested that it was true. It seemed very likely that the new pro-Roman heir to a great estate might resent the claims of a passionately royalist bastard cousin. It seemed very likely that the second cousin would try to undermine or destroy his adversary's support, and if that happened to include an Egyptian trader with a valuable and vulnerable cargo—it could easily be done. Another false accusation, trouble with the customs office, a party of hired thugs to loot the ship—a rich man who had the favor of a new government could do anything he liked. Ani ought to be grateful that Arion had explained the situation and would leave them voluntarily.

He just wished he didn't feel so certain that Arion was taking himself off to Hades—and that the prospect didn't hurt so much. He just wished that he had, after all, ordered Melanthe not to listen to Arion at all.

It was a very subdued party which started off on the final leg of the journey next morning. The somber mood was not lifted when, midmorning, they neared the riverside terrace of Hermogenes and found that the statues Arion had mentioned were in the process of being removed. Half the dancing animals were already gone, and there were Roman soldiers working on a lyre-playing leopard, levering it up to shift it into a waiting straw-filled crate.

"Why do they have to do that?" asked Serapion miserably.

"The man who owns them must have sold them," Ani replied. It was, he knew, a half-truth. In the current circumstances, it was very likely that the owner had been compelled to give up the statues by a Roman who admired them—or that he'd been executed. Clemency undoubtedly had limits.

There were, nonetheless, still many beautiful pleasure gardens flanking the Canopic canal, leading down from many beautiful houses, and Serapion soon cheered up again, and began rushing from one side of the boat to the other to see everything. There were statues and exotic trees, an aviary full of birds, an exquisitely landscaped mini-marsh, complete with flamingos and fish, a crocodile chained to a post by a foreleg in its own beautifully designed pond. Melanthe, however, who normally would have copied her little brother, stayed miserably in the cabin. Arion sat motionless at the prow, staring moodily at the river from under his wide-brimmed hat.

The canal ran at last into a wide, brackish lake, brilliantly blue in the sun, and in the distance could be seen a shining mass of white walls and red roofs, towers and domes and gardens, a green, cone-shaped hill rising against a blue sky, and a spark of pure gold from some unseen monument or statue erected to the gods. They had reached Alexandria at last.

CHAPTER IX

Caesarion watched Melanthe reading through the letters, his throat tight. Her thick black hair hung down, hiding her face, but he knew that she was still angry. Her small hands with their charming round nails moved the pages with sharp jerks, and her voice as she read over the words was a furious mutter. They were alone in the stern cabin. From behind the partition to the forecabin he could hear Serapion talking to his nurse, and outside on deck Ani was discussing the mooring with the crew.

He felt trampled inside, muddied and confused. When Ani had made his offer the previous evening, a part of him had astonished the rest by leaping up with a shout of "Yes!" Ludicrous idea—the last Lagid monarch working for a Coptos import-export business! Ridiculous! Insulting! Insane!

And yet he had never in his life been as happy as he had

been these last few days. He had wanted the journey to go on forever. He had saved *Soteria*, and everyone was grateful to him (except Apollonios, who could be ignored) and nobody was disappointed in him, and Melanthe had stopped pitying him, and looked at him with those marvelous dark eyes full of admiration and gratitude. The crew had despised him, but they'd changed—not out of fear of punishment, but because of something he had done. He had *earned* their respect. They had no idea that he was the queen's son, they knew he had the disease—yet they liked and admired him! Small, stupid, simple thing; ridiculous to worry about their opinion, anyway—but it delighted him to the core. And Melanthe—beautiful Melanthe, with her skin like dark honey and her wonderful eyes, who had inherited her father's intelligence and strength of will—Melanthe liked him, too. Or had.

It was obviously stupid to become infatuated with a cameldriver's daughter, to stand here writhing inside because she was angry with him. There had never been any possibility of a connection between them, quite apart from the fact that it would probably aggravate his condition if there were. Ani plainly adored his pretty daughter. He couldn't possibly injure a man he so much liked and respected by seducing the girl—even if she'd let him, which was by no means clear. Yes, she liked him—but she wasn't weak. She wouldn't disgrace herself and her family by parting with her virginity before her wedding night. He didn't even want her to—not if it would hurt her, which it would. And the idea of *marriage* was absurd. The law didn't even allow it—and anyway, he was in no situation to undertake such a commitment.

His mother probably would have had Melanthe flogged if

she'd discovered that he could even bring himself to contemplate such a thing without laughing aloud. He was glad she was gone, and couldn't.

He hauled his mind back, astonished at himself. And yet, Cleopatra *had* been cruel and arrogant sometimes. He thought again of Rhodopis. Rhodopis had been his first love, his childhood sweetheart. The queen had had no call to sell the girl in the public market! If she felt she had to get rid of her, she could have freed her and given her a dowry. He'd said so at the time, and the queen had replied, "If the palace slave-girls get the idea that your bed is a route to freedom, we'll be hauling them out of it every night."

He had gone down to the slave market himself, found the man who'd bought Rhodopis, and bought her back for twice the price. Then he'd freed her and provided the dowry himself, without telling his mother. It hadn't been easy: his allowance hadn't covered the cost, and he hadn't dared ask money from the chamberlain, who would have told the queen. He'd sold a racehorse to one of his companions, and given Rhodopis the dowry in cloak pins and rings.

Sixteen, he'd been, and officially a king, and yet he hadn't been able to buy the freedom of a girl he loved without resorting to subterfuge. He had never been given any real authority. He should officially have come of age at sixteen, and been enrolled in the ephebate, the corps of young citizens who were given military training. His mother had hired tutors to provide the training, but he had not been enrolled—not until the next year, after Actium, when the queen had wanted to reinforce the shaky loyalty of the populace by showing that she believed the dynasty would survive. Shrewd of her—but he'd known even at the time that she was signing his death warrant by it. There had been just a slim chance that Octavian would spare a child, even one named Caesar. There was no chance at all that he would spare a man by that name.

. . . and she hadn't taken him to Actium, which still rankled bitterly. He had been old enough to join the army for the campaign, he had expected to be given a military command—titular, of course, with some older, experienced man to do the real work, but an opportunity to watch and learn how it was done. Instead he had been left in Alexandria with his little brothers and sister, subject still to tutors and schoolwork. "Your condition," his mother had said—and yet, how many times had she told him that his *father's* condition had never stopped him from conquering all the available world?

He felt, with a sudden intense passion, that he had never been anything at all—the child of two divinities, but a cipher himself. Cleopatra had wanted a male Lagid as colleague; she had seen advantages in bearing a son to Julius Caesar. She had wanted, though, only a baby and obedient child. A grown man who could lead armies and think for himself—she'd never wanted that at all. *Arion* was more of an individual than Caesarion had ever been.

He found himself remembering, bitterly, the doctor who had wanted to cauterize his brain. He'd been fourteen, weakened by a year of drugs, purgings, and bleedings. The fellow had argued that drilling a hole in the top of the skull and heating the membranes of the brain with red hot irons would clear the head of phlegm and enlarge the ventricles of the brain, thus making further seizures impossible. Caesarion had heard similar promises before dozens of other torments, and had begged to be spared. Olympos, Cleopatra's own doctor, had, bless him, backed his plea with a declaration that the procedure carried a risk of death or permanent injury and was unlikely to produce any benefits. Cleopatra had considered . . . and finally refused permission. But she'd allowed the enthusiast to try the irons on the back of Caesarion's skull, behind the ears, to see if they produced any improvement.

Apollo and Asklepios, it had hurt! He had the scars still— they must be visible now, with his hair so short. He reached up and found one, a smooth indented bar of bare skin amid the cropped fur. He had begged his mother not to let the man touch him—begged her in tears—and she had told him that he was a king, and must be brave.

He should not be remembering such things about his mother now, so soon after her death. He should be mourning. Only . . . he could not help feeling glad that Melanthe, and Ani, would never meet her.

"What's this?" Melanthe asked sharply, breaking into his thoughts with a resentful glare.

He took the sheet of papyrus from her. "Sample reply to an inquiry about the incense," he told her.

Melanthe was going to be her father's scribe while the party was in the city. She could read and write tolerably well and had a clear, legible hand, though her spelling was erratic, her Greek far too colloquial, and she did not know the correct forms for business letters. Caesarion had already written all the letters Ani had asked for—the requests for an interview with each of Aristodemos' old suppliers. He had also drafted several other, supplemental letters, asking for an interview with alternative suppliers—the headings left blank, since he

didn't know any names. He had written out everything he
knew about Alexandria's harbor and trade regulations, its syn-
dicates and corporations—information he thought might be
helpful—and he had composed several careful specimen
responses for Melanthe to adapt if there was any need. There'd
been time for that on the voyage, and he'd discovered that he
very much wanted Ani's enterprise to succeed.

"And this one?" demanded Melanthe.

"Sample reply to a merchant offering tin."

She leafed through the remaining letters, set them down.
"That's all, then," she said forbiddingly.

"Melanthe, please!"

"What?"

"I've got to leave now. Don't be angry with me!"

She banged the sheaf of papyri down on the strongbox and
glared at him. "You expect me *not* to be angry, when you
think it's better to *die* than to go into partnership with my
father?"

"I don't . . ."

"My father is a good man! He got his money by hard work
and good ideas: does that make him so much worse than somebody who just *inherits* it? He's benefited everyone in our neighborhood: all the men earn extra from the flax, and the women
from the weaving. He has never cheated anybody, he honors
the gods and loves his family. How *dare* you despise him!"

"I don't!"

"You do! You despise all of us. You said we degrade ourselves like slaves because we help each other. And now you're
going to go off and get yourself *killed*, rather than work with
my father any longer! You expect me *not* to be angry?"

"Melanthe, I . . ."

"All that talk about how you don't want us hurt!" Melanthe rushed on, growing more angry with each word. "It was *lies*, all of it! There wouldn't be any danger at all if you just *avoided* this cousin of yours. He thinks you're a Roman prisoner, or dead, or gone off into exile. Even if he finds out you're still alive, if you're not bothering him—if you're not asking your mother's old friends to make trouble for him!—why would he bother you? There's only danger if *you* go and stir things up! And you don't *need* to stir things up; you could work with my father. But no, you're too proud! You expect me to say, 'Oh, that's all right, I understand that we're just dirt, go off and die with your own kind and my blessing'? I won't!"

"I don't think that!"

"Yes you do," she replied, glaring at him, her eyes full of tears. "You know you do."

"A little," he admitted. "Not as much as I used to. Melanthe, please, try to understand . . ."

"I don't!" she said flatly.

"I have a brother," he told her, surprising himself by the admission. "A half-brother, about the age of Serapion. I don't know where he is, or even if he's alive or dead."

The glare faded a little. "What do you mean?"

"I have to find out what happened to him. That means I have to talk to my mother's friends. That means I have to risk one of them going to my cousin—and *that* means I don't dare stay with you, in case it draws trouble here."

"This is the first time you've mentioned a brother," she pointed out suspiciously.

"O Zeus! I don't dare tell you about myself, Melanthe, I

don't *dare*; especially not here in Alexandria. I do have a brother, I swear it by Dionysos and all the immortals. His name's Ptolemy. He's six years old."

The rest of the glare died. "I'm sorry," she whispered, and wiped her eyes. "I'm sorry. I always seem to say horrible things to you." Her lip trembled. "It's just that I don't want you to go."

He took two steps forward, caught her elbows, kissed the face that raised itself to his own. He felt for a moment as though he were indeed a god, and that it was divine ichor, not blood, that ran within his veins. He kissed her again. Her arms lifted, locked round his shoulders, and her lips, clumsy and unpracticed, opened to his.

A door opened, and they both looked round to find Ani staring at them accusingly.

Caesarion let go of Melanthe and took a step back hastily. "I . . ." he began.

"You were just saying farewell," Ani told him firmly.

"Yes," agreed Caesarion, face hot.

"I wish you much joy," Melanthe told him, wiping her eyes. "And good luck, and be careful—please, be careful, and, and . . . let us know what happened, if you can."

"I'll try," he said, swallowing. "I wish you very much joy, Melanthion."

He reached down, fumbled up the basket that held his other tunic and the books, stumbled out onto the deck. It was early in the afternoon, and the lakeside harbor was quiet, boat crews and dockworkers alike resting during the heat of the day. The rest of the party on *Soteria* crowded around him, shook hands, wished him joy. Tiathres presented him with some bread and olives, wrapped in a linen handkerchief. Serapion ran out of the forecabin and hugged him. He rumpled the little boy's hair and wished him joy and health.

Ani cleared his throat. "I'll walk you as far as the dockyard gate," he announced.

The two of them started along the empty quayside in the hot sun.

"I'm sorry," Caesarion found himself saying. "About Melanthe."

Ani shot him a sideways look and tugged on his lower lip. "So am I."

"I didn't intend . . . I meant no disrespect, to her or to you."

"Was that true, what you were telling her?"

"You were listening?" Caesarion demanded indignantly.

"As I live, of course I was! You think I'm not going to keep an ear open when a young man is speaking privately to my daughter? Was that true—you have a little brother?"

Caesarion trudged on for several steps, not looking at him. He had, he realized, told Melanthe about Philadelphus because he'd known that she would accept him as a valid reason for leaving her. But Philadelphus was only part of his true motives. Another part was, undoubtedly, the pride of which Melanthe had accused him. A third part, though, was the truth about himself. If he were caught, the whole party could be killed for having harbored him, and that possibility had become intolerable. Better if they never knew.

"I do have a little brother," he answered Ani. "I wasn't lying. I want to help him, if I can."

"You've never trusted us at all," Ani said flatly. "Not even with things that are to your credit."

Caesarion met his eyes. "That's not true. I think I do trust you as much as I've ever trusted anyone in my life."

Ani stopped. "Lady Isis, boy, you must have had a miserable life! First you say that no one was ever kind to you without expecting something for it, and now you never trusted anyone!" He made an impatient gesture. "Sorry. You don't like to be called 'boy.' "

"Actually," Caesarion told him, "I don't mind it anymore." He tried to smile. "You know your offer—the partnership? I wish I could accept it." It was the shocking truth. He had a nasty suspicion that it was because he'd sunk to his natural level, but even that didn't affect the itch to accept, and to go on being happy.

Ani was looking at him with a curiously hurt expression. He reached out and touched Caesarion's upper arm. "Why don't you?"

The scent of carrion, and a sudden vast irrational horror. Caesarion grabbed the remedy, sat down at the side of the road.

"Isis!" exclaimed Ani, recognizing the signs. Caesarion was aware of him hurrying to get behind him, to catch him if he fell, and was comforted.

A choir was singing a hymn to Isis: "Hail, Queen of rivers and winds and the sea. Hail, Queen of war . . ." Cleopatra sat on a gilded throne, shaded with purple awnings, dressed as the goddess and wearing the serpent crown. Caesarion, on his own golden throne a step below, shifted in his stiff, jeweled cloak to watch her. Little Ptolemy Philadelphus, farther down

still, tried to take off his diadem and was stopped by his body-
guard. The crowds cooed at him.

The river flooded, red-brown with mud. The priests led a
white heifer to the altar for the thanksgiving sacrifice. The
head priest waited with the knife shining in his hand.

He was being violently sick. Everything stank, and it was
fearfully hot. "That will get rid of the poison," said the doctor,
with satisfaction.

The man lay on the table, facedown, his arms and legs
bound to it with thick ropes. They'd peeled his scalp off the
back of his head—it lay, inside out, above his ears—and cut
off the back of his skull. "You see here the ventricles of the
brain," said the doctor, prodding with a scalpel. The victim's
hand twitched, and Caesarion cried in horror, "He's still alive!"

He was sitting in the sun at the side of the road. Ani was
crouched behind him, supporting him, one hand holding the
remedy steady before his face. He groaned, leaned back into
the support, felt . . . safe.

"Over?" asked Ani softly.

Caesarion nodded. He leaned forward, found the remedy
again, breathed it. The scent was growing faint: he would have
to have a new one made up . . . if he survived the next few
days.

Ani let go of him and came and sat beside him. "I don't
think it's anything to do with phlegmatic humors," he declared.
"Or moisture. You have seizures when your spirits are disturbed—when you're distressed or in pain."

"So why doesn't everyone?" Caesarion asked him sourly.

Ani shrugged. "Well, then, you're naturally *inclined* to have
them, and you'd have some anyway, but you have more of

them when you're distressed, or hurt, or tired and hungry. If it was phlegmatic humors you would've been throwing fits all the time on the river, and would've had hardly any in the desert: instead it was the other way around. You can't argue with it, boy. It's obvious. I don't think you need to avoid women at all. I certainly wouldn't, if I were you." He hesitated, then went on. "*Who* is still alive? Please tell me. You say that every other seizure, and I've started imagining things."

"Oh." He had never told anyone that private nightmare—but there didn't seem to be any harm in informing Ani, if it was bothering him. "I don't know his name. He was a criminal—I think they said he'd murdered a woman. He had the sacred disease, like me. One of the doctors at the medical school of the Museum asked if they could cut him open, and my mother took me along to see it. She wanted me to see what was wrong with me."

"They cut him open while he was still alive?" Ani asked, staring. "Isis and Serapis!"

"The doctors of the Museum do dissections of dead subjects regularly. Dissections of living people . . . not so often, and it needs royal permission, but it is done. They use criminals who are going to be executed anyway. They drugged this man, and tied him to a table, and cut off the back of his head. I thought he was dead." Caesarion suddenly found himself shaking. "Then the doctor said, 'Here you see the ventricles of the brain!' and poked, and the poor man's hand moved." He shut his eyes. "I've seen it in seizures ever since."

"Merciful Lady Isis! Your *mother* took you to see that? How old were you?"

"Thirteen. I was thirteen. She didn't know it was going to upset me that much."

"How could she not know? Any normal person would be upset, and to show a child who suffers from the same disease . . ."

"She didn't know," Caesarion said wearily. "I suppose we aren't normal people. Are *you* normal, Ani? You're not like anyone I ever met before."

"I'm more normal than *that*!" Ani declared disgustedly.

Caesarion smiled. "I'm very glad I met you." With an effort, he got to his feet. "I must go. Don't walk me to the gates: we'll say farewell here. Ani, I am grateful, very grateful, for all your kindness. Thank Tiathres for me again, and tell Melanthe I . . . I hope she is happy. I wish you much joy."

Ani jumped up, stood facing him a moment, his face moving as though he were about to speak—then embraced him. Caesarion stood very still. Like his mother's death, this seemed to catch him in some place he could not guard with a pang of bitter loss. When Ani let go he touched the other man's arm, hesitantly, not daring to look at him—then bent, picked up his basket, and walked away.

He walked blindly as far as the Mareotic Gate, trying to tell himself that this sense of bereavement was ridiculous. He had known Ani for a month, the rest of the family rather less than that, and they were all common Egyptians. They were *not* important to him, and he should not feel as though they were . . . Certainly he shouldn't feel the way he did—the way he'd felt when he rode out from the palace stableyard and left Philadelphus.

There were Romans guarding the Mareotic Gate in the Alexandrian city wall. The gate itself was open, though, and the
Romans merely sat in the shade of the archway, watching the
passersby. Caesarion walked through, onto the Soma Street,
the wide throughfare which crossed the city from north to
south. Here he paused, wondering where to go. Some of his
mother's supporters had stayed loyal to the end; a few might
even be pleased to find him alive. Some of these, however,
would very probably be under Roman surveillance, if they
were alive and free at all—Seleukos, who'd been finance minister; the chamberlain Mardion; Diomedes, the royal secretary—none of them would be safe to approach. Nikolaos of
Damascus, who'd tutored Caesarion in history? No. That was
an ambitious man, bitter at having backed a loser: he'd turn
traitor in an instant. Olympos, who'd been Cleopatra's personal doctor, was probably trustworthy, but didn't have the
resources to do much.

He should have thought this through before arriving in the
city. That he hadn't *wanted* to think about it was no excuse.
He walked slowly on up Soma Street. The shops were closed
for the afternoon, and the great thoroughfare was quiet. A few
beggars rested in the shade of a portico, together with some
flea-ridden cats; at the public fountains women gossiped over
the water, but apart from that, the street was abandoned to
the sun. That was just as well. His face was familiar to far too
many people in this city, and his incipient moustache wasn't
going to be much of a disguise. He had examined it in the
mirror again that morning, and had found it no thicker than
it had been in Coptos.

Just before the center of the city where Soma Street met

the east-west Canopic Way lay the precinct of the royal tombs. This was an enclosed park where the mausoleums of eight generations of Lagids stood amid date-palms and bushes of flowering cistus. Caesarion paused at the wrought-iron gate— then opened it and went in. He needed to sit down and think about how to proceed.

He had often visited the tombs before. The grand domed mausoleum which loomed above him as he came in was that of the fifth Ptolemy, Epiphanes, "the god manifest," and of his queen, who had been the first queen of Egypt to bear the name Cleopatra. The greatest names of the dynasty—Ptolemy the Savior and his wife Berenike; Ptolemy and Arsinoe, the Loving Siblings—had smaller tombs on the north side of the enclosure. His mother's tomb was not in the precinct, which was some comfort. She had had a splendid mausoleum built not long before, next to the temple of Isis. He supposed that she was buried in it—beside Marcus Antonius, if the report was to be believed. He had never liked Antonius—a loud, swaggering man, vigorous, crude, and inclined to drunkenness. He did not like to think of his mother lying beside that lout for all eternity—but he supposed that she might have been planning just that when she chose the site for her tomb. Antonius was not a Lagid, and could not lie in the royal precinct. Cleopatra had, for reasons never clear to Caesarion, genuinely loved the lout, and wanted to be with him in death.

Led by habit, he retraced the familiar route to the left of Epiphanes' tomb, down a ramp, past the round monument of the seventh Ptolemy, "the Benefactor," to the tomb of his grandfather, the twelfth Ptolemy, called Auletes, "the Flute-Player." There was a sunken garden next to it, with a fountain under a colonnade that ran into a fish pond overgrown with feathery papyrus. He had often sat there as a child while his mother conducted an annual remembrance at her father's tomb, and he remembered it as a haven of quiet.

It was quiet now, but not undisturbed: as he walked down the steps into the garden, he saw that someone had removed the fountain and replaced it with a marble altar on which rested a tall urn of polished porphyry. He glared at it, more hurt than he'd expect by such a trivial alteration. What would happen to the *fish*, without the fountain?

There was a wooden placard with a painted notice leaning against the base of the altar and he walked over to it to see what excuse it could offer for the desecration.

PTOLEMY CAESAR

read the notice,

THEOS PHILOMETOR PHILOPATOR
Heir to two kingdoms and inheritor of none
Death, not kingship, came to Cleopatra's son.
Farewell

He stared at it, stunned, then raised his eyes to the urn. Someone had draped it with a wreath of bay leaves and roses, and two oil lamps stood on the altar beside it: both had gone out. A bronze incense burner was full of gray ash.

It made sense, he supposed. The Romans could not have tipped his supposed ashes into the public sewer: that would have been impossibly provocative. They would not, however, want to build him a monument, either. Putting the remains in the royal precinct but somewhere unobtrusive was the best solution, and someone must have remembered that he liked to sit here. Someone had put up the notice in place of an inscription. Someone had tended the tomb. He wondered who. He could not think of anyone, among the hordes of noble companions, tutors, and slaves who had once accompanied him, who would be likely to risk offending the Romans by the gesture. Maybe the Romans had appointed someone them-selves, so as to preserve the proprieties. They were like that.

He sat down on the bench under the colonnade and watched a bird singing from a perch on a tall papyrus frond. They hadn't killed the fish after all, he saw: there was a bit of lead piping sneaking from behind the altar and into the pond, and the carp swam shadowlike in the dark water, just as they al-ways had. Not a bad place to be buried, really. He could wish that his ashes were indeed in that urn, that he could rest here forever, and never face the struggles and very probable be-trayals of the next few days.

He knew, bleakly, that he would in the end fix on someone to approach—and in all likelihood either his helper would betray him, or someone in their confidence would betray him and his helper both. There would be an arrest, an arraignment, an execution or two, and he would end up back here in this garden, this time inside the urn. His heart ached with weari-ness. He was not sure anymore even what he hoped to achieve. It was very unlikely that he could be any help to Philadelphus. If the emperor had decided to kill the little boy, he would already be dead; if the emperor had decided to spare him, a bungled rescue attempt would only make his situation worse.

Even if by some miracle the rescue succeeded, where could they go and what could they do? He had still in the back of his mind a vague fantasy that they might buy some land somewhere and live together quietly—but he could not believe they would succeed in doing so. There was no place for them in a world which belonged to Rome.

He'd seen in Ptolemais that there was no point in going on. He'd given up on suicide for a time, first because he was needed, and then because he was happy. Perhaps the best thing he could do now would be to buy a knife and finish what he'd started . . . only he did want at least to *know* what had happened to his little brother.

There was a sound of feet coming down the steps. He leapt to his feet—and saw Rhodon, former tutor and undoubted betrayer, on the pavement at the other end of the sunken garden. He wore a plain dark cloak, and his dark hair and philosophic beard were neatly trimmed. Two attendants were still on the steps behind him, one carrying an oil flask, the other a basket.

Rhodon noticed him and paused. For the first instant he simply looked annoyed. Then he realized who was facing him, and his face went white. His mouth opened, but no sound came out. Caesarion stepped back, glancing frantically about the enclosure. The stone walls were too high to vault. He cursed himself for having walked so casually into a place he couldn't get out of.

The attendant with the oil flask dropped it. It shattered loudly on the stone, spattering the steps and the wall with thick oil and releasing a reek of attar of roses. The attendant tried to run backwards, and sat down heavily on the steps.

Caesarion rushed forward, hoping he could somehow get past before the man found his feet again.

"Nooo!" screamed Rhodon—a shriek so appalling that Caesarion stopped in shock. His tutor fell to his knees, wringing his hands. "I didn't mean to," he gasped. "I swear I didn't, but you rushed straight at the spear. What was I supposed to do? I only meant to hold you there until the Romans could come. It was the emperor's order, not mine!" His teeth were chattering. "Go away; please go away! O Herakles, please, go away!"

He was kneeling in front of the steps. "Get out of my way," Caesarion said reasonably, "and I will."

Rhodon scrambled to his feet and backed away into the garden, his eyes fixed on Caesarion with a look of glazed horror. Caesarion hurried past him, then was forced to stop. The two attendants, side by side on the steps, blocked his way. They were both familiar faces, two of Rhodon's favorite slaves; they both clearly recognized Caesarion, and were apparently too frightened even to move out of the path of his vengeful ghost. Caesarion hesitated—and heard Rhodon stir behind him. He looked around quickly, and saw that Rhodon's eyes, no longer glazed, had registered the basket Caesarion was still carrying over one arm.

"You're alive," said Rhodon incredulously.

Caesarion dropped the basket, whirled on his betrayer, and hit him hard in the face. The blow was hard enough to hurt his hand, and felt quite extraordinarily satisfying.

Rhodon fell backward, cracked his head against the garden wall, and slipped down it into a heap. Caesarion went after him, kicked at him wildly, felt his foot connect. Rhodon, his hands clasped over his face, uttered a muffled scream for help. Caesarion kicked him again. One of the slaves came up behind and grabbed his arm. He elbowed the man in the ribs, hard, hooked a leg round his shin, pushed him over, turned—and ran straight into the second slave. The slave threw an arm around his neck, trying to bend him over in a headlock. He caught the man round the waist, another wrestling hold, dropped to his knees, and threw his opponent over his shoulder.

But now the first slave was up again, flinging himself back into the fight. There was a brief, hot, panicky tussle, and then Caesarion found himself pinned panting on the pavement, a knee in his back and his right arm bent up against his shoulder blade. He struck the ground furiously with his free hand.

"How can you possibly be alive?" Rhodon's voice demanded from above him.

He craned his neck. Rhodon was on his feet again, braced against the garden wall. His nose was streaming blood, which was thick in his beard and dripping over the front of his dark tunic, and there were dust and dead leaves in his hair. He was shaking visibly.

"You bugger-arsed *whore!*" Caesarion said thickly. "Isn't killing me once enough?"

Rhodon pushed himself away from the wall, knelt down slowly by Caesarion's head. Blood from his nose dripped on the stone before Caesarion's eyes. "The spear went right into you," he said faintly. "Zeus, I couldn't pull it out! And then the tent caught fire, and I dragged you out of it, with the spear waggling about in the air. You weren't breathing, I swear you weren't. And Avitus pulled the spear out, and stabbed it in again, to see if you were dead, and you were. How can you possibly be alive?" He reached out and touched Caesarion's cheek, jerked his hand back again as Caesarion flinched convulsively.

He looked at the blood on the ground, then pressed the back of his wrist against the stream from his nose. "You had a seizure, didn't you?" he asked, his voice muffled but growing a little steadier. "I knew you did, when the spear went in— but I thought it was because you were dying. Zeus, we *burned* you, though! I watched the pyre burn!"

"You had the tent awning over it," Caesarion told him. "You didn't lift it to see if I was still there, did you?"

Rhodon stared at him, his hand still pressed to his nose, his keen dark eyes oppressed with memory. "No," he said at last. "No. They'd already displayed the body to the whole camp. Nobody wanted to watch it burn. No one was happy about it, anyway. I know I wasn't. Zeus!" He sat back on his heels. He wiped at his nose vaguely, then pinched the bridge of it to stop the bleeding. "All this time, I thought I killed you. No one has wanted anything to do with me, because I killed you. My mistress and children are spat at in the street, because I killed you—and here you are, alive!"

"You betrayed me," Caesarion said bitterly. "You swore an oath to me, to my mother, to my house, and you broke it. You meant me to die. You think people are going to think *better* of you because you made a mistake the first time, and had to come back for a second try?"

"No," whispered Rhodon. His face was still white, marked with blood in a ghastly mask. He glanced at the slave who had Caesarion pinned and ordered, "Let him up."

There was a moment's hesitation, and then the slave let go of Caesarion's arm and got off. Caesarion pulled himself onto hands and knees. He glanced toward the steps, and saw that both slaves were still in the way. His side was hurting from the tussle, and his wrist throbbed. He couldn't escape, and had no appetite for another fight. He sank back onto his heels and examined his sore wrist. The scab was cracked.

"What's that?" Rhodon wanted to know.

Caesarion looked across at him sullenly. "I tried to kill myself when I heard that my mother was dead," he said, lowering the wrist again. "What are you going to do?"

"I don't know," Rhodon replied. "What are you doing here? Why did you come back to Alexandria?"

"There was nowhere else to go. I went to Berenike, but the Romans had taken the *Nemesis*. I thought if I came back perhaps I could help my mother—or at least Philadelphus."

"Philadelphus?"

"I always liked Philadelphus. I thought the twins would probably be heavily guarded, but I might be able to get to Philadelphus. I thought perhaps someone would help me, that I could get him out, and get away, and live quietly with him . . . somewhere where people don't know us." He met Rhodon's eyes. "You think I came here to raise a rebellion? I'm not that stupid. Everyone who mattered has already either betrayed my mother or surrendered. If they wouldn't fight for Marcus Antonius and my mother, they certainly won't fight for me."

"Who have you approached?" asked Rhodon.

Caesarion sighed. *That* was the question which would interest a great many people, and which might, if the answer

was not believed, lead back to engulf the *Soteria* and everyone
on it. "I have approached no one," he declared firmly. "I arrived in the city about noon today, and I came here to think
about how to proceed. I traveled on a common sailing barge
with people who had no idea who I am. Give it a moment's
thought, and you'll see that I've had no time to do anything.
It's a long way from Berenike, and I've been ill—thanks to
you. It was a deep wound. Do you know what happened to
Philadelphus? Is he alive?"

"Alive, unharmed, and in the palace," Rhodon said at once.
"Under close guard."

Caesarion closed his eyes a moment, trying to smother the
passion of relief.

"I believe that he and the twins have their own servants
with them," Rhodon went on.

"His own nurse?" Caesarion asked eagerly. The nurse had
raised Philadelphus from his infancy, and was in many ways
more important to him than his mother. No one would comfort him more.

"So far as I know. The emperor hasn't said what he intends
to do with the children. When your mother was alive, he
threatened her that he would kill them if she committed suicide, but he hasn't done it, and it's clear now that he won't.
I don't think he could, to tell the truth. They're the children
of his brother-in-law Antonius, after all, and he has thousands
of former Antonians among his own forces now. There was
enough of an uproar over Antyllus, and people accept that sort
of thing when a city falls far more easily than they do a month
later."

"What happened to Antyllus?" Caesarion asked, with trepidation. Marcus Antonius' eldest son, by his Roman wife Fulvia, had been about his own age, and they'd often shared lessons and excursions. There'd been a lot of rivalry between them, and they'd disliked one another's parents and each other, but they'd known one another fairly well.

"Beheaded," Rhodon said grimly. "He was betrayed by a tutor as well: Theodoros told the soldiers where he was hiding. He ran into the temple of Caesar, in the hope that that would protect him, but they hauled him out and put him to death." He paused, then added, "You know that emerald pendant he used to wear, the one he said brought him luck? Theodoros stole it from his body, and the Romans found out. They crucified him."

"*Crucified* him?" Caesarion repeated, more shocked by this than by the execution of Antyllus. Antyllus, after all, was the eldest son of a man who had been the emperor's rival and who still commanded loyalty among the troops, and he had, like Caesarion, officially come of age. It was understandable that Octavian would order his death. Theodoros, though, who'd tutored Antyllus—and occasionally Caesarion—in rhetoric, was freeborn and an Alexandrian. He should not have suffered the punishment of slaves.

"Crucified him," Rhodon confirmed, with a ghastly smile. "Nobody likes a traitor."

"That surprises you?" Caesarion asked sarcastically.

"I never expected to be liked for it," Rhodon replied, trying to wipe his nose. "Though, I have to admit, it's been much worse than I expected."

"So why did you do it?" Caesarion asked, the angry bewilderment he'd felt when he first realized what Rhodon had done to him stinging afresh.

"In the first place, because I have a woman and children in Alexandria," Rhodon replied, with that direct honesty that Caesarion had always liked. "I didn't want to abandon them and run off into exile. In the second place . . . the war was lost. Everyone knew that. Yet you had every intention of raising an army and continuing the fight. More lives lost, more wounded, more money spent on mercenaries in a land which was already impoverished. All that stood in the way of peace was one emotionally unstable epileptic boy. I thought I was serving the greater good."

"What do you mean, 'emotionally unstable'?" Caesarion demanded hotly.

"It would be a wonder if you weren't," said Rhodon sourly. He got up, went over to the fish pond, and rinsed off his bloodied hand in the water. "On the one hand, expected to behave like a king; on the other, required to be totally obedient." He wiped his face with his dripping hand and looked round at Caesarion again. "I used to wonder sometimes what you'd be like if you ever came into power. It used to frighten me."

Caesarion's eyes stung. Rhodon had never mentioned this opinion of him before, and he was bewildered to find that he still cared what the man thought. "That is totally unjustified!"

"Is it? Zeus, your mother used to frighten me, and your father, by all accounts, was a monster. You have, I know, read his own account of the siege of Alesia."

He had, and it had shocked him. Caesar had besieged the

Gaulish city of Alesia. To save food, the Gaulish leader Vercingetorix had turned all the old people, women, and children out of the city. They had begged Caesar to let them pass through his lines: he had refused. Then, more humbly, they'd begged him to accept them as slaves: he had refused again. He had watched them die of hunger and thirst between the two armies, unmoved and unashamed.

"That was as much the fault of Vercingetorix as of Caesar," he said defensively.

"He was a man without mercy or natural kindness," said Rhodon quietly. "And your mother was another of the same stamp. How could you learn something neither blood nor nurture would teach you? And the disease you suffer would eat away a sanity far more firmly founded than your own."

"This is mercy, is it?" Caesarion demanded sharply. "To insult and revile me when I can't retaliate and can't escape? I never did *you* any harm!"

Rhodon stared at him blankly for a moment, then wiped his nose again. "You asked me why I did it," he said. "I was trying to explain."

Caesarion got to his feet. "You have explained that you always judged me harshly without telling me what you thought or giving me any opportunity to defend myself. I am repaid: I misjudged you as well. I used to like you."

Rhodon winced. "I liked you, too. I didn't mean you to die."

Caesarion snorted in disgust. "You've just told me your real opinion of me! You mean that you didn't want the guilt of having killed me yourself."

"No! I hoped the emperor could be persuaded to spare your life."

"That was never a possibility," Caesarion said vehemently. "Never. He would not dare even to parade me in the triumph. Cleopatra—oh yes, the malevolent seductress of Roman virtue humbled at last, a magnificent spectacle; Cleopatra's children— a pathetic sight for the crowd to coo over; Julius Caesar's son, in chains behind the chariot of Julius Caesar's grand-nephew— he would not *dare!*"

"They say you're not Caesar's son."

"I know what they say. They know what the truth is, and they don't really expect to be believed."

"The emperor did consider sparing you. I have it on good authority he did. Areios persuaded him otherwise. 'It is not good to have too many Caesars,' he said, misquoting Homer. Areios has great influence with him, and is much in favor."

Areios was an Alexandrian philosopher who had studied under the same teachers as Rhodon, spent years at court, failed to obtain the royal appointment he felt he deserved, and departed for Rome to advise Ocatavian on Alexandrian affairs. It was undoubtedly true that he was hostile to the royal house and that he would have advised the emperor accordingly—but the emperor was unlikely to have asked for advice on such a point. "I do not trust that story," Caesarion said coolly. "Octavian probably put it about to deflect criticism from himself. My death was ordered before he ever reached Egypt, and if you thought otherwise, Rhodon, you deluded yourself. What was it you used to tell me? 'Wishful thinking is the enemy of truth'?"

"He's trying to forge a stable peace," Rhodon said earnestly. "I do believe that. There have been very few executions." He paused, then added, "Far fewer than last autumn, when your mother returned from Actium."

"I am tired of this," Caesarion said sharply. "Finish it. What are you going to do? Hand me over to your master, or dispose of me quietly and pretend that it was me in the urn all along?"

Rhodon glanced vaguely at the urn. "Who *is* in the urn?"

"I should imagine it's a mix of Eumenes, Megasthenes, Heliodoros, and some camel saddles. I was astonished that nobody counted the skulls and came looking for me."

Rhodon gave him a startled look. "It was a very hot pyre." He rubbed his mouth. "I can't think. I'm not going to kill you. You say that you want to take Philadelphus and go away somewhere where no one knows you. I can't get Philadelphus. Would you go without him?"

Caesarion stared at him in silence, unable to grasp what he was saying. Rhodon left the fish pond, came over and stood facing him. "I'm not going to kill you," he repeated. "I thought I had, and I bitterly regretted it. Telling the Romans—they would not be pleased to discover that a dead king has come back to life: it is altogether too miraculous and would disturb the people. For you to disappear into quiet retirement seems to me the very best thing that I could hope for. I can help you. Will you trust me?"

Caesarion couldn't think how to answer. He turned away, went over to the bench under the colonnade, and sat down. "I do not trust you," he said at last. "I would be a great fool to do so. Anyone else *might* betray me; you've already proved that you will."

"I can help you," Rhodon insisted, urgently now. "There are too many people in this city who know you for you to walk about it in safety. I have been back for ten days now, and I have access to the Romans: I know how people stand with the new order. I know who is still loyal to you. The Romans believe they own me, and don't care what I do. I can go anywhere, approach anyone. Listen to me, O king! I want to help you. If I wanted to destroy you, I could do so, here and now. You said so yourself. But I want to *help* you. I beg you, give me the chance!"

He sounded sincere. He had lied before, of course, and Caesarion had believed him. And yet—was he any more likely to turn traitor than anyone else Caesarion might choose to rely upon? Had *anyone* remained faithful to the end?

Rhodon could have had him strangled by now, his body hidden in the garden to be removed under cover of darkness and dumped into the harbor, weighted down with stones. It was, in many ways, the most practical course for Rhodon to take. Instead, Rhodon asked to be allowed to help.

Rhodon had been tending the tomb. The oil whose thick scent of roses still hung in the heavy air had been intended to refill the lamps on the altar. That argued a genuine remorse, a real desire to atone.

"What do you want me to do?" he asked at last.

Rhodon crossed the garden in a rush and dropped to a knee beside the bench. "Come back to my house now," he said urgently. "Stay there. Let me do the rest."

He stared at the man's earnest face. Rhodon's nose was starting to swell, and there was blood in the beard and under the nostrils. His eyes were eager, full of hope.

"You will give me a sharp knife," he said in a low voice. "You will make no effort to take it from me at any time. If I suspect that you are betraying me again, I will use it on you first, if I can, and then on myself. I will not, under any circumstances, be arrested and questioned."

Rhodon winced, but said only, "I agree to your condition."

CHAPTER X

All her life Melanthe had wanted to see Alexandria. Now she was here, and had no interest in it.

Part of the problem was that Arion had told her about it, and now every sight reminded her of him. The wonderful mechanical toys in the temple of Serapis; the view from the terrace of the Paneion; the light of the Pharos; even the sea anemones in the harbor—they all reminded her of Arion. She found herself wondering, again and again, whether he'd found someone to help him, or whether his second cousin had found him first. She discovered that she had a clear picture of the second cousin in her mind—a small, twisted, sour-faced shrill-voiced man in magnificent crimson clothing—and she kept seeing Arion dragged in before him by thuggish cronies. The second cousin would gloat, then order his slaves to cut Arion's throat and dispose of his body secretly. Sometimes she imagined Arion's little brother—the rightful heir to the estate, of course—weeping at a barred window while the slaves carried the bloodied corpse away.

Of course Arion had been bound to *try* to help his little brother. She could never have abandoned Serapion without even learning what had become of him. But where she would proceed with reasoned caution, she was sickly certain that Arion would be reckless. He did not value his own life. *She* did, but he would throw it away as though it were worthless, even though she wanted, more than anything in the world, to cherish it within her own.

She tried to tell herself that there had never been any possibility of that, that he would never have married her. It made no difference to the hot misery inside her, and she found it only too easy to convince herself that he *might* have married her. After all, his family were dead and wouldn't be arranging a grand marriage for him. An orphaned bastard, even one from a very great house, would be content to marry the daughter of a well-off merchant—wouldn't he? And he had liked her. She was sure he had.

There had been boys she'd liked in Coptos. They all seemed so shallow and silly now, compared to Arion. He was so . . . *everything*. Brave, brilliant, cultured, noble . . . even the thought of his staring fits didn't bother her anymore. What had once seemed pitiable now seemed only another example of courage and strength: not even illness could subdue him. She wanted, desperately, what she had had for one shining instant and could never have again: his mouth against her own and his body warm and secure within her arms.

Tiathres and Papa spoke to her very seriously, saying that

they understood how she felt, but that the world was full of sorrows, and she must set this one behind her and make the most of the joy at hand. She did not see, though, how they could possibly understand how she felt. Tiathres had married Papa when she was seventeen, a marriage arranged by her family, and she had never been in love with anyone else. As for Papa—he was a man, and men never understood how women felt, everyone knew that. How could they expect her to enjoy Alexandria when her heart was dead?

So she declined to go on most of Tiathres' sightseeing excursions, and instead stayed with Papa and tried to help with the paperwork. That reminded her of Arion as well—she heard his beautiful voice in every long vowel of the sample letters—but at least it provided her with something to do which she didn't have to pretend to enjoy.

The business part of the expedition was having mixed success. The glass manufacturers Aristodemos had dealt with were happy to deal with Papa instead, but the tin importer wouldn't even grant an interview. Papa thought Aristodemos must have sent him letters full of lies. The market for incense, ivory, and tortoiseshell, however, was buoyant—apparently all the Roman soldiers in the army of occupation wanted exotic goods to take home—and at first Papa was too busy disposing of the cargo at a huge profit to search for another supplier for the tin.

After five days in the city, however, Kleon's cargo was all sold, and Papa turned his attention to tin. He asked the glassworkers who might supply it. The glassworkers didn't know, but referred him to a bronzesmith who would. Papa took the bronzesmith out to dinner. The bronzesmith referred him to his own supplier. Melanthe copied over one of Arion's letters, filling in the blank with the supplier's name. The supplier wrote back very cordially, saying that he had no tin to spare, but referring them to another supplier who might. Melanthe copied over another letter. The second supplier responded at once, inviting Ani out to a lunch to discuss the matter.

Papa set off to meet the supplier at about noon on the seventh day after they'd arrived in Alexandria, looking, Melanthe felt, very distinguished in a long cloak draped like a gentleman's—another trick of Arion's. She kissed him goodbye, then sat down in the stern cabin to copy over the accounts from the sale of the cargo.

Soteria was quiet. Tiathres and the nurse had taken Serapion and Isisdoros to see if the gates to the palace quarter were open and they could visit the menagerie; Apollonios and Ezana were off at some sailor's tavern, together with Pasis and Petosiris, the free helpers from Coptos. Of the four slaves, Achoapis had gone with Papa, and Mys was off seeing the city on his own. Only Harmias and Pamonthes remained on board with her. Harmias was sleeping off a hangover, and old Pamonthes sat playing the flute, producing little rills and ripples of melody that hung in the heavy air. It was a breezeless late-September day, and the cabin was hot and close. The columns of figures were very dull, and after a while Melanthe found herself chewing the pen, staring out the open door, and wondering if Tiathres and Serapion and the others had succeeded in seeing the snake. Was it really as big around as a man's waist? And would it really lick its keeper's ear?

Perhaps Papa and Tiathres had a point, after all. When they

got the tin they would go back to Coptos, and when they got
back to Coptos she would be very sorry that she hadn't seen
the snake—or the Gymnasium, or the Temple of Isis, or the
famous Museum . . .

Nobody had been to see the Library yet. She did want to
see the Library. Arion had said that it contained more than
three hundred thousand books. The library at the gymnasium
in Coptos wasn't supposed to have more than a hundred.
Three hundred thousand books! Who could imagine such a
thing? Three hundred thousand books must contain an answer
to every question anyone could think to ask. Books like stars
in the sky, a vast and uncharted ocean of knowledge!

And Arion said there were statues there of all the famous
poets and philosophers. The different philosophical sects, he
said, kept interfering with the statues of the founders of rival
sects, so that one day Zeno was holding a sausage instead of
a scroll; and another, Epicurus wore a wig. It would be fun
to see that.

Maybe she could suggest that they go to the Library tomorrow. Papa would like to see the Library, too, and if they
got the tin, he'd be free.

She remembered for the first time that Papa had loved and
lost her own mother. He had known her far better and loved
her far more profoundly than she had known or loved Arion.
He still felt the loss—you could see from his face when he
was thinking of her. But he was a happy and affectionate husband to Tiathres. The heart, she realized, can heal, though the
scars may ache in bad weather. She would not forget Arion,
but . . .

There was an enormous crash from somewhere just outside. Melanthe dropped the pen and ran to the cabin door to see what was going on.

A gangplank had been thrown across onto *Soteria*'s deck, and a group of half a dozen rough-looking men were running aboard. They were carrying cudgels and knives. Pamonthes, who'd been sitting in the bows, was staring at them with his mouth open.

Melanthe ran back into the cabin, slammed the door, and bolted it. She looked back at the pile of papyri littering the table. If the legal documents were lost, they could not be replaced. She crammed them hastily into the strongbox, jammed the lid shut. From outside on the deck came the sound of shouting, then a splash. She locked the strongbox and looked around wildly for somewhere to hide it. Somebody tried to open the door.

Robbers? she wondered. Or thugs hired by Aristodemos? That would be worse: robbers would merely steal valuables, but thugs would destroy everything they could.

There was more shouting from outside, and the sound of hatches being flung open. Nothing to worry about there: Kleon's cargo was all gone, and the glass hadn't been loaded yet. Most of the money from the sale was on deposit in a bank: Papa hadn't wanted to keep such a large sum aboard *Soteria*. There was some silver in the box, though, under the papers. Where, where, where to hide it?

She darted across to the corner of the cabin, plonked the strongbox down on top of a sleeping-mat, and rolled it up. She stood it in the corner, went over to the next mat, rolled that up, and stood it next to the first. She treated the third mat the same way, then tossed the sheets and headrests on top of them.

There was another burst of shouting from on deck—Harmias, she thought, aroused from his hangover and trying to fight. Somebody rattled again at the door, then struck it with some force. The bolt bent visibly. Melanthe grabbed the table, tipped it over against the door, and sat down with her back to it.

Papers and silver weren't the only valuables in the room, she realized. There was also herself. Pretty young girls sold for a high price, and they, too, could be stolen by thieves or destroyed by thugs. She pressed her palms against the underside of the table, trying to stifle the sick terror.

There were other boats moored next to *Soteria*. There was a city watch in Alexandria. There were guards on the city gate. Surely somebody would soon come to help?

A series of heavy blows landed on the door, and the table jumped against her back. She braced her heels against the floor and pushed hard. Another blow, and she heard the bolt crack. Outside, somebody gave a yell of triumph. A thud, and a man's weight hitting the door: the table skidded forward, and she scrabbled frantically and managed to force the door shut again. Another thud, another . . .

The table was forced along the floor as the door opened until its legs were touching the cabin wall. Melanthe cowered behind it as three men rushed in. They glanced round, saw her. One of them yelled and dived forward to grab her wrist.

She screamed, slapped him with her free hand, screamed again. He leaned over the tabletop, got both her hands, hauled her to her feet. She kept screaming. Another man slapped her, and she screamed harder. He swore. The man who was holding her hands shoved her back against the wall, hurting her. She found that she was crying. The man who'd slapped her put his hand over her mouth. Her nose was blocked from crying, and she couldn't breathe. She stopped trying to scream and fought instead for air.

The man took his hand off her mouth, holding it ready to put back again. "Where does your master keep his silver?" he demanded.

"In the bank," said Melanthe, swallowing. "He put all of it in the bank."

"He must keep some here! What about spending-money?"

"He took most of that with him," she replied, choking. "He went to see a man about tin. He gave some to Tiathres, too, but she's taken the little ones to see the menagerie."

"What happened to the cargo? There was supposed to be a rich cargo!"

"It's all sold."

The man swore again. The third man was prowling around the room, looking for valuables. He pulled some of the sheets and headrests off the heap in the corner, kicked at the rolled-up mats.

"Papers," said the first man. "Where are the ship's papers?"

Melanthe began to cry in earnest. "In the b-bank! They t-told us it w-wasn't safe to k-keep valuables on a b-boat!" In fact, keeping the papers anywhere else would have been impracticable—but the robbers didn't need to know that.

There was a shout from on deck. The first man hurried out the door. From the furious exclamations it sounded as though a lookout had spotted someone running to fetch help. The first man stuck his head back into the cabin. "Take the girl, anyway!" he ordered, and vanished again.

The man who was holding Melanthe's wrists pulled at her. She screamed shrilly and sat down, where she was, behind the upturned table. He swore, tried to pull her up. She braced her feet against the table and wouldn't budge. He cursed, let go of her wrists to pull the table out of the way. She kicked at him, caught him in the eye as he bent over. He roared and lashed out at her with his feet. She rolled out of the way.

Then the third man came over and grabbed her ankles, and the other stormed through her wild flailing and got her arms again. The two of them hefted her into the air between them and carried her out of the cabin. She screamed with all her strength and struggled madly.

The deck of *Soteria* was littered with smashed jars of oil and spilled lentils, while sleeping mats and a sack of flour bobbed in the surrounding water. Harmias was lying on the deck next to one of the open hatches, his head covered with blood. She couldn't see Pamonthes, and hoped that the first splash she'd heard had been him jumping overboard to swim for help. The four other men were standing impatiently on the quay with a chest she recognized as Tiathres', waiting for the last two to join them.

She saw in a flash that they still had to maneuver her off the boat, and decided that if she could make herself too difficult to carry they would have to leave her. She rolled wildly in the men's hands, got a foot free, kicked. They cursed, set her down, slapped her. She kicked some more, rolled, scratched, tried to bite. The larger man picked her up, despite all she could do, threw her over his shoulder, and got her across the gangplank in a staggering run. She saw a woman on the next boat staring at her, and she stretched an arm out pleadingly and shouted, "Help me!"

Nobody helped. She had a hand clapped over her mouth again, fought, couldn't get air, fainted. She woke up across a man's shoulder, limp, aching, and dizzy. She gathered her strength, tried once more to get away, and found a beefy hand clamped against her neck, choking her.

There followed a confused nightmare of being carried, dragged, and pushed along dark alleys which stank of stale urine and cats, of buffeting and curses. It seemed to go on for a long, long time. Eventually, though, there was a narrow tenement, and stairs, and finally a dark, dirty room full of boxes where an old woman sat spinning.

Melanthe's captors shoved her forward into the room. She stumbled, caught herself, and turned to see that all six robbers had filed in after her. One of them was dragging Tiathres' traveling-chest. She backed against a wall and stood braced there, sick and shaking.

"What's she?" asked the old woman, staring at her.

"Almost the entire proceeds!" replied the man who'd questioned her on the boat, who appeared to be the leader. "No cargo, no money, and one of them swam off and fetched the watch from the Mareotis Gate. We had to run. The slut's a she-wolf, too. She kicked Zeuxis in the eye. She wants to be tied up."

They spoke in Greek, which Melanthe found peculiarly shocking. In Coptos, crude dirty bandits would have been Egyptian: only the upper class spoke Greek all the time. Things were different in Alexandria.

The old woman got to her feet and came over to inspect Melanthe. "Pretty, though," she remarked, and pinched her cheek.

Melanthe raised her hands defensively, but did not quite dare hit the old woman. She felt instinctively that she would be brutally punished if she did. "Please," she said breathlessly. "Please let me go! My father will pay to have me back."

The old woman's eyes narrowed. "*Will* he? And who is he?"

"His name's Ani," gasped Melanthe. "It was his boat."

At this there were grunts, a sigh, and a collection of angry, reassessing glares. They had, she realized, assumed that she was a slave.

"Freeborn!" said the leader in disgust. "That's all of a piece with everything else about the job, that is." He went over to the wall, picked up a large jug, and drank thirstily.

"Perhaps the man will pay for her," suggested the largest of the robbers, going over and catching the jug as it was lowered.

The leader shook his head. "He won't dare keep anything to connect him with what happened. No, we'll have to sell her to Kinesias." He sat down heavily on the floor. "We'll be lucky if we get two hundred!"

The old woman had gone over to Tiathres' chest and was looking through it. It contained only items of spare clothing which had belonged to various crew members, and one pair of earrings. The old women examined Serapion's dirty tunic, then tossed it back in the chest. "Hundred, maximum!" she said in disgust. "What happened to the cargo of spices?"

"Already sold, according to her," said the leader, with a wave of the arm at Melanthe. "It wasn't on the boat, that's certain. And the money from it was banked. The whole job's going to be worth less than four hundred, and the watch are buzzing like hornets. What a disaster!"

"My father would pay more than two hundred to have me back," Melanthe ventured.

The robber leader looked at her thoughtfully and picked his nose. "How much are you worth to him? Five hundred?"

"He . . . he might not have that much right here," she quavered. "The money from the sale of the cargo belongs to his partner." She was quite certain that Papa would spend every last obol of it to redeem her, and worry about how to repay it later—but there was no sense in letting the robbers know that. "But he'd give you everything he could. He's a merchant, and he loves me." The final words caught in her throat unexpectedly. He did love her. All her family loved her. What would they feel when they found that she'd been dragged off to slavery and rape?

She had to get away. She could not, could not, end up that way.

"That's no good," a snaggle-toothed robber objected impatiently. "Who's going to go tell him we're willing to sell? *I* won't!"

The leader scratched his bristly chin. "I don't suppose you can write?" he asked Melanthe.

"Yes," she said, her breath catching. Was it possible that she might yet escape from this nightmare?

"So you could write a note telling your father to meet us somewhere, and exchange you for, say, four hundred?"

"It's still too risky!" protested the big man. "You *know* the guard are looking for us. That fellow on the boat called them in, and it makes them look bad if boats get looted in harbor in broad daylight. They need to impress the Romans or they'll be disbanded. They'll be watching that merchant whether he wants them to or not."

Snaggle-Tooth agreed. "I think we may have killed the other fellow on the boat. If we get caught, the Romans will crucify us. We can't risk it. Sell the bitch to Kinesias: at least we know that's safe."

The old woman cackled suddenly. "I know! We go to the one that started it, tell him that there wasn't any cargo or any money, and all we got was his enemy's daughter. We tell him we want another four hundred or we sell her back to her father."

There was a silence around the room, then wide grins. "That's good!" exclaimed the leader appreciatively. "He'll pay. He's boiling with hate, that one."

"And when he's paid," said the old woman, "we sell her to Kinesias. Six hundred, clear profit, plus whatever we can get for the chest."

"No! Please!" cried Melanthe frantically. "Please, my father will pay you more than Aristodemos!"

"Oh, Aristodemos, is it?" said the leader. "And you know about him?"

"He hates my father," Melanthe said, trembling. "He told lies about us before. He got us arrested by the Romans, but they found out that he was lying, and they said they would charge him if he didn't take it back. My father has a letter from the Roman general Gallus saying what happened, and he'll try to get Aristodemos arrested, I know he will. You can't count on getting anything from Aristodemos!"

"He won't be arrested," the leader replied confidently. "Not because of some Egyptian with a letter. He's a gentleman. Still, I'm interested. Where's he from?"

"Coptos, like my father. He's angry because Papa took his place with a Red Sea trader. He swore, right in the market-place, that he wouldn't endure that."

"That's enough."

"Please, you . . ."

"Quiet, you!" ordered the leader. "—Thrason, tie her up and keep her quiet. I'll go find Aristodemos. Zeuxis, you go and talk to Kinesias."

Thrason, who turned out to be the big man, pulled a coil of rope out of one of the boxes and tied Melanthe's hands and feet. By the time he'd finished, she was crying, so he did not gag her, merely shook the remaining rope at her and assured her that she would be both gagged and beaten if she made any noise.

She spent the rest of the afternoon lying in the corner of the dirty room among the boxes while the robbers drank and talked among themselves. She was afraid at first that they would rape her, but—perhaps because of the old woman— they showed no interest in her at all. The old woman, it gradually emerged, was the mother of two of them—including the leader, who appeared to be called Nikokrates—and the aunt of Thrason. She sold the proceeds of the men's robberies to a variety of shops around the Mareotic quarter of Alexandria, and she debated with them where to sell the clothes and the earrings. Melanthe listened fearfully for some discussion of the "Kinesias" who was her intended purchaser, but none was forthcoming.

Zeuxis, a tall thin man with a black eye from Melanthe's kick, returned early in the evening in a good mood, carrying a fresh jug of beer. "Kinesias is interested!" he announced to his friends. "He says he'll pay two hundred for her if she's sound and a virgin. And the best part is, he's sailing tomorrow morning!"

Melanthe lifted her head from the floor with a whimper of terror. *Sailing.* Of course. Selling a free person as a slave was difficult, if not impossible, in their own country. It was a crime which the enslave person was almost certain to disclose. However, cross the sea, and free birth became impossible to prove. Victims of piracy or kidnapping could end up on the block next to those born to slavery and prisoners of war. Selling to Kinesias meant getting less than a pretty young girl would normally fetch because Kinesias was a ship captain who had to transport his wares—and he was sailing in the morning.

"I thought he wasn't going to do another trip till the end of the month!" said Thrason.

"Somebody changed his mind," replied Zeuxis. "Somebody with a lot of money, by the look of things. They were putting carpets in the passenger cabin when I was there, and silver lampstands. Is the little bitch a virgin? I told Kinesias she was, but he's sure to check."

They checked. Thrason and Zeuxis held Melanthe down while the old woman examined her. She curled up in her corner afterwards, sobbing bitterly. *Sailing in the morning.* Sailing off to a life of slavery, where her virginity was merely an increment on her price, and she would never see anyone she loved ever again.

Nikokrates, the robber leader, arrived back while she was still weeping. With him was Aristodemos.

Melanthe swallowed her sobs and tried to sit up straight: she would not give this wicked man anything more to gloat about than she could! Aristodemos came straight over and stared down at her, his eyes half-lidded, his lips curled in distaste.

"Well?" asked Nikokrates.

"It's his daughter," Aristodemos admitted grudgingly. "But the shameless wretch still has the documents! He's been waving them at the harbor authorities and accusing *me*! I *paid* you to destroy them!"

"You *paid* us a hundred drachmae to hit the boat," replied Nikokrates. "You said the god-hated thing was loaded with spices and ivory, and that we'd easily make a fortune from it. But all we've got is the girl and trouble from the guard. We're going to have to spend every obol you gave us on bribes to keep them off. I tell you, the best thing for us would be to sell the girl back to her father cheap, because then they'd leave us alone. It's only because you paid us that we're even giving you a chance to get your revenge. If you don't want it, we'll sell her back to her father, and he can go away happy and stop bothering us."

Aristodemos bit his lip.

"Why do you hate my father so much?" Melanthe asked in agonized bewilderment. "He never cheated *you*. You got rich out of cheating *him*!"

"You filthy little bitch!" snarled Aristodemos. "He's an upstart Egyptian peasant who thinks he's better than a Greek. He never knew his place, and he refuses to learn it!"

"You know he's a better man than you," Melanthe said, suddenly understanding.

Aristodemos bent over and slapped her, then spat on her. "Very well," he said, turning to Nikokrates. "I'll give you the four hundred. But if I'm buying her, I keep her and do whatever I like with her."

Nikokrates looked at Zeuxis. Zeuxis made a cupped-palm gesture with one hand, then held up two fingers.

"Do you think that's a good idea, Lord Aristodemos?" asked Nikokrates smoothly.

Aristodemos gave him a look of startled alarm, and Melanthe realized that he hadn't told Nikokrates his real name. No wonder the robber had been interested in what she had to say about Aristodemos: it gave him a hold on the man.

"You're a known enemy of this man Ani," Nikokrates went on. "You've already been in trouble because of it. One of those papers you're so worked up about is a letter from a Roman general detailing how you made a malicious accusation against your enemy. I don't think it's a very good idea for you to take charge of the girl, do you? —Particularly not if he's already accused you to the harbor authorities."

Aristodemos' face darkened. "I won't be threatened by the likes of you!"

"Threatening you? Me? I'm simply pointing out that you don't want to dirty your hands. Let *us* dispose of the girl."

"How?" demanded Aristodemos. "I don't want her father to get her back."

"There's a ship leaving for Cyprus in the morning," said Zeuxis.

"In the morning?" asked Nikokrates, startled. "I thought not until the end of . . ." He checked himself.

"In the morning," Zeuxis repeated, with a confirming nod to Nikokrates. "We'll get the girl aboard, and the captain will sell her in the market at Paphos."

"There you are," said Nikokrates, turning back to Aristodemos. "Aphrodite's city always needs fresh whores. You'll have the satisfaction of knowing that your enemy's daughter is servicing sailors in a foreign port, and no one will be able to say a word against you."

Melanthe was unable to stifle her whimper of horror. Aristodemos glanced at her quickly, and his lips curled in satisfaction. He was however, still reluctant to pay out more than he had to. "Get the girl aboard?" he asked suspiciously. "*Sell* her, you mean!"

"The captain doesn't pay much," warned Nikokrates. "It's not like a legal business. His arrangement with the port authorities costs him plenty."

"If I'm paying for the girl," Aristodemos said mulishly, "I ought to get the money from this captain."

They argued about it for a while. Eventually Nikokrates agreed to split the purchase price with Aristodemos—except that the purchase price quoted was a hundred drachmae.

Melanthe didn't correct him. She didn't feel able to speak. Her thoughts went battering about her head like a frightened bird in a cage. She *had* to come up with some way to escape from this nightmare soon, or it would be too late.

Aristodemos didn't trust the robbers, and insisted on seeing the ship captain Kinesias for himself. Nikokrates eventually agreed to this as well. Melanthe, it seemed, should be moved to the ship that evening anyway, as the captain wanted to leave early.

They set out at once. Melanthe had hoped that perhaps she could summon help or slip away from her captors while they crossed the city, but she was given no opportunity. Nikokrates gagged her with a rope, selected an empty crate from the stacks along the wall, and stuffed her into it, still bound hand and foot. He fastened a lid on top, and in this fashion, blind and half suffocated, she was carried down the stairs, loaded onto a handcart—she knew it was a handcart, because there was no sound of an animal—and jolted across the city.

She thought, oddly, of the dancing animals from the terrace by the Canopic canal. "Why do they have to do that?" Serapion had asked, as the Romans packed the statues away. Papa's response, she saw now, didn't really answer the question. Serapion had meant, *Why do people have to take things that other people love?* and Papa had only replied, "Because they can."

The cart stopped after a while and sat still for what seemed hours. Melanthe tried not to cry, because that made it hard to breathe. At last she felt herself lifted and carried up an incline, then lowered again. The lid of the crate was removed to a glow of lamplight, and Melanthe blinked up at a sour, big-nosed man who was gazing down at her.

"This is the girl," said Nikokrates. "Pretty, eh?"

The big-nosed man only grunted and waved for people to take her out. Nikokrates and Zeuxis heaved her out of the box and set her down on the floor. She looked around, and saw that she was in a room made of wood—thick, dark wood—and that besides the two robbers and the big-nosed man there was a thin old man holding the lamp. Aristodemos was watching from the doorway. Iron shackles lay heaped into a pile in a corner.

The thin old man handed the lamp to Big-Nose and knelt to untie Melanthe's bonds.

"Stay still if you know what's good for you, girl," growled Big-Nose, glaring at her. He picked up the length of rope the old man removed from her ankles, doubled it, and slapped it significantly against the wall.

Melanthe lay still while the old man examined her, looking at her eyes, her teeth, her hair, pulling up her tunic and touching her breasts, and finally checking, as Zeuxis had expected, whether she was a virgin. The other men all watched. She felt sick and frantic and wanted to lash out and run, but she forced herself to behave like a fledging bird grounded, seeking invisibility by the absence of motion. Let them only think that she was too frightened to move!

At last the old man nodded at Big-Nose, whom she was now nearly certain was the ship captain Kinesias. "Healthy and intact," he proclaimed, in a reedy voice. "Do you want to test her with the wheel?"

The test for the hidden defect of the sacred disease. She thought wistfully of Arion, wished that she'd slipped up to him one evening and suggested that they go for a walk along the riverbank . . . wished that she had had the chance to kiss him more than just the once . . . far, far better to have lost her virginity to him than to a sailor in a brothel.

Kinesias shook his head. "Never caught anyone like that anyway." He turned to Nikokrates. "Very well. You . . ."

Melanthe leapt to her feet in one convulsive motion and ran straight for the door. Aristodemos threw wide his arms in startled denial, and she turned sideways without breaking step, raised her arm and smashed her elbow into his face with all the weight of her body behind it. He screamed and fell backward. She vaulted over him. Her left foot came down on his chest, making her stumble, but she regained her balance and dashed along a dark, narrow hall where men and women lay shackled amid crates and huge amphorae—the ship's hold, she realized. Behind her, the shouting had begun.

There was a ladder at the end of the hold and she pelted up it, emerged in another narrow passageway, this one flanked by doors and lit dimly by a lantern halfway along. One of the doors opened, and a man's head poked out. She glanced up: there was another ladder beside her, disappearing into the dark. She shot up it, hearing the sound of feet scrambling up the first ladder just below. At the top of the ladder was . . .

. . . a solid barrier. She fumbled at it frantically, found hinges, pushed at the side opposite them . . .

It refused to budge. She fumbled again, this time searching for a bolt. A hand from below seized her ankle, and she screamed.

She clung to the rungs of the ladder, but was dragged, still screaming down to the corridor floor just below. There were more doors open now, more shocked faces staring. Nikokrates grabbed her hands and wrestled them behind her back, and Kinesias slapped her.

A door at the end of the corridor, behind the ladder, opened in a flare of lamplight. "By all the immortal gods!" exclaimed a voice—a beautiful, cultured, educated, *familiar* voice: "What is going on?"

"Arion!" she screamed, searching for him with her eyes, and he replied, in amazement, "Melanthe!"

He was standing framed in the doorway, dressed in a dark tunic that caught the light here and there with a glitter. There was another man in the light behind him.

"No need to trouble yourself, sir," said Kinesias, moving between them. "It's simply a slave-girl, trying to run off. If you just . . ."

"That is an outrageous lie," Arion said sharply, pushing him out of the way. "I know this girl. Her father saved my life. Melanthe, what are you doing here?"

He was right in front of her. He was real—the same cropped hair, the same ready show of blood in the cheeks, the same proud eyes. Only the tunic was different—a black tunic, worked with gold, very rich. She wanted to throw herself into his arms, but Nikokrates was holding her arms twisted behind her back, and she could only gasp at him.

"Lord," the man who'd been behind Arion said urgently, "let me handle this." He'd come out of the cabin behind Arion, a slim man, older than Arion, dark-haired and bearded, soberly but expensively dressed.

"This is not your business," Kinesias told the two of them. "Go back to your cabin, sirs, and let me get on with my trade."

"I told you, this girl's father saved my life," Arion replied. "She is to be released and returned to her family at once. There is no bargaining to be done."

"Lord!" protested Arion's friend, looking warily at Kinesias. "I said, let me handle this!"

Kinesias was shaking his head. "She can't be released. The

guard are looking for her already. If she goes back, they'll come here to see what else I've got."

"You assured us that the authorities had been bribed," said Arion disdainfully.

Kinesias grimaced. "Silence comes in quantities. I paid for only so much of it. This would cost more than I can afford."

"You can sell the girl to my friend, though, surely?" said Arion's friend, with a false smile. "All that will mean is you getting your money here instead of at Paphos, and her traveling to Cyprus in the cabin instead of the hold."

Kinesias at once looked far less forbidding, but: "No," said Arion flatly.

His friend shot him a look of annoyance. "Be reasonable!" he protested. "The girl will be safe and well treated, the captain will be happy, and our security will be preserved."

"You didn't listen to me," Arion said sharply. "She isn't a slave. She's the free daughter of a merchant who saved my life. Her father adores her. Am I supposed to repay him by enslaving her myself?"

"Keep her as your free concubine, then, if you want her so much!" cried the friend in exasperation. "But we can't afford trouble with the guard!"

"How am I to learn what neither blood nor nurture will teach me?" Arion asked, with an edge to his voice that seemed to bring his friend up sharp. "The answer, Rhodon, is that I might have encountered such things elsewhere—only, you know, I never did, until I met Melanthe's father." He turned to Kinesias. "You can be reasonable. Say you bought the girl in good faith, that you didn't know she was freeborn. I will pretend to believe it. If you've paid out money. I will reimburse you. I will repay you twice what she cost you. You will have your profit from her, and my custom as well. Otherwise I will take her back to her family myself, and you will lose both."

"This is not wise!" protested Rhodon. "Not if the guard are looking for her. And we cannot afford to wait and look for another ship!"

"You could let me go in morning, when you leave," Melanthe offered, very faintly. "Then I could go to the guard, and say I was hiding on the docks all night, and I never even saw the ship."

"What about *us?*" demanded Nikokrates suddenly. "Kinesias, you pimp, you don't sell *us* like this! You don't take this bugger's money for what you haven't yet paid for yourself!" He glared at Arion. "Who are you?" he demanded. "I've seen you somewhere before."

There was a thump from the next ladder, and then Aristodemos struggled up, helped by the old man. There was blood all over his chin and down the front of his tunic, and he had a hand clasped to his mouth. He glared venom at Melanthe—then recognized Arion.

"You!" he exclaimed—and coughed blood. She saw, with amazement, that she'd knocked in his front teeth.

"The situation becomes clear," Arion said drily.

"I think you should go back into the cabin," Rhodon advised him urgently. "The situation may be clear to you, but to me it's starting to look dangerous." He glanced down the corridor—where, Melanthe saw, all but a few doors were now open and at least a dozen people were watching them.

Arion did not move. "I do not trust you to see this as I do," he said evenly. "Rhodon, I will pay for this girl's safety with my own, if need be."

"That's *ludicrous!*" exclaimed Rhodon, staring at him.

"What am *I* supposed to do in Cyprus anyway?" demanded Arion. "One can live quietly, or die, as well here as there."

"The object is to *live!*" Rhodon told him.

"To what end?" Arion asked, unmoved. "If I die now, it will not be your doing. You have done everything you could. I acknowledge it freely."

"And you'll throw away everything I've done, because of some *Egyptian* girl?" cried Rhodon furiously.

"I owe her father a debt," Arion replied. "I will not purchase my life at his expense, or hers."

"This is a criminal fugitive from the Romans!" exclaimed Aristodemos, finally gathering the energy to speak.

Three of the men who'd been watching from the nearest doorways came out suddenly and silently. One of them caught Aristodemos' shoulder. Melanthe had a sudden sense that things were becoming unbalanced, like too much crockery stacked on the edge of a table—and that the teetering stack was much taller and far, far heavier than she'd realized.

"A criminal fugitive," Nikokrates repeated, staring at Arion. "Not our kind, though." He glanced over at Aristodemos, who was glaring indignantly at the man who held him. "The Romans are after him, you say?"

"Take your hands off me!" Aristodemos ordered. "—Yes, he fled the king's camp when . . ."

He stopped, gasping. The man who'd been holding his shoulder caught him as he slumped and lowered him gently to the floor. His eyes stared intently at nothing.

Nikokrates shivered. Suddenly he shoved Melanthe hard, sending her stumbling into the opposite side of the corridor. She caught herself on a shoulder, turned in time to see Nikokrates, a knife in his hand, crashing into Arion.

There were shouts of alarm, several of them, and a flurry of body against body. Then the robber was standing behind Arion and holding a knife to his throat. "Nobody move!" ordered Nikokrates. "Anybody moves, and he dies!"

Everything went very still. Two more of the men had come out of the doorways, but stood frozen. One of them had a knife in his hand. Aristodemos was lying on the floor, his eyes still staring madly. Melanthe realized that he wasn't breathing.

"What is this supposed to achieve?" Arion asked calmly. He stood very straight, his head back, the knife gleaming golden against his pale skin.

"I think your life is worth a lot more than the girl's," said Nikokrates softly. "I think your friends here would pay a fortune for it. So would the Romans."

Arion sighed. His right hand moved slightly. Then he spun about where he stood, his left hand came up fast to catch at the knife, and his right hand moved again, fisted, against Nikokrates' side.

Nikokrates' knife leapt wildly into the air, fell to the floor. Nikokrates grunted and folded over. His friend Zeuxis yelled, ran toward him, and one of the strangers leapt after him and brought him down with a crash. The stranger's hand rose and came down: Zeuxis screamed horribly. The stranger's hand rose and fell again, and the scream stopped.

Arion crouched over Nikokrates a moment, tugging at something buried in the robber's side. He straightened slowly, holding a knife of his own, its blade red. "I didn't think I was going to need it," he remarked, looking at it.

Then he dropped it and fell to his knees. A look of horror came over his face, and his bloodied hand began to claw at the neck of his tunic—then stopped as his eyes fixed in the ghastly stare of a seizure. Blood was trickling slowly from a scratch at the angle of his throat, where Nikokrates' knife had caught him as he turned, but it was clear he did not feel it.

Kinesias looked at him, at the three bodies littering the floor, at the grimly silent men who'd come out of their cabins—to protect Arion, Melanthe finally understood, not to guard the captain. He looked back at Arion. A look of sheer panic convulsed his face. "Get off!" he ordered shrilly. "I didn't know what I was getting into. I'm not carrying you, not for any price!"

CHAPTER XI

Caesarion sat at the desk in the cabin, trying to compose a letter. It was just before dawn—the ship's captain had grudgingly agreed that he ought to remove himself and his chattels from the ship in good order by daylight, rather than pack them off helter-skelter in the middle of the night and risk drawing the attention of the watch. Now the slaves were packing the last of the carpets, hangings, and furniture. There remained only this desk, and the lamp by which he must write the letter.

The goods and slaves really belonged to a Friend of his mother's. Not a Kinsman or First Friend: Archibios had been outside that select circle. He had been merely an extremely wealthy private citizen who was occasionally received at court—yet when the queen died, he had offered the emperor the astonishing sum of two thousand talents of silver to leave her statues and monuments intact. This, Rhodon had told Caesarion, was in stark contrast to many more exalted figures, including several Caesarion might have approached. When the queen was a prisoner, her finance minister Seleukos had informed Octavian where she'd hidden the treasures she'd hoped to use as bribes, and even Olympos, her trusted personal physician, had warned her captors that she was planning to die rather than grace a Roman triumph. Others Caesarion might have turned to—the chamberlain Mardion and the royal secretary Diomedes—were dead. He would never have thought of going to Archibios. Rhodon had certainly proved his value there.

Rhodon had been a surprise generally. Caesarion had had only the vaguest notion that his tutor owned a house near the Museum, and had not known that he had a mistress and children at all. The house had proved to be a small but lovingly furnished mansion, and the mistress a stunning red-haired Gaulish woman whom Rhodon had bought as a slave ten years before and freed. It could not be a legal marriage, but the couple were obviously devoted to one another: a major concern was how to legitimatize their children so they could inherit from their father. Caesarion found that he could now easily imagine Rhodon's anguish at being required to abandon his family and depart into exile while the Romans were marching on Alexandria. It plainly hadn't helped that the Gaulish woman had been enslaved during one of the campaigns of Julius Caesar, and had little love for Caesar's son.

Rhodon's remorse for his treachery was clearly sincere. He had thrown himself with passionate enthusiasm into finding Caesarion a refuge, and turned at once to Archibios.

Archibios had at first refused to admit Rhodon to his house, but had eventually done so out of curiosity. Shortly afterwards, the old man had himself appeared at Rhodon's house, and had wrung Caesarion's hand and wept for joy. He had, he said, a large estate on the island of Cyprus: would Caesarion accept it? They could make out a fictitious bill of sale, and such a sale would arouse no suspicion: he was having to sell a lot of land as it was, to cover what he'd promised the emperor for the statues. It would give him such joy, he said, to know that he could use the property to secure the livelihood of the divine queen's son.

Caesarion had asked again after Philadelphus. Archibios and Rhodon both had promised to see what they could discover, but nothing had come of it, except confirmation that at least the little boy had his own nurse to look after him. In the meantime, the voyage to Cyprus progressed from suggestion to plan without his ever having formally agreed to it. Archibios and Rhodon had, between them, located this dubiously reputed ship which could slip out of the harbor without an inspection. Archibios had selected attendants—armed bodyguards, in case the ship's captain was tempted to rob his passenger—and provided slaves and furnishings from his own house. He had been so eager to help that Caesarion hadn't felt able to refuse— even though the thought of being trapped trying to run an estate on Cyprus filled him with a sense of panic.

Now he had to write Archibios and inform him that all his efforts had been for nothing. It was not easy to do: he found that he was, on the one hand, ashamed to have wasted so much effort, undertaken with such goodwill and at such risk— but on the other hand, he felt no regret whatsoever. He had saved Melanthe and would restore her to her family, and that was worth more than the miserable scraps of his life. He was, however, sorry for Archibios.

Ptolemy Caesar to his Friend Archibios, son of Diodoros, greetings, he wrote at last.

I hope you are in good health. It is with great regret that I must inform you that the voyage you arranged cannot now take place. When I went on board the vessel you hired, I recognized, among the slaves who form the principal cargo, the daughter of the merchant who saved my life after I was wounded near Berenike. She had been kidnapped through the malice of an enemy of her father, and Kinesias, the ship captain, refused to release her, although I offered to redeem her. I insisted upon her release—my debt to her family demanded nothing less— and in the course of the argument which followed, I was rec- ognized. Although the men you lent me acted with commendable speed to prevent the matter from progressing any further, the captain has nonetheless realized who I am, and refuses to carry me.

I am fully aware that my position is too delicate to endure the delays and upheaval involved in a search for a different ship, and I am therefore resolved not to endanger my friends further by making the attempt. My regret is not for myself— indeed, I fear that if I had taken up the property you so kindly offered me, I would soon have come to grief. I am, however, very sorry for the waste of your efforts, which have been loyal and generous, and have greatly comforted me after betrayal by so many others. I would be deeply grieved and ashamed if your kindness to me led to your ruin. I therefore return to you, with this letter and my thanks, all the people and property you were good enough to place at my disposal. I beg you not to concern yourself with me further, but to ensure your own safety. I will escape from Egypt by another road.

I thank you for your loyalty to myself and to my mother's memory, which you have done so much to protect. I pray that the gods prosper you as you deserve, and I wish you very much joy.

He sat for a moment, watching the ink dry, feeling strangely at peace. He should, of course, have died at Kabalsi—and yet, the last month had been, for all the suffering, well worthwhile. He had met real kindness and real loyalty; he had discovered that even traitors could seek atonement; he had saved some people who were worth saving; he had fallen in love.

The cabin door opened, and he glanced round to see that Rhodon had come in. The philosopher had stayed on the ship all night, helping to arrange the orderly departure. He gestured at him to wait, then blew on the ink, scrolled the letter, and inserted it in one of the elegant little letter-cases provided, with the desk, by Archibios.

"May I see it?" asked Rhodon.

He hesitated—then handed him the unsealed letter.

Rhodon took it out of the case and began to read it in a rapid mutter, then stopped at the end of the second paragraph and looked up accusingly. "What other road?" he asked.

"You know the one I mean," Caesarion replied, in a low voice. "Do not, I beg you, distress Archibios by naming it. Tell him I hope to find a ship at one of the Red Sea ports."

"Because of a *girl!*" exclaimed Rhodon in dismay. "Because of a sixteen-year-old black-eyed Egyptian!"

"You betrayed me for your mistress and children," Caesarion pointed out. "There are worse causes. But it isn't just because of her. Rhodon, I never wanted to go to Cyprus anyway, and I owe Melanthe and her family a great debt. It made no sense to cling to a life I hate at the cost of betraying people whom I love."

Rhodon lowered the letter and stared at him unhappily. "*Love?*"

Caesarion felt his cheeks heat, but did not look away. "They are good people who were kind to me without expecting anything in return. You're a philosopher. Don't all the schools hold that what we are by birth is an accident, and that in the essence of our souls we are all equal, all mortal? I honor and esteem Melanthe and her family, and I will not betray them."

Rhodon made a noise of exasperation. "I never adhered to any of the schools, as you know very well. And your birth was no accident. Your mother decided that she wanted a son by Julius Caesar, and she got one."

"That's still an accident in the philosophical sense, isn't it? Not intrinsic to my nature as a man."

"Zeus, I don't know anymore what's intrinsic and what we become by choice. You were never really willing to leave without Philadelphus, were you?"

"I suppose not," Caesarion admitted. "Rhodon, if I'd gone to Cyprus without Philadelphus to care for and worry about, what would I have done? Drunk to excess, and probably *talked* while I was drunk, and got you and Archibios into trouble. I was not brought up to live quietly. I was brought up to be a king, and I can no more change that than I can cure myself of the disease. I have no *purpose* anymore!"

Rhodon looked away. He gazed down at the letter, then rolled it up silently and put it back in the case. "I suppose," he said—and his voice was thick, "that I wanted you to go to Cyprus to ease my own conscience. If you were safely alive there, then it didn't matter that I'd betrayed you."

"It didn't matter anyway," Caesarion told him. "You were quite right. The war *was* over. To go on fighting would have done nothing but cause death and suffering for no benefit whatsoever."

Rhodon shook his head. "I was wrong. I was quite wrong." Caesarion saw with surprise that he was in tears. "I thought you were like your mother—that you had no capacity to feel the suffering of others. I was wrong. You would have been a great king."

He was moved and bewildered by the unexpected tribute. "No one can say what sort of king I would have been," he replied at last. "I was never going to reign. Egypt was living on Roman sufferance before either of us was born. My mother believed that she could forge a partnership with Rome, but my death became inevitable the moment that failed. I don't even understand why she bothered to send me out of the city at the end. She can't possibly have expected me to do anything except prolong the war."

Rhodon stared at him in astonishment. "She wanted you to *live*. The gold was for *you*, not to pay soldiers. Didn't you realize that?"

It had never occurred to him. She hadn't said why she was sending him away. She had simply summoned him suddenly one night, early this same summer, and ordered him to go. He had expected to stay in the city until it fell—as they had all known it would. "You must escape," she had told him, taking his hand and looking into his face. "He may spare others, but he will not spare you. I have arranged a ship and money. You must go quickly, while we still control the Nile. I will join you if I can." Then she had embraced him. She had done that regularly, but usually it was perfunctory, intended as a gesture to satisfy the court that he was hers and still in favor. That time had been different: she had clung to him, pressing her face against his hair, then leaned back and looked at him for a long, long moment.

For the first time he realized that she had known that she would never see him again. Rhodon was right. The ship and the gold had not been an injunction upon him to continue the struggle, but, very simply, an attempt to preserve his life. He had *always* known that she'd borne him as a tool, to unite in his person the rulers of Rome and the heirs of Alexander. The idea that she would wish to preserve his *life* when she knew he would never fulfill the purpose for which she'd created him—that was new, shocking, and profoundly moving. He sat still, his heart pounding in his ears. Then, hurriedly, he dug out the remedy and inhaled it, afraid the revelation would provoke a seizure.

"Thank you," he said to Rhodon at last.

"You never realized that?" asked Rhodon.

He shook his head.

"She was not a kind or loving mother," Rhodon commented quietly. "I suppose you simply didn't credit it."

"She was bitterly disappointed when I was struck by the

disease," replied Caesarion. "She tried very hard to find a way to cure me. It . . . damaged things between us."

"She did want you to live," said Rhodon softly. "You could. Still. What about *really* trying one of the Red Sea ports? Archibios would provide you with money."

"No." Caesarion wiped his eyes and lowered the remedy again. "I endanger everyone who helps me. Rhodon, I was questioned by the Romans twice on my way to Alexandria, and I had to pass through three customs posts. I survived because I was traveling with Melanthe's father, a genuine merchant with a legitimate, well-documented cargo. To travel as a fugitive, with a large sum of money—I would be caught."

"You could go back with your merchant," urged Rhodon. "He seems to be your friend anyway. We could . . ."

"No," Caesarion insisted. "I will not put him at risk. How can I ask good people to risk death and ruin to keep me alive, when even I see no point to it? You said it yourself. I am not worth any more lives." He wiped his eyes again. "I'm tired of it, anyway. The lies and the bad choices, the treachery and the disease. It will be a relief to have it over."

There was a long silence, which was interrupted by a hesitant knock on the door. "Yes?" called Caesarion.

The eldest of the three female slaves Archibios had given him stuck her head into the cabin. "Master," she began nervously—and then Melanthe pushed past her.

Caesarion found himself on his feet with his arms open before he was aware of moving. Melanthe went directly into them as though it were her natural place, and pressed her face against his shoulder. It was an embrace for comfort, not love, but his whole body seemed to open to it like an eye. He kissed her hair, stroked it, suddenly and intensely happy. Melanthe was whole and free this morning because of him. That was an achievement to be proud of.

He had thought of taking her home the previous night— but the terror and violence had taken their toll, and as soon as she understood that it was safe to collapse, she'd done so, in tears and fits of shivering. He'd ordered the female slaves to look after her, and they'd given her a dose of warm honeyed wine mixed with opium and put her to bed. Now she was awake again—and, it seemed, washed, anointed, and throwing herself into his arms.

The slave-woman was looking amused. "You are willing to see the girl, then, master?" she asked—unnecessarily, as she'd plainly seen that he was more than willing.

Caesarion nodded. "Thank you for caring for her."

The woman bowed and withdrew. Melanthe lifted her face and looked at him. One side of her mouth was still swollen from the blows she'd sustained the previous day, and there was a cut on her left eyebrow, but her eyes were as beautiful as ever. "*Are* you their master?" she asked.

He wondered how much of what had happened she'd understood. He thought, probably not much—yet. She was observant and far from stupid, but she had been far too shaken to have reasoned her way through it yet. "Only temporarily," he told her. "They belong to one of my mother's friends. They're going back to him as soon as we finish packing."

Melanthe flinched. "Because of me? Because there was a fight over me, and the captain won't take you anymore?"

"It's for the best," he told her firmly. "I didn't really want to go to Cyprus anyway."

"What happened to your little brother?"

He shook his head. "He's alive. He has his own nurse with him. I don't think he's going to be harmed. I have to be content with that, since I can't improve on it."

"What about your second cousin? Does he *know* you're here?"

"Second cousin!" exclaimed Rhodon in surprise.

Caesarion had forgotten he was there. He glanced around. "He is, you know. Once removed."

"Not as far as he's concerned," Rhodon remarked darkly. "You're the one removed, in his view. —Young woman, good health."

To Caesarion's disappointment, Melanthe let him go. She eyed Rhodon warily. "Good health, sir. You are a friend of Arion?"

Rhodon was not disconcerted by the name: Caesarion had already decided to keep it during the voyage. "I would wish to be," he told Melanthe calmly. "But I fear that he is resolved to have no friends now. I have been trying to persuade him to accept help, and he refuses it. Is it true that your father does business down the Red Sea?"

"Yes, sir," agreed Melanthe, still very wary. "He has a partnership with a captain called Kleon, who sails out of Berenike."

"I very much wish that Kleon and your father could persuade Arion to sail out of Berenike, as a third partner, perhaps with a second ship. Given the piracy common in those waters, a convoy would surely be safer than one ship on its own. I and my friends have some money we could invest. I understand that it's a profitable trade."

"Rhodon!" protested Caesarion, shocked and dismayed. It

had never been any part of his intention to involve Melanthe in the discussion of what to do next.

Melanthe looked at him wide-eyed, then at Rhodon. "My father offered Arion a partnership," she said. "He refused it."

Rhodon lifted his eyebrows. "Did he? I would like to meet your father. He must be a remarkable man. My young friend here esteems him greatly, and members of his family are not easily impressed."

Melanthe visibly swelled with pleasure and satisfaction. "I thought he was just too proud to accept it!"

"If he refused, it's probably out of fear of his second cousin," Rhodon told her. "Personally, I think that so long as he stayed out of Alexandria there would be little danger. His cousin believes him dead, and will not go looking for him." He tapped the letter-case against his chin. "You know, the more I consider it, the more it seems to me that Arion would do very well commanding a ship on the Red Sea, fighting pirates and ne-gotiating with barbarians. It is much closer to what he was brought up to do than managing an estate on Cyprus."

"Rhodon, I can't!" Caesarion cried angrily. "You know I can't!"

Rhodon met his eyes. "You could endure it more easily than your friends could endure your death." He glanced over to Melanthe. "He intends to kill himself as soon as he's returned you to your family."

"Arion!" cried Melanthe accusingly, whirling back to him. "Is that true?" She looked into his face searchingly—then flared into a blaze of indignation. "It *is* true! You mean, you were going to go manage an estate on Cyprus for this gentleman, and I ruined it, so now you're going to kill yourself? You *mustn't*! You saved my whole family at Ptolemais, and last night you saved me. I would *die* to repay you. Papa would, too, I'm sure! You can't go off and kill yourself without saying a word! If we ruined one plan, you must let us provide you with another!"

"Melanthion . . ." Caesarion began hesitantly.

She seized him by the shoulders, shook him urgently. "You *mustn't*! Maybe you don't care about yourself, but your *friends* care, my family cares, *I* care! Doesn't that matter to you at all?"

Caesarion glared over her shoulder at Rhodon, who smiled and spread his hands in a gesture of helplessness, looking quite insufferably pleased with himself.

"It *does* matter to me," he told Melanthe. "That's why . . ."

"He is resolved," Rhodon interrupted. "And he is very stubborn and headstrong, like all his family. He thinks his life is no longer worth living, and I have no hope of changing his mind. But you might be able to."

Melanthe digested that in a blink. She looked searchingly into Caesarion's face. Then she let go of his shoulders, caught his left hand, turned it over, and traced the red weal across the wrist. "When you did that," she told him, looking up seriously into his eyes, "it hurt me, too. Only a little, though, because then I didn't care so much. If you did it again, I would feel the knife on my heart." She lifted the hand and kissed the scar; the touch of her lips made his skin tingle. "You mustn't do it. Please, Arion. You're precious to me. You mustn't, there's no need. You can come back to *Soteria* and stay there quietly until we leave Alexandria. We're going very soon. Papa may have the tin already. Your second cousin doesn't know about us, he won't suspect a thing. If your friends want to invest in another ship for you, they can write to Papa and Kleon. No one would even know you were with us. It would be perfectly safe."

"It would be natural for our friend Archibios to invest in a ship," Rhodon put in eagerly. "He has several such investments already."

Caesarion extracted his hand. "Go back to the women and get ready to go," he ordered Melanthe sternly. "Tell them to find you a cloak. I need to discuss this."

"You mustn't kill yourself!" Melanthe insisted. "I won't let you!"

"I will discuss this with my friend!" snapped Caesarion, and pushed her toward the door.

She went, though with a defiant backward glare that said he had not heard the last on the subject. Caesarion closed the door and leaned against it.

Rhodon laughed. "O Aphrodite, daughter of Zeus, you are greatest of all the immortals! Not even kings can contend with you."

Caesarion glared at him furiously. "That was *unjust*! She doesn't know who I am or what she risks!"

"She doesn't care," replied Rhodon. "She has put a line through your name and marked it with an obelus: I want *this* one! And you're very pleased with that. Don't try to deny it: it was plain on your face. Nothing wrong with that, either. I'd be pleased, too, to have a brave, beautiful girl like that in love with me. If that isn't worth staying alive for, what is?" He came over and set the letter case down on the desk. "Write another letter," he urged. "Tell Archibios that you have found a Red Sea trader who has accepted you as a partner, that you will depart in a few days for Coptos and Berenike. Invite him to write to the merchant and invest in a ship."

Caesarion found that he didn't know how to reply. All his resignation to his fate had left the room with Melanthe, and his treacherous imagination was building another flimsy edifice for him: Ani welcoming him back as a full partner; Melanthe smiling at him, kissing him, holding him; voyages out of Berenike into the wonders of the south . . . "And won't Archibios be grieved and ashamed, to find that I would sink to working as a merchant?" he managed, trying again to marshal his sense that the whole idea was ludicrous.

"Why do you think Archibios had two thousand talents ready to hand over to the emperor?" said Rhodon. "To be sure, he owns land. But he has always invested the income from it wisely. He has no contempt for trade—and he wants you to *live*, O king. He wants to know that the blood of the Lagids still flows in Egypt, that the old order endures within the new, that the glories of our inheritance are not altogether destroyed. That is precious to him—as it is to me. I will tell him that I think you are much better suited to activity and danger than to idleness on an estate, and I think he will agree. He knows the history of your house."

"The risk . . ."

"Is not great! *I* chose to take it; *Archibios* chose to take it; the girl would have no hesitation. You are dead, remember: your ashes are in that urn. I don't think our preparations hitherto will have created much stir, and Kinesias is certainly not going to take his story to the authorities. In Alexandria you might be recognized, but if you stay out of Alexandria you should be safe. And in a year or two, if you grow a beard, you'll be safer still." He pulled the letter out of the case, held it toward the lamp. "Let me burn this," he urged. "Write a new one. Live. Give the girl what she wants. She is promising you life and love. Why should you choose death?"

He bit his lip until he tasted blood. "I will not ask them to commit themselves in ignorance," he whispered at last. "I will take Melanthe home, and I will tell Ani the truth. *Then*, if he agrees, we will take the course you suggest."

Rhodon smiled and held the papyrus in the flame from the lamp. It flared and smoked. Rhodon held it up by one corner after another, finally dropped it to the cabin floor and ground the ashes into the rough wood with his foot. Caesarion took out another sheet of papyrus, dipped his pen in the ink, and wrote a new letter.

When he'd finished it and put it in the case, he took out a final sheet of papyrus and wrote out carefully:

I, King Ptolemy Caesar, Theos Philometor Philopator, decree in respect of my tutor, Rhodon, son of Nikanor, that his children by the freedwoman Velva are to be regarded as legitimate. They are to be enrolled as citizens of Alexandria and are to be permitted to claim their inheritance from their father. Witnessed, this twenty-eighth day of June, in the twenty-second year of the reign of Queen Cleopatra, which is the fifteenth year of my Kingship, by
Second Witness:

He handed it to Rhodon. "I don't have the royal seal," he said. "But if you want to make use of it, you could tell Archibios that I ask him to sign it. If you sign it as well, that should be sufficient to sway a court of law. The Romans may, of course, disallow it, but they have ratified most of the ordinary acts and ordinances of the realm, and they would have no reason to spite you."

Rhodon stared at the paper, his face white. "The date?" he whispered.

"Just before we left Alexandria," said Caesarion. "You must remember it thus. We were about to leave. You begged me to do something to provide for your children, and I wrote this. We happened to be near Archbios' house, so we asked him to witness it. He took charge of it, and was to have obtained the seal from my mother, but in the confusion of the siege he did not do so, and when he learned of your treachery he resolved not to return the document at all. Recently, however, you visited him, and explained that you had been misled by Roman promises. Seeing that you had been deceived and were stricken with remorse, he returned the paper to you— which provides an explanation for your recent visits to one another, if anyone takes an interest in them."

Rhodon stared at the paper a moment longer. Then he touched it to his lips and slid it into the front of his tunic with a trembling hand. "Thank you," he said. He knelt and prostrated himself—the formal salute to a reigning monarch, which Alexander's heirs had adopted from the Persians, and which the Persians had used before their kings and their gods.

"Get up!" Caesarion hissed in alarm. "This isn't the place for that! Zeus, someone might come in!"

Rhodon stayed down. "I beg your forgiveness, O king," he said formally, "for my treachery, and for the injury I did you."

"I've already forgiven you," whispered Caesarion. "I would hardly have written that if I hadn't. Get up!"

Rhodon got up, moved hesitantly toward him for the embrace a royal Kinsman would expect after making the prostration; stopped in shame. Caesarion completed the movement himself, and found himself clasped hard in Rhodon's trembling arms. The papyrus crackled, the remedy made a lump against his chest, and the sheath of the knife—concealed in a hidden pocket behind the thick gold border of his tunic—pressed uncomfortably against his side. "I'm sorry," choked Rhodon. "I should have gone to you, exactly like that. I didn't think you would pay attention."

"I might not have," Caesarion admitted. His heart was pounding hard and he felt sick with too much emotion. He extricated himself as quickly as he could, sat down again, got out the remedy. The herbs had been renewed, and the scent was strong again. He breathed it deeply, fighting off a sense of panic. Suddenly he wanted all this to be over: he wanted King Ptolemy Caesar, the focus of so much passion and danger, dead and buried. He wanted to be Arion again.

"Seal the letter," he ordered. "We should go."

Two slaves were waiting outside the cabin to remove the desk and the lamp. Caesarion nodded to them, started up the ladder, and heard them collapsing the desk-legs as he emerged onto the deck. Rhodon followed him in silence.

Kinesias' ship was moored in the Eunostos Harbor, to the west of the Pharos, in a run-down area beyond the stone-walled central quays favored by more respectable vessels. Archibios' people were already waiting in a solid bunch at the end of the tumbledown pier, and the two mule-drawn carts were piled with the rest of the luggage.

Kinesias was on deck, and came over when he saw Caesarion emerge. He rubbed his hands together nervously, gave what was probably intended as an appeasing smile but came out as a sick simper, and ducked his head. Slave-trader, thief, pimp, and smuggler though he was, he was still in awe of a king. "Lord," he said, "I hope there are no ill-feelings."

Caesarion tossed the end of his cloak over his shoulder and pulled on his hat. The cloak was new—dark, and unobtrusive—the hat the one Ani had bought for him in Berenike. "If I am caught," he said levelly, "be certain that I will do my utmost to ensure you are beheaded, as you deserve for your abuse of free people. If I am not caught, I can only pray that the gods allot you the punishment I cannot provide. May you be accursed, Kinesias, now and forever." He nodded briskly at Kinesias' ghastly stare, and strode down the gangplank and along the pier.

Melanthe was waiting with the others. The women had indeed found her a cloak—respectable girls did not wander about the city dressed only in a tunic—and he had not at first registered her presence. It was a plain cloak of bleached linen—there had been no reason to bring anything more elaborate for the three slave-women—but Melanthe still contrived to look unusually pretty in it. She watched him anxiously from under the draped hood.

He nodded to her, then to the attendants and slaves. He waited for the final two men to arrive with the desk, then held up his hand for attention.

"As you all know," he began, "our plan has miscarried, and I am sending you back to your lord. I have written him a letter which explains the situation and which makes it clear that you are none of you at fault in any way. You have given me good service in the past few days, and I thank you for it—and yet I am pleased to be able to send you home. You serve a good and loyal man, and I cannot believe that you left his service gladly, or that you are not at heart pleased to return to it.

"I have advised your lord that I am going to try another route out of the city. I will make arrangements for it through someone else, however, and you will not be required to do anything more. It would be best if you took the road along by the harbors, where your carts will attract no attention—though if you are questioned you should say that you are moving goods from a property your lord has recently sold. I will say farewell to you here." He gestured a summons to Chaireas, the leader of the free attendants; the tall man came over and bowed deeply. Caesarion handed him the sealed letter, and Chaireas bowed again and slipped it into the front of his tunic.

There was a shuffling, and then Chaireas cleared his throat and asked hesitantly, "Lord, shouldn't some of us go with you?"

"No," Caesarion replied at once. "I wish to attract as little attention as possible." This was true, though he also wanted as few people as possible to know the name and situation of *Soteria*: it seemed safer that way. "I will go very quietly, with just the girl I am taking back to her family."

Sosias, the butler who was responsible for ordering the slaves, looked unhappy with this. "What about your luggage, lord?" he asked, waving at the large traveling-chest full of clothing. "You'll need someone to carry it."

"Too conspicuous," Caesarion told him, with a disdainful glance. "Too conspicuous to move, and most of it too conspicuous to wear. Give me a spare tunic and cloak in a basket, and that will be enough."

"You'll still need someone to carry it, lord," insisted the butler, shocked. "A gentleman can't carry a basket, like a slave!"

"I'll carry it," Melanthe declared suddenly.

Caesarion looked at her soberly. "*You* are not a slave."

"But I'm used to carrying baskets," she replied. She glanced defiantly around the slaves. "In Coptos, free people often do!"

The slaves looked as though they found this hard to believe. "We will sort it out in due course," said Caesarion, trying not to smile. "Just pack the spare clothes."

Muttering unhappily about the state of a world where gentlemen of *the very noblest blood* were obliged to set off across the city on foot with their luggage in a basket, the slaves found a suitable basket and packed it—then had to be told to pack it again, with less conspicuous garments. Then there was another delay while the strongbox was opened and a purse full of money taken out—"Lord, my master would be most distressed if he discovered that I had permitted you to depart like a beggar!" protested Sosias. At last, however, he was able to wish the slaves and attendants very much joy, and watch the carts rumble off along the harborfront.

That left Rhodon and Melanthe. "Am I permitted to come with you?" Rhodon asked drily. "I must point out that this is not a good part of the city, and three would be safer than two—or, for that matter, one unfortunate philosopher all on his own."

"You can come with us as far as the Heptastadion," Caesarion conceded. "After that I think I'd prefer it if you went to see Ar . . . to see our friend and tell him how things stand." He picked up the basket.

Melanthe at once came over and took it from him. "I said I'd carry it!"

"It isn't heavy," Caesarion told her, halfheartedly trying to take it back.

"Then let me carry it! *They* thought you shouldn't. You think so, too, really." She arranged the basket over one arm and faced him challengingly. "Have you decided what you're going to do?"

He gave her a lopsided smile. "I will explain the whole situation to your father. Then, if he agrees, I will go back to Coptos with you on *Soteria*, and my friends here in Alexandria will arrange the investments needed for a ship."

Her challenging look gave way slowly to a wide, white smile of delight. "Really?" she asked breathlessly. "Oh, I praise Isis!" She flung her arms about him, basket and all, and beamed into his face. "It will be all right, you'll see!"

He was not convinced, but that lovely face smiling into his own was impossible to resist. He kissed her. She pressed against him, and her hand came up and touched his hair, traced the line of one of the scars on the back of his head. When he lifted his head, she was still smiling, her eyes alight with love. He shivered, suddenly dreadfully afraid, and let her go.

"*If* your father agrees," Caesarion said grimly.

He started away from the pier, along the harbor in the wake of the carts. Rhodon was quite right that this was not a good part of the city, and they'd be safer staying out of the backstreets until they were farther east.

"He'll agree!" Melanthe declared, hurrying after him happily. "You know he will. He wanted you as a partner even without any money. When he hears that not only are you going to join him, but your friends are buying you a ship so he'll have to expand the business—he'll think he's arrived in the west, where the gods live and all things are perfect."

"The esteem, it would seem, is mutual?" Rhodon asked. Caesarion glanced back, and saw his tutor looking amused.

Melanthe looked down in embarrassment. "My father does esteem Arion, sir, yes. He's . . . Well, you see, we're Egyptian, and my father never had much opportunity for education, but it's something he values very much. Arion is so well educated and he knows so many things, and . . . my father has a great respect for him."

"So it seems I can take some credit for the mutuality of admiration," said Rhodon, the amusement now open.

"Rhodon was one of my teachers," Caesarion explained.

"Philosophy and mathematics," confirmed Rhodon.

"Really?" asked Melanthe, her eyes brightening. "You're a philosopher? What sort? A Stoic?"

"I thank Zeus, no," said Rhodon. "Indifference to earthly goods and freedom from emotion are no goals of mine. I adhere to none of the schools. I find something to dislike in all of them. I could be a Cynic, I suppose, but I find the posturing tedious."

"He was a good teacher," Caesarion told her. "He taught

me what all the schools say, and helped me pick holes in it. He taught me to think critically."

"You needed little help with that," Rhodon said, smiling. "It was your natural instinct." He turned back to Melanthe. "He was a good student. Very sharp, very fast. More interested in natural philosophy and practical mathematics than in abstract speculation, but that is something of a tradition in his family."

"My father would love to meet you, sir," said Melanthe, her eyes still very bright. "He is interested in philosophy, but the only sort of philosophers we've ever had in Coptos are Stoics, and they just preach."

"I want to meet your father," Rhodon replied. "If an uneducated Egyptian can make such an impression on . . . Arion, he must be a truly remarkable man."

"Not yet," Caesarion said firmly. "If Ani agrees to this plan, we can make arrangements. Until then, I think it is better if there is no evident link between him and my friends here in Alexandria. There is still far too much that can go wrong." He shivered again. Writing the first letter, he had felt calm and unafraid: now all possibilities filled him with terror. Melanthe had touched the place in his heart which he had never been able to guard completely, and the bitter thirst for love which resided there had never given him anything at all but pain.

They arrived at the Heptastadion, the causeway that led to Pharos island, with Rhodon answering Melanthe's eager questions about philosophy. Beyond it the Great Harbor curved in a dazzling vista of blue water against white marble. The Temple of Caesar was just along the road, an imposing building in the Ionian style, where the statue of the deified Julius stood in gilded bronze—where Antyllus had fled for sanctuary, and from which he had been dragged to his death. A mile away, on the other side of the harbor, the Lochias promontory shimmered in red, gold, and green—the palace quarter, where Caesarion had been born. Caesar Octavian was there now— having breakfast in the Nile Room, perhaps, or a morning bath under the mural of Dionysus and the Pirates, while his guards changed shift and marched to the spacious barracks.

Somewhere over there Philadelphus would be getting up— sitting, perhaps, at a window while his nurse combed his hair, and wondering what would happen to him; perhaps mourning a brother he believed dead.

Caesarion turned away. He could not help Philadelphus, and would never see him again. He remembered the little boy's soft arms around him, and a wet kiss on his cheek, one aching afternoon when he'd had a seizure; remembered Philadelphus in his little purple cloak standing in the stableyard biting his fist as he rode away. The pain was a physical thing, a knot in his heart.

He was feeling dizzy. He dug out the remedy and held it to his face.

"What is the matter?" Melanthe asked in alarm. "Are you . . ."

He shook his head. "I was just thinking of my little brother." He gathered himself up and turned to Rhodon. "We part here," he decreed.

Rhodon hesitated, then held out his hand. "Only for a few days, I hope. Send me a letter confirming the arrangement as soon as you can, and I will come and discuss the details."

Caesarion shook the hand. "*If* Ani agrees."

"Papa is certain to agree," Melanthe declared confidently. "We will see you aboard *Soteria*, sir, soon."

"If he does not agree," said Rhodon, clasping Caesarion's hand in both his own, "come back to my house, I beg you. We can arrange something else. I am deeply in your debt, lord, and I would welcome any chance to repay you."

Caesarion gave him a sickly smile, not trusting himself to speak. He pulled his hand away, and started along the cross-street that led from the Heptastadion to the Temple of Serapis. He was aware of Rhodon gazing after him, a worried look on his face.

They were back in the respectable part of the city now. It was still early in the morning, but late enough that shops were open, and as they approached the Canopic Way the street became crowded. Carts and handcarts rolled along the paving-flags, and hawkers cried their wares at every corner. Caesarion pulled the brim of his hat down and the edge of his cloak up and walked swiftly, in silence. Melanthe hurried after him, bumping passersby with the basket, and eventually caught up and took his hand. "Are you all right?" she asked him anxiously.

"I am afraid," he admitted. "If your father says no, I don't know what I'll do. And he may say no, Melanthion. I've never told him the truth, and when he learns it he may simply decide that the risk is too great."

"He isn't going to say no," Melanthe said, leaning forward to peer into his face. "Arion, he helped you when he didn't even know who you were, and last night you *saved* me, at the cost of losing . . . what your friends had arranged for you. He *can't* say no, you must see that!"

He stopped walking, caught both her hands in his, gazed at

her for a moment. People on the street were looking at them. He ducked into the shadow of a portico of shops and towed her into the shelter of a column. "I'm afraid," he told her again.

"If your cousin thinks you're dead, surely there isn't much danger?"

"I don't trust this! Something will go wrong. Melanthe, at Berenike, I was afraid that if I came back here as your father's secretary I'd turn into somebody else, and I was right, I have. On the ship . . ." He caught his breath, not sure what he was trying to tell her, or why. He only knew that his heart was pounding with dread at some imminent catastrophe, and the prospect of meeting Ani seemed to lie beyond some fearful barrier which he did not believe he would ever surmount.

She looked up at him seriously, her eyes enormous. The world seemed to revolve around those eyes. "Are you ashamed of what you've become?"

"No," he said, and it was true. "I feel I ought to be, but I'm not. Before—before and on the ship, which is the same thing—they didn't *really* know who I am, but they knew who I'm supposed to be. *I* always knew that, too, but I also knew that I couldn't live up to it, because of the disease, and because . . . because I'm not *enough*, not good enough or wise enough or strong enough. They reverence what I'm supposed to be, but me . . . the me that is here, now, talking to you—they don't even see. If I do something that makes them notice me—like have a seizure, or fail—then they're embarrassed, and they try to pretend it never happened. Only you and your family, you know what I *am*, because the other is a thing I never told you. So I'm afraid, you see?—of everything you might think and feel when you know the truth. I can face dying, but losing myself just when I'm becoming myself for the first time . . . I can't face that. But I'm not making any sense."

She laid a finger against his lips. "I love you," she told him seriously. "I know I'm young, and I know I haven't known you very long, and I can see there's lots you've never told us—but I love you, and it's not going to change."

He leaned his forehead against hers, breathing in the scent of her hair. She stroked his head, her fingers tracing the narrow indentations of the scars. The overpowering sense of dread gave way suddenly to joy, a joy so intense that it seemed to explode out of his heart and fill the entire universe with light.

"Melanthe," he said, and the world shattered.

CHAPTER XII

Melanthe told herself afterwards that she should have recognized the signs for what they were. Arion had gone
very pale, stared with a desperate intensity, and seemed terrified of nothing. But she did not recognize the signs, and the
seizure caught her totally unprepared.

It was not a small seizure, either. She had not seen a major
one before, had had only a vague idea what one was like. One
moment he was saying her name, about to kiss her—the next
he was uttering a fearful shriek and falling on top of her, every
muscle rigid.

She caught him, sank to her knees. He slid out of her arms
and rolled onto the dirty paving of the portico, rigid, his back
arched and his lips pulled back in a horrible grimace. His eyes
had turned upward in his head so that only the white showed.
All around them, people were staring in alarm.

"Arion!" she cried, and hung over him in helpless horror.

"A man's having a fit!" exclaimed one of the shoppers to her neighbour.

Several people spat at them, to deflect the contagion, and backed off. All of a sudden Melanthe found herself surrounded by a ring of people, all of them watching Arion with fascinated disgust. She finally realized that yes, he was having a fit. He was not dying, had not been struck suddenly by a demon or possessed by a god: he was suffering a paroxysm of the brain of a sort he'd had many times before. Trembling, she knelt down by his head and tried to cushion it. Arion's lips were turning blue. His hat had fallen sideways, and the cord was biting into his neck; hurriedly she pulled it loose and set it down on top of the basket, but he did not start breathing again. She did not know what to do, and fought not to cry: it wouldn't help anyone if she had hysterics.

Arion suddenly drew in a deep breath. His body jerked from head to foot in a convulsion, then went limp. Another convulsion, and froth leaked from his mouth . . . but he was breathing again. Melanthe caught his hand and held it. More people spat at them.

A man came out of the nearest shop—a cheesemaker's— and threw up his hands in dismay. "What's this?" he demanded, glaring at Melanthe. "Get that lunatic out of here!"

"Gladly!" she said tearfully. "Lend us a cart!"

"Cart? I'm not lending anything to a lunatic and his whore. Get him away from my shop!"

"I'm *not*!" she cried indignantly, "and *he's* not! And how am I suppose to take him away without a cart?"

"Just get him away!" shouted the shopkeeper. "Filthy disease! They shouldn't let them out!" He kicked Arion, who was lost in another convulsion and felt nothing.

"Leave him alone!" Melanthe screamed furiously. "You can't do that! He's a gentleman!"

"Gentleman!" replied the cheesemaker derisively, and spat directly into Arion's oblivious face. "Filthy lunatic! Ought to be locked up!"

She suddenly remembered the money the slaves had handed Arion that morning. She had been shocked to see that Arion had neither asked nor checked how much it was, but the purse had looked quite heavy. She pulled a fold of his cloak loose, found the purse, still securely attached to Arion's belt. "We have money!" she shouted, indicating it triumphantly. "We can *hire* a cart. Who'll rent us a cart?"

The cheesemaker stared in astonishment at the heavy purse, and at the gold-worked edges of the tunic Melanthe had revealed beneath the plain cloak. For a moment something like recognition flickered on his face. Then Arion convulsed once more, and the recognition was replaced by revulsion. Arion went utterly limp. The whites of his eyes showed under the half-closed lids, and froth trailed from his slack lips onto Melanthe's cushioning knees.

"I'm not renting my cart to a lunatic, even if he does have money," the cheesemaker decided. "Don't want the filthy disease anywhere near my goods, no. I want him away from my shop: people expect my cheeses to be wholesome!" He kicked Arion again, then tried to shove him toward the gutter with the flat of his foot.

"You leave him alone!" Melanthe screamed shrilly. She moved Arion's head carefully off her lap, then leapt up. The shopkeeper at once gave Arion another shove toward the street, and she flew at the man, hitting him in the chest and forcing herself between him and his victim. "I'll take him away!" she screamed into the startled and indignant face. "I'll take him away as fast as I can, but I can't *carry* him!"

"My master wants to know what the matter is," said a new voice. Melanthe looked around to see a bored-looking man studying Arion's body with distaste. The crowd, she realized, had grown, and was spread out into the road. In the sunlit street beyond it stood an ornate four-wheeled carriage, drawn by white mules and surrounded by attendants dressed in red tunics, enticed by the crowd to a stop.

"My friend has had a seizure," she said, sensing an authority which could impose order. "I want to take him home, but I need a cart—or a hand-cart, a mule, *anything*! I need to take him to my father's boat, which is moored in the Mareotic Harbor. Sir, we are respectable people. My father is a merchant from Coptos. Arion is his partner. We have money, we can pay."

The man's lip curled, but he went back to the carriage to report. The cheesemaker glared at Melanthe, but he did not hit her or try to push Arion into the street again. *Authority* had arrived, and he would await its verdict.

The door of the carriage opened, and a small bad-tempered man in an elaborate crimson cloak got out and stalked over. "Can't anyone in this city sort anything out for themselves?" he complained angrily—and then he saw Arion.

For a moment Melanthe thought he was about to have a seizure as well: his face went white, and he stared at the unconscious young man with an expression of amazement. "O

Father Zeus!" he whispered. "Immortal gods, it's not possible!"

"He's had a seizure, they said," the senior attendant told his master, puzzled. "The girl there wants a cart to move him."

The man from the carriage edged closer to Arion, still staring. Melanthe saw his eyes fix for a moment on the scars. Amazement was joined on his face by horror. "O Zeus, Zeus!" he muttered. "It is. It's impossible, but it *is*." Then, snapping into a fervent activity, "Get him into the carriage at once!"

"Lord?" asked the attendant, as though he'd misheard. "You want him in *your* carriage?"

"Get him off the street this instant!" shrieked the man in crimson.

The puzzled attendant flinched, summoned several of his fellows with a wave. The man in crimson looked at Melanthe. He had weak blue eyes in a pinched face. "Who are you?" he demanded. "What are you doing with this . . . this person?"

He was the second cousin. Melanthe was all at once certain of it. He looked exactly as she'd imagined. She took a step back, appalled at what she'd done. "Sir," she said, "who . . . What . . . what do you want with my friend?"

The attendants were clustering around Arion. They pulled his cloak straight, bent over and got their hands under him. His head rolled helplessly.

"He's your *friend*, is he?" asked the man in crimson grimly. "Come with us."

Melanthe took another step back. The attendants picked Arion up and carried him out of the portico. "No!" Melanthe shrieked, so loudly that they paused and looked around. She ran over to them, hesitated helplessly: there were five of them, and Arion was deeply unconscious in their hands. She could not take him away from them. "Where are you taking him?" she demanded frantically. "You're his enemies, aren't you? Let him go! I'll call the watch!"

The men snorted with derision and carried Arion on toward the carriage. The man in crimson came over and caught Melanthe's arm. "Don't be a fool!" he snapped. "Do you know who I *am?*"

"No," she replied shortly, "but I can tell you don't mean any good!"

"I am Areios Didymos," said the man in crimson, drawing himself up to his unimpressive full height. "I am a friend of the emperor. All Alexandria knows that. You must come with me, girl, and explain . . ."

Melanthe stamped hard on his foot, wrestled her arm free, and bolted.

She fought her way through the crowd, ignoring the shouts, then hitched up her tunic and dashed along the road. In half a block she found herself bursting onto the carriageway of a much wider street. She darted behind a cart, dodged a horse, skipped over a curb, and arrived under another portico. There she pulled her cloak over her head and forced herself to walk—a brisk, businesslike walk, fast, but with nothing fugitive about it. The portico was crowded, and many of the women and girls had cloaks very similar to her own. She heard more shouting behind her, but she did not look back, and it faded.

Melanthe kept walking, trembling now. Some of the people were looking at her oddly, and she pulled a fold of linen across her face. Her nose had started to run, and her eyes blurred.

She should have prevented it. She should have . . . kept her temper, talked *reasonably* to one of the other shopkeepers, got a cart and moved Arion quietly, before there was a commotion. She should never have *summoned*, O sweet Isis, *summoned* some unknown rich man to help: she should have *known* that it was dangerous. She'd panicked, she'd lost her head, and now Arion was going to die.

She had told him that she loved him. He had fallen almost on those words, and when he woke—if he ever woke!—he would be in the hands of his enemy, and she wouldn't be there, and he would think she'd betrayed him, O Lady Isis!

But she would fetch help for him. Papa would be able to think of something to do. Arion had saved him once: he'd surely find some way to save Arion. Areios Didymos, the Friend of the Roman emperor—he *had* to be the second cousin. Everything about him fit what Arion had said, and his name was similar to Arion's. Families often did use similar names for all their members. Probably Papa had heard of Areios Didymos from his new rich Greek associates. They might have told him something that would be useful. He'd discover some way they could help.

She bumped into a stout woman with a basket of vegetables. "Careful!" snapped the woman; then, looking at her more closely, "Child, what's the matter?"

"I'm lost," gasped Melanthe, pressing the palms of her hands against the blinding tears. "I need to find my father. His boat is at the Mareotic Harbor, but I don't know the way."

The stout woman tut-tutted, led her to the next corner, and pointed out the way to the harbor gate.

The Mareotic Harbor looked much as it had when she left it: a maze of boats and quays, warehouses and trolleys and cranes. She hurried through it, blind and stumbling, unable to remember where, among all these barges and skiffs and sail-boats, *Soteria* was moored. Then she heard her name called, and turned, and saw through tears her father running toward her.

"Papa!" she screamed in relief, and ran to him.

"Melanthe!" he cried again, and threw his arms around her.

She clung to him, sobbing bitterly. "It's all right now," he told her tenderly. "It's all right now, Sunbird, you're safe now."

It wasn't all right, but she couldn't speak.

Papa held her, rocking back and forth, and eventually led her along the side of the dock, and there was *Soteria*, and then Tiathres was beside her, and her brothers, and all the others were clustered around, fetching her cold clothes to wipe her face, and cups of watered wine, and telling each other not to crowd her.

Almost all the others. Harmias, whom she'd last seen lying on the deck with his head covered with blood, was absent.

"Harmias?" she asked at random, and the sudden quiet told her what had happened even before Papa admitted, "He died before I got back. Oh, my darling girl, we were so afraid for you!" He spoke in the Demotic he very rarely used to her. "My baby. Are you all right? Did they hurt you?"

"They have Arion," she told him.

In the confused silence that followed, she realized that, of course, the others knew only that she'd been dragged scream-ing from *Soteria* by a band of robbers. "He—he rescued me," she tried to explain. "They took me to this ship, and they were going to sell me, but Arion was there. He was going to

Cyprus, on the same ship. He told them to let me go, but they wouldn't, and there was a f-fight. Aristodemos got killed. I . . ."

"Aristodemos was there?" asked Papa, his face darkening.

Melanthe nodded. "He paid them a hundred drachmae to rob *Soteria*, and he promised them the cargo, only it wasn't here. He told them to destroy all the papers, but I hid them. You found them, didn't you?"

"Yes," said Papa, and patted her shoulder. "You were a clever girl. The harbor authority was all over us after the robbery. *Someone* had sent them a letter saying that our cargo was stolen goods from the start. Without those papers we would have been in trouble. I knew Aristodemos was behind it. I told those buggers to arrest him, but they wouldn't do any such thing, not to a Greek gentleman. He's *dead?*"

"They k-killed him," Melanthe stammered, remembering it and starting to shake. "I never saw how. I don't know what happened to his body. He just g-gasped and stopped talking, and they put him on the floor. He was staring and staring, and then I saw that he wasn't breathing. It must have been a knife. They had knives. Arion had a knife hidden in his clothes, and I didn't see it until he t-took it out of Nikokrates—he was the chief robber; he was horrible, I'm *glad* Arion killed him! They were going t-to sell me to a brothel on Cyprus, and Nikokrates got Aristodemos to p-pay him to do that, instead of selling me to you, b-because Aristodemos hated you so much he'd p-pay to make you unhappy." She swallowed. "And then Kinesias, the ship captain, said he wouldn't carry Arion, and ordered him to get off the ship.

"So we left the ship this morning, and Arion's friend said

that Arion was going to kill himself, and he asked me to persuade him not to do it. He was going to go to Cyprus and
manage an estate, but he couldn't, because of the fight, and
they said it was too dangerous to arrange another ship, and he
didn't want to get his friends into trouble, so he was going to
kill himself. And Arion's friend said we could help, we could
persuade Arion to go back to Coptos with us instead, and his
friends would invest in a ship for him—a *second* ship, Papa,
that would make a convoy with *Prosperity*. So I begged Arion
to agree, and finally he said he would explain the whole situation to you first, and we were coming back here so he could
do that, and he had a seizure." She started to cry again. "He
fell over in front of a shop, and the shopkeeper kept kicking
him, and everyone was spitting at him and calling him a dirty
lunatic and telling me to take him away, but I *couldn't*, without
a cart, and they wouldn't lend me one, and this rich man came
along, and I thought he would *help*, but he's Arion's second
c-cousin, and he t-told his men to take him and put him in
the c-carriage, and I c-couldn't help, and they're going to k-
kill him!" She pressed her hands against her face. "If it weren't
for me, he'd be on his way to Cyprus!"

"Hush, hush, hush!" said Tiathres, holding her.

"Calm down," Papa ordered. "Take a deep breath. Now, do
you *know* that this man was Arion's second cousin?"

She felt a rush of desperate relief, and wiped her nose. Papa
would think of something to do. "I think he was," she said
eagerly. "He was rich, and he said he was a friend of the
emperor. He recognized Arion right away: when he saw him
he shouted, 'O Zeus, it's impossible, but it is!' and ordered
his people to put Arion in the carriage. He said his name was

Areios Didymos, and that's a lot like Arion's name."

"Areios!" exclaimed someone on the fringe of the group, and she looked up and saw that it was Kleon's man Apollonios. "Areios is supposed to be the most powerful man in Alexandria!"

"What do you know of him?" Papa asked quickly. "I've heard people mention him a few times since we arrived, but I don't know anything about him."

Apollonios sneered. "I suppose *Egyptians* never hear about anything. He's a philosopher. He used to be at the queen's court, but he never rose very high, so he went to the emperor, and rose right to the top. When Caesar first came into the city, he had Areios beside him in the chariot. He told the city he spared it partly because of Areios' intercession. Areios has asked Caesar to spare this man or that, and the emperor has given him what he wanted every time. Everyone wants to be his friend. He's a very, very big man just now."

"He's little and ugly," Melanthe said hotly. "He tried to put *me* in the carriage, too, but I got away."

"Just as well," said Apollonios. "That's not a man to cross."

Melanthe glared at him, then looked pleadingly at her father. "What can we do?" she whispered. "It's my fault this happened. Arion would be safely on his way to Cyprus if it hadn't been for me."

"It's not your fault that you were kidnapped," Papa told her, very firmly. He sighed, rubbed his hands through his hair, suddenly looking utterly exhausted. "Sunbird, I don't know! I . . . I suppose I could go to Areios and tell him that his cousin isn't claiming any of the inheritance, that if he lets him go I'll take him off and he need never see him again."

"Are you *insane?*" demanded Apollonios. "If Areios thinks that epileptic boy is his enemy, then that boy is *dead*. There isn't a man in Alexandria will raise a hand to save him. Arion knew that: he told you you didn't want to touch it. Zeus, even if Areios didn't do anything to you, you'd have everyone who *heard* about it making trouble for you in the hope of pleasing him!"

"I *owe* the boy!" Papa said, with a glance at Melanthe.

"It isn't your cargo!" shouted Apollonios, getting to his feet. "It's *Kleon's*. Kleon sent *me* to keep an eye on things, and you are not—you are *not*—going to ruin the whole of a profitable venture for the sake of your daughter's boyfriend!"

Melanthe burst into tears again.

"Arion never injured his cousin," said Papa quietly. "He does not deserve such hatred."

"You don't *know* that!" Apollonios snarled. "You don't know anything at all about Arion, except that he refuses to answer questions!"

"I know the important things about him," Papa replied, sharply now. "I know I like him a lot better than I like you."

Apollonios sneered. "Yes, that's been pretty clear for a while. Nice Greek boy with a beautiful voice, well born, well educated, shame about the disease, pity he's too proud to look at you. Were you hoping to give him to your daughter, or share him with her?"

Papa jumped to his feet. "You buggering Greek!" he roared. "Don't you smear *me* with your own filth!" He waded through the ring of others and swung wildly at Apollonios.

Apollonios staggered back against the railing, then pushed himself off it again and flung himself back at his adversary.

Tiathres screamed. Papa and Apollonios fell to the deck, Papa underneath, both of them cursing and hitting each other.

All the men except Ezana were Papa's, and they stood about yelling encouragement to Papa and trying to kick Apollonios.

Tiathres jumped up, found a bucket, lowered it off the side of the boat, heaved it up, and flung the dirty harbor water over the combatants. They broke apart, coughing. Ezana slid in next to Apollonios, grabbed him, and wrestled him off toward the stern, where he began arguing with him earnestly. Tiathres, meanwhile, dropped to her knees beside her husband and put her arms around him. She began to beg him not to fight, not now, not with his partner's man. Papa sat dripping in the middle of the stern deck, wiping at a cut on his cheek, swearing, and looking murder at Apollonios.

Melanthe covered her face. Papa was a man, not a god. She should never have expected him to work a miracle. There would be no rescue. Arion had chosen to help her rather than ensure his own safety, and he would die for it.

What was more, she realized, with a hot stab of shame, she had abandoned him. If she'd gone with the man in crimson, she might have been able to help—but she'd run away and left him to die alone. She understood now how he had felt in the temple at Ptolemais, when he realized that he'd failed those he'd pledged his heart to; she understood why he'd wanted to die.

Soteria gradually calmed down. Apollonios was persuaded by his comrade to offer a grudging apology, which was reluctantly accepted. Melanthe lay down in the stern cabin with a sheet over her head. Her father went down to the harbor office and informed the authorities that his daughter had returned safely, and the harbor office offered to inform the city watch, who would want to send someone to ask what had happened to her.

"If you don't feel able to speak to them, say," he told her, when he returned. "I can ask them to come another time."

Melanthe took the sheet off her head and looked up at him miserably. His face, which had always seemed to her so wise, was bruised from the fight, and he looked exhausted and ashamed. A trickle of compassion eased its way into the choking pain. He was not a god—but he loved her, and he had been frantic for her safety. He would have helped if he could, even at the risk of his own life.

She sat up and hugged him, and he held her. "I'm so sorry," he said vaguely.

"There's nothing to be done," she choked. "I'll see the watchmen when they come. Papa, what should I tell them about Arion?"

He let her go, looked at her seriously, blew out his cheeks. "I don't know," he said finally.

"I want to tell them the truth—that he saved me. But if Areios is really so powerful, then that might cause trouble. And I don't really understand why Arion was on that ship. He said he didn't want to attract attention, and he was worried about the port authorities, but I don't understand why. I don't understand why he couldn't wait at his friend's while they looked for another ship, either. There was . . . there was a lot about it that was strange. And his people killed Aristodemos. That might cause trouble, for him or for his friends."

" 'His people'?" Papa asked, confused. "I thought the robbers killed Aristodemos."

"No," said Melanthe. "One of Arion's people did. I don't know who they were. They weren't slaves. They were armed. I saw them holding knives, but there were spears in one of the rooms I saw, too. He had slaves, too, though, about a dozen of them. There were three women who looked after me. He said really they all belonged to a friend of his, and he sent them back to the friend when we left." She sat silent for a moment. The events of the previous night and morning now seemed dreamlike, unreal, blurred by too much emotion. "He had a cabin with carpets and silver lamps," she told her father, slowly waking to the strangeness—a strangeness quite independent of her own feelings. "He sent those back to the friend, too. And he had clothes made of silk, which he made them take back, because they'd attract attention. The slaves wanted to send someone with him, to carry his things, but he thought it would attract attention. They all called him 'lord.' Even his friend called him that."

"Are you certain of this?" Papa asked her, frowning, holding her hands.

"Yes." She was frowning as well now. "Arion said he was going to explain it all. He was afraid, though, that you wouldn't help once you knew the truth. I told him you would."

Papa shook his head unhappily. "I *want* to help, Sunbird. I would have tried. Perhaps there's still something we can do. You mentioned a friend who was with him. Do you know his name?"

"Rhodon," Melanthe said at once. "He was a philosopher. I didn't like him at first, because he . . . he didn't want them to let me off the ship, in . . . case it attracted attention from the authorities. He told Arion to take me to Cyprus with him instead. But this morning he was very friendly and polite, and he said that you must be a remarkable man, to have impressed Arion so much, and that he wanted to meet you."

Papa was surprised, flattered, unhappy. "Rhodon," he repeated. "I think Arion's mentioned him. I've heard that name."

"Arion said he used to be his teacher."

Papa frowned. From outside on the quay, there was a shout of alarm.

They looked at one another, suddenly afraid, and both got up in one movement and went to the door.

A troop of Romans were quick-marching along the quay, led by an anxious harbor official. There were about thirty of them, in red tunics trimmed with gold, polished strip armor, and shining helmets with tall crests of red horsehair.

Melanthe gaped. She had not told Areios who she was: this couldn't be because . . .

She had told Areios' servant, though, that her father was a Coptos merchant moored at the Mareotic Harbor. Trade from the Red Sea was still scarce: there probably weren't any other Coptos merchants moored here. None, probably, who'd brought their daughters along—and the harbor authority would be very well aware that Ani, son of Petesuchos, had a daughter, after the events of the previous day.

"Papa," she said wretchedly.

"O Isis!" groaned Papa. "Sunbird, I think we've been out of our depth from the start."

Apollonios, catching the sudden spread of sober silence, looked up and saw the Romans too. He turned furiously back to Papa and screamed, "This is *your* fault!"

CHAPTER XIII

Caesarion woke with a sense of profound joy and gratitude, a feeling that something wonderful had happened to him, though he could not quite remember what. He lay relaxed, breathing evenly and looking up at the painting on the wall. It was the *Odysseus in the Underworld* of Apollodoros, which meant that he was in the private audience chamber in the Great Palace. He could not remember going there, but that was all right: he knew he had had a seizure. He felt weak and tired and ached all over, as he always did after one of the major ones, but the usual sense of guilt and shame was quite absent. In a moment, he thought dreamily, someone would come with a cold drink, and he would ask them to prepare a bath.

"He's awake," someone said.

There was something not right about it. The voice . . .

. . . had spoken Latin. He struggled up to a sitting position—and found that he'd been lying on the floor, and that his hands were tied. He looked down at them in disbelief: lashed together in front of him with a bit of dark leather that looked like a piece of horse harness. He looked up, and saw a man standing over him and regarding him thoughtfully.

He was in his mid-thirties, pale, good-looking in a frail way, with a wide forehead and a small round chin; his brown hair fell in heavy locks across his brow and over his ears. He wore a white tunic that bore the wide purple stripe of the senatorial order, no cloak, and a heavy gold signet ring on his right hand. His face was familiar, but Caesarion could not remember ever having met him.

"You are in the palace," the man told him, in Greek. "You had a seizure on Serapeion Street, near the Canopic Way, and, unfortunately for you, my friend Areios found you and brought you here." He retreated a little, and sat down on a couch, facing Caesarion.

Caesarion looked down again at his bound hands, looked back up at the man. He remembered now where he had seen that face: statues and coins. "Octavian," he said, his throat dry.

The emperor sighed. "My name is Gaius Julius Caesar, like my father."

"*Adoptive* father," Caesarion shot back. "You were Gaius Octavius until you were my age."

"And you," Octavian replied, "were Ptolemy Caesar from the moment you were born, and given the title 'king' at the age of three. But I am emperor, and you are not." He steepled his fingers. "How is it that you're alive?"

His heart began to beat in a slow, sick rhythm he could feel in his gut. He wondered if they'd found his knife. He did not dare check, not while they were watching him. He glanced around the room, saw another man—dark, powerfully built, plainly dressed, but not, he thought, any sort of servant— standing leaning against the doorframe, also watching him. A third man—one he knew, Areios Didymos, philosopher, for- mer courtier, and ambitious traitor—was sitting very quietly on a stool by the opposite wall. Apart from that, the room was empty.

The private audience chamber had two doors, one of which led into the Red Hall, the other into a long private corridor and tunnel which went directly to the stables by the gate, so that people could be brought in and out of it without being seen by other visitors or by the palace staff. Probably someone had brought him in that way. There were guards on the gate, of course, and probably there were more guards in the Red Hall, just the other side of the larger door. Presumably the reason there were no guards in the room was because the emperor did not want people to see him and know that he was alive. That wasn't going to help him get away. He was bound, he was still weak from the seizure, and the dark man who was not a servant was standing beside the smaller door, the one that led into the private passageway. He was not going to escape. He was going to die.

He looked down at his hands again, then reached up with both of them and felt for the remedy. It was not there.

"We took your drug," said the emperor. "Also the knife stitched into your tunic." He moved a foot, and Caesarion saw both possessions, on the floor under the couch, only feet away and quite, quite out of reach. "Answer the question, son of Cleopatra."

He was going to die, but first they wanted him to talk. He must not betray any of his friends. He closed his eyes, made himself take a deep breath, opened them again. "When my camp was attacked," he told Caesar Octavian, and was relieved to find that his voice stayed level, "I had a seizure and fell into a stupor. I was stabbed as well, in the side, a deep wound. The men you'd sent to kill me apparently believed that I was dead, and put me on the pyre. When I woke, it was day, and they were not watching, so I simply walked off. They had put a tent awning over the pyre as a shroud, and apparently they never moved it, and didn't realize I had gone. There was no treachery, O Emperor—apart from Rhodon's to me." He paused, then added, "The drug you took from me is a help for the sacred disease, not a poison. You have no cause to deprive me of it."

"I had heard before that you suffered from the disease," Octavian remarked thoughtfully.

"I inherited it," Caesarion told him. "From my father."

The emperor smiled. "And who might that be, O King? Do you even know?"

"Yes," Caesarion said evenly. "As you do."

The smile vanished, was replaced by a look of cold assessment. "So. It was, you say, simple misapprehension, and not treachery, that let you survive your execution. I have seen very deep stupors following epilepsies, and you have certainly provided evidence that you are subject to them, so I suppose I must believe you. How did you escape, and what mischance brought you here?"

It was no good, sitting on the floor like a frightened child.

Caesarion got slowly to his feet and straightened, trying with all his strength to look like a Lagid and a king. "If the men you sent to take our ship have returned, you will find that they report that an Alexandrian named Arion turned up in Berenike, and attempted to contact the man left to watch for it. The centurion, Gaius Paterculus, was deceived by the false name I employed to guard myself, and by the assurances of his comrade at the camp that I was dead. I told him that I had been an officer on the staff of Eumenes, the commander of my guard and he believed this. He decided that, since I was young, wounded and unarmed, I posed no danger to the state, and he left me, in accordance with your policy of clemency."

Octavian's eyebrows shot up. "A serious error."

"What danger do I pose to you now?" Caesarion asked bitterly. "You have Egypt. I could not even flee into exile, and became instead a fugitive in my own country. I started back to Alexandria in the hope that I could help my mother, or at least my little brother, but I had the news of my mother's death on the journey and my brother has proved to be beyond my reach. The only plan I had left was to disappear quietly and live out the rest of my life under a false name."

"Who helped you?" asked Octavian implacably. "You could not have reached Alexandria on your own."

"I reached Alexandria by common means. I told no one my real name or condition. If you must know, I wrote letters to pay my way. I arrived in the city only a few days ago, and I was still trying to determine the state of things when that traitor there found me." He glanced disdainfully over his shoulder at Areios.

"You had a girl with you," Areios put in, low-voiced. "An Egyptian girl, who said her father was a Coptos merchant, and that you were his partner."

Caesarion kept his face still, fixed in the public expression of kingship he had worn for innumerable ceremonies. "A nobody. One of the people I met on the journey. If you saw her, you know why I had her with me, but I never told her anything. Did she really say I was her father's partner? Herakles, she was hopeful!"

"You also had a purse containing forty drachmae," Octavian said quietly. "And you wear a very fine tunic which is *not* military, and has that interesting little pocket for the knife. Do you claim that these were provided for the pyre, or that you obtained them as the wages of a scribe?"

He wished passionately that he had not accepted the money, and that he had worn his plain red military tunic. He had put on this one because of its pocket for the knife—much good it had done him.

"Well?" asked Octavian.

Caesarion shook his head. "Some friends gave me money and wanted to arrange a livelihood for me. No one has asked me to contend with you, O Emperor, nor have I asked help from anyone to do so. The plan was, as I said, for me to disappear quietly. I think that objective is one you share."

"Who helped you?" demanded the dark man beside the door.

He spoke in Latin, in a deep, growling voice. Caesarion glanced at him, looked back at the emperor. "I will not name them," he said evenly, in Latin to acknowledge the intervention. "I assure you, there is no plot against you. Their only crime was wanting me to live."

The emperor raised his eyebrows. "Your Latin is as fluent as it was reported to be." He, too, had shifted to Latin. "But you were raised in the hope of ruling over Romans, weren't you? I fear that we cannot accept your assurances."

The dark man left the door and stalked over. A heavy hand descended on Caesarion's shoulder. He forced himself to stand calmly and did not look around. "How many people know that you are alive?" the deep voice asked in his ear.

He stood straight and still. "They will soon know that I am dead." *Then* he allowed himself to look around into the louring face. "I presume you are Marcus Vipsanius Agrippa?"

The emperor gave a slight snort of amusement. Agrippa scowled. It had been a fair presumption: the emperor's chief general and right hand would be involved in resolving all his most sensitive problems. Areios' demeanor suggested that he was only here because he'd been the one to bring Caesarion in. He probably couldn't even understand them, now that they were speaking Latin.

"You pose us a difficulty," Octavian told him, still in Latin. "You have been publicly proclaimed dead. Your ashes have been paraded down the Nile and displayed in every town between here and Coptos. Your return has the appearance of a miracle. If we admit that we made a mistake, people will doubt all similar pronouncements we make in future. The next bad harvest will see a crop of pretenders."

"A whole rank of Caesarions, returned a second time from the dead," growled Agrippa, "with perhaps a Cleopatra or two to keep them company."

"I do not expect a public apology for the mistake," said Caesarion, and was pleased with his own coolness. "You are perfectly able to correct it privately."

"The question is whether we can," Octavian told him. "How many people know that you are alive?"

"Very few," Caesarion told him. "Emperor, you know yourself how freely our friends betrayed us. If I'd asked help from three, one at least would have turned me in."

"What *two* helped you, then?" demanded Agrippa.

Caesarion stood looking straight before himself and did not answer. The hand on his shoulder tightened its grip, and another hand caught his chin and forced his head round, so that he looked directly into the deep-set eyes. "You are officially dead," Agrippa told him. "No one will know what we do to you. Do you think we can't force the truth out of you?"

He swallowed involuntarily, and saw with shame that Agrippa noticed. Caesarion remembered how easily Hortalus had broken him in Ptolemais. He had not believed then that anyone would dare abuse him. He believed it now.

Agrippa let go of his chin. A heavy thumb rubbed at the scars on the back of his head. He remembered Melanthe touching them that morning, exploring them curiously, with love, wanting to know more of him. He closed his eyes, shuddering.

"What did that?" asked Agrippa.

O Apollo, no, please.

He heard the emperor get up and come over to look. An imperial finger traced the line where the red-hot iron had burned its way into his skull.

"I've heard of this," said Octavian. "My uncle mentioned it

once. It's a treatment for the sacred disease. Hot irons."

"On a *king?*" asked Agrippa, surprised.

"I imagine the queen wanted him cured," said the emperor. "I have never heard that he was able to oppose her in anything." He went back to his couch and sat down again. "Or did you undergo that willingly?"

Caesarion did not answer. The memory of the cauterizing irons tightened his throat, and he knew that his voice would come out shrill if he did. He wished they would give him the remedy. O Dionysos, it would be so humiliating to have a seizure now!

"My uncle would never let a doctor near him," Octavian informed him. He leaned forward. "Would you undergo that treatment again? You know more about what pain is like than many, no doubt. How much of it do you think you can endure?"

"Areios, do you understand what they are saying?" Caesarion cried loudly, in Greek. "They will torture me to obtain the names of the friends who helped me. You approve this, do you?"

Areios tried to shrink into the wall. Caesarion looked back at Octavian. "Will even the torturers approve?" he asked, still in Greek, wanting to make sure that everyone in earshot understood him. "I am a Lagid, a god and the son of a god. I am also your own kinsman, the child of the adoptive father whom you profess to honor. Even your friends flinch from this deed, and what would it gain you? One or two names of men who will, you may be very sure, never admit to having seen me alive anyway. There was no plot. You have *won*, Caesar.

Egypt is yours, my mother is dead, and I soon will be."

"We do not like having to take your word about the plot," said Agrippa, from behind him.

"I do not like being asked to betray my friends," replied Caesarion. "You would silence them forever. Probably I cannot endure very much pain—but I will try. I will not give you their names freely."

The emperor sighed and gestured to Agrippa. The big man left Caesarion and came over to sit down beside his friend. The two of them regarded him soberly, side by side.

"I would not have your friends put to death," said Octavian.

Caesarion gave a snort of derision. "No, of course not."

"Who was it? Timagenes? Athenion? Hermogenes? Archibios?"

Caesarion said nothing. He hugged to himself the thought that they would never even consider Rhodon.

"I will not harm them!" Octavian repeated impatiently. "Can't you see that it's getting too late for executions? I killed everyone I was going to kill within the first few days. To start beheading royalists *now* would attract precisely the sort of attention we wish to avoid!"

"You are king, or something more than one," Caesarion replied. "There is no check upon your actions but your own will. If you know who my friends are, the opinion of the people will not protect them."

"I am not a monster!" exclaimed the emperor. "I fought to obtain Egypt, but now that it's mine, I want it to prosper in peace. I have been clement and merciful. I will be generous to your friends, too."

"Isn't that what you told my mother?" asked Caesarion.

"That you would treat her generously? But your intention was to display her in your triumph, and when you feared she might escape you in death, you tried to prevent her by threatening to murder her children. That is the true measure of your clemency!"

"I did not kill them."

"There would have been no point, would there, when she was already dead? Caesar, you have just threatened *me* with red-hot irons. Do you really expect me to believe that you would spare my friends?"

"This is going nowhere," said Agrippa. "Lock him up, and see what else we can find."

Caesarion realized, with a catch of the heart, that they had never had any intention of torturing him. It was, as he had said, something even the emperor's friends would flinch from; it was something the emperor flinched from himself. They had merely tried to frighten him into compliance. He felt ashamed to have believed them.

"Lock him up where?" asked Octavian. "The gossip's probably running wild already. 'Areios drove up to the palace in a great hurry with a body in his carriage; it was rushed to the private chamber with a cloak over its face, and the emperor and Agrippa are both closeted there now: gods and goddesses, who do you suppose it was?' "

Areios stirred. "I did the best I could, lord!" he protested. "My attendants didn't recognize him, and I tried to prevent anyone else from seeing him."

"It was not a criticism," Octavian said at once. "You did very well. My point was that there will already be gossip about this. People will be itching to discover what's going on, and if they see *him*, the rumor will be all over the city within the hour. 'Ptolemy Caesar has come back from the dead and is a prisoner in the palace!' There'd be a riot by nightfall. If we move him with a cloak over his head and pick guards whom we know to be trustworthy and silent, that will only show the rest that we have something we badly want to hide." He rested his chin on his fist and stared angrily at Caesarion.

"We could put him in the corridor for now," suggested Agrippa. "Shackled, with two trustworthy men to watch him. It's private, and it saves us rearranging shifts in the prison. Or we could have him strangled immediately. It's not what I'd recommend, not without knowing who he's seen, but it would prevent any outcry about him being alive."

Octavian sighed and straightened. "The corridor," he decided. "See to it at once. And ask Longinus if he's managed to trace the girl yet."

Caesarion pressed his hands together, trying to keep his face still. *Trace the girl. An Egyptian girl, who said her father was a Coptos merchant . . .*

O Zeus, knowing that, they *could* trace Melanthe. Ani had made a stir about her disappearance, and the guard had been looking for her. Any merchant from Coptos would use the Mareotic Harbor, and there were not many such merchants about at the moment.

"I've already told you," he said, managing to keep his voice steady, "the girl's nobody. I never told her or her father anything about myself."

Octavian and Agrippa both looked back at him. He realized, with a sick lurch, that he should have volunteered nothing.

They had assumed that she *was* unimportant, and he had just showed them that she was not.

"She was with you long enough to know who you were visiting, was she?" Agrippa asked, smiling for the first time.

Melanthe *did* know who else had helped him. She had met Rhodon. He had tried not to name Archibios in front of her, but probably she had heard the name, from the slaves, if from no one else. She probably didn't even understand what would happen to the men if she named them, but if she did, and if she tried to keep silent, she would be tortured. The scruples which protected him would not extend to an Egyptian girl at all.

He was going to destroy everyone who had helped him— Rhodon, his red-haired mistress, his little children; Archibios, that loyal and generous old man; Ani; Tiathres and Serapion and little Isisdoros; the slaves and helpers; beautiful Melanthe, who had promised she would love him whatever he told her about himself. They were all going to die—because they had made the huge mistake of helping him.

He imagined them using the irons on Melanthe.

"Please," he heard himself say, and heard his voice crack. "The only offense these people have committed is to help me. The girl and her family don't even know who I am. They are not your enemies, Caesar. I beg you, do not harm them."

There was a silence, and then Octavian asked incredulously, "You *beg* me?"

"I beg you!" Caesarion repeated recklessly. "Do you want me to kneel? To prostrate myself? I will, if you will spare them. The shame will be yours, Caesar, for requiring it." He dropped to his knees. "I beg you, Caesar, show mercy to innocent people who have committed no crime against you!"

Octavian took a step back in alarm. "Get up!" he ordered. "I do *not* require it."

"Swear that you will punish no one merely for helping me!"

"You are in no position to make demands!" Agrippa broke in angrily.

"I am not demanding," Caesarion told him fiercely. "I am begging. I am a Lagid, and I am on my knees, begging your friend to spare people who have never harmed him in any way at all. O gods, witness it!"

"Get *up*!" Octavian cried. "Apollo! I did not ask this!"

Agrippa hurried out of the room.

"You did not ask this," Caesarion agreed, meeting the emperor's eyes. "You asked instead that I betray my friends. You felt no shame in asking it, or in threatening me with torture when I refused. Are you ashamed now, because you have forced me to beg you for mercy for them—no, it is not even *mercy*! It is mercy to spare the guilty, but to spare the innocent is *justice*, Caesar! Will you not grant it?"

Agrippa came back in with two men in the strip armor and old-fashioned high-crested helmets of the Praetorian Guard. From the amount of gold on their harness, they were both high-ranking. "Take him out," he ordered them, pointing to Caesarion. "Keep him in the private corridor outside this room until we summon you. No one is to come near him or speak to him, and you are to tell no one anything that you may see or hear in connection with him—not your brothers or lovers, not your own officers. He is Ptolemy Caesar, the son of Cleopatra, and no rumor of his survival must reach the city. I will send Longinus to you presently with some shackles for him."

The two guards stared at Caesarion in shock, but they saluted Agrippa and stamped over. Caesarion got to his feet as they reached him, knowing that the alternative was to be dragged off on his knees. He did not resist as they took hold of his arms. They marched him over to the small dark door. He glanced over his shoulder and saw that Octavian was still watching him. Their eyes met and held as the door opened and he was forced through; and then the door shut and he was trapped in the dark passage with the guards to secure him there and no hope at all.

CHAPTER XIV

The arrest in Ptolemais had been worse, Ani told himself, watching as the Romans secured *Soteria* and posted a guard on it. There'd been shouting, blows, screaming children. The soldiers making the arrest had barely spoken Greek, and everything had been confusion and pain. This was very orderly: "Are you Ani son of Petesuchos, a merchant from Coptos?" asked the commanding officer, in good Greek. "Is this your daughter? We have orders to arrest you." They would not say why he was being arrested, but they were willing to explain—without shouting!—that this was because they'd not been informed themselves. A couple of the men leered at Melanthe, but their officer rebuked them. They carefully ascertained who everyone was, checked that there was no one missing, and bound each man in turn, neatly and without violence.

In a way, though, the very restraint was frightening. Ptolemais had been what an Egyptian expected of Greek justice, but this orderliness, this methodical pinning down of everyone and everything involved—this had the feeling of an action from above, commanded by a power the soldiers themselves were afraid of. And this time, they were arresting everyone. Even Tiathres. Even the children.

One of the Romans finished making an inventory of the boat's documents. He signed it, set it on top of the sheaf of papyri, and put it in the strongbox. He tucked the strongbox under his arm and nodded to the officer in command. The officer called an order and the troop set off, the Egyptians roped together in the middle and the Romans flanking them.

Ani had been given the position of lead prisoner in respect of his status. Like all the men, his hands had been tied behind his back; a rope around his neck secured him—to their mutual dismay—to Apollonios, who was next in line. The women and children had been left unbound, the children because they were too small and the women because they were needed to look after the children. Tiathres and the nurse took turns carrying Isisdoros, who was too young to walk far, and Melanthe clasped Serapion's hand tightly. The little boy had cried when they tied up his father, but he was not crying now, only staring with huge frightened eyes.

Ani's position placed him near the Roman officer. When they were under way he hurried to the limit of the rope, ignoring Apollonios' protest, and called out, "Sir—please?"

The officer glanced back at him disapprovingly.

"Sir, where are you taking us?" Ani asked.

"The palace," was the short reply.

"The *palace?*" Ani repeated incredulously. "Why?"

"I've already told you. I obey my orders. I don't ask my commander to explain them. Be quiet."

"But, sir, we are common, ordinary people!"

"If there has been a mistake, they will sort it out when we arrive. Be quiet."

It was a long walk: through the Mareotic Gate, up Soma Street past the precinct of the royal tombs, past the mausoleum of the city's founder, Alexander the Great, past the great Museum and the famous Library. The streets grew steadily wider, the buildings which flanked them more splendid. Ani's bonds rubbed his wrists raw, and his shoulders started to ache from walking with his hands behind his back. He found, though, that he did not notice it as much as he should have done: too much of himself was stifled by a sense of horrified awe. It was as though he had received some terrible and vital revelation, but he had somehow forgotten it—or as though the part of himself which had grasped it was too appalled to yield it up.

They came at last to a wall, and to a gate guarded by men in the same uniform worn by their captors. There the Roman troop halted with a double stamp, and the prisoners stumbled to a stop.

"That's the palace," Serapion said, his small voice carrying through the sudden hush. "We tried to go in yesterday to see the menagerie, but they wouldn't let us in."

The officer turned and looked down at the little boy with a grim smile. "They will let you in today, child. If you are lucky, they may even let you out again." He marched over to the gate and spoke to the guards, and the great iron-bound doors swung open to engulf them.

The palace was not a single building but a vast complex.

From the gate they could see a mass of domes and porticoes set amid the abundant green of lavish gardens. It was a fantasia of marble and palms, gilding and grapevines, airy and spacious and spectacularly beautiful. Their guards, however, turned to the right, into a courtyard flanked by a barracks and a stable. They halted there and stood in the sun of the barracks yard while the officer went off to report to his superior.

It took a long time. They were all hot, tired, and thirsty from the long walk. Isisdoros began to cry. Tiathres knelt in the dust of the square and rocked him on her lap. The nurse, poor frightened woman, sat curled up with her hands over her head. Melanthe sat down beside her and held Serapion.

At first the Romans ringing them just leaned against their spears, but after a while they allowed the male prisoners to sit down where they were, and half the guards went off and sat down in the shade in front of the west wall of the barracks.

At last the officer came back. With him was a man in a short red cloak and gilded armor—a superior officer of some kind, though Ani did not know enough about Romans to put a name to the rank. The guards in the shade stood up, and the guards on watch prodded the prisoners to make them stand up. The superior officer regarded the Egyptians with distaste. "Which of you is in charge?" he demanded.

Ani straightened his aching shoulders. "I am, sir," he said. "Ani son of Petesuchos. Sir, I think there has been some mistake. I am a merchant, sir, I . . ."

"You are from Coptos?" asked the man in gilded armor.

"Yes, sir. I am acting as agent for my partner Kleon, a cap—"

"You have a daughter, about sixteen?"

"Me," said Melanthe, tugging a fold of her cloak farther over her head.

The man in gilded armor regarded her with narrowed eyes, then nodded. He said something in Latin to the officer who'd arrested them; the officer replied. The commander gave an order, and the officer saluted.

"You and the girl are to come with us," the officer told Ani. "The others will stay here."

Serapion began to cry. Tiathres tried to comfort him. As the soldiers untied the rope around his neck and separated him from Apollonios, Ani looked longingly at his wife and sons. He looked back at the officer. "Sir," he asked humbly, "please may my people have some water to drink?"

The officer hesitated—then snapped his fingers and gave an order in Latin. "I have told the men to fetch water," he said.

"Thank you," whispered Ani.

The officer nodded and jerked his hand in the direction of the main gate. Ani bowed his head, and started to walk as he'd been told.

"Not that way!" said the man in gilded armor.

The officer looked startled and confused. His superior snorted, then pointed in the opposite direction—across the barracks square toward the stables. The officer looked still more confused. The commander set off in the direction he'd indicated, and the officer herded Ani and Melanthe after him.

They went into the stable, and there, among the stalls for the horses, was a locked door. The commander took a key from his belt and opened it. A flight of steps ran down into darkness. After the hot sun of the square outside, that entrance looked as black as the mouth of the Underworld. The gilded commander stood aside for them, holding the door and the key, ready to lock it again when they had passed. He spoke briefly to the arresting officer—an order, it sounded like, and a warning.

The officer became afraid. Ani could see the fear settle over him, and felt his own skin prickle cold in response. The Roman glanced at Ani and Melanthe in confusion—then nodded and started down the stairs, his feet loud in the silence.

Melanthe balked, stood trembling at the top of the stairs, gazing down into the darkness. "What is this?" she asked, in a frightened whisper. "What are you going to do to us?"

"This is another way into the palace," said the commander impatiently. "A private way. You are to see the emperor."

Her head jerked up, and she stared at him in terror. "The *emperor*? Why? W-we haven't done *anything*!"

Ani felt some balance shift inside himself. Outside in the barracks yard sat his wife and sons; in the Mareotic Harbor his livelihood lay impounded. Before him was only this—a journey into the Underworld, from which it was unlikely he would return. But he had no choice. In his heart he committed himself and his daughter to Isis and Serapis, who alone could overcome Fate. "We'll find out why they want us soon enough," he told Melanthe. "Come on, Sunbird. I'll be right behind you."

Melanthe caught her breath—then walked slowly down into the darkness. Ani followed her. The gilded commander came last, and paused to lock the door.

The passageway was not, after all, unlit. Shafts at regular intervals allowed daylight to filter in and illumine the smooth flagstones of the floor. The walls were smooth, whitewashed plaster, and from overhead came sounds—horses, at first, and the voices of men; then noises of water, of a garden being dug, of people talking, too remote to be understood. Their own walk was in silence, apart from the sound of their footsteps—the clicking thud of the hobnailed sandals of the two officers, the softer slapping of his own feet and the whisper of Melanthe's. After a time there was another flight of steps, this time going up, and after that the passage had more the appearance of a corridor, with a boarded floor. It twisted and turned corners, as though it were working its way deep into a building. Sometimes there were windows instead of skylights, but they were always too high up to allow more than a glimpse of treetop or sky. Once there was a door, and the officer, in the lead, paused and looked back questioningly at the man in gilded armor, but the commander shook his head.

Just when it seemed to Ani that the passage would go on forever, they rounded a corner and came upon people. Two of them were soldiers who wore the same uniform as their captors, and stood leaning on their spears; between them another figure sat on the floor, its back against the wall and its head resting on its knees.

"Arion!" cried Melanthe, somehow sensing the identity of what was only a dark shape in a dim corridor.

The figure on the floor lifted his head, and it was indeed Arion. There were leg-irons about his ankles and shackles on his wrists. The faint gray light caught in the gold on his tunic. His face was pale. Then the nearer of his two guards stepped between them and lowered his spear threateningly at the newcomers. "Consistete!" he ordered.

The commander called out something, then squeezed past

the prisoners and began speaking to the guard, who raised his spear again at once.

Arion got to his feet, clanking, bracing himself against the wall. All the Romans looked around at him quickly, as though alarmed.

"Melanthe," he said, in a low, hoarse voice. "Ani." He took a deep breath. "I'm sorry."

"Tace!" a guard told him urgently.

"You should have left me in the road by Kabalsi," said Arion, ignoring him. "I wish you had."

Ani expected the guards to hit him, to threaten him into silence—but they did not. It was as though they were afraid of him. Instead, one of them gestured urgently for the new-comers to go past. The officer hurried by, and the commander caught Melanthe's arm and dragged her after him. She dug in her heels.

"I'm so sorry!" she told Arion breathlessly. "If it wasn't for me you'd be on your way to Cyprus."

Arion gave a sick smile and shook his head. The man in armor hauled Melanthe on by brute force, past Arion. Ani was now last. He thought of saying something, but he didn't know what to say, and it looked as if Arion's guards would hit him if he said anything, so he edged past in silence. The corridor was narrow, and his shoulder almost brushed Arion's chest. The young man's eyes were fixed on him with a desperate intensity, anguished and ashamed. He wanted to stop, to take the boy's arm and tell him it was all right—but it was not all right, and he could not, his hands were tied.

He was past. Behind him, Arion slumped to the floor with

another clank, and buried his head in his shackled hands.

There was a door at the end of the corridor. The man in gilded armor knocked on it, and it opened.

The room beyond was about the size of an ordinary dining room. On the wall, facing the door by which they entered, was a painting, about six feet long, which showed a man by a dark river, reaching out one hand pleadingly to the shadowy figure of another man, who had turned away. Insubstantial ghosts ringed him, and his friends had covered their heads in grief. After what had just happened in the corridor the image struck against Ani's heart like a hammer and for a moment he could do nothing but gaze.

"It's the right girl," said a voice, and Ani looked away from the painting. There were three men in the room: a small man in a crimson cloak, who had spoken; a large, dark man, plainly dressed, who was leaning against the wall by the door they'd just used; and a slim pale man in a purple-striped white tunic, who sat upon an ivory couch.

"That's Areios," Melanthe said, drawing close to her father and glaring at the man in crimson.

"It seems the recognition is mutual," said the man in the purple-striped tunic with satisfaction. "And you, fellow—are you this girl's father?"

"Yes," Ani whispered. His mouth was dry. "Ani son of Petesuchos. Sir . . . Lord . . . forgive me, I don't want to be insolent, but I'm a stranger to the city, and I don't know much about powerful people. Are you the emperor?"

"Yes," the other replied, very calmly. "I am." He smiled very slightly. "In time, Egypt will learn to recognize me."

Ani knelt, clumsily. He knew you were supposed to prostrate yourself to a king, but he had no idea how you went about it.

"Do not prostrate yourself," Octavian said, gesturing for him to rise. "It is an oriental custom we Romans despise." Ani struggled to get back to his feet without the use of his arms. "Do you know why I have had you brought here?"

Melanthe took a deep breath. "It's because of Arion," she declared—boldly, though she stood close enough that Ani could see how she was trembling. "That man Areios has told you some lie about his cousin Arion."

"His cousin Arion?" repeated the emperor in surprise. "Who and what do you mean?"

Ani wished that the emperor had allowed him to kneel: his knees were weak, and his bowels wanted to give way. The terrible fact he had grasped had at last revealed itself to him. "O Isis!" he whispered. Melanthe looked at him in confusion and alarm.

"His name isn't really Arion," he told her, swallowing. He looked back into the emperor's cold eyes. "It's *Caes*arion, isn't it?" he whispered.

"But that's the king," Melanthe said—and then her face went still, and her eyes widened and darkened with horror. "The king's *dead*!" she protested. "I *saw* the urn with his ashes in it!"

Her voice betrayed her, its sharpening shrillness proclaiming that she knew what she said was untrue.

"He told me, right at the start, that the Romans thought he was dead," Ani told her, and his own voice was unsteady. "He said they anointed him for the pyre, and he woke up while they were asleep, and walked off. I thought he was just feverish and confused."

"So he did tell you about himself," said the emperor grimly.

"No," Ani replied numbly. "No. He told us very little. I've been working it out . . . since your guards came for us." He looked back at the implacable face of the new lord of Egypt. "When he said that his second cousin would kill him over a disputed inheritance—it wasn't Areios he meant, was it? It was you."

"Yes," agreed the emperor, satisfied.

"Second cousin?" asked the dark man.

"If one accepted Cleopatra's account of his paternity," replied Octavian, "I would indeed be his second cousin once removed."

Ani could not meet his eyes. A thousand small senseless things crashed together into a sense so inevitable and overpowering that he knew he should have seen it long, long before. He remembered Arion's distress at hearing that the queen was a prisoner, his alarm when Caesarion was first mentioned, his surprise when the centurion in Berenike had addressed him by the name he had given Ani. He remembered the boy, wounded and wretched, saying that the Romans had thought he was dead; later, when he heard that the king had been in the camp, and was dead, he had not remembered it, had not considered, even for a moment, that a young man who'd been in that struggle and been presumed dead—a young man who was clearly aristocratic and exactly the right age—might actually *be* the king. All the things he had learned about Arion since then—the Roman father, the grief at the queen's death, the increasingly open references to a powerful enemy whose attention Ani must at all costs avoid—all of them he had ignored, or misconstrued into some ludicrous fantasy of estates and legacies. Why had he been such a blind fool?

Because he was an ordinary man, and ordinary men did not invite fugitive kings to write letters for them. Because the more he got to know Arion, the more he had seen him as fragile and human and likable, and the more impossible it became to associate him with the divine son of Queen Cleopatra and Julius Caesar.

"He has the sacred disease," he said stupidly. "I never heard that the king had the sacred disease."

"It is not something one would boast about," replied Octavian. "I had heard, from those who were well informed about the court," he glanced at Areios, "but on the whole the queen succeeded in suppressing any discussion of her son's infirmity."

"He said his father had it. I never heard that . . ."

"My adoptive father," said the emperor, "did suffer from the disease. I do not accept, of course, that Ptolemy Caesar is his son. The queen saw many advantages in claiming that her child was Caesar's." He tapped the arm of the couch. "You understand now, I think, that your situation is very serious. You have given shelter and assistance to King Ptolemy Caesar, whom I sentenced to death. I had believed that my sentence was carried out. It was not pleasant to discover that a man whom I believed was safely reduced to ash has in fact been wandering freely about Egypt for the past month. If you wish to live, you will tell me everything you know—where he has been, what he has done, and, most particularly, who he has spoken to. It is clear that, whether you knew who he was or not, you have been rather closer to him than he wished to admit. You have a daughter"—the eyes glanced at her and lingered a moment—"and, so I have been informed, a wife, sons, slaves, and friends who are in my hands. They will die—believe it!—if you lie or prevaricate in any way."

Ani stood under the chill gaze, aware of Melanthe shivering beside him, of the pain of his chafed wrists and the ache in his shoulders. He thought of Tiathres sitting in the dust and sun of the barracks yard, comforting their children. For the first time the stifling horror eased enough to admit another emotion—a trickle of anger.

"I found him on the road to Berenike," he said. "Near the waystation of Kabalsi. It was the night of the fourteenth or fifteenth of August. He was lying in the road, wounded and unconscious. I picked him up and helped him for no other reason than that he would have died if I hadn't, and I couldn't let a young man die when it was within my power to save him. He told me his name was Arion, that he was from Alexandria, that he'd been in a camp belonging to the queen's forces which your troops had just taken. Later, when I learned that the king had been in the camp, he added that he'd been a Friend of the king. He tried to meet a ship in Berenike and leave Egypt, but your people had already taken it. I was planning to go to Alexandria on business, so I offered to let him come with me if he would write my letters. I am an uneducated man, lord—an upstart peasant, if you like: I grow flax and make linen goods, and just this summer I've been trying to become a merchant. I'd gone to Berenike with a load of linen goods which I placed with a ship-owner captain named Kleon, who agreed to a partnership with me. Kleon entrusted me with a cargo of spices to take to Alexandria and sell on commission; I was to buy glass and tin with the proceeds. It is not easy for a man like me to get Alexandrian merchants to accept him, and I knew that to have an educated Greek to write letters for me and advise me would help. Arion agreed to write the letters, and they *have* helped. Your men took all the papers from my boat, and if you like you can see everything he's done. He wasn't happy about it, particularly at first; he thought it was degrading, and since he's a king I suppose he was right. But that's what he did, and there's nothing he did which was political in any way. When we reached Alexandria, seven days ago, I pressed him to stay with me and offered him a partnership, but he told me that he had an enemy who would destroy me for helping him, and left us. I didn't see him again until just now in the corridor outside this room. That, lord, is the truth, as I love life."

"Your daughter was seen with him this morning," said the dark man.

Ani met his eyes. "My daughter, lord, was dragged off my boat yesterday afternoon by robbers who killed one of my slaves. If you doubt me, you can ask the harbor authority and the city watch, whose doors I was battering down for news of her all night. She turned up back at my boat again only a few hours ago. She says Arion rescued her and was bringing her home when he suffered a seizure and fell into your hands." He realized that he was still talking about "Arion." Knowing the boy's real name didn't seem to have changed how he thought of him.

The boy. Arion. King Ptolemy Caesar, the God Who Loves His Father and Mother, the son of a woman who had claimed to be the living incarnation of Isis . . . He could not fit the titles to the young man he knew. Sweet Lady Isis, what had he gotten into?

The emperor gave Melanthe another thoughtful look. Then he glanced at the gilded commander, who saluted.

"I have seen the documents the merchant referred to," he said. "Most of them are, indeed, concerned with customs dues, incense, and tin. There is also, however, a letter from Gaius Cornelius Gallus, saying that the merchant was arrested on a charge of fomenting sedition, which he investigated and found to originate in mistaken information obtained from a rival merchant."

The emperor looked back at Ani, suddenly all ice.

"I have an enemy called Aristodemos," said Ani. He found that he was able to speak quite firmly and clearly: *nothing* that happened now could make his situation any worse. "He used to be the partner of Kleon, the Red Sea trader who is now working with me, and he was very angry that I had, as he saw it, stolen his place. He met Arion briefly in Coptos marketplace when we went to pay the dues on the cargo, and heard that he was a Friend of the king. On the strength of this he went to Ptolemais Hermiou and told General Gallus that Arion was a rebel trying to stir up trouble, and that I was helping him, funding him with the cargo we were carrying. But it was all lies, and the only reason he said it was to make trouble—for me; he didn't know or care a thing about Arion. He didn't even know that Arion spoke Latin. He probably would have chosen a different lie if he had, because it was Arion's Latin that got us out of that mess, since he was able to persuade the Ro—General Gallus' men, to listen to our side of the story. My daughter says that Aristodemos is the one who set the robbers on to our ship as well, and I've discussed *that* with the city watch, too. You can prove even with the documents you have that we weren't fermenting any sedition. I paid my customs dues in Coptos on the third of September. General Gallus had us arrested in Ptolemais Hermiou on the sixth, and released us on the seventh, as his letter should tell you. We passed the customs post at Babylon on the twentieth and registered with the harbor authority in Alexandria on the twenty-third. It's a long way to Coptos, lord, and my boat's heavy and was running with eight oars: there wasn't *time* for us to ferment sedition. And I didn't fund anything with the cargo: I brought it straight here to Alexandria, sold it, and spent the proceeds on glass and tin, apart from Kleon's profit and my commission, which are deposited in a bank. I'm an honest man, and it's all accounted for." He met the cold eyes steadily. "I didn't fight for the queen, either. I don't even think she was a good ruler. All up and down the Nile there's good land going to desert because the money and the men that should have repaired the dikes and ditches went to support her foreign wars. Now that you are ruler of Egypt, lord, I hope you will do a better job, and spare something to improve your land."

There was a silence. "Egyptian," said the emperor, "you are insolent."

"I'm sorry," said Ani at once, sincerely. "I didn't mean to be. As I said, I'm a plain man and I don't know the right manners to use to a king. I'd prostrate myself, but you say you don't like that."

Octavian's mouth twitched. He leaned back. "Very well. Say I accept your account of yourself and your dealings. In that case, we know that Ptolemy Caesar was innocently en- gaged in trade between his supposed death on the—the four- teenth of August, wasn't it, Marcus?—the fourteenth of August, and your arrival in Alexandria on—when was it again?"

"The twenty-third of September," said Ani, in a low voice. *Did* the emperor accept his account? Did he dare hope for anything?

"The twenty-third of September," repeated Octavian. "My birthday, as it happens. Apollo, what a birthday present! Today is the twenty-ninth. By your account, you parted from the king seven days ago, and know nothing he's done since—apart from the alleged rescue of your daughter." He surveyed Ani and Melanthe, his eyes cold again. "He has, I know, ap- proached certain of his friends for help. I need to know who they are. If you can tell me, I will conclude that you are not rebels, and I will be able to be merciful, to you and to the rest of your people who are in my hands. If you refuse to reveal them, I will know that you are part of a plot, and treat you accordingly."

Ani still wasn't sure whether he dared hope, but his sense of calm was gone. His heart beat wildly, and he wished again that the emperor would allow him to kneel. "I don't know who he went to see," he croaked. "Melanthe, if you know anything—tell him."

Melanthe looked at the emperor, her eyes enormous.

"All our lives depend on it!" Ani urged her.

"I . . ." she began. She bit her lip. "Sir—please. What will happen to Arion's . . . t-to the king's friends? They were only trying to help him. They weren't trying to rebel against you."

"If that is the truth, then they have nothing to fear," said Octavian, without hesitation. "You know who they are, do you?"

"I . . . I think so. Sir, there was one man who was with Arion, his friend, and there was another man who'd lent him money and attendants and slaves and things. If there was anyone else, I don't know anything about them."

"With him where?" the dark man, Marcus, asked sharply. "Where was this?"

"On a ship, sir. The . . . the robbers took me to this ship. I don't know what it was called, but the captain was named Kinesias, and it was going to sail to Cyprus. The captain bought free people and sold them as slaves overseas. Arion was there, as a passenger—I suppose because Kinesias had bribed the port authorities so he could leave without anyone seeing what he had on board. Arion had a lot of people with him. He was going to go to Cyprus to manage a friend's estate there, but when he saw me he tried to make them let me go, and there was a fight and . . . I can see now that the captain realized who he was, and refused to carry him because of it. I didn't understand it at the time. So we got off the ship, and Arion sent all the people and things back to their master, and he said he would find another way out of the city. The friend who was with him told me that Arion meant to kill himself, and we tried to persuade him to be my father's partner instead. But sir, please believe me, nobody at all was saying anything about fighting you!"

"The names!" said Marcus impatiently. "Two of them, you said! Two names!"

"The man who had the estate, who owned the slaves—he

was called Archi-something. I never met him, and I didn't hear his name more than once or twice: Arion tried not to use it. But the slaves mentioned him. Archi . . . Archib—"

"Archibios?" asked Marcus.

"Yes," said Melanthe. "That was it."

Marcus smiled in relief. He looked at Octavian.

"It makes sense," said the emperor. "And we can easily confirm, too, whether he owns an estate in Cyprus. Very good, girl. And the other friend, the one you did meet?"

"Rhodon," Melanthe said at once. "He said he was a philosopher, and he'd been Arion's teacher."

Ani abruptly remembered why he'd heard that name. Rhodon was the young king's tutor who'd betrayed him, on whose spear he'd been reported to have died. He remembered suddenly the first time he'd questioned Arion: *"Why weren't you wearing armor?" "I was asleep. Rhodon came, and . . ."* and another of those maddening halts, which had led him—hot, thirsty, itching, and irritable as he was—to goad the boy: *"Rhodon your lover?"*

No, Rhodon was the one who'd made the hole in his side. So what was Rhodon doing on a ship with Arion, happily accepted as Arion's friend? It didn't make sense—unless you postulated that there had been some kind of plot all along, that King Ptolemy Caesar's death had been staged, that there were real and serious plans for rebellion, and Rhodon had always been a part of them.

There had been no plan. Ani could know that: he had seen the wound, the muddle and confusion. But the emperor could not know, and the doubt and alarm were growing on his face.

Melanthe was still staring at the emperor, puzzled now,

aware that something had gone wrong but not knowing what.

"Rhodon," said Octavian sharply. "You're sure of this?"

The little man Areios pushed himself off from the wall and, for the first time, tried to make himself noticed. Here in this room "the most powerful man in Alexandria" seemed so insignificant that Ani had almost forgotten him. "Caesar," he said.

Octavian looked at him.

"I, uh . . . well, Rhodon and I studied together, and . . . well, I have spoken to him a couple of times since . . . He has been very remorseful. He hadn't meant to kill the boy, he said; he only meant to take him prisoner and bring him back here to the city. He thought you could be persuaded to spare him. I . . . I don't think there was any plot. I think he believed the young man was dead, and when he found that he was still alive, he seized the opportunity to make amends."

Octavian kept looking at him. Areios ducked his head. He did not give up, though, and Ani realized that this was actually a decent and merciful man, eager to protect his friends—that Melanthe had misjudged him. "Lord, I *know* Rhodon," he persisted. "He is direct to the point of being simple. I can't imagine that he would be capable of *pretending* remorse and shame while he knew that in fact the young man he was believed to have killed was still alive. He's not a good actor, Caesar. He wouldn't convince anyone. And—lord—your own men reported that Ptolemy Caesar was stabbed by his tutor and died. If the man who was stabbed wasn't Ptolemy Caesar, then who did the merchant find wounded on the road? And if the merchant and his daughter are part of the plot, and found no one on the road, why would they name Rhodon now? And if they weren't part of the plot, and found no one, how do they know the young man at all? Caesar, the proposition is alarming at first glance, but the more it's examined, the more contradictions it reveals, and the weaker it becomes."

Another slow relaxation. The emperor nodded. He turned to the silent guard commander. "Tell the men in the corridor to bring the young man in," he ordered. "Tell them to take the irons off his legs first. No need to make him shuffle."

The commander bowed and went out.

There was a thick silence. Melanthe stood very still, trembling, her hands pressed together, watching the door with a hopeless look that Ani found still had the power to hurt him. He remembered when he had been a few years older than her, and had met her mother. O Isis, to have such a fire in the heart for a creature who had always belonged to another world, and who would soon be dead.

They might all soon be dead, he reminded himself.

The door opened again, and the little procession came through: the commander; the first guard; Arion; the second guard. Arion still wore the shackles on his wrists. He had lost his cloak, and there was dirt on the expensive gold-worked black tunic. His eyes were red. He held himself, though, like a king. He always had, Ani realized: on a camel or a boat, in company or alone, half naked on a pallet under an awning with a hole in his side, he had always had that air of disdainful assurance, that absolute grace. Ani himself had felt it from the start, had been irritated by it, had later approved its effect on others. He had never understood it for what it was.

Arion glanced at Ani unhappily; looked for a longer moment

at Melanthe, then turned his eyes to the emperor—as though, Ani thought, he were the one in command and the emperor merely someone who must report to him.

"Archibios," said Octavian levelly, "and Rhodon."

There was a flicker of grief. Arion's eyes went again to Melanthe, and for a moment the look again became one of anguish. Then they went back to the emperor, and the mask of disdain settled again.

"Rhodon is a surprise," said Octavian. "When was that arranged?"

"It was a chance meeting," Arion replied, his voice completely steady and as beautifully modulated as ever. "When we arrived in Alexandria, I went to the precinct of the tombs to consider what to do. I found a certain urn in a garden where I used to like to sit. Rhodon came there to tend it. He was very surprised to find me, as he had sincerely believed me dead. For my part, I would have fled him if I could, but he prevented me. However, after some discussion, and after I told him that I wished only to disappear quietly, he asked me to allow him to help. I stayed at his house, and he approached Archibios. Neither of them suggested anything against you, O Emperor. They are innocent men whose only crime is that they tried to save the life of a friend. Will you grant my request?"

Arion's look was one of proud challenge; the emperor, seated, returned a gaze of cold appraisal. "Rhodon is still a surprise," Octavian insisted. "He betrayed you. By all accounts, he injured you severely."

"He did so," Arion said at once. "If you do not credit the

account of a whole century of your own men, Caesar, the evidence is in my flesh. I am sure you will not scruple to examine it, and I cannot prevent you."

The emperor gazed at him a moment impassively. Then he nodded to the guard commander.

The guards did not want to press any indignity upon a king. They took hold of Arion very tentatively, tried to see if they could work the tunic off his shoulders without taking it off. The tunic was stitched, and could not be slipped off, and the shackles were in the way. They fussed with the stitching and the chains. Arion, his face burning but expressionless, finally fumbled at his own belt with his chained hands, unfastened it and let it drop. At this the soldiers finally pulled the tunic up, over his head, exposing his body as though it were a slave's. The new scar stood out on his right side, still red and swollen with blood. Octavian nodded again, and the guards pulled the tunic down and fastened the belt back on in embarrassed silence.

"The centurion in charge was a reliable and trustworthy man," said the emperor. "I am sure Rhodon wounded you, and you appeared dead. Yet you trusted Rhodon. You did more than that: when I asked you to name him, and threatened you with torture, you refused. This surprises me."

Melanthe put her hands over her mouth, appalled by the revelation that she'd betrayed something Arion had been willing to endure torture to suppress.

"I forgave him," said Arion. The color was still hot in his cheeks. He had not, Ani realized, expected the emperor to take up the offer to examine him, and he was humiliated and furious. "I understand why he acted as he did. I did not want him *dead* Caesar. I do not want anyone to die for helping me. Will you grant my request?"

Melanthe caught her breath, and Arion looked round at her quickly, his face suddenly unguarded again.

"He said he wouldn't hurt anyone if all they'd done was help you," Melanthe whispered.

"Melanthion, kings lie," Arion replied. "This man has lied, and lied, and lied again; he has signed treaties full of promises and broken them all. But you were not to know. What else did he tell you? That he'd spare you if you told him what he wanted to know?"

"Yes," said Melanthe, trembling. "And he said he'd kill all of us, even my brothers, if we didn't."

" 'Kings lie'!" Octavian broke in sarcastically. "She should have learned that from you, *Arion*. Girl, I have no reason to kill your brothers. As for your request, Ptolemy Caesar, I have not yet decided whether to grant it or not. Whether or not you believe it, I wish to be clement where I can."

"Were you *unable* to be clement," Arion asked savagely, "when you and your colleagues published the proscriptions and sentenced the best men in Italy to death? —Over two thousand of them, I believe."

"That was twelve years ago," said Octavian, sharply. The cold was suddenly shot with real anger. "And those men were all enemies. Archibios and Rhodon have both, in their ways, rendered me service."

"Two thousand talents of silver," Arion sneered, "and fifty of gold. Of course, proscriptions raise a lot of money, too.

Your clemency has always been weaker than your greed. Were you clement to Mardion and Diomedes and Alexas? To Antyllus? To my mother? To me?"

Octavian's fists clenched.

"Boy!" said Ani, through his teeth, and Arion looked at him angrily. "You're not helping. If the man says he wants to be clement, don't, for life's sake, talk him out of it!"

There was a silence. Arion's cheeks were flaming, and his eyes were hot. Ani realized that he'd just called him "boy" in front of all of them.

It seemed, however, to have cooled the imperial temper again. Octavian gave Ani an ironic glance, then turned his attention back to Arion. "You forgive Rhodon and understand why he acted as he did," he prompted.

Arion stood in silence for a moment, his cheeks still burning. "He has a mistress and children here in Alexandria," he said at last. "He did not want to leave them unprotected when the city fell. And he said—quite rightly—that the war was over, and that to continue it was simply to waste more lives and money upon a cause that was already lost." He lifted his head. "My mother could oppose you, Caesar, only because she allied herself with Antonius. I have no Roman allies: they are all yours, or dead. I am Caesar's son, but you are his heir. If I were free, and king of Egypt, still I could not contend with you. The most I could do against you would be cause you some trouble and expense; any war I began would be over within a year, and my own people would suffer for it most. You alone have the power to create peace. And therefore I agree with Rhodon that it is better for me to die. What I have asked you—and the only thing I have asked you—is that you act justly and spare those who never committed any offense except to help me."

There was a long silence. "You surprise me very much," Octavian said at last.

"Will you grant my request?" Arion asked again.

The emperor leaned forward and rested his chin on his hands. "Let us be clear about what your friends were doing. If they had taken and concealed a treasure which was forfeit to the state, they would expect to die for it. If they had been found stockpiling weapons and engines of war, they would be executed—even if they claimed they wished only to preserve the things, not use them. You would be a very great treasure to any rebellion which might arise, and a very dangerous weapon in any future war. Your friends were well aware of that."

"These two here were not."

"They are, however, now aware of many things which I do not want revealed."

"If you will not grant them mercy," Arion said, speaking faintly but with great deliberation, "will you let me buy it for them?"

The eyes narrowed. "Anything you possessed is now mine by right of conquest. What do you think to offer me?"

"A letter," Arion replied, his face white. "Release them, Rhodon and Archibios, and leave them all their households and property intact, and I will write a letter in which I confess that my mother once confided to me the name of my real father. I will date it to a time earlier in this year, and address it to someone who might reasonably be supposed the recipient of such a confidence."

There was another silence. "I am astonished," said Octavian at last. "Who was your real father, then?"

"Caesar," Arion replied, with a curl of the lip. "As you are aware. But I will name whomever you please. I trust you will not insult Caesar's memory by requiring me to say that my mother deceived him with someone utterly unworthy."

After a moment of hesitation, Marcus shook his head. "It would be no use," he told the emperor. "Such a document would have to have his personal seal attached if it was to carry any weight, and we've destroyed that. Those who believe he is Caesar's son would dismiss it as a forgery."

"They'd do so even if we still had the seal," Octavian replied. "They would say, 'If he wasn't Caesar's son, why was he put to death?' Still, an extraordinary offer. Two years ago I would have pardoned a dozen traitors for it, and paid a shipload of gold. Today . . . I think it simpler and better if I decline."

Arion's shoulders slumped and he lowered his head.

"I grant your request," said the emperor.

Arion's head came up again, his eyes wide in disbelief.

Octavian gave a self-satisfied smile. "My clemency is given, not bought. First I wish to confirm, as far as I can, the story these two have told. If they prove to have told the truth, I will require them to swear an oath never to tell anyone what they know of you—and then they may go free. Rhodon and Archibios I will question; if their account matches yours, I will release them on the same oath. When we last spoke, son of

Cleopatra, you were pleased to say that, because I am a king
or something more than one, there is no check upon my action
but my own will, and that if I wished to kill your friends,
public opinion would not protect them. This is, undoubtedly,
a lesson you learned from your mother, and believe. She told
my father the same thing. My father, however, died on the
steps of the Capitol with twenty-three stab wounds in his
body, and your mother might have learned from it that she
was mistaken in her view of the importance of public opinion—but she did not. She told Antonius what she had told
Caesar, and now Antonius is dead, and so is she. They might
have survived, even after Actium, had their people remained
loyal—but everyone deserted them as soon as their cause fal-
tered. Why do you think that was? Your mother never cared
whether she was hated, so long as she was obeyed. I do care,
and I hope to rule longer than she did. Archibios is a man well
liked and well respected; Rhodon is known to have done me
a service; these two here are common people who never even
understood what they had become involved in. I will be clement."

Ani understood that Octavian had realized some time before
that he could be clement safely, and that, in fact, it would be
easier and less trouble to him than being vindictive—but he
had spun out his granting of that clemency because he wanted
Arion to appreciate it, to ask for it, to thank him for it. It
was, he felt suddenly, an outrageous demand—that Arion
should thank the man who had invaded his country, killed and
imprisoned his family, taken from him everything he owned,
and sentenced him to death.

Arion hesitated. Then he bowed, a slow inclination of the

head that left his shackled hands still, and said, with real feel-ing, "I thank you, Caesar, for your clemency."

Octavian gave another satisfied smile. "Very gracefully done. Tell me, whose life was so important to you that you were willing to beg and to slander your mother for it? I think not Rhodon's, however much you've forgiven him. Are you that much in love with this girl?"

Arion straightened, his face royal again. "I do love the girl. But I would have begged for any of them. The shame I took upon myself is nothing compared to the shame of knowing that I destroyed my friends."

"Where did *you* acquire a conscience?" asked Octavian. "It was bred out of your mother's line long ago."

"I would not have obtained such a commodity from my father's people," Arion replied, with that slight curl of the lip. "Let us agree that we are responsible for our own hearts." Then he glanced over at Ani and added, "And this man here showed me the value of such things."

Ani was astonished. The emperor gazed at him a moment, thoughtfully. Then he lifted a commanding hand. "Marcus," he said, "go find the documents the merchant mentioned; look them over and confirm the story. Areios, go with him. Lon-ginus, get a horse, ride over to the harbor office, check the story about the robbers. Vitalus, go question the merchant's people about their journey to Alexandria; check that the pris-oner never left the boat on his own to talk to people we don't know about. Don't tell them who he is. You two"—Arion's pair of guards—"take the prisoner back to the corridor. Let the girl go with him; let them talk, if they want to. I will speak to this merchant."

Marcus nodded and departed out the larger door. Areios bowed and followed him. The gilded commander and his subordinate each in turn saluted and left by the smaller door, into the passageway that led to the stables. The remaining two guards escorted Arion, and Melanthe, back through the small dark door. Ani stood bewildered where he was, alone in a room with the ruler of the world.

Octavian stood, glanced around, and picked up from a place on the floor beneath his couch a sheathed knife, about the length of a man's hand, with a plain black hilt. He walked over behind Ani and sawed through the rope that bound his hands. Then he went back to his seat.

Ani eased his stiff arms straight and looked at his chafed wrists. He glanced warily at the emperor, who sat toying with the knife. "Thank you, lord," he said—it seemed safe enough to say that. "And thank you, very much, for your clemency." He essayed a weak smile. "I have a wife, sir, and children I will be very glad to see again."

Octavian nodded an acknowledgement. "You are no danger to me, I hope. You remind me a bit of my stepfather."

Ani gave him a startled look, and Octavian added, "Not in appearance, but there is a certain . . ." He wiggled his fingers expressively. ". . . a certain quality in common."

"With your stepfather, lord?" Ani asked incredulously, wondering who the emperor's stepfather was—not Caesar, surely?

"Lucius Marcius Philippus," said Octavian, as though he'd heard the thought. "My mother's second husband. A good man, as you appear to be."

That was a surprising tribute. Isis: the emperor was well endowed with fathers—natural, adoptive, and now a stepfather as well. He wondered what the man wanted with him. He did not like him, and distrusted that promised clemency. He wondered whether Tiathres and the children and the men were still sitting in the barracks yard, or whether they'd been locked up in a prison. O Isis, to see them again . . .

It was something, he told himself, that this cold, calculating, mean-spirited man wanted to be praised for clemency, rather than, say, magnificence or power or military glory. It was a far more humane ideal than the ones chosen by most other rulers. Give him credit for it: this was someone who at least *wanted* to be a good man.

"I am curious," the emperor told him. "What did you do to Ptolemy Caesar?"

"Lord?" Ani asked in astonishment.

"He credits you with teaching him the value of a conscience. You called him 'boy,' and he heeded you and checked himself. That is a Lagid! Probably a Julian as well, though I deny it, but undoubtedly a Lagid. He begged for your life. He called the gods to witness it, and well they might, for I don't imagine they've seen such a thing as a Lagid begging before—certainly not a Lagid begging for the benefit of someone else."

"Lord, nobody wants to ruin their friends. Arion . . ." He hesitated.

"His name's Ptolemy," Octavian pointed out.

"It's the name I know him by, sir. Lord, I think Arion has had very few friends, and so he greatly treasures the ones he does have. If you want the truth, lord, I think he's had a miserable life."

He stopped. It sounded a stupid thing to have said, now that he'd said it. Arion—*Caesarion*—was, after all, the son of a queen and a god. This room, this palace, this city, and the whole kingdom of Egypt had been his until that very summer. Ani plunged on, however, justifying himself. "He's told me that nobody else was ever kind to him without expecting something for it, that he never trusted anyone, that flatterers put maggots into your heart that eat you alive. His mother apparently believed it would be good for him to see someone with the sacred disease cut open while they were still breathing—which tells me, at least, that she wasn't a woman I'd entrust with any child, let alone one like that."

"Like what?"

Ani shrugged. "High-strung, passionate, and imaginative."

"You speak as though you were his father."

Ani felt his face heat. "I know what I am, and what he is. But I found him injured and helpless, and I looked after him, and I suppose that yes, the nature of what I feel for him is fatherly. My daughter's not much younger. If that's insolent, I can't help it. I didn't know he was a king."

Octavian gave a snort of amusement. "Probably you would have made him a fine stepfather. But not at Cleopatra's court. The queen would have punished your insolence severely."

"Isis! I'm not *that* insolent. I'm not a man who would have been admitted to the palace at all, except perhaps at the goods entrance."

"She was an extraordinary woman. Even at the end, as a prisoner. When she was in a room, everyone else seemed to fade. A glorious creature. I never intended her to die. I think, though, that she cannot have been a comfortable companion. I can't imagine having such a woman as a mother, and she would never permit her colleague to be anything like an equal.

I think you're right, he had a hard life. The disease itself is a cruel affliction, too—I remember how my uncle suffered with it."

"*Uncle*," now—and Ani suspected that this time Octavian did mean Caesar. He wondered again why he'd been selected as imperial confidant. "He remembers things in it, he says," Ani volunteered hesitantly. "Horrible things, over and over again."

"My uncle suffered that," said Octavian in a low voice. "He used to wake up from his fits and weep." He met Ani's eyes, and went on, very quietly: "It's strange how much he reminds me of my uncle—my *father*, I should say, since he adopted me, but if I'm honest I still think of him as Great-uncle Julius. When they brought him in, unconscious from the fit, it all came back. Marcus and Areios were rattling on about what was wrong with him and when he'd wake up, and I *knew*, because I'd seen Uncle Julius in the same condition. He has that same trick Uncle Julius had, too, of looking at you like he's just stepped down from Olympus, and that headlong look when he's moved. Not the charm, though. Not his mother's charm, either. No, you're right, he's had a miserable life."

There was a silence, and then Ani said hesitantly, "Lord, what are you going to do to the boy?" He did not so much want as *need* to know, but he also felt that, for some strange reason, Octavian *wanted* him—him specifically—to ask that.

"He is too dangerous to be allowed to live," Octavian replied at once. "You call him a boy, but I was that age when my uncle died and I was named his heir. Many people—Marcus Antonius among them—thought I was too young to be taken seriously. They were egregiously mistaken."

"But he doesn't *want* to contend with you," Ani dared, still feeling for what was allowed, afraid every moment to be slapped down again for insolence. "You heard him. Lord, you want him to disappear quietly, and that's exactly what he wants himself. Ptolemy Caesar has been dead for a month. Couldn't you say that Arion is just a young man who happens to look a bit like him? Nobody would believe that the son of Cleopatra was working as a Red Sea trader."

Octavian regarded him with an amused twist to his mouth. "You *are* like my stepfather. He never gave up on anything, either. You *still* want that young man as a partner. Did he sleep with your daughter?"

Ani felt his face heat again. "No," he said shortly. "—Not so far as I know. She's a good girl, and I'm sorry she ever met him, because she won't get over him in a hurry."

Octavian looked down at the knife he was still holding. He began to toy with it again. "I will tell you something. When Caesar named me as his heir, my stepfather advised me to refuse the inheritance. It would destroy me, he said, one way or another—and by that, he meant that either I would be crushed and killed in the contention, or that the deceits, cruelties, and betrayals I would have to practice in order to succeed would kill my soul. I loved Philippus, and I did consider doing as he said. Certainly I think he was wise. My soul is not quite dead, but I have felt pieces of it go: here a principle, there a cherished hope, and there a man betrayed."

"You want to spare him," Ani said, suddenly understanding why he was there.

Octavian looked up at him with another twisted smile. "When Cleopatra was my prisoner, she showed me some of my uncle's letters to her. He did love her. When I was a boy I adored Uncle Julius, and as a man I owe him everything. He acknowledged Caesarion as his. He had no other son of his body. And that *is* his son, whatever I may say to the world. I was not convinced of it before, but I am now. Uncle Julius would not want me to kill him." He sighed. "The boy annoyed me, with his assumption of superiority and his prating about the proscriptions. He has, though, exceptional courage, together with intelligence, eloquence, loyalty to his friends, and a conscience. I wish I had not met him. It was much easier to order his death before I had."

"But you are the emperor!" exclaimed Ani. "Why should you do something you don't want to do?"

"Leaving that young man alive would be like defeating an army and leaving it intact with all its weapons and its pay-chest," said Octavian. "He is a threat to peace as long as he draws breath. *Now* he wants to disappear quietly, *now* his friends want the same—but a few years from now? Some unforeseen mischance—a failure of the inundation, a foreign invasion—and Egypt may be crying for a savior. Wouldn't he appear again then?"

"Lord, you heard him! He *knows* that if he did it would start a war and make everything worse. He acknowledged that only you can create peace. What, you think he was lying when he said he agreed that it was better for him to die? It hasn't crossed his mind that you might spare him!"

"I'm certain that he was saying what he believes to be the truth—now. But circumstances change, and kings, if they want to survive, adapt to them."

"He's only a threat if he's Ptolemy Caesar," said Ani, com-

GILLIAN BRADSHAW

ing closer and dropping to one knee to look the emperor in the face. "Arion's no threat to anyone. And if he's been Arion for a few years, who'll believe he was ever Ptolemy Caesar? You killed Ptolemy Caesar, and everybody knows it. You could let Arion live."

Octavian slid the knife into its sheath and clenched both hands on it. He looked up into Ani's eyes.

"It wouldn't be a life fit for a king," Ani admitted. "It would be a merchant's life. But he would be alive, and you would know. You would know that your uncle's son still saw the light of day, that his blood still ran in living veins—perhaps that his line continued, however humbly, that you were not responsible for exterminating it. You could have both things: your enemy dead, and your cousin alive."

"Would you be responsible for him?" Octavian asked, in a low voice. "Would you pledge your life, and the life of every member of your household, that he would *remain* Arion, whatever happens?"

Ani thought for a minute, then took a deep breath. "Yes, lord. I would pledge my life to that, and the life of every member of my household. Give him to me, and I will be responsible for him. I don't know, though . . . I don't know whether he'll accept it. He is desperately proud, and he doesn't value his own life. I think in many ways he regards death as a release."

"He loves your daughter," said Octavian. "I will make him the offer. If he accepts, I will hold you to your pledge." He got to his feet and strode to the door, flung it open.

A short distance away down the dim corridor, Arion and Melanthe were standing together among the guards. Melanthe was inside the hoop of Arion's shackled arms, and she was stroking his head. Everyone looked around at the open door.

"Bring them back in," ordered the emperor.

There was a shuffling as the party reordered itself. Melanthe ducked out under the shackles then caught Arion's arm. The little procession trooped back into the audience chamber.

Ani remembered Arion on the boat between Ptolemais and Alexandria—the slow, shy, nervous unfurling of happiness. He felt a sudden desperate desire for that to go on. Arion, though, had been Arion only for one month. He had been Ptolemy Caesar all his life. How could he be expected to renounce everything he had been for something that had barely begun?

Octavian sat down and inspected his prisoner again. "I have been discussing the situation with your friend Ani son of Petesuchos," he announced. "He has made a suggestion. Are you familiar with the *Electra* of Euripides?"

Arion stared a moment in baffled incomprehension. Then his face went white. "Caesar," he began—and stopped.

"Of course, in that play, the commoner did not fulfill the queen's expectations," Octavian went on remorselessly. "I would not permit such conduct from you."

"Caesar," whispered Arion. "Caesar—I do not ask this."

"Ptolemy Caesar is dead. He must remain dead. If you live, it would be as Arion son of Gaius. You would renounce your former name and condition, and swear never to reveal it to anyone. You would leave Alexandria as soon as you are able, and never return. I would inform Archibios and Rhodon that I have had you put to death, and you would make no effort to contact them or anyone else who knew you in your former life. You would remain in the household of Ani son of Petesuchos, who has agreed to be responsible for your conduct, and who has pledged his life and the life of every member of his household that if I give you to him you will never disturb the peace of Egypt. Are you willing to accept your life on these conditions?"

Arion said nothing. He turned a stunned face to Ani, then to Melanthe, who was suddenly ablaze with hope. He made an incoherent sound, clawed at the top of his tunic, then dropped to his knees. His eyes fixed on nothing with an expression of horror.

"It's a fit," Ani said hurriedly, afraid that the emperor would be offended and withdraw his offer. "He's—he's overcome. You'll have to wait until it passes, lord."

Octavian regarded the young man with clinical detachment. Arion had started to grind his teeth. He whimpered in horror. "He hasn't fallen down," he objected.

"He doesn't, with this sort," Ani told him, obscurely ashamed to be discussing the affliction with such knowing calm. "He has this sort much more often than the other, but they don't last long."

Octavian sighed. He looked around himself and then, from the same place under the couch where he'd taken the knife, lifted a familiar silk bag on a fine gold chain. "He said it was a remedy," he remarked, and handed it to Ani.

"Yes," agreed Ani, and hurried over to hold it before Arion's tortured face. "I can't say I've noticed it doing anything to stop a fit, but I think it makes him calmer after one."

"Lord," said Melanthe, looking at the emperor with shining eyes, "you are kind, and good, and I thank you with all my heart, and I pray that you rule Egypt in health and prosperity until my children are old."

"He hasn't agreed yet, girl," said Octavian—but he smiled smugly.

CHAPTER XV

A rion finished the oath and lifted his hand from the small pile of signets and amulets, all of them engraved with symbols of different gods, which they had used for the swearing—the private audience chamber could hardly accommodate an altar and a sacrificial victim. He found himself staring at the hand in the flickering lamplight. It looked no different than it had, but ten minutes before, it had been the hand of a deposed king, and now it was the hand of—what?

He didn't know. He didn't know, and a part of himself was screaming that this was wrong, wrong, wrong; that he should have died—at Kabalsi, at Berenike, at Ptolemais, and certainly here in Alexandria, before he ever abased himself so far as to disown his very name.

The rest of himself was wildly relieved.

Melanthe was gazing at him rapturously. Part of himself

wanted to kiss her; the rest stood, stunned and bereft, furious with her for being the cause of his destruction. She started toward him, but Ani checked her, somehow aware of the agony of his division. Arion was grateful to him.

"I hope I do not regret this," said Octavian.

"I hope neither of us does," Arion replied. "If you wish to change your mind, I will not protest it."

Agrippa was scowling. He disapproved. He had tried to talk his friend out of this extreme and unwarrantable clemency. Arion still didn't understand why Agrippa hadn't succeeded. He suspected, though, that Octavian had done it because he wanted exclusive possession of the name of Caesar—a thing which Caesarion would otherwise have kept even in death. Octavian had been unable to resist humiliating an enemy— twice: once in the degradation itself, and again in his own acceptance of it.

He wondered if he would have agreed if he hadn't already lost all dignity and resistance through the treachery of his own diseased brain. It was pointless, though, to try to imagine what things would be like without the disease. The disease was a part of him, and without it he would be another man entirely.

"I have been considering what explanation to provide for today's events," said Octavian. "I have not been able to think of anything remotely satisfactory."

Ani coughed. "You thought we were someone else?"

"Who?" asked the emperor. "I would prefer to avoid any mention of King Ptolemy Caesar."

"Spies," Arion suggested, from the other side of the division he had made in himself. "You had received some intelligence which suggested that the king of Ethiopia had sent spies down the river to determine the strength and the nature of the new regime. Ani and I matched one description of the spies. After thorough investigation and intensive questioning, however, you concluded that we are merely merchants, and that the description you received was inaccurate or malicious."

"The king of Ethiopia?" Octavian asked curiously.

"Ethiopia has a long-standing dispute with Egypt over mutual raiding on the border, land ownership, and the rights of certain temples at Philae and Syene," Arion informed him wearily. "The king was wary of my moth—of the queen, but I would expect him to make a test of your strength within the next year."

"Indeed! I do not believe I have ever before had cause to consider the situation to the south of Egypt. Is the king likely to send spies?"

"He has almost certainly done so already."

"Indeed! I had not been aware. The story will do very well, then—and I will ask Gallus to keep an eye on Ethiopia." He eyed Arion. "I am appointing Gallus as governor of the province, and leaving him three legions, which, as I am sure you will appreciate, should be more than enough to deal with any trouble that arises—from Ethiopia or from any other source."

Arion bowed slightly.

"I myself will be returning to Rome, setting out next month. I will, however, inform Gallus about you, under conditions of the strictest secrecy. Nothing will be committed to writing, and his closest confidants will not know. He will, however, be able to find you—and your friend Ani—if anything goes amiss."

Arion bowed again.

"Marcus says that Gallus mentions in his letter that he offered you a job."

"As his secretary. For the languages, mainly. And some of the same tastes in poetry."

Agrippa made a noise of disgust. "He's much too fond of poetry—especially his own. To offer a job to a young man he knew nothing about, who might have been, and was, anyone— the man's a fool."

"I like poetry, too," Octavian replied tolerantly. "But Marcus, secretaries who can manage Greek *and* Latin with elegance aren't so common, and if you want one with the native language as well—which your mother must have insisted upon, yes?"

"Yes," agreed Arion.

"I don't think Gallus was a fool," concluded Octavian. "The blood is still worth something, even if the trappings are lacking." He looked at Arion levelly, then held out his hand. "I wish you joy."

Arion took the hand. It was cool and moist. Octavian, he thought, had the true phlegmatic humor. "I wish you joy," he said, feeling something within him die—when they had parted, it would be done. He would have disowned his inheritance forever.

He remembered at that thought one other thing he desperately wanted of this man. "Caesar," he said, suddenly urgent, "my brother Philadelphus—what are your plans for him?"

Octavian raised his eyebrows. "Why Philadelphus? You have another brother and a sister."

"I loved Philadelphus," he replied honestly. "I never knew Alexander or Selene very well."

"They will all three adorn my triumph," said the emperor. "On a carriage, I think, with a painting. No chains. The people will like it. After that, my sister has offered to take them. They are, after all, the children of that lout I made her marry. She is already raising Antonius' other children, the ones Fulvia bore him."

Except for Antyllus, Arion thought to himself.

"My sister is noble, gracious, and kind," Octavian went on. "Your brother will be well cared for."

Cleopatra had loathed Octavia. *Cold, smug, supercilious little prig,* she'd called her. Cleopatra, however, had been jealous: Octavia had married her man. Certainly Octavia had a reputation for piety, grace, and good behavior. She would undoubtedly see to it that Philadelphus was treated properly, that he was fed, clothed, educated, and provided for. As for love— well, a Roman matron of Octavia's standing would hardly look after the children *herself*, anyway. Philadelphus would have his nurse. Maybe he'd learn to love Alexander and Selene, or his half-brothers and -sisters, the children of Antonius and Fulvia. It was the best that could be had.

"Thank you," Arion whispered. "I am in her debt."

He wished that he could see Philadelphus, if only to say good-bye. But they had parted before, and the little boy had heard that he was dead. Probably that wound was beginning to heal by now. Better not to reopen it.

"Then, again, I wish you joy," he told Octavian.

"And you, cousin," replied the emperor.

Arion looked at him in surprise, but the emperor was signaling to the guards, and they opened the door to the private passageway and ushered his cousin away.

It was night, and the guards had brought torches. Arion walked in silence, his shoulders hunched. He was very weary, and body and soul alike seemed one indistinguishable ache. He wondered, vaguely, what had happened to his cloak and hat, or the basket of spare clothing Melanthe had been carrying when he had the seizure. Abandoned on the street, probably, no doubt to the delight of some beggar. The money would certainly not turn up. At least Octavian had given him back the remedy. He touched it for reassurance, and wished he still had the knife. He heard Melanthe pressing close behind him, knew that she wanted to take his hand, but he did not look back.

They emerged at last into the stable. He remembered coming here with Antyllus for riding lessons, remembered his beautiful bay stallion Perseus. He wondered if Perseus was still here, whether if he went to its stall the horse would recognize him and come over in quest of an apple from its master. If he did, would that be a breach of his oath to approach no one who had known him in his former life? Did a horse count as *someone?* He felt substanceless, a ghost caught in a shadowy dream.

Longinus, the commander of the Praetorian Guard, looked at him with alarm. "Sir, move out of sight!" he ordered. "And you," to one of the guardsmen, "get him a cloak and something to cover his head. You, put out that torch. Jupiter, most of the grooms and the servants *know* him!"

"Sir, are my people still in the yard?" Ani asked the commander eagerly.

"I'll find out," the commander said shortly, "after we've got your friend covered up."

Arion moved into the darkness of an empty stall and stood waiting quietly. Melanthe was watching him, but he did not look at her. Ani fidgeted, desperate to see his wife and sons again.

At last the guardsman came back with a plain cloak of black wool and a wide-brimmed traveling-hat very similar to the one he had lost. He put them on. The cloak was too heavy for the hot September night, and the hat was slightly too large. He tilted it forward so that it shaded his face, and pulled a fold of cloak high enough to cover his chin. The commander regarded him a moment, then nodded in satisfaction.

Ani's people had been locked into the guards' prison, just beyond the barracks. There was a certain amount of fussing and signing of releases, which Ani plainly found hard to endure, and then finally the prison door was unlocked, and the group was ushered out into the balmy night. There were tears and embraces. The story about Ethiopian spies was told. Tiathres at once blamed Aristodemos, and loudly thanked the gods that he was finally dead and could cause them no more trouble.

Arion watched from a distance, unmoved. Even when the others at last realized he was there, he managed to avoid any embrace. The ache in his heart was growing as the sense of dreamlike numbness began to fade.

Then at last they were walking back along the streets of the city. The four Praetorians who'd watched him in the audience chamber stayed with him, but another, ignorant man had joined them, carrying *Soteria*'s papers.

Apollonios sidled up. "What happened with your cousin?" he asked.

Arion stared at him blankly, still too stunned to feel more

than a remote astonishment. "What do you know about that?"

"The girl said Areios Didymos took you off unconscious in his carriage. Isn't he the cousin you were talking about?"

"No," Arion said in bewilderment.

"He isn't?" Apollonios was surprised and disappointed. "Why did he take you, then?"

Arion repeated the story about Ethiopian spies. Apollonios looked as though he didn't believe it. "So who is your cousin?" he asked.

"No one you know," Arion replied wearily. "Leave me alone."

"But what were you doing going to Cyprus?"

"Who says I was going to Cyprus?"

"Melanthe. She said you were going to Cyprus to manage an estate for a friend."

"Then that must be why I was going to Cyprus, mustn't it? I asked you to leave me alone."

"But why are you coming back? You insisted you weren't going to stay with the likes of us. You left. Why have you come back?"

"I'm going to marry Melanthe. Leave me alone."

"Do as he says," ordered Longinus, coming up behind Apollonios and making him jump.

Apollonios gave the commander of the Praetorian Guard a frightened look and moved away. Arion walked the rest of the way to the Mareotic Harbor shadowed by the guards, who were blessedly silent.

There were more documents to sign at the harbor before *Soteria* was released. It was very late by then, and the little boy Isisdoros was asleep in his father's arms. At last, however, all was settled, and they were allowed back to the boat.

It looked as dirty, battered, and degraded as it had the first day Arion saw it. He stood on the side of the dock gazing at it wretchedly while the others climbed joyfully aboard.

"Remember your oath," Longinus told Arion, as the guards prepared to depart.

I have made a mistake, he wanted to tell them. I didn't mean it. I will come back with you; Octavian can have me strangled. I will sleep in the urn in the garden, among my ancestors. I will die as a king.

Somehow, he didn't manage to say it. He nodded, silently, and went aboard the boat.

Soteria was just as he remembered it—cramped, squalid, and dirty. He lay down on his mattress in the stern cabin, between Ani and Apollonios, and spent the night staring at the ceiling.

In the morning he told the others that he felt ill—which was true—and stayed in the cabin. The others left him there. They were busy, anyway. It seemed that Ani had succeeded in finding a supplier of tin, as well as in buying a quantity of glassware, and all day they were running back and forth arguing about how much space the cargo would take up and what part of it should go where. *Soteria*, it emerged, was not large enough to carry everything at once. The difficulty was resolved when it turned out that the tin supplier did not actually have the tin on hand. Ani went off to talk to him, to bargain about whether the supplier would ship the tin to Coptos or whether Ani should come back for it. The others began to load the glass. None of it seemed real.

Tiathres came in to see him several times, bringing cold drinks, and thanked him warmly for rescuing Melanthe. Me-

Ianthe came with her stepmother the first time, but he asked her to go. In the light of the new day the thing he had done to himself seemed more appalling and less excusable.

In the middle of the afternoon he had a seizure, a small one, that was, oddly enough, comforting. All the memories were pleasant ones—Philadelphus playing marbles, Rhodon explaining philosophy, a garden with a carp pond. He had not, he realized, seen the man on the table since he'd told Ani about him. Zeus, it would be wonderful if he'd managed to escape that particular nightmare!

Ani reappeared in the cabin in the evening, when the others were on deck eating supper.

"How are you?" he asked.

Arion stared up at the cabin roof. The answer that occurred to him was, *You know the Galli, the priests of Kybele who castrate themselves in ecstatic rituals? I feel like one of them, the day after.* He did not utter it. It would be unfair to this man who had pledged his life to ensure his own survival, who he trusted as he had never trusted anyone before, who he was sure loved him, whom—he could now admit it—he loved like the father he had never known. "I will live," he said instead.

Ani squatted next to him and pulled on his lower lip. "Be a waste if you didn't, after all that. What happens in the *Electra* of Euripides?"

"The princess Electra, the daughter of Agamemnon, is married off to a common peasant so that she cannot bear sons who will revenge her father's murder."

"Oh."

"In fact, the peasant, out of respect for the royal house,

never consummates the marriage, which is dissolved by the end of the play."

"Well, don't tell that to Melanthe. She's miserable enough as it is."

He remembered the brief interval with Melanthe in the corridor when he believed that he had secured her safety, but would soon die. The touch of her body, her lips, her hands on his head, her voice whispering that she loved him . . . it had seemed at the time that to live and possess her was worth far more than a name. Perhaps it would seem that way again; right now he felt he was a degraded coward and a fool.

Dionysos, how could he disown his *name*?

"I don't know who I am anymore," he told Ani, his eyes filling with tears.

"It isn't *her* fault," Ani said. "*She* knows who you are. You're Arion, who saved her family and her freedom, the man she loves. To us, you're what you showed yourself to be."

"You *own* me!" he exclaimed angrily, sitting up. "In Berenike it was thirty drachmae; by the time we reached Coptos, it was much, much more, and now—he *gave* me to you, he said. Am I to be your slave?"

"What I offered was a partnership," Ani replied sourly. "You don't have to marry Melanthe. There's others would be happy at the chance."

He caught his breath. "Leave me alone. Please. It's too soon, it still hurts too much."

Ani sighed, blew out his cheeks, nodded, got up. "You want anything to eat?"

"No. Thank you."

"Clean tunic? That one looks like it itches anyway."

"Later."

In the morning they finished loading the glassware, packing it in baskets lined with palm leaves. Ani went to the bank he'd chosen, which had a branch in Coptos and a seasonal office in Berenike, and arranged letters of credit, to avoid risking the money on the voyage. He went to his supplier and finalized arrangements for the tin. Arion stayed in the cabin. Tiathres brought him a clean tunic, plain bleached linen. It had belonged to Harmias, whom the robbers had killed.

By now, he supposed, Rhodon and Archibios have been told that I am dead.

He remembered their offer to invest in the Red Sea trade, to buy him a ship. Ani would have liked that. On the other hand, Ani's business looked to be prospering very well without their help. The profits this time would be Kleon's, apart from Ani's commission, but they were large profits, and the outbound cargo would be better than it had ever been. The next voyage was likely to produce a very fine sum indeed, and a full half of it would be Ani's.

He supposed he would be very useful to Ani in the business, even if he couldn't go to Alexandria. He could deal with authority, Greek or Roman, and let Ani deal with trade. It was likely that they would prosper.

He shivered, imagining himself living in Ani's house, married to Melanthe, fathering children . . .

He wasn't sure whether the prospect was blissful or appalling.

*   *   *

ARION HAD THOUGHT he would stay in the cabin until dark, but when *Soteria* began to move he put on his cloak and hat and came up on deck.

The heavily laden boat moved slowly out onto the lake. Alexandria rose from the blue water like a fantasy city in a painting, a dream of light and shading, too beautiful to be real. His city, always his city: founded and built up by his ancestors, creation of his blood. The thought that he would never see it again was a loss as raw, almost, as the loss of Philadelphus. He leaned against the stern rail and watched it until it was out of sight. The north wind pressed against his cheek, tugged at his hat, and made the black cloak flap loudly. He thought of the black sails of Theseus, returning to Athens after he had traced the labyrinth and slain the minotaur and abandoned his lover sleeping on the shore of Naxos. He could feel Melanthe watching him, but he would not look at her.

They made their way back along the Canopic canal, mainly by tacking across the wind, occasionally with some help from the oars. It was after dark when they reached the Nile.

They moored *Soteria* very close to where they had secured it on their outward voyage. Tiathres lit the fire and cooked supper, and Ani went off and bought some wine. They gave Arion a cup and a roll of flatbread with cheese and olives, and he thanked them, and sat on the deck to eat them, apart from the others but no longer quite shut away. He decided it was safe to leave off the cloak and hat. Nobody questioned him, not even Apollonios. It seemed to have been accepted that he had given up his chance of reestablishing himself as a gentleman in order to save Melanthe, and everyone treated him with solemn courtesy.

The Egyptians were at last beginning to recover their spirits after the stresses and strangenesses of the past few days. Pamonthes got out his flute and played folk songs, and presently some of the others began to sing. Arion remained on deck, silent, separate, but listening. He could feel Melanthe watching him again.

After a while she came over and sat down near him. He said nothing.

"Are you angry with me?" she asked at last.

"It wasn't your fault," he told her wearily.

"Papa says it hurt you so much that you can't bear anyone to touch it yet."

He found himself giving a choked grunt of acknowledgement.

"I didn't understand that it would hurt you like that," she said humbly. "I was just happy, because it meant you wouldn't die. I thought you'd be happy, too."

He looked down at his left wrist and rubbed the scar.

"Do you wish you had died?" she asked in a small voice.

"Some of me does," he admitted. "It's who I was, Melanthion, everything I was, everything I had. I disowned it, and I don't know what's left."

"Everything," she told him breathlessly. "You're no different. You're still *you*. You told me, just before you had your seizure, that the 'you' people saw, before, was really only what you were supposed to be, and not who you are. You said they reverenced that, but ignored you—that they pretended not to see you, because they were embarrassed."

He'd forgotten that he'd said that. He thought it over: it was true. "I was never enough," he told her. "I could never be what I was supposed to be. I tried, but there was the disease, and it couldn't be cured."

"*Nobody* could be enough! How could anyone live up to being the son of Cleopatra and Julius Caesar?"

"Hush, hush, hush! Don't say it, *don't* say it! That man is dead."

"But only a god could be enough! And you *are* enough, for me. You are more than I ever dreamed existed. And that's *you*, Arion, not that other person!"

"That other person is who I was *born*," he told her. "It's like the disease, innate and incurable. One can learn to live with the disease, but it won't go away. Never expect that."

She caught his hand, twisted her fingers with his own. "But you're alive. You're free. You have people who love you, things you can do. Can't you be happy?"

He looked into her face—the eyes, wide and coal-black in the moonlight, the lips trembling. Then he reached over and pulled her against himself. Tense muscles relaxed, melted against his side. She shivered, and leaned her head on his shoulder.

"I think I may learn to be," he told her.

AFTERWORD

or, What Really Happened and What I Made Up

Caesarion really did exist, though the question of whether Julius Caesar was his father has been hotly debated, in antiquity and ever since. It is easy to see why Cleopatra would wish to claim that he was, and equally easy to understand why Octavian would deny it. The strongest argument against Caesar's paternity is that, despite a legendary promiscuity, Caesar had only one acknowledged offspring—his daughter Julia, born a good thirty-five years before Caesarion. On the other hand, most of Caesar's affairs were with married women, whose offspring could not be acknowledged as his. Rumor made him the real father of at least two noble Romans, and there may have been obscure bastards as well. Caesar undoubtedly knew more about his own fertility than does any modern historian, and all the evidence is that he believed himself to be Caesarion's father. Marcus Antonius, in fact, claimed that he acknowledged it. That may have been propaganda, but it is unquestionably true that during Cleopatra's visit to him in Rome—which is generally agreed to have occurred after Caesarion's birth—Caesar lodged her in one of his own houses and placed a golden statue of her in the temple he had built for the goddess Venus Genetrix, the supposed ancestress of his own clan—an utterly exceptional honor in Republican Rome, and one which Caesar never afforded his wife. It is hard to believe he would have done this if he believed she was trying to pass off another man's child as his own.

The real Caesarion was, almost certainly, killed in 30 B.C. by order of Octavian. There are two accounts of his fate: both agree that he was supposed to flee Egypt via the Red Sea ports, and that he was betrayed by a man called Rhodon, who was one of his tutors. Plutarch, however, says that Rhodon lured him back to Alexandria with a promise of pardon, while Dio Cassius says that he was overtaken and killed on the way into exile.

That he was epileptic is my own invention, and I'm afraid I inflicted him with the condition because it made him more interesting to me. I had no such plans when I started researching this book, but I came reluctantly to the conclusion that Cleopatra was a nasty piece of work, and that her son wouldn't have been much better. Giving him a disability to overcome made him sympathetic again. (I *wanted* to admire Cleopatra, but I couldn't. She was too ruthless, and showed far too much interest in conquering the world and not enough in looking after her own kingdom. She displayed the sort of behavior I deplore in "Great Men," and, in good conscience, could not approve in a Great Woman.)

In defense of the invention, all I can say is that it is within the bounds of possibility. Julius Caesar was epileptic, which would have made his offspring four times more likely to develop the condition than the norm, and the history of incest among the Lagids must have increased that risk. If Caesarion *had* developed the condition, the Greeks and Antonians would have suppressed the news because of the stigma attached to the illness, while the Octavians would have kept quiet about it because it would be evidence of Caesar's paternity. Caesarion is not much in evidence during the last years of Cleopatra's reign—there's no mention of his presence on any campaign, despite the fact that he was old enough, and there's no hint of any marriage arranged for him, though two of his younger siblings were betrothed. This *could* be because there was something wrong with him. (Of course, it could also be because Cleopatra was paranoid about sharing her own royal power.)

For the attitudes toward, and treatments for, epilepsy in antiquity, I am indebted to Owsei Temkin's *The Falling Sickness*. The pathology of the disease which I have Caesarion relate to Ani is derived from the best doctors of the time. (I hasten to add that it is, in fact, wrong. Epileptic attacks occur when the brain produces an abnormal pattern of electrical discharge, either globally or in a specific area. Temporal lobe epilepsy, which I chose for Caesarion, begins in the temporal lobes, as the name implies, and may or may not spread to the rest of the brain.)

I have, with some reluctance, followed the habit of historians and referred to the Roman emperor as "Octavian," in spite of the fact that nobody at the time seems to have done so. (He called himself "Gaius Julius Caesar"; his enemies called him "Octavius.") He later solved the problem of what to call him by taking (in 27 B.C.) the title "Augustus," the name by which he is best known.

I have assumed that Greeks of Cleopatra's time knew the use of the monsoon winds and were trading directly with India. This may or may not have been the case. The periodic nature of these winds is said to have been discovered by a Greek called Hippalos, but we do not know his dates. He may have lived as early as the generation before Cleopatra or as late as the generation after Octavian. The Red Sea ports, however, and the caravan routes to them from Coptos, had been operating since the early Ptolemaic period, and my suspicion is that the winds were discovered sooner rather than later.

The Romans used the caravan routes heavily, improved them, and established mines in the mountains nearby. They also repaired the irrigation systems along the Nile, which the later Lagids had neglected. For a brief time Egypt flourished as a Roman province. However, very little of the wealth which flowed out was reinvested at home, and the Augustan period was followed by a steady decline. Ultimately, Roman rule was a disaster.

Cleopatra's children by Marcus Antonius were brought up by Antonius' ex-wife, Octavian's sister Octavia. (It amuses me how few people seem to realize that Cleopatra *had* children. Cleopatra the sex-goddess obviously appeals to the popular imagination in a way that Cleopatra the unwed mother of four, or even Cleopatra the ruthless politician, does not.) Cleopatra Selene was eventually married to King Juba II of Numidia (later Mauretania), at which point Alexander Helios and Ptolemy Philadelphus were "given" to her. Nothing more is known of their fate.

Gaius Cornelius Gallus was governor of Egypt during its first three years as a Roman province. He was an energetic administrator, supervising repairworks to irrigation systems, crushing a couple of rebellions (one in the south of the country), and receiving the ruler of Ethiopia into Roman protection. However, his success went to his head, and led him to set up statues of himself and inscriptions boasting of his achievements *without reference to the emperor*. In consequence he was recalled and struck off the list of the emperor's friends. When the Senate began treason proceedings against him, he committed suicide. Augustus, who was absent at the time, is supposed to have lamented that the Senate had not left him free to quarrel with his friends.

Augustus Caesar, son of the deified Julius, ruled the Roman empire with clemency and humanity for the next forty-four years, and his reign was afterward regarded as a Golden Age.